Robert Muchamore was born in 1972 and spent thirteen years working as a private investigator. *CHERUB: Brigands M.C.* is his eleventh novel in the series.

The CHERUB series has won numerous awards, including the 2005 Red House Children's Book Award. For more information on Robert and his work, visit **www.cherubcampus.com**

Praise for the CHERUB series:
'If you can't bear to read another story about elves, princesses or spoiled rich kids who never go to the toilet, try this. You won't regret it.' *The Ultimate Teen Book Guide*
    'My sixteen-year-old son read *The Recruit* in one sitting, then went out the next day and got the sequel.' Sophie Smiley, teacher and children's author
    'So good I forced my friends to read it, and they're glad I did!' Helen, age 14
    'CHERUB is the first book I ever read cover to cover. It was amazing.' Scott, age 13
    'The best book ever.' Madeline, age 12
    'CHERUB is a must for Alex Rider lovers.' Travis, age 14

BY ROBERT MUCHAMORE

The Henderson's Boys series:

1. The Escape
2. Eagle Day
3. Secret Army
coming spring 2010

The CHERUB series:

1. The Recruit
2. Class A
3. Maximum Security
4. The Killing
5. Divine Madness
6. Man vs Beast
7. The Fall
8. Mad Dogs
9. The Sleepwalker
10. The General
11. Brigands M.C.

Look out for CHERUB: Shadow Wave
coming late 2010

BRIGANDS M.C.
Robert Muchamore

Hodder
Children's
Books

A division of Hachette Children's Books

A Catalogue record for this book is available
from the British Library

ISBN-13: 978 0 340 98903 6

Typeset in Goudy by Avon DataSet Ltd,
Bidford-on-Avon, Warwickshire

Printed in Great Britain by
Clays Ltd, St Ives plc

The paper used in this book is a natural recyclable product
made from wood grown in sustainable forests.
The hard coverboard is recycled.

Hodder Children's Books
A division of Hachette Children's Books
338 Euston Road, London NW1 3BH
An Hachette UK Company
www.hachette.co.uk

WHAT IS CHERUB?

CHERUB is a branch of British Intelligence. Its agents are aged between ten and seventeen years. Cherubs are mainly orphans who have been taken out of care homes and trained to work undercover. They live on CHERUB campus, a secret facility hidden in the English countryside.

WHAT USE ARE KIDS?

Quite a lot. Nobody realises kids do undercover missions, which means they can get away with all kinds of stuff that adults can't.

CHERUB T-SHIRTS

Cherubs are ranked according to the colour of the T-shirts they wear on campus. ORANGE is for visitors. RED is for kids who live on CHERUB campus but are too young to qualify as agents (the minimum age is ten). BLUE is for kids undergoing CHERUB's tough one-hundred-day basic training regime. A GREY T-shirt means you're qualified for missions. NAVY is a reward for outstanding performance on a single mission. The BLACK T-shirt is the ultimate recognition for outstanding achievement over a number of missions. When you retire, you get the WHITE T-shirt, which is also worn by staff.

Part One

1. PATCHES

The Brigands Motorcycle Club began in California in 1966, founded by an armed robber named Kurt Oxford. There were dozens of clubs just like it: mean dudes on big bikes, oozing menace and scaring regular citizens.

The Brigands weren't the largest biker gang, nor the toughest or most notorious. Many thought Kurt Oxford's death in a 1969 prison shooting would be their end. But instead of breaking up or being absorbed by a larger club – 'patched over' in biker speak – the Brigands expanded.

As he cruised Los Angeles freeways on his Harley Davidson, Kurt Oxford never could have imagined that his motorcycle club would one day have seventy chapters spanning the United States and a hundred more, from Sydney to Scandinavia. In 1985, Brigands membership was estimated at more than three thousand full-patch members, and ten times that number of associates and hangers-on.

Only a full-patch member of the Brigands is entitled to wear the club's colours: an embroidered logo depicting a caped highwayman brandishing a sawn-off shotgun.

Excerpt from *Riding with Kurt and the Brigands* by Jane Oxford

*

Out of eleven British chapters, the South Devon Brigands ranked second only to London in power and seniority. Their clubhouse was a creaky affair, converted out of a pair of barns on fifteen acres close to the wealthy enclave of Salcombe. On a clear day the video cameras mounted around its corrugated metal fence could peer over the barbed wire at millionaires' yachts moored in the marina below.

Dante Scott was eight years old, son of Scotty, the vice-president of South Devon Brigands. Dante was a tough kid who'd swing at anyone who took the mickey out of his tangled red hair. He liked hanging out with his dad at the Brigands clubhouse, which was usually on Wednesday and Friday nights when his mum drove to Plymouth for evening classes.

Bikers played pool, drank, smoked dope, swore and didn't want kids under their feet. Nobody ever cleaned the compound outside and Dante's mum told him never to play out because of broken glass and jagged metal, but he'd never been hurt and his dad didn't mind if it kept him occupied.

Dante would get behind the wheel of a wrecked Ford and pretend to drive, or make a ramp with bits of rotting wood and send empty beer kegs crashing down the hill.

Mostly there were other kids around. The ground was too sloped for football, so they'd play hide-and-seek or tag, which was most enjoyable in the dark with torches. Best of all was when Teeth came and coached kids in the boxing ring.

None of the Brigands were exactly teddy bears, but Teeth looked scary even by their standards. Huge and muscular, he wore sharp spurs on the back of his boots and greasy jeans held up with a length of bike chain that could be ripped out and used to beat the shit out of anyone who messed with him.

Biker names were usually ironic. Little George was the size of a house, Fats as thin as a rake and Teeth had nothing but squishy gums and a couple of brown molars at the back. He'd never say how he lost them. Dante asked one time and Teeth just said, *you should have seen the state of the other guy.*

Teeth was a nightclub bouncer with a sideline in drug dealing, but he wanted to be a pro wrestler. Sometimes he'd get a few weeks' work at a holiday camp in the summer and he'd wrestled on TV a couple of times, though he wasn't one of the big stars who got in the wrestling magazines stacked up in Dante's bedroom.

Teeth would take Dante and any other boys who were interested into the big room at the back of the main barn which contained an ancient boxing ring with frayed ropes and a warped floor. He'd taught Dante how to box properly, how to do Karate kicks and headlocks and all kinds of other stuff that he wasn't supposed to tell his mum because his dad said she'd go spare.

Every Brigand in the world has to attend a Wednesday-night clubhouse meeting known as church. Church night was Dante's favourite. Wives and girlfriends of the chapter's sixteen full-patch members would make food and get drunk at the bar while the men had their meeting in a little outbuilding known as the chapel. There were always other kids around.

Joe was always there. He was the son of the Führer, the chapter president. Dante and Joe were in Year Four at the same school and they were good mates. On this particular Wednesday the pair had stuffed themselves with chicken wings, cocktail sausages, oven chips and cola before each getting a hard smack and a threat of worse to come after dumping an older girl called Isobel into a puddle by the line of motorbikes out front.

After some loud belching to stop Joe's geeky eleven-year-old brother Martin from concentrating on his book, the pair ended up wrestling each other and chasing around the outside of the boxing ring. When they got breathless they'd run back to the bar and fuel up on cup cakes and Fanta.

This got repetitive after a while, so Dante and Joe were pleased when church ended and Teeth came out of the meeting room. Most of the Brigands joined the women and club associates at the bar, but Teeth sauntered past the pool table and blinking fruit machine to stick his head between the elasticised ropes of the boxing ring and give the two eight-year-olds high fives.

'How's my little champions?' Teeth asked, as he cracked a big gummy grin. His lips curled into his mouth and he couldn't sound Ss and Ts properly, but nobody was ever going to take the piss.

The two eight-year-olds were covered with grime and dust off the floor of the ring. They had bright red faces and glistening brows.

'You gonna show us a new move?' Joe asked, panting as he sat down with his legs swinging over the side of the ring.

'Kickboxing drills,' Teeth said seriously.

Both boys groaned.

'That's *so* boring,' Dante complained. 'Show us something cool, like that secret move you told us about where you hit the guy in the back of the head and his eyeballs shoot out of their sockets.'

'You're too young,' Teeth said cheerfully. 'Fancy moves do not a good fighter make.'

As Teeth spoke, he pulled off his boots and hung his leather Brigands jacket on the ring's corner post.

'Tell you what,' he said, as he jumped into the ring, with holey socks and a giant foam sparring pad over his right hand. 'Show me some decent kicks and punches. Then I *might* just show you a good way to dislocate someone's shoulder. Dante, you're up first.'

Over the next quarter hour Teeth worked up a sweat as the two boys chased him around the ring punching and kicking his sparring mitt. A couple of older girls also came in, and while Dante and Joe leaned against the ropes watching, Teeth showed the girls a devious thumb lock that could be used on any boy whose hands wandered into places they shouldn't.

'I don't know why you bother, Sandra,' Dante chirped. 'You're so ugly no boy's gonna come near you anyway.'

Sandra was thirteen, with her hair scraped back tight and a mouth like a foghorn. 'I dare you to come down out of that ring and say that,' she yelled. 'I'll rip your bloody little head off.'

'My cousin reckons you've already slept with half the boys in Year Ten,' Joe added.

'Oh does she indeed?' Sandra said, placing her hands on her hips. 'Like she can talk after everything she got up to with—'

Teeth interrupted. 'Now, now, children! Play nicely. If you're gonna start shrieking and whining I'm off to the bar to get drunk.'

Dante blew Sandra a cheeky kiss as Joe turned back into the ring and picked up the sparring mitt.

'You wanna put on your gloves and spar some more?' Joe asked.

'Too knackered,' Dante puffed, as he glanced at the clock on the wall behind the ring. 'Let's get a drink.'

As the boys jumped out of the ring, their dads – the Führer and Scotty – came into the room. The two men had been holed up in the club office for more than an hour after church finished.

Scotty was a big man, thirty-four years old, square jaw, rugged looking and with the same tangled red hair as his son. The Führer was twenty years older. Short and squat, with a titchy Hitler moustache and his arms fully inked with tattoos. His bald head and fat belly meant that

Dante could never look at him without being reminded of a bowling pin.

'Is Martin in here?' the Führer barked, so angry that all the tendons in his neck stuck out. Then he turned to Teeth. 'Has my boy Martin spoken to you?'

Teeth shook his head. Dante thought it was weird because Martin was the last kid on earth who'd jump into a boxing ring.

'I told him to speak to you,' the Führer said, before steaming off to the other room.

Joe grinned at Dante and whispered cheerfully, 'My geeky brother's about to get his butt kicked.'

Before Joe could explain, the Führer was back, dragging eleven-year-old Martin by his white school shirt.

'What did I tell you, brat?' the Führer shouted. Sandra and the other teenage girl backed off as Martin got bundled against the wall.

'Talk to Teeth,' Martin replied sheepishly. 'I forgot.'

'And what did you do?' the Führer yelled, as he ripped the book out of his son's hand. 'Harry Potter!' he snorted. 'You spend the night reading some book about dragons and tomorrow you'll go back to school and get your arse kicked again. What's the matter with you?'

'Screw you,' Martin shouted defiantly. 'Fighting never solved anything.'

There was a sharp crack as the Führer slapped his son's face. He turned towards Teeth and Scotty and began an explanation.

'Yesterday I caught this little bag of bones in the kitchen, crying to his *mommy*. Saying that some kid's picking on him at school. Can you imagine that? My son, the school punchbag. So I brought him down here tonight and told him to get Teeth to show him some moves. So what does he do?'

Joe seemed to enjoy watching his big brother getting whacked and couldn't resist stirring it. 'He can't help it, Dad,' Joe blurted. 'He's a natural born geekburger.'

Teeth spoke more sympathetically. 'It's not hard you know, Martin? Four or five sessions will teach you enough to stick up for yourself. I'll be happy to meet you up here a few afternoons after school and help you out.'

'I *don't* want to learn to fight,' Martin said angrily. 'I'll deal with this my way.'

'What's your way?' the Führer roared. 'Cry to mommy? Pay off the bully with a bag of sweeties?'

'I'm a pacifist,' Martin said, as he scowled at his dad. 'I'm not like you, Dad. I don't want to pick up an iron bar and break a guy's back, like with that dude you put in a wheelchair.'

The Führer wrenched Martin forward before thumping him against the wall again. '*You'll* be in a wheelchair if you don't get up in that ring. And the next time I see you reading I'll shove the damned book up your arse.'

Martin got hitched off the ground and thrust violently between the ropes around the ring. He moaned as his hip slammed down on the planks. People had heard the ruckus and were filtering through from the bar to see why the Führer was yelling.

'One step out of that ring and I'll break your skinny neck,' the Führer warned.

Martin clutched his painful hip as he staggered towards the far side of the ring, but he wasn't trying to escape. He'd eyed Teeth's Brigands M.C. jacket hooked over the corner post and when he got there he picked it up by the collar and spat on the patch.

Dante's jaw dropped. A biker's patch is a sacred object. It wasn't unknown for people to get a beating for accidentally brushing up against a patch in a crowded bar. If any adult had spat on Teeth's patch in a Brigands clubhouse, they'd be unlikely to make it out alive.

'That's what I think of your stupid ass motorcycle club,' Martin shouted defiantly, as he spat again and then gave his dad the finger.

'You little *bastard*,' the Führer snarled, as he grabbed the top rope and started clambering up into the ring.

'Oh you big brave man,' Martin shouted back. 'Let all your cronies cheer while you beat up your eleven-year-old son.'

Joe didn't like his brother much, but he didn't want to watch him die either. 'Martin, shut your *stupid* mouth,' he begged. 'Dad's gonna kill you!'

'Screw you as well,' Martin yelled back. 'You just copy everything Dad does.'

More people were coming into the back room from the bar. Outrage flashed through the gathering as everyone found out that Martin had spat on Teeth's patch.

The Führer had a vile temper, and Teeth didn't want his president doing something to Martin he'd regret later. So he grabbed him around the waist and pulled him down off the ropes. Teeth was twice the size of the Führer, but he struggled to keep hold. Scotty and another biker waded in to help.

'He's a kid acting out, boss,' Scotty said. 'Calm down. I know you don't really want to hurt him.'

'That's not my son,' the Führer screamed, as he pointed at Martin. 'When I get my hands on you I'm gonna smash every bone in your body.'

Teeth wasn't happy that some kid had spat on his patch. He reckoned Martin deserved a slap, but he didn't want to see him get stomped by a grown man.

'It's my patch to defend,' Teeth said, as the Führer finally settled down enough for the three bikers to let him go. 'But I'm not fighting a little kid and neither are you.'

'He *can't* get away with that,' the Führer answered. 'He's old enough to know what the patch means to us.'

'Someone his own size,' Teeth said, before looking down at Dante. 'Hey Dante, you wanna defend the club's honour?'

Dante had sloped off to the corner of the room with Joe and was startled to find everyone looking his way. 'Eh?' he gawped.

Teeth ducked down beside Dante and spoke in a whisper. 'Martin's a head taller than you, but he's skin and bones. You can take him easy. Will you get up there and fight for the honour of my Brigands patch?'

Dante didn't know how to answer. Teeth was one of his favourite grown-ups and he'd normally do anything

Teeth asked, but it wasn't exactly normal for an adult to ask you to jump into a ring and beat up another kid.

Dante's dad, Scotty, crouched down opposite Teeth.

'We've got to do something to satisfy the Führer,' Scotty explained in a whisper. 'You know what his temper's like. If we let him deal with Martin, the boy's gonna end up in hospital with his skull caved in.'

Dante looked warily at Teeth. 'So you want me to go easy on him?'

Teeth shook his head. 'The little prick spat on my patch. He deserves *some* pain. I just don't want the Führer killing him.'

Dante looked left and right at the two men he admired most in the world. 'OK, I'll fight him.'

Ever since his outburst, Martin had hung back at the far side of the ring looking increasingly scared. He'd seen his dad dragged off the ropes, but had no idea what was coming next until Teeth dinged the bell at ringside. By this time there were nearly forty people in the room.

'Ladies and gentlemen,' Teeth shouted. 'Following the desecration of my beloved Brigands patch by the skinny young chap now cowering on the far side of the ring, I'm pleased to say that cool heads have prevailed. The honour of defending the Brigands Motorcycle Club will be taken up by someone his own size. Namely, young Dante Scott!'

Most of the crowd was drunk and cheered noisily as Teeth lifted Dante into the ring and his dad led a chant in his name. The ring felt huge and its height gave a strange sense of isolation.

'Kill the geek, Dante,' Sandra shouted. 'Smash his brains out!'

'Put your fists up, Martin,' Joe shouted. 'Stop being a pussy.'

Everyone was yelling something, except poor Martin who stood on the far side of the ring with his arms at his side. Dante's brain ran at full pelt. Two things occurred to him. First, he wasn't wearing gloves, gumshield, or any other safety equipment and nobody had laid out any rules. Second, he thought about school and how his teacher made kids shake hands and sit together for the whole of the following lesson if they got in a fight.

Dante felt like he lived in two different worlds. The world of his mum and his teachers, where you weren't supposed to swear or fight and always had to be nice to everyone. Then there was the Brigands' world, where men sold drugs, stabbed snitches, got drunk, stole cars and found it perfectly acceptable to stick you in a boxing ring and tell you to beat the crap out of another kid who'd spat on a jacket.

'Stop stalling, Dante,' the Führer shouted. 'Wipe the floor with the skinny prick!'

Dante stepped away from the ropes and saw Martin backing into the opposite corner of the ring. Getting cornered is the worst thing a boxer can do, but Martin had never boxed in his life and held his arms crossed meekly in front his face.

Dante closed fast and threw a punch. He was surprised by how swiftly Martin dodged and he thought – almost hoped – that the fight would be more even than everyone assumed. He followed up with a Karate kick and his trainer sank deep into Martin's undefended stomach.

The crowd shouted wildly as Martin stumbled sideways. With everyone cheering him on, Dante got a taste of bloodlust as the older boy hit the ropes and bounced back towards him. He pounded Martin's face and stomach before an especially satisfying blow hit the squishy part of Martin's nose.

Blood spurted up Dante's arm and across the front of his T-shirt as Martin's legs gave out. The crowd was going insane and Dante felt wonderful and terrible at the same time. At the front of the crowd, Sandra was jumping up and down and screeching, 'Kill him, kill him. Scramble his brains!'

The amount of blood was shocking, but all the cheering made Dante feel like he was king of the world. Martin was sobbing and clearly had no intention of getting up, despite a few unsympathetic souls telling him to be a man and find his feet.

Teeth symbolically held his Brigands jacket aloft and rang the bell at ringside.

'Honour restored,' he shouted, before looking at the Führer. 'Are you happy with that, boss?'

The room went quiet as the Führer considered his reply. 'My boy got what he deserved,' he nodded. 'I'll settle for that.'

Teeth looked relieved as he stepped into the ring. 'Could someone get me some ice for Martin's nose, please?'

As Dante ducked between the ropes to leave the ring he found the Führer standing right in front of him.

'Sweet-faced little bulldog,' the Führer beamed, as he gave Dante a quick hug and slipped a ten-pound note into his palm. 'You gonna wear a Brigands patch one day?'

'Sure,' Dante said, as the other Brigands gathered around, saying stuff like *you saved the club's honour* and taking it in turns to shake his hand.

Two metres behind, Teeth had Martin sitting up. The boy's nose dripped blood on to the wooden boards. As Teeth held a handkerchief over a split lip, Martin kept saying thank you because he knew he'd have come off far worse if his father had done the beating.

Joe chased his friend as Dante walked away from the ring, looking at the clotting blood spattered up his arm as he crossed into the deserted bar.

'You were *lethal*,' Joe said enthusiastically. 'When my brother's nose burst! Oh man, I wish I'd been allowed to do that!'

Dante kept walking silently, until he was out in the night air facing a line of bikes.

'You OK?' Joe asked uncertainly. 'He didn't even hit you, did he? *And* you got a tenner off my dad.'

'Just shut *up* a minute,' Dante said, as he tried getting his head straight. He felt really confused and if Joe hadn't been standing there, he probably would have started crying.

2. ANIMAL

It was eleven by the time they left the clubhouse. Dante strapped on his helmet and locked arms around his dad's waist as the V-twin engine rumbled to life. Some Brigands ran beautiful bikes with custom paint and expensive chrome components. Scotty preferred what's known as a rat bike.

His twenty-year-old Harley-Davidson Softail had clocked 178,000 miles and was finished in matt grey, streaked with rust. The leather seat was cracked so bad you could see the springs inside and only Scotty's love had kept it running, long past the point where it would have been cheaper to buy a replacement.

The Scott family lived amidst farmland a fifteen-minute ride from the clubhouse. Dante loved riding with his dad, especially after school pickups when he got to put on a cool leather jacket and a crash helmet while his mates clambered into people carriers. But it was two hours past bedtime, the roads were near deserted and the whole way home Dante was scared that he'd drift into sleep and fall off the bike.

Scotty didn't want to wake his other three kids, so he cut the engine and freewheeled down his front driveway. The house got a lot less love and attention than his Harley. The driveway was badly overgrown and the kitchen light shone through a boarded window that Dante's brother Jordan had smashed with a cricket ball several months earlier.

Scotty pulled up under a car porch next to a stack of kids' bikes. Dante yawned as he stepped off the Harley and unbuckled his helmet.

'Kitchen light's on,' Scotty said. 'Your mum'll be waiting in ambush. Whatever you do, *don't* tell her about the fight.'

Dante raised an eyebrow as he unzipped his leather jacket. 'I know, Dad, I'm not stupid.'

'Oh!' Scotty blurted as he saw the dried blood all over Dante's T-shirt. 'Take that off.'

'It's freezing,' Dante complained.

'Hurry up, before she comes out to see what we're up to,' Scotty said, as he put his key in the front door. Dante pulled his shirt over his head, but he had no pocket big enough to tuck it into so he threw it behind a shrub as his dad stepped into the hallway.

Dante's mum, Carol, stood in the kitchen doorway. She wore a pink dressing gown and slippers, but a tattoo of coiled snakes ran from her ankle up to her left knee and marked her out as a biker chick.

'Don't give me a hard time,' Scotty begged, giving his wife pleading eyes as Dante pushed back the front door.

Carol was angry, but kept her voice down because eleven-month-old Holly was sleeping in her parents' room at the top of the stairs.

'A hard time!' she hissed. 'You've got a bloody nerve. Dante's eight years old and he's got school in the morning. Do you know the job I'll have getting him out of bed?'

'I'm sorry,' Scotty said quietly. 'I was discussing the development deal with the Führer and it just dragged on forever.'

Dante put his foot on the bottom step.

'Wee and teeth,' Carol told him stiffly. 'Then straight to bed and keep the noise down. Everyone's asleep up there.'

'Can I get a glass of water?' Dante asked.

'I'll bring it up for you,' Carol said. 'And where's your shirt?'

Dante couldn't think of an excuse so his dad butted in. 'He got hot running around with Joe and took his shirt off. We had a look around, but we couldn't find it. I've got to go back tomorrow morning and do some work on the bike. I'll take a proper look in daylight.'

Dante found his mum's fluorescent pink fingernail waggling under his nose. 'I'm *fed* up with you losing things, Dante. If that shirt doesn't turn up, the replacement's coming out of your birthday and Christmas money.'

Normally Dante would have protested, but he was so tired he could barely keep upright.

'Goddammit, Scotty,' Carol said, as Dante crept up the stairs. 'Two nights a week is all I ask and you can't even bring him home at a decent hour.'

Dante was one of four kids, and their dirty clothes and damp towels were spread thick across the scruffy little bathroom. Along with puddles on the floor were his big brother's mud-crusted rugby kit and sixteen-year-old Lizzie's stash of deodorants and beauty products.

After a leak and a twenty-second excursion for his toothbrush, Dante headed down a narrow hallway and quietly opened the door of the room he shared with his brother Jordan. The thirteen-year-old snored, with a foot hanging over the side of his bed and his duvet mounded over his head.

Jordan was moody and Dante was likely to get a punch if he disturbed him, so he crept towards his bed. He took off tracksuit bottoms, undies and trainers with a single sweep and slipped on a pair of pyjama bottoms before straightening his pillow and rolling under the sheets.

*

Dante woke on his back with Jordan leaning over his bed. The older boy held the curtains open and peered through the window.

'What are you doing?' Dante moaned sleepily as his brother's briefs hovered above him. 'Get your damned nuts out of my face.'

'Do you know that car?' Jordan asked seriously.

Dante pressed the button on his projector clock making 02:07 flicker in red on the ceiling. As he slid out from under Jordan he heard men speaking downstairs and his heart quickened when he realised they were angry.

'Maybe it's the police,' Dante said edgily, as he shuffled up to the window next to Jordan and looked down on to the driveway.

There were no streetlights out here in the country, so it was usually pitch black at night, but the living-room and kitchen lights were on downstairs and enough light escaped through the blinds to illuminate the outline of a Ford Mondeo and a customised Harley Sportster.

'That's the Führer's bike,' Dante said.

Jordan shook his head. 'He drives a Sportster but that's not his.'

Dante took pride in knowing something his older brother didn't. 'It is so. Remember the Barcelona run last summer? That's the one he took when he couldn't get his orange one running.'

'You're right,' Jordan admitted. 'And I've seen that Mondeo at the clubhouse before as well.'

As the two boys peered out, blurred words from the three men downstairs came up through the floorboards.

'I'm gonna sneak down and listen,' Dante said as he hopped off the bed.

Jordan grabbed his arm. 'I wouldn't. Dad'll go ape shit if he catches you.'

'I'll be casual,' Dante said confidently, as he pointed to the shelf beside his bed with his clock and a box of tissues on it. 'Mum never brought my water up so I'll just say I'm thirsty.'

Jordan let go. He was fond of his little brother, but he was also curious to know what was going on and it was no big deal to him if Dante got yelled at.

'Just be careful,' Jordan said. 'Don't hang around.'

The lights were on in the hallway and bathroom. Dante crept down in socks and pyjama bottoms. By the time he reached the hallway he'd worked out that the three voices belonged to his dad, the Führer and a big hairy Brigand who everyone called Felicity because he looked like some actress in an old TV show called *The Good Life*.

They were arguing about the redevelopment of the clubhouse. Dante was only eight and didn't know the ins and outs, but understood that the land on which the Brigands clubhouse was built was worth a lot of money. Some members of the chapter, led by the Führer, wanted to knock down the barns and build shops, restaurants and a block of apartments. A smaller group led by his dad said they liked the clubhouse the way it was and didn't want to sell it.

It was risky standing at the bottom of the stairs where he'd be spotted through the archway into the living-room, so Dante moved into the kitchen. He quietly slid the toaster out of the way and leaned across the worktop to peer through the wooden slats in the serving hatch above the washing machine.

They didn't have a separate dining-room, and his father sat at a small dining-table, the back of his head less than half a metre from Dante's prying nose. There were documents spread across the tabletop. Felicity sat opposite, while the Führer stood up jiggling Dante's Wrestlemania pen between his thumb and forefinger.

'Just sign,' the Führer said, his voice the calmest it had been since Dante awoke. 'You're the only one blocking this, Scotty.'

'Bull crap,' Scotty said, as Dante watched his head shake. 'The vote was nine to four, two abstentions.'

'Those guys are with *you*,' the Führer said. 'If you change, they'll change. And the vote doesn't matter anyway. It's your signature that we need: president, vice-president and club secretary can authorise the land deal.'

The Führer leaned on the back of the couch and spoke louder. 'You know how many palms I had to grease to get permission to build on that land, Scotty? Half the county council have had their houses decorated gratis; the mayor's wife is wearing a three-K watch. All that came out of my building company, not club coffers.'

'It's just money with you,' Scotty shrugged. 'But what's gonna happen to the club? We lose thirty years of tradition and spend three years without a clubhouse. Members will drift away, the chapter will die.'

The Führer gave Scotty the kind of *silly boy* look that Dante got off his Year One teacher when he poured PVA glue in his lap.

'We'll hire a church hall or a school gym,' the Führer said. 'And when the project's finished South Devon will have the best Brigands clubhouse in the country, probably the world.'

'The barns have got soul,' Scotty explained. 'Sure it'll be swank, but you can't buy history, you can't buy class.'

Felicity interrupted, 'Scotty, guys like me and Big Ted need the money. We're looking at two hundred grand for each full-patch member.'

'Guaranteed, up front from Badger Properties,' the Führer added. 'Look around you Scotty. You're living in a shithole. You can pay off your mortgage, fix this place up, buy a decent bike and still have enough left to take the kids to Disneyland or something.'

Dante had only previously heard his dad's side of the argument: how the Führer's plans would turn the club compound into a tourist trap, how the members would take their money and drift away. But the instant Dante heard the word Disneyland he flipped sides and wanted his dad to take the pen and sign.

But Scotty stood up and looked at his watch. 'It's two in the morning,' he yawned. 'We've been over this six, ten, maybe even twenty times. Everyone knows where I stand and now I'm going to bed.'

Dante grimaced as Mickey Mouse and a trip on an aeroplane vanished in a puff of smoke. Then he jolted and slid down off the cabinet as his mum crept up and touched his shoulder.

'Nosey parker,' she said irritably as she dragged her son towards the fridge-freezer. 'You should be asleep. If you start up whining when you've got to get up for school in the morning I'll make you *damned* sorry.'

Dante studied his mum's expression. Sometimes she got so angry that you had to do exactly what she said or she'd go bananas, but he wasn't getting that look and decided to play for sympathy.

'I came down because *you* forgot to bring my glass of water.'

His mum took a tumbler out of a cabinet and slammed the door shut before filling it from the cold tap. 'There,' she said, as she passed it over. 'Now scram.'

Dante reached the hallway as hell broke loose in the living-room. His dad shouted. Then the table grated across the floor and the Führer shouted back.

'I've put my own sweat and money into this, Scotty. I'm not leaving this house until these papers are signed.'

'You think you can bully me?' Scotty screamed. 'You don't know me at all, do you? Get out of my house you short-arsed son of a bitch.'

Scotty stepped out from behind the table, muscles swollen beneath his vest and looking like he could break the Führer in half with a sneeze. Dante swelled with pride, but the balance of power changed when Felicity pulled a handgun from beneath his leather waistcoat.

'You sit down and sign it,' the Führer ordered, as the Wrestlemania pen smacked down on the table.

'You think you can muscle this?' Scotty shouted incredulously. 'After all these years? You'd better kill me because this is way out of order. I'll have this put to a vote and you'll be out of the club.'

The Führer smiled. 'The accountants found some irregularities in the books from last year when you were club secretary. I've already discussed it with the London chapter and the national president. They've left it at my discretion for now, but you're looking at a disciplinary hearing and being kicked out of the club in bad standing.'

'Trumped up bullshit,' Scotty hissed. 'How much did you bribe them?'

'Enough,' the Führer smiled. 'That's all you need to know.'

Dante had the best view in the house. As well as a clear view into the living-room, the crashing table had brought Jordan and Lizzie out on to the top of the staircase behind him. In the kitchen, his mum stood on an upturned bucket and pulled a shotgun wrapped in a bin liner down off the cabinet.

'Dante, upstairs,' his mum shouted, before ratcheting the shotgun, heading into the living-room and aiming it at Felicity. 'I think it's time you boys said goodnight.'

Scotty was alarmed and raised his palm. 'Carol, you be careful with that thing,' he warned. 'It's loaded.'

'Well you don't say,' she carped, as Dante got halfway up the stairs and stopped. 'Now I don't give a shit about your development, but it's two in the morning. I'm awake, my kids are awake and I want you two out of my house. Is that crystal clear?'

The Führer looked at the barrels of the gun and smiled. 'Carol, why don't you put that thing down?'

'You know what?' Scotty said, eyeballing the Führer. 'I don't need this shit any more. I'll sign the papers and take my two hundred grand. I signed up for a brotherhood not a business, so you can take my Brigands patch and stick that too.'

As Dante's mum lowered the shotgun, his dad bent down to pick the pen off the floor. The Führer set the table straight and told Felicity to help pick up the papers and find the pages that Scotty needed to sign.

Carol looked back into the hallway. 'You kids get back in bed,' she shouted. 'Don't make me come up there.'

Dante moved up a couple more steps, but his two teenage siblings didn't like being spoken to that way and stayed defiantly still on the top landing.

'Don't make me come up there, you three,' their mum repeated.

'I'm trying to get past,' Dante protested.

This earned him a withering look from Lizzie at the same moment as a baby's squeal came out of their parents' room.

'Aww great,' Carol said, as she turned back towards the three men. 'That's an hour getting Holly back to sleep.'

'I'll get her,' Lizzie said wearily, as she headed towards the cot in her parents' room, mumbling, 'Don't mind me, I've only got a Spanish exam tomorrow,' to herself.

In the living-room the papers were back on the table. Scotty reached between toy cars and blocks underneath the sofa to grab Dante's pen. As he straightened up, he saw Felicity's handgun pointing limply at the carpet. Felicity's eyes stared dumbly at the Führer, awaiting his next order.

'OK,' the Führer said, as his titchy moustache bristled in a self satisfied way. 'Three signatures by the Post-it notes.'

Scotty was serious about signing the documents, but the Führer's smile and the happy little bounce of his size eight Dr Marten boots made him angry. Scotty loved the Brigands as much as – maybe even more than – he loved his family and the thought of handing in his patch and burning off his highwayman tattoo was too much to take.

With a powerful movement, Scotty sprang to his full height while simultaneously driving the pen through Felicity's windpipe. Blood gurgled; Dante and Jordan nervously came down the staircase to see why their mum had screamed.

'Shoot him now, Carol!' Scotty shouted.

Dante's mum raised the shotgun as Felicity staggered back to the wall. The giant still had the pen sticking out of his throat and he was choking on his own blood, but he managed to raise the pistol slightly.

Two triggers were pulled in the same second.

The shotgun erupted with two orange muzzle blasts, spraying shot over a wide area concentrated around Felicity's head and torso, but also peppering the surrounding wall with tiny holes. The pistol made a sharper bang. Felicity hadn't the strength to raise it high but the final act of his thirty-eight years on earth was to shoot a bullet into Scotty's kneecap at such an angle that it bored on down, shattering his right fibula and exiting through the back of his calf after severing the main artery in his leg.

In the seconds before he passed out, Scotty groaned as he hit the carpet and reached for Felicity's pistol.

The Führer had ducked under the table and he too crawled towards the pistol as Carol pumped the shotgun to reload.

Carol had known the Führer since she'd been a fourteen-year-old tearaway hanging around the Brigands clubhouse looking for free marijuana. She knew that the Führer would kill her now that he was riled, but she felt calm as the empty cartridge flew out to her left.

To Carol the consequences of murder were nothing compared to her need to protect her kids. But as she pushed the barrel forward, there was lightness to the action and a hollow sound from inside. The shotgun was empty.

3. WITNESS

Carol turned. She saw Jordan at the bottom of the stairs and Dante halfway up as she dropped the gun and charged towards the front door.

'Run,' she screamed to her boys. 'Get out of the house, now!'

Jordan followed his mum towards the front door, Dante started going downstairs but ducked out of the way when the Führer fired Felicity's pistol. It was a wild shot from under the dining-table that punched through the wall and clattered into saucepans inside the cupboard on the other side.

The Führer sent the table flying with his boot and took proper aim with his second shot. It hit Carol in the back as she held the latch on the front door. Her body slumped against the frosted glass, blocking the doorway and forcing Jordan to turn back into the hall.

The Führer stepped out of the kitchen doorway, trailing blood from the rapidly growing puddle around Scotty.

'Come on, Jordan!' Dante pleaded, as he headed back up the stairs and charged towards the door of his parents' room.

But Jordan knew he wouldn't win a race to the top of the stairs with a bullet. Possibly hoping to save his own life, but more likely knowing he was doomed and trying to give Dante a better chance to reach his parents' room, Jordan grabbed the only thing that came to hand and charged at the Führer.

The metal waste basket was filled with umbrellas and a collection of Holly's toys. As the items flew through the air Jordan made a desperate lunge. He was as tall as the Führer, and his flying foot plus the debris forced the Führer back into the living-room – but not before he'd pulled the trigger and shot Jordan in the stomach.

The teenager crumpled against the tiled floor. As the umbrellas, Duplo bricks and Beanie Babies landed, the Führer pointed the muzzle of the pistol down and shot Jordan through the head.

Dante reached his parents' bedroom. His legs felt hot, his stomach was somersaulting. It was a cramped space, with clothes piled out of the broken wardrobe doors and eleven-month-old Holly's cot shoehorned at an angle between the double bed and the radiator. Holly lay on the bed kicking the air, gnawing her fist and making a low rattly groan that meant she wanted someone to pick her up and cuddle her back to sleep.

Lizzie had seen everything downstairs. She'd opened the window and considered jumping down and running for help, but she didn't want to leave Holly and didn't think she'd be able to jump safely with the baby in her arms.

The Führer stepped over Jordan and raced upstairs as Dante slammed the bedroom door and bought a few seconds by turning the key.

'Go by the window,' Lizzie shouted, as she gave Dante a shove, then reached up high and grabbed the front of the double wardrobe.

She tugged with all the strength she could muster and the fragile chipboard and melamine wardrobe creaked and groaned as it crashed down in front of the door. Wire hangers clanked inside and the seldom used suitcases on top puffed clouds of dust.

'Come out now and I'll kill you fast,' the Führer shouted, as a shot skimmed through the top half of the door. Dante and Lizzie ducked and the bullet only hit the wall.

'What do we do?' Dante screamed, as the Führer shoulder-charged the door.

'That time Jordan dared you to jump out of the window and you twisted your ankle,' Lizzie said rapidly, as the Führer slammed into the door again, popping the lock and shifting the tilted wardrobe several centimetres. 'Do you think you can do it again without hurting yourself?'

'That was two summers ago,' he nodded. 'I'm bigger now.'

'Right,' Lizzie said. 'You drop, I'll lower Holly down to you and I'll jump last.'

'OK,' Dante nodded.

The Führer slammed the door again. The opening was now almost wide enough to squeeze through. Holly hated the banging and started to cry as Dante swung his leg out over the window ledge. He'd noticed his legs feeling warm, but it was only now that he saw the dark green patch around his crotch and realised that he'd pissed himself with fright.

'Come *on*,' Lizzie urged, as Dante stared down. It was a three-metre drop on to a shaggy lawn softened by the recent rain, but his mind flashed back to the previous jump and he hesitated until the Führer slammed into the door again.

A sharp pain went up Dante's leg as he landed, bare shoulder squelching into the mud. By the time he stood up, Lizzie was leaning out of the window, with Holly dangling off the end of her arm, kicking and screaming.

Dante went on tiptoes and gripped Holly's chubby ankles.

'Have you got hold?' Lizzie shouted.

'I think so,' Dante said. He was at full stretch, and wasn't a hundred per cent sure which way the baby would topple when Lizzie let go.

There was a huge bang behind, indicating that the Führer had triumphed over the wardrobe blocking the door.

'Take her,' Lizzie screamed. 'Don't wait, start running.'

Dante stumbled backwards as Holly's weight

transferred into his hands. The baby's head and body were heavier than her legs and with Dante holding her ankles her body pivoted awkwardly.

Dante gasped in horror as Holly's skull scraped the pebbledashed wall of the house. She let out a desperate scream, but in a frenzy of flying arms and trying not to fall over Dante saved her from hitting the ground head first, ending up with the baby clamped awkwardly to his waist.

Up above the Führer was in the bedroom. Lizzie couldn't jump safely until Dante and Holly had moved out of the way and the Führer grabbed her arm before she got a chance.

'Wish I had more time with a sexy thing like you,' he laughed as he dragged the teenager away from the window.

Lizzie kicked, spat and elbowed the Führer, but it only delayed the inevitable by a couple of seconds. The last thing she saw was her own nose squished against a cracked mirror as the pistol touched the back of her head.

The shot echoed through the darkness around the farmhouse. Holly wriggled and screamed as Dante tried to run with her. The wind was cold on his chest and his socks slipped on the mud.

Dante dared a backwards glance and saw the Führer aiming his gun through the bedroom window. It was open ground, but it was also dark and the Führer was no marksman. He fired two shots. The first was hopeless, the second close enough for Dante to hear it whistle over his head and lash through branches and leaves at the end of the garden. No more shots came and Dante realised the Führer had run out of bullets. It was Felicity's gun, so even if there was a spare ammunition clip the Führer wouldn't have it.

Dante reached the bottom of the garden, ducked under a slatted fence and began running across a fallow field belonging to a neighbouring farmer.

'Please Holly,' Dante begged, stroking his sister's hair as she fought and kicked. 'You've got to be quiet.'

The top of her head oozed blood. He remembered his mum telling him never to touch or prod Holly's head because babies' skulls are so delicate. What if he'd done her brain damage when she'd hit the wall?

The ground underfoot was soggy, and with no shoes and Holly's weight slowing him down Dante knew he'd never make it across three fields to Mr Norman the onion farmer's house before the Führer caught him.

Dante had played around these fields all his life and knew plenty of hiding places, but they weren't much use with Holly screaming her head off. He thought about abandoning Holly and running for help. A baby was no use as a witness, so there was no rational reason for the Führer to kill her, but when riled the Führer wasn't a rational man and Holly might have some value as a hostage.

Part of Dante wanted to sink into the mud and cry. After seeing his mum, dad, brother and sister die, death almost seemed like the best option, but a bigger part of him was determined not to let the Führer win.

'Sssssh,' Dante sniffed, as he stopped walking and ducked low behind a bush before gently bouncing Holly to soothe her. His curling breath caught the moonlight and his socks squelched in the mud.

Then Dante had a flash of genius. He wiped his little finger on the least muddy part of his pyjama bottoms and then gently introduced it to Holly's mouth. Holly was teething and bit down so hard that he normally would have yelped, but with something to bite on her noise reduced to a gurgle. She also wriggled less which made it easier for Dante to hold her.

Dante saw the Führer step out into the back garden, quickly flashing a torch across the lawn, illuminating the bush behind which Dante crouched. Then the Führer stopped and pulled out a mobile telephone.

'I'm not Scotty,' he began. 'It's me; I can't use my own phone. Just shut up and listen. I've got a big mess up at Scotty's place. I need you to come up with some petrol. We've gotta burn everything . . . I'm not giving details on the phone; just do what I'm asking. I've got to track down his bastard kid before he mouths off. Get the petrol and be here as fast as you can.'

As the Führer tucked Scotty's phone in his leather jacket, Dante considered his options. He'd never make it across the onion fields before the Führer caught him in the torch beam. He could probably make it to the road without being seen, but the roads around here were dead at this time of night. He wouldn't get far carrying Holly, and the first people to spot him would most likely be whoever it was that the Führer had just called.

He thought about going back to the house and sneaking inside to make a 999 call, but if he was seen he'd be trapped and he had no key, so the only way in was through the back door where the Führer was currently standing.

Dante realised that his best chance was the push-bikes stacked up beside the house. His own bike was a BMX, which was pretty useless because there was no way he could ride fast and hold on to Holly. But the bike Lizzie rode to school each morning had a big vinyl pouch over the back wheel which she'd stuff with her backpack and hockey kit.

It wasn't a great plan, but it was the only one Dante had. As the Führer reached the bottom of the garden he crossed into the field where he'd seen Dante heading a couple of minutes earlier. The youngster used the trees and bushes on the edge of the field as cover, moving sideways and then running across the concrete towards the car porch at the side of the house.

The bikes were kept leaning up against the brickwork, with the battered Harley taking pride of place on its kickstand alongside them. The lights were still on inside the house and Dante was horrified by what he saw.

His socks and the cuffs of his pyjama bottoms were thick with mud, the rest of his body was spattered and the dark patch of urine around his crotch had grown. He imagined what Jordan would say if he saw that he'd wet himself in fright. A hammer blow hit when Dante realised that his brother was never going to say anything again, *ever*.

Dante looked back cautiously and was pleased to see the Führer heading deeper into the fields. The house provided visual cover, but he'd still hear if Holly started bawling and Dante needed both hands free to move Jordan's racing bike and wheel out Lizzie's.

He crouched slowly and moved Holly's head back from his shoulder. Dante never usually carried her any further than the walk between the house and car and she was surprisingly heavy if you held her for long enough.

'Good girl,' Dante whispered, but as he moved the hand away from Holly's neck he saw the huge triangle of blood that had run from the cut on her head and soaked into her sleeping suit. Holly made no sound as he rested her on the concrete and pulled his finger from her mouth.

The baby looked still, eyes closed and a glaze of sweat on her cheeks. She was breathing, but there was stiffness about her and a dead look that reminded him of a plastic doll.

'I'm sorry I hit your head,' Dante said quietly as he wheeled Lizzie's bike away from the wall and ripped open the Velcro cover on the pouch.

After hurriedly throwing out Lizzie's GCSE history textbook and science folder, he cradled Holly and lowered her carefully into the pouch. He pulled down the Velcro cover, but deliberately left it loose so that she could breathe.

Dante was much shorter than sixteen-year-old Lizzie. His feet didn't reach the ground from the saddle and he had to tilt the bike uncomfortably to one side to push off, but after a wobbly start he took a final look back over his shoulder as he pedalled up the drive.

The trees overhanging the road gave him cover, but he worried that whoever the Führer had phoned would pull into the driveway before he made it out. When he got up to the road he reached forwards to flip on the headlight before looking both ways and swinging out.

4. HANDS

Salcombe wasn't exactly a crime blackspot. The police spent most of their time dealing with parking offences, low-level drug dealing and burglaries of rarely used second homes. Even the Brigands knew better than to piss in their own backyard and usually kept whatever trouble they caused behind the high fences of their clubhouse.

A burned out house with five bodies inside was the biggest crime in decades. Twenty-six-year-old constable Kate McLaren had never known anything like it. The fire brigade's first impression was arson, but the house didn't burn completely and the charred corpse blocking the front doorway had an obvious bullet wound in her back.

The media had poured into the area, split between the crime scene and the car park around Kingsbridge police station four miles away. Photographers, journalists and TV vans fitted with satellite dishes were double parked in the street awaiting a press conference.

There had been no official announcement, but it was common knowledge that two of the dead were Brigands and many journalists jumped to the conclusion that an old grudge had flared between the Brigands and a local gang known as the Headless Corpses.

The key witness lay silently in a small room filled with toys and cushions. There was a two-way mirror, a video camera mounted above the doorway and anatomically correct dolls that little kids could use to re-enact the horrible things that adults did to them.

As the only woman on duty, Kate McLaren had been asked to play mother. Dante's clothes had been taken for forensic purposes. After comforting him during a doctor's examination and taking him upstairs for a hot shower, she'd persuaded the manager at Woolworths to open early so that she could buy underwear, tracksuit and trainers for age 7–9. Through all of this, and the four hours that followed, Dante hadn't spoken.

The child-friendly room felt too warm as Kate stepped inside. Dante was warmer still, having buried himself under every cushion and soft toy he could find. The click of the door made his eyes swivel and he flicked some hair off his face before going back to being dead.

'You didn't eat any of your lunch,' Kate said softly, as she stared at the tray on the floor.

She didn't know what Dante liked, so there was milk, juice and cola, along with two different sandwiches, packets of cookies, pieces of fruit, crisps and chocolate bars.

'I could get anything you wanted, Dante. Fish and chips, bacon sandwich, a Happy Meal.'

The cushions above Dante shifted and the boy made a dry grunt. Kate smiled, hoping she'd finally made a breakthrough.

'Did you say you'd like a Happy Meal? What's your favourite, Dante? A burger? McNuggets?'

'Will it make me happy?' Dante said sarcastically.

Kate ached with grief as she tried to imagine what Dante had seen. Getting him to speak was a breakthrough, but she wasn't a psychologist and had no idea what to say next.

'I used to collect Smurfs when I was your age,' Kate said. 'They were little blue men with white hats. My parents got coupons when they bought petrol and you needed ten tokens to get a Smurf.'

Dante sensed Kate's desperation. He felt cruel, making her sit there worrying about him and asking questions that he ignored, but there was darkness in his head like he'd never felt before. Everything hurt: colours hurt, sounds hurt and so did the rubbery smell from his new trainers and the itchy label in the back of his shirt. He wanted to speak, but at the same time thinking of even the tiniest movement filled him with dread.

'Would you feel more comfortable speaking to someone else?' Kate asked. 'Like your teacher? Or maybe you'd prefer talking to a man instead of me? Because we don't want to push you Dante, but you can really help by telling us what happened.'

Dante thought about his dad. He'd been let out of prison to witness Dante's birth, before returning to serve the balance of an eighteen-month stretch for possession of drugs and assault. He'd told Dante that the cops fitted him up. He said it was better to sort your own problems. The cops were scum. Snitches and informants were lower than paedophiles.

But Dante wasn't grown up. He'd have a long wait if he wanted to get on his Harley and settle a score with the Führer with a gun or a knife. So should he be a snitch or should he wait until he was old enough to get revenge?

Dante rolled slightly on the cushions and felt a burning pain in his bladder.

'I need to pee,' he blurted, aching with dread as cushions and teddies flew about. He stood up and glowered at Kate with manic eyes and knotted hair.

Kate led Dante briskly along a peeling corridor, past offices filled with desks and computers. The men's toilets were through the last door before the fire exit at the end of the corridor.

The frosted windows had been swung open and Dante got a chill blast as he stepped up to the urinal and started pissing. After shaking off he looked at the sinks and decided to wash his hands. He didn't usually wash if he'd only peed, but he liked the fresh air in the washroom and wanted to delay going back to the stuffy air and the pile of cushions.

Dante turned on the tap and repeatedly tugged the lever under the soap dispenser until a bright pink lake filled his palm. When he slapped his hands glistening strands flew in all directions, spattering the white tiles behind the sink.

He concentrated on the soap, finding innocent relief in swiping it up and down his hands, then rubbing them together until a lather mound pirouetted and shrank into the plughole. Dante imagined that his mum was watching him from heaven or something. She'd undoubtedly be pleased that he'd washed his hands.

She always said he should wash his hands every time he went, even if it was just to pee. Also if he came in after playing out in the fields, and before he ate dinner, and if he stroked Mr Norman's golden retriever. If Dante had washed his hands all the times his mum wanted he'd probably have to do it thirty-seven times a day. On the other hand, Dante's dad didn't care about that sort of thing. He'd come inside after working on his bike, and get a filthy look as he wiped greasy hands on his jeans and picked up a sandwich.

But which one of them was right?

A flushing noise came from one of the stalls behind Dante. A big man emerged in a red tie and cheap suit. He slapped a copy of *The Times* on the tiled ledge above the sinks before starting to wash his hands.

'Did I need that,' the man said, as he gave Dante a relieved smile. 'Better out than in, eh?'

Dante didn't respond. His eyes were fixed on his hands, but his mind was back in the boxing ring from the night before. He thought about the difference between the world of his mum, where you said *please* and *thank you* and washed your hands and the world of his dad where fighting, swearing, selling drugs and farting out loud were perfectly acceptable.

'Name's Ross Johnson,' the big man continued, despite the fact that Dante had ignored his first remark. 'I've come down from London. I'm a police inspector, but I'm also a psychologist. I specialise in interviewing and supporting child witnesses. You must be Dante Scott.'

The words drifted over Dante as he scrubbed under his nails and between his fingers, struggling to wipe off all the soap. All Dante's life his dad had been the cool one and his mum had seemed bossy and strict. But if all people were like his mum, he wouldn't have had to watch her get shot in the back. Or have seen his brother and sister die, or Holly get hit on the head or . . .

'A crime is like your dinner,' Ross explained. 'You want to get right on the case while it's hot. Information you give us today is more valuable than the same information might be tomorrow.'

Dante was finally listening to Ross Johnson. As he turned the tap off, he looked up and saw that the big man was holding out paper towels to dry his hands.

'My dad didn't like the police,' Dante said nervously, as he dried between his fingers. 'He told me never to speak to cops if they came to the house. But I don't think that's what my mum would have wanted. It was the Führer, trying to get my dad to sign papers letting them knock down the clubhouse. Felicity was there. He pulled a gun when my dad said no.'

Ross was excited by this information, but at the same

time raised a hand indicating that he wanted Dante to stop talking. 'Dante, what we need to do is take you to an interview room where I can get everything you say on tape, OK?'

Ross opened the door and Kate was stunned to see Dante chatting away. She didn't complain, but felt miffed that after all of her efforts to get Dante to come out of his shell he'd opened up after a chance encounter in the gents.

'I want a cheeseburger and chips from Bay Burgers and loads of ketchup,' Dante said confidently as Kate led him back down the corridor with Ross striding behind.

Dante suddenly felt odd, but also important. His brain ran at fifty times normal speed and the aches in his head were replaced by sparks of energy.

'And I don't want to go back in that horrible room,' he added. 'It's too stuffy.' Then he stopped suddenly and turned towards Kate. 'My sister Holly! What was it you told me about Holly?'

Kate smiled. 'Holly is in the hospital. She had some stitches and lost a lot of blood. She'll be in hospital for a few days but she's going to be fine.'

Kate opened the door of the little room with the cushions and toys, but Dante was repelled by the dead air and the sense of gloom he'd felt as he lay on the cushions.

'I hate this room,' he said.

'It's just for a minute until we find somewhere else,' Kate explained.

'We'll find a room with a window that opens,' Ross

said warmly. 'You can eat your burger while I set up the tape recorder.'

An image of Jordan and Mum flickered in Dante's mind. He felt like he was balanced on a cliff's edge. He was terrified that the room and the cushions would send him back into the aching black space where his mind had spent the last six hours.

'I can't go back in there,' he said, breaking into a loud sob. 'I want my mum back. Why did this have to happen to *me*?'

Kate went down on one knee and scooped Dante into her arms. His grip felt surprisingly strong as he grasped her with tears streaking down his face.

5. POOL

Three hours later Ross Johnson came out of an interview room looking stressed. Five long strides took him into an incident room. Chief Inspector Jane Lindsay was the uniformed officer in charge of the murder inquiry. She stood by the window, peering into darkness at the press gathered in the car park downstairs.

'They can wait there all night,' she sighed. 'They've had the only statement they're getting.'

Ross furrowed his brow as he followed the senior officer's gaze. Most of the journalists sat on the low wall around the car park or in the open doorways of their cars. A vaguely familiar face from the BBC wore a high-necked black coat. She was going out live on twenty-four-hour news, while the correspondent from Sky stood behind her camera trying to put her off by making dickhead gestures.

'So,' Chief Inspector Lindsay asked, as she looked back at Ross. 'How's our star witness holding up?'

'Dante's in shock,' Ross said. 'He's having what we call a manic response: one minute he's full of beans, the next he's crying and asking for his mum. But he held it together for long enough to record a decent witness statement.'

'Do you think he'll make a good witness in court?' Lindsay asked.

'He's only eight, but I'd say so,' Ross nodded. 'I had a brief conversation with his teacher. She said Dante's one of the two or three brightest kids in his year. Good all-rounder, confident and popular. Only trouble is he can be a bit rough in the playground, but she says they've got a few bikers' sons at the school and they're all the same. They idolise their dads and the macho posturing rubs off on them.'

'We might need a strong witness,' Lindsay said. 'The Führer had half an hour to clean up the house before Dante reached the payphone and forensics reckon he did a pretty thorough job. All the bodies are badly burned and what wasn't burned got a soaking when the fire brigade doused the flames.'

'What about away from the scene?' Ross asked. 'Tyre tracks, petrol cans, eyewitnesses?'

'Not yet, but we're hoping,' Lindsay said. 'I've dealt with Brigands cases before. The Führer will have torched his clothes and shoes. The weapons will have been taken away and melted down.'

'Has the Führer been pulled for questioning yet?' Ross asked.

Lindsay shook her head. 'We thought he might choose to disappear for a few days, but he seems confident. We knocked on his door, asked him a few questions and explained that we wanted to impound his bike in conjunction with a murder investigation. He told the officers to go ahead, but they found the bike on the floor of his workshop in a hundred and sixteen pieces, fitted with a brand new set of tyres that'll make it impossible to trace tyre tracks.'

'Shit,' Ross said, shaking his head. 'What about the other Brigands, someone must know something?'

'They'll never speak to cops,' Lindsay said.

Ross raised an eyebrow in surprise. 'But in this instance. I mean, two of their own people dead. A woman, two kids . . .'

'Someone in the gang might have a problem,' Lindsay acknowledged. 'But if they do, they'll deal with it within the club and the first we'll know is when another body turns up. So, unless forensics find something spectacular, or an eye witness comes forward, I'd say that this case is going to hinge on the quality of Dante's eye witness testimony. I just hope he's not telling any fibs.'

'I think he's solid,' Ross said. 'Except for the bloody T-shirt.'

'What T-shirt?'

'Forensics found one of Dante's T-shirts in a bush alongside the house,' Ross explained. 'It was covered in blood. I asked the boy and he said his friend Joe had a nosebleed while they were playing.'

'So are they following the story up?' Lindsay asked.

Ross sighed. 'Joe is the Führer's youngest son. Same age as Dante, same class at school. The thing is, the way the blood is spattered across the shirt it doesn't look like any nosebleed that I ever saw. And when I mentioned it to Kate, she said that Dante had dried blood on his arm and under his fingernails when he got here. The doctor who examined him took swabs and photographs.'

'Dammit,' Lindsay cursed.

Ross shrugged. 'I'm guessing he caught this Joe with his elbow or something and doesn't want to tell me because he's scared he'll get into trouble for fighting.'

'Most likely,' Lindsay nodded. 'But the fact that Dante lied undermines his credibility as a witness.'

'Still,' Ross said, 'Dante's given us an hour's worth of testimony. I don't think anybody will believe that an eight-year-old is capable of making up a story in that kind of detail.'

Lindsay shrugged. 'Let's hope, eh?'

'What are we gonna do with Dante?' Ross asked. 'Did you get anywhere trying to track down a relative?'

Lindsay shook her head. 'Scotty was a product of the care system. No known father, mother deceased. There's an uncle, but he's in Wandsworth prison and won't be available for babysitting duties until 2011. On Dante's mother's side there's one grandparent, but she's in a psychiatric hospital and there's no aunts or uncles.'

'Shit,' Ross said.

Lindsay shrugged. 'A healthy boy with a tragic sob-story background and cute baby sister. They'll get snapped up for adoption. I know it's sad, but in the long run it's probably better *not* being brought up by some biker scumbag.'

Ross nodded. 'I was actually thinking about tonight. Dante's the only witness. The Führer's going to want him dead. We can't have an eight-year-old living in a police station, but we've got to find somewhere safe.'

'Could you deal with that?' Lindsay asked. 'Maybe take him under your wing for a few days, until we find a foster home in a safe location? You're the only person he's responded to. We'll find a couple of nice rooms in a hotel.'

'Sounds reasonable,' Ross said. 'I'm a London boy, so I've got to find a hotel anyway. I'd suggest somewhere at least an hour's drive from Salcombe. I'll need some shopping money as well. He's got nothing except the clothes he's standing up in.'

*

Every time Dante woke up he hoped it was a dream. He wanted to find himself back in his own bed with the floor piled with junk and Jordan's teenage odour in the air. But this was the third morning he'd woken in a king-sized bed at the Bristol Park Hotel, after a night of drug-induced sleep.

Nothing could compensate for the loss of Dante's family, but the plush hotel did at least provide some novel distractions: room service, mini bar, on-demand movies and best of all swimming pool at the end of the hall.

Dante's family weren't rich. He'd never stayed in a hotel before and he'd worn hand-me-downs from Jordan all his life. It felt satisfying peeling sticky labels and tags from new BHS boxers and socks each morning. Devon police had also granted him enough money for an Adidas tracksuit, two nice pairs of jeans, some warm tops, a camouflage coat and a pair of blue Etnies skateboarder shoes that were the coolest item of footwear he'd ever owned.

Ross slept in the adjoining room and the doors in-between were propped open. Dante strolled through and found GMTV on Ross' television with the sound turned low. Ross himself was in the bathroom using his Philishave.

'Morning,' he said, when he saw Dante reflected in the bathroom mirror. 'Did you sleep well?'

Dante smiled a little. 'Those pills are like pressing a magic button. You take one and ZONK: fast asleep.'

'I probably need to reduce the dosage. You don't feel groggy at all? No headaches?'

'Nope,' Dante said, as he sat on the bed and eyed Ross' laptop on the desk nearby. 'Are they saying anything about us on the news?'

Ross wiped his face on a towel and came into the bedroom dressed in his boxers and a vest. 'I've only been up for about ten minutes but the story seems to have died down.'

Dante felt disappointed. The story was out of the news after four days, but it would be the biggest thing that ever happened to him if he lived to be a hundred.

'Your mood seems quite even this morning,' Ross said. 'You know you don't have to hide your emotions from me? I'm here to support you.'

'I know,' Dante said. He crashed back on Ross' unmade bed and stared at the ceiling rose. 'I still feel upset when I think hard.'

'But you feel like you're beginning to move on?' Ross said.

Dante shook his head. 'I feel weird because everything is different. Like, on Monday I'd never even met you. Now you're like, my only friend in the world.'

Ross was flattered and couldn't help smiling. 'This is just for a couple more days until we find a foster family, Dante.'

'So,' Dante said thoughtfully. 'Have there been lots of boys and girls like me, who you've looked after when something horrible happened?'

'I've interviewed and counselled children all over the country. I carry on helping witnesses right up to when they testify in court. Even afterwards if they still need me,' Ross explained. 'But most children in your situation have a grandparent, or an auntie or an older cousin or something who they can live with. This is only the third time I've lived with a child in a hotel.'

Dante smiled. 'So I'm special.'

Ross laughed as he checked the time on the TV. 'Special like every other kid I've ever worked with. Now, if I order us room service for between nine and nine fifteen that gives us half an hour for a splash in the pool. Does that sound cool?'

'My swimming shorts are drying off on my towel rail; I'll go put them on.'

Dante's shorts were still damp from swimming the night before and he shivered as he pulled them up his legs. When he walked back into the other room, Ross was on the phone ordering breakfast and Dante was shocked to see the Führer's face on the TV screen. It was a black and white photo, and he looked much younger than the man Dante knew.

He found the remote on Ross' pillow and turned up the sound.

'Police say that fifty-four-year-old Ralph Donnington will appear in court later today. Donnington, who is the president of South Devon Brigands and more commonly known as the Führer, was arrested in the early hours of this morning. He is expected to be questioned in connection with the murder of four members of the Scott family on a farm near Salcombe on Wednesday.'

Dante hadn't seen the Führer's face since the murders three nights earlier and it chilled him.

Ross hurriedly put the phone down and stepped towards Dante. 'You OK?' he asked.

'Fine,' Dante lied, as Ross put a reassuring hand on his shoulder. 'How long will all this take?'

'Six months,' Ross said. 'But it could drag on much longer.'

'That's ages,' Dante tutted.

'The wheels of justice turn slowly I'm afraid.'

'You left my sleeping pills lying around yesterday,' Dante said after a minute. 'I thought about swallowing them all so that I could be dead like Jordan and Lizzie. But if I died now, the Führer would get away with *everything*.'

'He would,' Ross said, then changed the subject because Dante's emotions were so fragile. 'We'd better get to the pool now if we want to be back before breakfast turns up.'

6. GUILDFORD

Two and a half months later

Dante and Holly now lived with foster parents in suburban Guildford, two hundred miles from the South Devon Brigands. Donald and Linda Graves were full-time foster parents. More than a hundred children had passed through their care over three decades, most recently in a large detached house that was licensed to house eight foster kids at a time. Some only stayed a few nights, others for months or years.

Dante's room was on the first floor and his day always started with an invasion from Holly. He laughed to himself as her tiny hands battled with the doorknob outside, then buried himself under his duvet and pretended to be asleep as she charged into the room and dragged the covers away.

'I want to sleep,' Dante giggled, as his little sister

clambered on his mattress and whacked her sticky hand against his tummy. She couldn't manage to say Dante so she called him Ant.

'Ant, Ant!'

Dante hid his face under his pillow. Holly shrieked with delight, burrowing alongside and finding herself nose to nose with her brother.

'Up,' Holly giggled, as she thrust her finger towards Dante's face.

Holly had no sense of danger and Dante sat up quickly, an instant before she would have jammed her finger in his eye.

'Crazy baby!' Dante laughed, giving her a quick kiss before surveying a room lit through thin curtains.

There was an unused bunk above and his school clothes and backpack were scattered across the floor. Normally Dante rumbled with Holly for longer, but an electric wheelchair stood in the doorway.

Its occupant Carl was thirteen. He'd lived with Donald and Linda since he was a toddler and had severe cerebral palsy. Violent spastic movements contorted his hands and face as he nudged a control stick and whirred into the room.

'Happy birthday,' Carl said, holding out a gift as Linda walked in behind him.

Linda was short and chunky, with big glasses. Her permed hair was turning grey and her faded clothes seemed to have been through far more washes than was good for them.

Dante sat on the edge of his bed and smiled as he

studied the tissue paper wrapped around Carl's gift. It was all scrunched and the Sellotape was at weird angles, but Dante appreciated it because simple manual tasks like wrapping a present could take Carl a significant amount of time.

'Cool, thanks,' Dante said, as he tore the paper to reveal a travel chess set. The pieces were stored in foam slots under the board, which then folded in half to make a box.

'It's got pegs,' Carl explained. 'So I don't knock the pieces over when we play.'

Dante had never played chess before Carl taught him. 'We'll have a game after school,' Dante said. 'I'm gonna beat you one day.'

Carl cracked a big smile. 'You wish!'

Linda put a Woolworths carrier bag on the edge of the bed. 'Just some Haribos and a couple of extra tops,' she explained. 'Don't let the baby get the plastic bag.'

Almost as if she'd understood Holly stuck her hand down the bag and pulled out a glossy-covered WWE annual. It was the previous year's title, reduced to ninety-nine pence.

'That's the wrestling book you were looking for, wasn't it?' Linda said.

Dante nodded enthusiastically. 'I had it before the fire. It's got a *massive* section all about Goldberg in it.'

'Wrestling's stupid,' Carl said. 'It's all fake.'

'You're full of crap,' Dante snapped back. 'Those guys are so strong they'd pluck you out of your chair and toss you with one arm.'

'But I could beat them all at chess,' Carl smiled, as Holly opened out the annual and tried it as a hat.

While this was going on, Linda had picked dirty grey socks, pants and an ink-stained school shirt off the floor. 'Get in the shower and put on clean school clothes today,' she said firmly. 'What must people think of me, sending you to school covered in biro and mud?'

Dante smiled. He liked the way Linda fussed over details like a loose shoelace or a scratch on his face, although sometimes he got upset because she'd use the exact phrase that his mum would have done.

Dante realised that Holly was still in her night clothes. 'Do you want to come in the shower with Dante?' he asked, holding his arms out wide.

Holly made a fuss in the bath and showering with Dante was the easiest way to keep her clean, but Linda had an eye on the clock.

'I'll give madam a little bath in the sink once you're all at school,' she said. 'Otherwise you'll be late again.'

Dante didn't mind, but Holly knew what was going on and looked cross as she saw Dante grabbing the bath towel hooked up on his door and heading across the hall to the bathroom.

'Meeee!' Holly whined.

She was about to throw a fit, until she heard the hydraulic platform of Carl's wheelchair lift swinging out over the staircase.

'All aboard!' Carl said, as he rolled the chair on to its platform and pulled up the locking bar.

Holly raced across and Carl leaned forwards to lift Holly on to his lap for the ride downstairs.

*

Dante showered until Linda banged on the door and told him to hurry up because she was cooking him his favourite scrambled egg, bacon and potato cakes for breakfast. After putting on underpants and combing his hair, Dante bolted across the hallway and found that Linda had straightened his bed and laid out clean school clothes. He had football practice after school, so she'd put out his Astroturf trainers to wear and tucked his water bottle and shin pads in his school pack.

Dante sang *Happy Birthday to me* as he pulled up black tracksuit bottoms and a red school shirt before swinging his bag over his back and heading downstairs. But he gulped in shock when he reached the landing and saw an oversized Harley touring bike parked out front and a man in a leather jacket heading up the driveway. Dante didn't see enough to recognise who it was, but the Brigands logo on his helmet was unmistakeable.

The doorbell buzzed as Dante raced into the kitchen and yelled out: 'Call the cops! Don't let him in.'

But a twelve-year-old called Abby was standing right in the hallway by the front door and had already opened up.

'Good morning,' the biker said, as Linda realised who he was and rushed frantically down the hallway to block his path.

The staircase led directly into a kitchen and dining-room that had been knocked together to make a space large enough for Donald, Linda and eight kids to dine together. Dante looked one way, at Holly in her high chair, then the other, considering grabbing a knife from the kitchen drawer, but in the end he backed up the stairs and grabbed his mobile phone.

As a protected witness Dante was supposed to keep the phone with him at all times. Donald made sure it was fully charged every night and Dante even had special permission to keep it with him during school. The phone had been programmed so that pressing and holding down the zero key for three seconds dialled an emergency response number at the local police station.

As the phone rang in Dante's ear, he heard Linda frantically telling the biker on the doorstep to *sling his bloody hook*. The biker's accent was Dutch and Dante knew he'd heard it before.

'What's going on?' an eleven-year-old called Ed asked, as he looked up the stairs. 'What are you hiding for, Dante? That bloke's got a birthday present for you.'

Dante didn't reply because the police had answered his call. The police knew who he was from caller ID and he quickly explained the situation.

'Stay out of sight,' the female desk officer said. 'We'll dispatch the nearest car. It'll be there in five to ten minutes.'

Dante considered escaping, but the biker was out front and the back garden had a high fence designed specifically to keep children in. He crept back down into the kitchen and joined Abby, Ed and two other kids who leaned out of the door into the hallway to watch the scene unfold.

The Dutchman had moved a couple of steps into the hallway and was trying to calm Linda down. He looked like a typical biker: boots, denim, greying beard and mirrored sunglasses.

'I know it's the boy's birthday,' he explained. 'We're not all animals, you know. I'm ashamed of the situation with Scotty and his family.'

Dante leaned out between the other kids and recognised the biker's face. He went by the name of Doods, which was Dutch for death. Dante had met him at a summer bike festival in Britain and on the Brigands annual European run in Germany and Scotty had put on a big show of bear-hugging both times.

'I have a gift for the boy,' Doods explained. 'Please don't be frightened, lady. Scotty was a brother. We don't all condone what has happened to the boy and his family. I came to pay my respects on his birthday. I don't want to upset you or anyone. Take my gift and I'll leave.'

Linda sounded worried. Dante's location was supposed to be secret. He'd moved two hundred miles and even used a different surname at his new school so that people didn't recognise him from the news.

'Dante, get *back*,' Linda growled, as he slipped between the other kids and into the hallway.

But Dante was calmer now. He'd seen plenty of fights in his short life. Doods was easily strong enough to shove Linda out of the way and would have already done so if that's what he wanted.

'Kid,' Doods said, as he reached towards Dante with a big Toys R Us bag. 'I wanted to wish you a happy birthday. You're too young to remember, but I came off hard in a bend in Switzerland a few years back. Your dad pulled me out of the crash barrier. Gave me the kiss of life and made a tourniquet to stop my leg bleeding. I owe your dad, Dante. That's the only reason I came here today.'

Doods put the carrier bag down and backed up on to the doorstep.

'How did you know I was here?' Dante asked, as a distant police siren sounded.

'The Führer found out somehow,' Doods explained, with a shrug. 'They know you're here. They've been trying to get a Brigand from a chapter in Mexico City to come over and kill you. You're not safe here and I'd better go before I get hassled by cops.'

Doods dropped the toy bag at Linda's feet and jogged back to his Harley Tourer. He pulled out of their street seconds before a police car turned in at the opposite end. As Linda ran out on to the driveway and waved her arms to attract the attention of the approaching police car, Dante peeked cautiously into the Toys R Us bag.

The gift wasn't wrapped: a pair of radio-controlled Hummers with a giant bar of milk chocolate and a birthday card Sellotaped to the box.

'Cool shit,' Ed said. 'Make sure you plug them in to charge before school and we'll be able to race in the garden when we get home.'

7. MOVES

Two uniformed policemen stayed with Dante until Ross Johnson arrived. By this time Linda's elderly husband Donald had completed three separate school runs, leaving Dante and Holly as the only kids in the house.

'Will I have to move out?' Dante asked, as he slumped on a beanbag in the living-room. Donald and Linda were on the sofa, Ross in an armchair and Holly lying on her belly in front of the TV messing with a stack of DVD boxes.

'Basically,' Ross admitted. 'The alternative would be to keep you here and give you twenty-four-hour police surveillance, but we don't have the resources.'

Dante had got used to living with the Graveses and their menagerie of foster kids. He was disappointed, but he'd suspected that moving would be the only practical option.

'This Doods,' Ross said, as he pulled a flip photo wallet out of his briefcase. 'Is that the only name you've ever known him by?'

Dante nodded. 'That's how it works with the Brigands. Like, my dad probably knew the real names of all the guys in the South Devon chapter, but with other chapters it's just nicknames. And it's rude to ask.'

'And he was definitely from Holland? But no patch identifying his chapter?' Ross said. He opened the thick photo wallet about two thirds of the way through and passed it to Dante. 'Take a look and see if you can pick him out.'

Dante took the album and flipped through photographs of Dutch Brigands. Some were police mugshots, but most were surveillance shots taken at biker festivals, concerts and runs. These were the centrepiece of outlaw biker culture, taking place during the warm weather between Easter and September with bikers from all over the world meeting up at a central location.

Some events were Brigands only. The biggest were open to everyone from lone riders to members of the major international outlaw gangs and drew in up to ten thousand bikes. At the friendlier events, the South Devon Brigands would hire a pair of coaches and bring along wives, girlfriends, hangers-on and kids.

Many of Dante's best memories were of going on runs. You got muddy and didn't wash for a week, you slept in tents, ate food cooked on a fire or drove to the nearest town for takeaway. The adults got drunk and let kids roam free between motorbikes, beer cans and bonfires.

The pictures made him sad, because he'd become what bikers hated most: a snitch. Many of the bikers posed for the surveillance photos, flexing muscles, grimacing and mooning the camera.

Dante welled up when he recognised a small blond girl hanging off a man's leg. Dante and Joe had made friends with her a few years earlier. They'd been four years old and both lads were fascinated by the way she had to pull her jeans down and squat when she needed to pee.

Holly was at the age where she wanted whatever Dante had and with so much attention on the photo album she made a grab.

'Not for you,' Dante said gently. 'I'll play with you later.'

Holly squealed in protest until Donald came over and scooped her up.

'What I don't understand is how they could have found Dante here,' Linda said. 'I mean, this Doods was a big fellow. He could have come in with a gun or a knife and there's nothing Donald or I could have done to stop him.'

'Information leaks,' Ross said bitterly. 'The Brigands might only have sixteen full-patch members in South Devon, but there are four times that number of hangers-on, the Dogs of War and the Monster Bunch are basically Brigands puppet gangs with another fifty members, and they all have wives, girlfriends and other relatives. That's between a hundred and fifty to two hundred biker associates in South Devon. Somewhere amongst that lot there's bound to be someone who works as a cleaner in the police station, or a secretary at Dante's old school who saw where his school record was sent, or someone whose brother-in-law is a cop.'

Dante looked alarmed. 'You're saying I can *never* be completely safe?'

Ross shrugged uneasily. 'Dante, something has gone badly wrong and we underestimated the threat from the Führer and the Brigands organisation. We'll have to be more thorough and give you a complete new identity. That will take a while to put together and while you're waiting I'm going to suggest to social services that you move in with me.'

'Presumably he'll be much safer once the Führer is behind bars,' Donald added. 'I mean, they might hold a grudge, but nothing will get the Führer out of prison once he's convicted.'

'That's him!' Dante said, as he saw Doods standing in a crowd of full-patch bikers. They held beers and stared without interest at a stripper on stage in the background. 'Photograph number eight-one-four. This guy, third from the right.'

Ross grabbed a stapled paper index from his case before shuffling over the carpet on his knees so that he could see who Dante was looking at.

'Are you sure?' Ross asked as he looked up the index. 'It says here that his nickname is Bolts. Real name Jonas Haarden.'

Dante nodded. 'My dad saved him after some bike crash. He's got metal bolts in his legs.'

Linda was impressed that Dante had kept his head together through a very upsetting morning. 'So, Dante,' she smiled. 'These biker nicknames can change?'

'Only if something big happens,' Dante nodded. 'Like if you were in a bad accident or you're involved in some famous punch-up where you gouge out an eyeball or something.'

While Dante explained, Holly headbutted a pile of wooden bricks and Ross had his telephone at his ear, asking a police colleague to e-mail him a copy of any information on Jonas Haarden and get a warning put out to customs and traffic police to try and arrest him.

'He tipped us off though,' Donald pointed out, when Ross ended his call. 'He must have been trying to warn us.'

'Maybe,' Ross said, 'but I still want him in for questioning. He's our best link to whoever leaked Dante and Holly's whereabouts. And if he just wanted to tip you off, why ride all the way out here? Why not pick up the phone?'

'My dad saved his life,' Dante said. 'He wanted to buy me a present and make me feel nice.'

'I hope that's true,' Ross said. 'But I'm sensing something under the surface.'

As Ross said this his mobile rang. Dante, Donald and Linda only heard Ross' half of the conversation.

'You're kidding . . . No, wait. It's sealed I think . . . *Shit!* OK, OK, I'll call you right back.'

'Something the matter?' Donald asked, as Ross slid his phone shut.

'Where are the toy cars Doods bought?' Ross said urgently.

'In the hallway,' Dante said. 'I was gonna open them, but the policeman told me to leave them in the box because you might want them dusted for fingerprints.'

'We've got to leave the house, right *now*,' Ross said.

Linda was first to work out what was going on. 'Are you saying there's a bomb in my house?'

'There's a chance,' Ross said, standing up. 'Maybe only a slim one, but I'm not risking it.'

Donald scooped up Holly as Linda led the way out on to the front doorstep. Always a mum, she made sure the two kids had warm coats as they skirted around Dante's gift and walked between the two cars down the front driveway.

'My colleague will call the local cops,' Ross explained. 'They'll cordon off the road and bring in a bomb disposal team. They should be here within twenty minutes.'

'Why do we think it's a bomb all of a sudden?' Dante asked.

Ross explained. 'Doods, Bolts, or whatever you choose to call him was a member of the Brigands' Rotterdam chapter. They had a nasty little turf war with two other gangs, which ended when a clubhouse blew up and fourteen members of the rival gangs got blasted. Doods was implicated in the bombing. He's on the Dutch police's most wanted list and nobody's seen or heard from him in over a year.'

'But why go to the bother of a bomb?' Donald asked, as Holly yanked his ear.

'A bomb gives the killer time to put space between himself and the victim,' Ross explained. 'You can trigger a bomb by text message from the other side of the world.'

*

Donald and Linda Graves' six-bedroom house was in one of the best streets in Guildford. The neighbours were mostly wealthy, with two nice cars on the driveway, two or three brats and breadwinners who paid their mortgages with well-paid jobs in London.

This comfortable lifestyle jarred with the experience of most kids fostered by Donald and Linda. Over the years kids in their care had been blamed – usually correctly – for everything from vandalising street signs to lobbing fireworks at a show-winning chihuahua.

However, in more than thirty years of fostering Dante was the first kid who'd led to the entire street being cordoned off pending the arrival of a four-man bomb disposal team. They came with sirens and orange lights. Two soldiers drove an army-green Land Rover, followed by a truck with riot mesh over the windscreen.

Ross explained the situation, out of earshot of the gaggle of surprised pensioners evacuated from neighbouring homes and two sweaty women who'd arrived back from tennis. It was school time, so Dante was the only kid around.

The driver of the Land Rover took his time strapping on an armoured suit and approaching the Graves' home with a microphone-like probe held in a gloved hand.

71

Dante had spent more time with the package than anyone else, so a female corporal kept him on hand and asked questions about whether he'd moved the package roughly since receiving it, whether it seemed heavier or lighter than he thought it ought to be and if the packaging around the cars looked like it had been tampered with.

She seemed relaxed and let Dante ask questions back. 'What does the thingy your friend's holding do?'

'Ricardo's approaching the bomb with a sniffer,' the woman explained. 'It detects microscopic traces of explosives, rather like an airport security scanner. There's also a video camera built into the tip. The lieutenant and sergeant are watching the video feed and telling him what to do.'

Whilst Dante was captivated by the technology, Linda and Donald were staggered that they'd spent ninety minutes sitting within a few metres of a package that was now being approached by a soldier wearing titanium anti-blast armour.

Ricardo moved slowly up the driveway. After two steps into the hallway, the soldier backed out as quickly as forty kilos of metal armour would allow. The sergeant came out the back of the van and yelled out: 'Positive reading. Some kind of bonded plastic explosive. From the chemical signature I'd say C-4. We'll need Mabel.'

Dante had hoped the present had been a gesture of loyalty from a friend of his father. Only now did he believe that Doods had been trying to kill him.

The female corporal who'd been speaking to Dante

opened the back of the Land Rover and dragged out a ramp. Mabel was a compact bomb-disposal robot. She ran on four rubber tracks, each of which could pivot to enable the robot to climb stairs. Above the tracks were chemical sensors, a multiple jointed arm and a hose linked to four hundred litres of highly pressurised water.

Mabel sped down the empty street as the female corporal helped Ricardo out of his armour. The bony sergeant working in the van noticed Dante hovering like a lost sheep and called him inside.

Dante stepped warily into the van. It was filled with computer screens and keyboards. A handsome lieutenant sat in a padded chair manipulating the joystick that controlled Mabel's tracks. Even with the back of the van open the heat from the electronics sucked all the moisture out of Dante's mouth.

'What do you think of our toy box then?' the sergeant asked.

'Aren't you scared that the bomb will blow up?' Dante replied.

'If it does Mabel's the only one that'll get hurt,' the sergeant explained casually. 'I get nervous when I'm on a London building site, with some rusty old World War Two bomb in the middle of a waterlogged hole that's too deep for Mabel. Or when I was in the desert, scratching at a piece of wire sticking out of the dirt and wondering if it was going to trigger a bomb, or if some Iraqi was going to shoot me up the arse when I bent over to take a look.'

'So this is an easy bomb?' Dante asked.

The lieutenant answered: 'Nothing makes us happier than finding a bomb in a dry, easily accessible space.'

Dante managed to smile as he watched Mabel's progress on the largest screen. The lieutenant positioned Mabel's spindly arm above the handles of the shopping bag and looked at the nine-year-old.

'Did you move this bag around much after you received it?' the lieutenant asked.

'Not that much,' Dante explained. 'My friend Ed wanted me to put them on charge so that we could race the cars as soon as we got home from school. So I took them into the play room at the front of the house, but before I got the box open the police came in and told me not to pull it about because Inspector Johnson might want to have it checked for fingerprints.'

'In that case we'll try to save Mrs Graves' carpet,' the Lieutenant said.

Dante looked confused and the sergeant explained for him. 'Mabel has eight nozzles, like a shower head, except if you stood under those nozzles when the water came out the water would cut through your body like a knife. When we open the tank, four hundred litres will be blown out in a quarter second. The water flushes the bomb, literally blowing the components apart before there's any chance of detonation.'

As the sergeant spoke, Mabel's claw grasped the handles on the Toys R Us bag. She picked it up and wheeled it backwards, down the driveway and into the middle of the street.

'Arming,' the sergeant said, before lifting the safety

catch over a large red button with red and black hazard stripes all around it and flipping two switches marked *danger*. Dante thought it was exactly the kind of button he'd wanted to press his whole life.

Outside the female corporal told the dozen or so folks standing near the cordon to turn away in case of flying debris or in case the flushing operation went wrong.

On the lieutenant's nod, Dante squished his thumb against the button. There was a deep thud, and the sound of rattling plastic and rain. The accompanying shockwave set off whoops, shrieks and neh-nahs from car and burglar alarms.

As Dante jumped out of the van to see the damage, Ricardo and the female corporal ran up the damp street and stood in the gutters trying to prevent valuable evidence from going down the drain. Inside the van, the lieutenant used Mabel's cameras to survey the shattered pieces of plastic and metal. As he swivelled the camera he noticed the shattered faceplate of the cars' radio control unit. It lay face down with a piece of plasticine-like explosive taped to the back.

After zooming in to make sure that the water blast had imploded the detonator he waved to the sergeant.

'There's your explosive,' he explained.

The sergeant squinted. 'That's not even enough to blow the wheel of a car.'

'Yeah but think how Dante would have been holding that thing when he was driving the car,' the lieutenant said. 'It was probably rigged to trigger after the unit had been used for a few minutes. The full force of the blast would have hit him in the face and chest.'

'Pretty clever,' the sergeant said, nodding reluctantly. 'Someone sure wants the little guy dead.'

8. DREAMS

Dante spent the next two weeks living in Ross Johnson's London flat, while Holly stayed with a new foster family a few miles away. Ross was divorced, but his university-aged daughter Tina was home for Christmas holidays.

Following the bomb attempt the police were taking no chances with the only witness to a quintuple murder. Dante's third school in as many months was six miles from Ross' home and it had been chosen for its location on a dead-end street.

An armed police officer drove him each morning and sat in his car making sure nobody suspicious came through the school's only entrance. At lunchtime he'd swap with another officer, who'd take Dante home and stay until just before bedtime. A third officer kept guard through the night.

It was an isolated existence. At school Dante was

known as Kevin Drake. There were a couple of boys he got on with, but the other kids had settled into their own cliques which were hard to break into.

Things other kids took for granted were complicated by bodyguards and security details. Boy Scouts was out of the question because the church hall had an unlit car park and exits on three sides. An invite to a Saturday afternoon birthday party required a change in shifts and Ross having to fill in forms and negotiate overtime payments with the Devon police force who were paying for Dante's protection.

Dante had always been the kind of kid who terrorised the playground and wound up teachers. But now he withdrew, burying himself in wrestling magazines, wondering about death and dreaming up elaborate fantasies of killing the Führer. He seemed content to watch the world drift by, rather than to take part in it. He only livened up when he got to visit Holly. He always tried to bring her sweets, or make a paper windmill or do some little thing to get her excited. Holly's foster mum would take them out to a local swing park and her one-year-old innocence allowed him to be a normal big brother until he looked up and saw the plain-clothes officer walking behind with a bulge under his jacket.

Dante's teachers didn't know his background and thought he was just taking time to settle. Ross was a trained psychologist. He knew Dante was depressed but couldn't do much about it.

He'd sent e-mails to a few trusted psychologist colleagues asking if they had any ideas, but their replies told him what he already knew: Dante needed to start a new life in a safe location with Holly. This wouldn't be a miracle cure, but over time he'd make new friends, develop new interests and begin to put distance between the grief in his past and his new life.

But Dante couldn't lead an ordinary life while the Führer was walking the streets. There wasn't even a date for a trial because the Devon police hadn't even charged him with the murders. Ross tried to sound upbeat when Dante was around, but privately feared that the boy might be stuck in limbo for two or three years.

*

Dante's mind drifted as he pressed the light on his projector clock. It was one of the few items salvaged from his previous existence and despite a melted facia and a warped lens it still put a legible 00:17 on to the ceiling.

For as long as Dante could remember he'd taken sleep for granted. He'd stay up as late as he could get away with, then crash out until he woke early the next morning. He'd either watch cartoons for an hour before breakfast, or if he'd stayed up too late he'd get shaken awake by his mum yelling at him to put his uniform on before she whacked him on the arse. Now he'd fight to get to sleep, then he'd wake up with nightmares.

Dante pulled his duvet around his head and brought his knees up into a foetal position. He closed his eyes and imagined that he was in a concrete bunker deep underground. He was protected behind huge metal doors, with video cameras. He had weapons. He had huge muscles like a wrestler, and he was famous and had hundreds of bodyguards who'd batter anyone who tried to come near him.

Dante's fantasy got shattered by a deep belch from the policeman sitting in the living-room less than two metres away. Some of the bodyguards were nice and played video games and stuff, but Constable Fairport spent all his time studying his sergeant's exam textbooks and looked like steam would vent from his ears if anyone made noise.

Now that he'd stirred, Dante found his ear was itching. The pillow felt lumpy and he had to move because the position that had been fine twenty seconds earlier now seemed completely impossible. He pressed the button on the clock again: 00:19. He'd been in bed since nine and reckoned he'd slept for less than an hour.

Dante's brain ran in circles. Pressing the clock made him think about his mum again, and he fondly remembered the way she always yelled at him with a half smile on her face and threatened to whack him, even though she never did apart from two or three times when he'd done something totally crazy. Like the time he'd got up in the night and filled Jordan's school bag with mud.

*

Dante woke with a start, as if someone had poured ice down his back. In the dream he'd been locked in the cellar of the South Devon Brigands clubhouse and the men upstairs in the bar were about to set one of the guard dogs on him.

He touched the clock – 01:07 – and couldn't believe

that he'd only slept for another hour. As his hand moved under the covers it dragged through a wet patch. He smelled the pee as he lifted the covers.

'Stupid idiot!' he cursed to himself, before gritting his teeth and punching his mattress.

Dante had never wet the bed when his parents were alive, or even at the Graves' house afterwards. But ever since Doods and the bomb threat he'd woken up wet every second or third night. Sometimes even twice.

The first few times he'd been so upset that his crying woke everyone up, but even though Ross said it wasn't his fault after all he'd been through, Dante was embarrassed and didn't want lots of people waking up and making a fuss every time it happened. To ease the problem Ross had bought a mound of cheap duvets and sheets, along with a plastic mattress protector and loads of pyjamas.

Dante quickly stripped off his sheets and carried them along the hallway to the bathroom. He locked the door and put everything in the basket before standing over the toilet. He peed a little bit and stood over the bowl for ages trying to make absolutely sure that there was nothing else there. When he finished he threw his pyjama bottoms on top of the sheets and wiped himself off with a warm flannel.

Once he was done he pumped some spray disinfectant into the laundry bin and put the lid on tight so that the sheets didn't stink out the bathroom. As he headed out he realised that he'd forgotten to grab clean pyjama bottoms. He'd have to run back to his room half nude, but it was only a few steps so he didn't think it would be a problem.

But as Dante rushed into his room he bumped into Ross' daughter Tina. She was nineteen, quite short, with a curvy figure under her nightshirt and stripy socks over small feet. Dante realised that she'd wiped his rubber sheet, put a fresh cotton sheet on top of it and brought one of the spare duvets out of the cupboard in the hallway.

Dante gasped, stretching his pyjama top down over his penis and bum.

'Don't be daft,' Tina laughed and threw him a pair of blue bottoms.

They didn't match the top half and Dante didn't like this because it made it obvious to everyone that he'd had an accident, but he was too embarrassed to complain and he stepped back out into the hallway to pull them on.

'I didn't wake you up did I?' Dante asked, stepping back into the bedroom as Tina smoothed out the fresh duvet.

'Nah,' she smiled. 'I couldn't sleep.'

'I'm really sorry,' Dante said nervously. 'I could have done the sheets. You didn't have to get up.'

'Come here,' Tina said, as she sat on Dante's clean bed. 'You look sad, give us a cuddle.'

Dante smiled as Tina wrapped her arms around his back and squished him. Tears welled up as he sniffed her deodorant. The smooth skin and shoulder-length hair reminded him of his dead sister.

'I always wanted a little brother,' Tina said. 'I wanted him to be called Barnaby.'

Dante smirked. 'That's *such* a toff's name! He would have got battered at school.'

'I always saw him dressed in a little sailor suit and patent leather shoes. It wasn't a *terribly* realistic fantasy to be honest.'

'I wish I could stay here forever sometimes,' Dante said. 'Especially if Holly could come.'

Tina ruffled his hair and pulled back a triangle of the duvet. 'You'd better get in. You've got to be up early for the drive to Devon.'

'If I was dead I wouldn't have to sleep,' Dante replied. 'Or worry about getting bombed. Or wake up drowning in piss.'

Tina rubbed his back and gave him a kiss. 'You are so strong and clever, Dante Scott. I'd bet you my entire overdraft that your mum and dad wouldn't want you dead. They'd want you to grow up and become an amazing happy person, and that's exactly what you'll be.'

Dante smiled and took another breath tinged with hair and deodorant.

'Now try getting some sleep and I'm only next door if you need me, OK?'

Dante nodded before skimming across his bed and diving under the sheets. Tina flicked out his light and he went to sleep thinking about Tina and imagining having someone like her as a girlfriend or wife when he was older. Sleep came easier when he looked forward instead of back.

9. LIES

Ross made Dante dress in chinos and a smart shirt for the trip to Devon. It was a five-hour drive in an unmarked police car, with Ross at the wheel and Dante's armed guard Steve in the passenger seat. Dante had the back seats to himself and spent most of the trip on his Gameboy and reading every word of two wrestling magazines that Ross had bought for the trip.

It was eleven when they stopped off at Bridgwater services to piss and eat Burger King. Dante was pleased that Ross bought him a Whopper. His mum always said it was too expensive because he'd waste half of it.

'That big enough for you, boy?' the police bodyguard asked, before blowing on his coffee.

Dante smiled. He'd been delighted when Steve had turned up for the morning trip. Out of all the police guards, he was the one most likely to join him on the

Playstation and the previous Saturday he'd even shown up with a packet of cake mix and they'd made a sponge with orange-flavoured icing.

'We stopped here once on a Brigands run,' Dante said. 'A full-patch called Pigeon got knocked off his bike after a run up in Scotland. I was in the run truck . . .'

'What's that?' Steve asked.

'You can't carry much luggage on a Harley,' Dante explained. 'So when the Brigands go on a run, there's usually a truck or van that carries baggage, spare parts and stuff. When I was little I used to think it was cooler to ride in the truck than in the coach with all the mums and kids.

'So anyway, this other truck knocked Pigeon off the road. We followed the truck until it pulled in. They were all set to beat up the truck driver, but the man realised he was being followed and called the cops on his mobile. So we arrived to find all these pigs – sorry, I mean police officers – waiting. But when they asked what we were doing they just said that I'd been whining that I needed to use the toilet.'

'So nothing happened?' Ross said, disappointed at the flat ending.

Dante smiled. 'I said I remembered coming here. I didn't say it was a great story.'

'You seem happier today,' Ross noted.

'Because something's happening with the murder case at last, even if I don't exactly understand what.'

'I thought I explained,' Ross said.

Dante shrugged. 'I still don't get this whole CPS thing.'

'OK,' Ross said. 'It's called the Crown Prosecution Service. You know when you watch a court thing on TV they have lawyers who ask people questions?'

Dante nodded.

'OK, well in each court the person who's on trial has a defence lawyer who tries to prove that he's innocent. And the government has a lawyer called a prosecutor who tries to prove that they're guilty. The government lawyers work for the CPS.

'With a complex case like the murder of your family, the police and the CPS work together and decide when there's enough evidence to charge someone with a crime. The CPS lawyers tell the police what kind of evidence they need to get a conviction and they speak with witnesses because it's very important to know how well their evidence will stand up in court.'

'So that's why I'm going,' Dante nodded.

As Dante said this, a frail looking woman who was well into her sixties entered the restaurant. Her soft leather briefcase and lavender coat with gold buttons looked out of place in the sparsely populated Burger King, but she cracked a big smile when she recognised Ross.

'Hello, darling!' the woman said brightly, as she headed towards the table and kissed Ross on both cheeks. 'When did I last see you? It must have been the child development conference in Leeds two years ago.'

Ross shrugged. 'Three years, I think. I haven't been to the last two.'

Dante was curious because the meeting didn't seem coincidental.

'Would you like me to get you something to eat?' Steve asked.

The woman gave a look like she'd rather eat her own shoe. 'Just a tea. Two sugars, no milk, thank you.'

As Steve stood up to join the short queue at the counter, the woman slipped into the seat next to Dante and loosened the belt on her coat.

'Dante, I want you to meet Jennifer Mitchum,' Ross explained.

'Good to see you,' Jennifer smiled, as she gently tapped Dante's wrist before stealing one of Steve's fries. 'Ross and I have been swapping e-mails, but it's wonderful to finally meet you.'

Dante didn't know what to say, but he hated it when people stole his chips. 'I'm sure Steve will get you some chips,' he said. 'So you knew we'd be here?'

Ross nodded. 'Jennifer is a trained psychologist and counsellor. She specialises in dealing with children like you who need to make a fresh start.'

Sometimes Dante felt like a stray dog that got passed from one reluctant owner to the next. 'I thought *you* were doing that,' he said, trying not to sound as bitter as he felt.

'I'm not abandoning you,' Ross assured him. 'But I'm a police officer. I have to travel all over the country interviewing children after crimes. There's no way I can look after you once Tina goes back to university.'

*

The Devon branch of the CPS was headquartered on a business estate near Exeter, fifty miles from where

Dante's family had been murdered. Dante was photographed and given a name badge before following Jennifer and Ross through a full-height turnstile.

A lawyer called Vanessa shook Dante's hand and led him down a hallway with frosted glass doors branching off each side. She had big eyes and a bust that reminded him of the strippers the Brigands hired for their parties.

The office was small, but functional. Dante sat on a long sofa with Jennifer and Ross on either side. Vanessa rested on the edge of her desk and grabbed a folder full of notes.

'Has Ross explained who I am?' Vanessa asked.

'Sort of,' Dante nodded. 'You're like the legal person in charge of the murder case. You look at all the police stuff, and decide when there's enough evidence to charge the Führer.'

'That's it exactly,' Vanessa smiled. 'Our problem is that when your house was burned a lot of forensic evidence like fingerprints and things disappeared. We've not found a weapon or a piece of clothing that matches anything found at the scene.'

'What about the mud?' Dante asked. 'The Führer walked in the field. He must have left boot prints.'

'Yes,' Vanessa admitted. 'We have boot prints that match the Führer's size and the tread matches a pair of Dr Martens boots. But lots of bikers wear the same boots, and the Führer's a size eight, which is the most common male foot size.'

'So it's useless?' Dante asked.

'Not useless,' Vanessa explained. 'Just not enough. A

jury has to be convinced *beyond reasonable doubt*, which means they need more than a couple of boot prints to prove a murder. Right now, the only thing that's likely to put the Führer behind bars are the statements you gave to the police on the night of the murders and anything you say in court.'

Dante nodded. 'Have you charged the Führer yet?'

'No,' Vanessa said. 'We're reviewing all the evidence and we'll make a decision on whether to arrest and charge the Führer within the next day or so. I asked Ross to bring you down here because I needed to meet you and ask very important questions about your statement.'

'Well, I'm here, ask away,' Dante said brightly.

Vanessa smiled. 'Some of my questions might be quite upsetting, Dante. What you have to understand is that the Brigands Motorcycle Club has a legal fund into which every member pays several hundred pounds a year. That means they can afford good lawyers, the best forensic tests, the best expert witnesses. The whole case depends upon a jury believing what you say. All the Führer's lawyers will have to do is put a *tiny* doubt into the minds of one or two jurors and he won't go to prison.'

Dante understood this better than most nine-year-olds would have done: members of the South Devon Brigands were often in some kind of legal trouble and some of the wildest parties in the clubhouse happened when a member scored a not-guilty verdict in court.

'There are two problems,' Vanessa continued. 'The first is that you're not going to be the only witness. I guarantee that other people will take the stand, prepared to swear that the Führer was with them at the time of the murder.'

Dante nodded. 'My dad covered for a couple of London Brigands one time. He said they were at a bar in Salcombe with him when they were up in London robbing some woman's jewellery.'

'There's not much we can do about witnesses who lie,' Vanessa explained. 'But the really important thing is that *you* are a good, honest witness. I think we have one problem with that.'

'What?' Dante asked.

Vanessa produced a photograph of the T-shirt he'd worn at the clubhouse on the night his parents died, complete with the blood stains across the front. Then she read an excerpt from Dante's witness statement aloud.

'*I was playing with my friend Joe in the clubhouse and he got a nosebleed. He gets nosebleeds all the time and some of it got on my shirt.* The thing is Dante, forensics took one look at the blood. Do you see the way it's spattered across the shirt?'

Dante nodded.

'It wasn't really a nosebleed, was it?'

'No,' Dante said sheepishly.

'We also tested the blood and it doesn't match Joe's blood group,' Vanessa said. 'So whose blood is it?'

Dante looked guiltily at Ross and shrugged. 'It's Martin Donnington's blood. That's the Führer's other son.'

'So what really happened?' Vanessa asked.

'More importantly, why didn't you tell the truth?' Ross interrupted.

Dante shrank down into his chair. 'I didn't want to get into trouble for fighting. So I said it was a nosebleed.'

Vanessa sighed and looked at Ross.

'But all the other stuff I said was true,' Dante said. 'It's before the murders anyway, so why does that bit even matter?'

Vanessa looked cross, but Dante was only a kid so she took a deep breath and tried to explain in the friendliest way possible. 'Do you know what corroborated means?'

Dante shook his head.

'Corroborated means that you can check something out. For instance, you can corroborate the fact that David Beckham scored a goal for England because everyone in the stadium saw it and it was filmed for TV. If you go into your bedroom and score a billion points on your Playstation, but turn the machine off before anyone sees the high score, there's no way to corroborate what you said because you're the only one that saw it.'

'I get it,' Dante nodded.

'The thing is, out of all the evidence you gave, what you said about the bloody T-shirt is one of the few things that can be easily corroborated. And if you didn't tell the truth about that, it makes it much harder for people to believe other things you said that can't be corroborated.'

Dante looked angry. 'So you're saying I'm a liar?'

'No,' Vanessa said. 'I'm saying that because you lied about one thing, people are much less likely to believe the other things that you said. And when people are being asked to convict a man of murder based solely upon your word it could make their decision difficult.'

Dante looked down between his legs and sulked. 'So I ballsed everything up.'

Ross put an arm on his shoulder. 'You made a small mistake when you were tired and upset. It's not your fault.'

Vanessa nodded. 'Can you tell me what really happened to the T-shirt?'

Dante spent two minutes explaining how the Führer got angry after his son Martin spat on Teeth's Brigands patch, and how he'd then been asked to beat Martin up to save the club's honour and to save Martin from a much more severe beating at the hands of the Führer.

Vanessa looked increasingly surprised as the story unravelled. It seemed too convoluted for Dante to be making it up, but it wasn't every day you heard about a bunch of grown men encouraging a no-holds-barred fight between two boys.

There was an awkward silence in the room when Dante finished speaking. 'I swear that's the truth,' he said. 'But none of the Brigands will corroborate it. They'll say I beat Martin up to make me look bad.'

Vanessa combed her hands through her long hair. 'OK,' she sighed. 'I think the best thing is for us to find an interview room where you can record an amendment to your statement.'

'How would the Führer's lawyers find out about this, anyway?' Dante asked. 'I mean, we don't have to tell them do we?'

Vanessa laughed. 'Unfortunately we do. Everyone has a right to defend themselves in court and see all the evidence against them. Once the Führer is charged, his defence lawyers will have the right to see all the evidence we've collected, including your original witness statement.'

'Just my luck,' Dante said, banging his heel against the sofa.

Vanessa gave Dante a serious look. 'I want you to read through your statement again, and if there's anywhere else where you didn't tell the absolute truth you need to tell me. OK?'

Dante nodded. The comment about the nosebleed had seemed like such a harmless lie that he'd forgotten it before the interview with Ross even ended.

'I'm sorry I'm so useless,' he said sourly.

Ross put a hand on his shoulder. 'It's probably not that bad,' he said, as he looked up at Vanessa. 'The Brigands aren't the only ones who have smart lawyers.'

Vanessa walked across and opened her office door. 'Thank you for coming in, Dante. I'd like to have a private word with Ross now. Would you mind waiting outside with Jennifer for a few moments?'

10. LODGE

Once Vanessa's office door closed she crashed into her chair and buried her head in her hands. Ross stared at her, frustrated.

'How bad is it on a scale of one to ten?' he asked, keeping his voice down because Dante was outside.

'Seven or eight,' Vanessa said. 'I'd hoped Dante's explanation for the lie about the T-shirt would be something other than the fact that he got into a bloody fight with the son of the man he accused of murdering his parents a few hours later. And Dante's school record isn't great. He's been in fights *and* he's been accused of bullying.'

'He's hardly a violent hoodlum,' Ross said.

'I know, but the Führer's lawyers will try to portray Dante as a violent and disturbed kid who was severely traumatised by what he saw. He was young and tired and to top it all off they'll have proof that he's a liar.'

'What about the attempted bombing? Does that help us?'

'The judge would throw any mention of the bomb threat out of court unless we had clear evidence linking it to the Führer.'

'He's a smart kid though,' Ross said. 'He'll look good on a witness stand and there's a lot of incidental evidence tying Dante's description of what happened to the bullet holes and the position of the bodies in the house.'

'I know,' Vanessa nodded. 'Nobody will deny that he saw what happened. But there will be other witnesses including the Führer's own sons and other Brigands who'll swear him an alibi. They'll drag up some expert witness who'll explain how an eight-year-old who sees his whole family getting their brains blown out can be so traumatised that he'll leap to conclusions and see things that he really didn't.'

'So you're not planning to arrest the Führer and press charges?' Ross asked.

Vanessa shook her head wearily. 'I would if I had one strong piece of evidence *besides* Dante's testimony. A gun that matched the bullets in the house. One of the Führer's boots. A trace of firearms residue. But the Brigands had half an hour to clear up the murder scene and they did a bloody good job.'

Ross sighed. 'So the Führer stays a free man?'

'For now,' Vanessa said. 'It's not like the police are going to stop investigating a quintuple murder after less than three months. But we're going to need a significant breakthrough and the longer the investigation goes on the less likely that becomes.'

'Are there any more forensic angles to be worked?'

'Nope. The only thing that's going to break this case open is another witness. Maybe if we arrest one of the Brigands further down the line on another charge and offer a deal in return for information about the murder. Or maybe a member of the public will walk into the police station with a gun or some clothing that didn't burn properly. You never know.'

'Poor bloody Dante,' Ross sighed. 'He's such a great kid and he needs the Führer put behind bars so that he can get on with his life.'

*

Vanessa asked Dante and Ross to stick around for a few more hours in case she needed to ask more questions after a joint meeting with her CPS bosses and senior officers in charge of the police investigation.

In the end, nobody had any more questions for Dante, but by the time he'd recorded a new witness statement and waited around for the meeting to finish it was nearly 6 p.m. and Ross didn't fancy the long drive back to London.

Ross, Dante, Steve and Jennifer booked into a bland hotel on a motorway junction. Dante shared his room with Ross. Because they were back in Devon he smuggled Dante into the hotel through a side door and made him hide in the bathroom when room service delivered their dinner.

The room had two double beds, but Dante lay on a bed beside Ross, eating spicy chicken with rice, drinking Pepsi from a glass bottle and sharing chips out of a basket lying between them. Steve the bodyguard was taking a nap in his room, but Jennifer had joined them and sat across the room with her lasagne perched on a narrow writing desk.

'So Dante,' Jennifer asked. 'How are you feeling?'

Dante enjoyed Ross' company. He not only resented Jennifer's intrusion, but couldn't understand why she'd suddenly appeared.

'I don't want to discuss my feelings with you,' Dante said bitterly. 'I don't need any more people sticking their noses in.'

Ross gave Dante a *don't be rude* stare, but Jennifer only laughed.

'It doesn't seem fair, does it?' Jennifer asked.

Dante tutted. 'Can't I eat my dinner in peace?'

'Jennifer is here to help you, Dante,' Ross said. 'She's just trying to get to know you better.'

'Fine,' Dante huffed. 'If there's one thing I've learned lately it's that life *isn't* fair. The Führer kills my mum, dad, brother and sister. Then he tries to blow me up with a bomb. And he gets away with it, because apparently nobody on the jury will believe me because I told one stupid lie about a bloody T-shirt.'

'They're not saying they'll *never* prosecute the Führer,' Ross noted. 'They just need more evidence.'

'Blah, blah, blah,' Dante said, as he dumped his dinner plate on the bedside table. 'I *never* should have spoken to the cops. At least the Brigands *do* stuff, instead of having meetings, and waiting for evidence and all this other crap.'

'You have every right to be upset,' Jennifer said.

'You're all useless,' Dante yelled. 'When I'm old enough I'm going to get a sawn-off and a motorbike. I'm gonna drive up to the Führer's house and I'm gonna shoot him in the legs. Then I'll hook him up, and watch him bleed slowly to death.'

Dante felt tears welling in his eyes and he was annoyed because half a minute earlier he'd been eating his dinner with Ross and now he was in a state.

'It'll get better,' Jennifer said.

'Bollocks!' Dante screamed. He threw his dinner at Jennifer and started to sob. 'I'm sick of everyone going on about my feelings. I want everyone to leave me alone.'

The plate narrowly missed the elderly psychologist, but the carpet and chair were covered with rice and chicken.

'I'm so useless I can't even hit an old granny with a plate of food,' Dante shouted, steaming across the room, slamming the bathroom door and locking himself in.

He looked at his red face in the mirror, before lashing out and violently kicking the toilet seat. He hurled Ross' wash bag at the wall, then grabbed the little bin off the floor and threw it at the frosted glass window. Instead of crashing through the glass as he'd hoped, it bounced off and hit him on the head.

'Owwwwwww!' Dante screamed, collapsing to his knees as Ross banged on the door.

'Open up,' Ross shouted. 'You're just working yourself into a state. It's not doing anyone any good, is it?'

'Sod off!' Dante said, as he kicked the door, then crashed backwards and sat on the toilet lid.

A penknife blade slid between the door and the bolt and Dante lunged forward as he noticed the bolt turning. He expected Ross, but was surprised to find Jennifer's slim frame in the doorway.

Dante charged at her stomach, but instead of bowling her over he found himself being spun around. Jennifer twisted Dante's arm up behind his back, and held him in an uncomfortable restraining position as she pulled him out of the bathroom and sprawled him down across the bed.

'Calm down,' Jennifer soothed. 'I'll let go as soon as you stop fighting.'

Ross closed in as Dante sobbed hysterically.

'Keep him still,' Jennifer said. 'I'll get my med bag.'

As Ross sat beside Dante on the bed, stroking his back and trying to get him to calm down, Jennifer dashed across the hall. She opened her room with a credit card-style key and came back moments later with her handbag.

'How can the Führer get away with it?' Dante sobbed. 'He killed my whole family. There's got to be more evidence.'

Ross had grown attached to Dante and had wet eyes himself as Jennifer rummaged through her bag.

'Dante, sweetheart,' Jennifer said, as she twisted the

sterile cap off the syringe needle. 'I need you to keep still for two seconds.'

Dante looked back and saw Jennifer moving towards him, with a five-centimetre needle catching the light.

'No!' he screamed.

'Hold him still, Ross,' Jennifer said, as she pulled Dante's trousers down a few centimetres to expose the top of his left buttock. She dabbed his skin with a sterile wipe.

'He can't get away with it,' Dante yelled. 'Leave me alone. What are you doing?'

Ross pushed Dante firmly against the bed so that he didn't move as the needle sank into his bum. Jennifer drew a swirl of blood up into the syringe before pressing down to inject a dose of sedative.

After a few seconds, Dante felt himself relax and his eyes shot out of focus. Within twenty the sobbing had stopped, his breathing had gone back to normal and he'd drifted into a deep sleep.

Jennifer looked exhausted and wiped her brow on the back of her wrist. 'So much for waiting until he fell asleep,' she said.

Ross rolled Dante on to his back and felt sad as he saw the boy's tear-streaked face. 'I'm very fond of him, Jennifer,' Ross said. 'I still can't believe what you told me.'

Jennifer smiled. 'Nor will Dante when he wakes up in the morning.'

11. STRANGE *(REPRISE)*

At first Dante thought he was still in the hotel. But there was only one double bed. There was a wall-mounted TV, a kettle, a telephone and a miniature fridge. He didn't have a clue where he was or how he'd got here. The last thing he remembered was checking into the hotel with Ross Johnson and Jennifer Mitchum.

Dante burrowed around under the duvet and saw that he was naked, except for a thickly padded incontinence pad. He opened out the elastic around the waist and was relieved to find it dry inside.

'Ross?' Dante yelled curiously, as he sat up and looked out of the window.

The room was on a corner, six storeys up. A crane hovered a few hundred metres away, its driver lowering glass panels on to a banana-shaped construction site. In front of the building were lawns, a car park and two helipads. Most intriguingly a line of little kids in matching red T-shirts and combat trousers was heading out of a side entrance carrying a selection of archery equipment, including bows, arrows and target boards stacked on a big trolley.

As he stepped back from the curtains, Dante noticed clothes laid out on the floor. They were his size: white socks and boxers, pressed orange T-shirt, plus green military-style trousers and boots. Apart from the T-shirt colour it looked identical to what the kids outside were wearing. The boots seemed new, with a rubbery smell and shiny black soles. The T-shirt had a logo with a winged baby sitting on a globe and the word CHERUB cut through the middle.

So it was some kind of boarding school, and Dante was relieved because it definitely didn't look like the Brigands had got their hands on him. He spun around when a door clicked beside him.

'Hello,' a girl said warily, as she leaned in from an adjoining room.

She matched Dante in size and build, but had long blond hair and would have been pretty but for two shockingly black eyes. The girl wore boots, orange T-shirt and combat trousers, and Dante was embarrassed because he was wearing the giant nappy.

'Hey,' Dante said. He thought about moving back to the bed and covering up with the duvet, but instead he froze on the spot. 'Erm . . . Are you like, I mean . . . Did you just sort of wake up here?'

The girl's eyebrows shot up in recognition. 'Exactly,'

she nodded. 'The corridor outside is empty, but I heard you yelling *Ross*.'

'What's the last thing you remember?' Dante asked.

'I was in a kids' home called Nebraska House. I was supposed to have an evening appointment with my counsellor, but I waited in her office for ages. Then I got a call to say she'd had to go off to Devon for some emergency and she'd see me tomorrow instead.'

'Devon,' Dante said curiously. 'Was she called Jennifer by any chance?'

The girl nodded. 'Yes, Jennifer Mitchum.'

'I know her,' Dante said. 'What, is she going around abducting kids or something?'

'This place seems OK,' the girl said. 'I mean, there's tennis courts and kids running around outside. I'm Lauren by the way. Lauren Onions.'

Dante dithered for a second before deciding to use his real name. 'I'm Dante,' he said. 'So is your room like this?'

Lauren held the adjoining door open so that Dante could see inside. 'Everything's identical, except I didn't have a big nappy on.'

Dante looked embarrassed. 'I don't know *why* they put this on me,' he lied. 'So what do you reckon we should do? Maybe try to find someone?'

'Why don't you get dressed and we'll look around together? There's got to be an adult somewhere.'

After putting on the uniform Dante met Lauren out in the hallway. They were at the end of a long carpeted corridor, with doors off either side. Some doors were open and as the pair walked they saw rooms in various states of disarray.

'Looks like teenagers judging by the size of the clothes,' Lauren said. She noticed a bedside clock. 'Quarter to ten, so I guess they're all in lessons.'

'What happened to your eyes?' Dante asked, as they started walking again.

'My idiot dad,' Lauren said reluctantly. 'He came home in a mood. I said I needed some money for shopping and he went crazy and punched me in the face.'

'Jesus,' Dante said.

'It's nothing compared to how it looked at first,' Lauren said. 'I could barely see on the way to school the next day. My teacher reported it and that's how I ended up in Nebraska House. My half brother James was supposed to be there, but nobody could find him . . .'

'Maybe he's here,' Dante suggested.

Lauren felt dumb because she hadn't thought of this herself. 'Maybe he is,' she smiled. 'He's an idiot, but we kind of look after each other.'

As they reached the lift and stairs in the centre of the building a teenager burst out of her bedroom. She held a giant art folio and a pile of books on Picasso. She wore the same uniform as Dante and Lauren, but looked about fifteen and her navy T-shirt was spattered with paint.

'Hello,' Lauren said politely. 'Can you help us please, we're a bit lost?'

The girl held out her palm. 'Can't talk to orange,' she said firmly.

Lauren and Dante were baffled by the response. They followed the girl as she approached the lift. She was carrying too much stuff to press the button.

'Up or down?' Dante asked.

'Down,' the girl said reluctantly.

Dante pressed the button. 'So why can't you talk to us? All we want is directions.'

'Sorry,' the teenager said. 'But you've no idea how much trouble I could get into for talking to someone in an orange T-shirt. They'll be watching you on CCTV. Mac will find you when he needs you.'

'Who's Mac?' Lauren asked.

'Will you speak to me if I pull my T-shirt off?' Dante asked.

The girl laughed, then looked anxiously at the LED display and groaned with frustration because the lift hadn't budged from the ground floor.

'I'll walk then, shall I?' the teenager said to herself angrily. 'I *hate* these lifts! They always make me late.'

Before racing off down the stairs, the girl saw the worried expressions on the two nine-year-old faces. 'This is a nice place, you've got nothing to be scared of.'

Dante and Lauren looked at one another and shrugged.

'Well,' Dante said, 'one thing's for sure, today can't get any weirder.'

Lauren managed a half smile. 'Don't bet on it.'

Sod's law dictated that the lift started moving as soon as the overladen teenager set off down the stairs. Lauren and Dante watched the display as the lift rumbled inside its shaft. When the doors opened they revealed a lady with long dark hair and a lacy top stretched over a heavily pregnant belly.

'Hop in,' the woman said. 'I'll start your tour from the ground floor.'

'Are you Mac?' Dante asked, as the doors closed.

The woman shook her head. 'No, Mac is our chairman. He usually takes prospective recruits on a tour of campus, but he's in bed with a chest infection. He's in a real state and his wife's refused to let him come into work. I'm Zara Asker, one of the senior mission controllers.'

'Is my brother here?' Lauren asked, as they stepped out on the ground floor. They were in the main entrance hall. There was a reception desk, and a worried looking boy in a red CHERUB T-shirt sat on a bench outside an office.

'Yes, James is here,' Zara said. 'One second.'

Zara walked towards the boy, who looked about seven. She spoke with an authoritative tone. 'Jake Parker sitting outside the chairman's office, *what* a surprise.'

The red-shirt boy stood up. 'It wasn't my fault, Mrs. I didn't even start it. I was just . . .'

Zara interrupted. 'Jake, it's your lucky day. The chairman is sick, so go back to your lesson and try *behaving* for once.'

Jake nodded sheepishly. 'I thought you'd left until after your baby was born.'

Zara smiled and rested both hands on her belly. 'He's in no rush to come out. I'm in for a couple of hours to show these two orange shirts around. Now scram.'

She turned back to Lauren and Dante as Jake ran off. 'He's a terror, that one,' Zara said, smiling through gritted teeth. 'Now I expect you're wondering exactly where you are.'

'Can I see my brother?' Lauren asked.

'Now that's *slightly* complicated,' Zara said. 'He's in basic training. You can go and watch him, but you won't be able to speak to him at the moment.'

'What's basic training?' Dante asked.

'I tell you what,' Zara said. 'Rather than answer odd questions here and there, how about I take you on a tour of CHERUB campus and explain exactly who we are and what we do?'

Lauren and Dante nodded. Zara led them out of the main entrance and down five steps. In the gravel outside was a fountain. The sculpture inside it had a three dimensional version of the baby on a globe depicted on their T-shirts. Three small electric carts were parked alongside.

'I can't fit behind the steering wheel,' Zara said. 'Would one of you mind driving? It's not hard.'

Dante got excited as he sat behind the steering wheel. The controls were simple: a lever switched between forward and reverse and two foot pedals for accelerating and braking.

'They can go quite fast, but keep it below ten miles an hour because there are lots of kids running around,' Zara said as she squeezed into the front passenger seat. Lauren hopped into the back seat and Dante jabbed the accelerator pedal.

'We've just left the main building,' Zara explained, as the little buggy drove slowly around the fountain and on to a gravel path. 'It's where all CHERUB agents eat; it's also where many of our staff live, along with the older agents. There are administrative offices, an archive in the basement and our mission control centre up on the top floor.'

Lauren looked curiously towards the roof. 'Mission control,' she repeated. 'That sounds like NASA or something.'

Zara laughed, but then they went quite hard over a bump and she told Dante to drive more slowly and take the next left on to the main path that led through the centre of campus.

'We don't launch rockets,' she explained. 'Our missions are the undercover variety. CHERUB agents are trained spies aged between ten and seventeen.'

Dante glanced at Zara's face to see if she was being serious. Apparently she was.

'Why?' Lauren asked. 'What's the point of using kids as spies?'

'Turn right again,' Zara said. As she continued, the buggy passed around the side of the main building. After a dense copse of trees they broke out into a clear December day. There were tennis courts alongside and a view over most of CHERUB campus, including rugby and football pitches, a dozen or so buildings ranging from storage sheds to a medieval chapel. In the far distance was a lake, beyond which lay dense woodland.

'We use kids as spies because nobody suspects them,'

Zara explained. 'The example Mac always uses is of a grown man knocking on an old lady's door in the middle of the night. Most people would be suspicious. If he asked to come inside, the lady would say no. If the man claimed to be sick she'd probably call an ambulance but still wouldn't let him in.

'Now imagine the old dear answers the door and it's a young boy, crying. *My dad's car crashed. I think he's dying. Please help me.* The old lady opens the door. The man jumps out of hiding, bops her on the head, goes inside and robs the place. Terrorists and criminals have been using tricks like this for years. CHERUB turns the tables and uses the same techniques to catch them.'

Dante smiled. 'So kids are actually better at being criminals or spies than grown-ups.'

'In many respects, yes,' Zara said. 'Because people don't suspect them.'

She pointed over her right shoulder. 'That's our swimming and diving pool complex. Do either of you like swimming?'

Lauren and Dante both nodded.

'I never get to go swimming though,' Lauren said. 'My mum got embarrassed because she was overweight and my brother James is a total wuss. He turns green and says he's gonna puke if you even go near a swimming pool.'

Zara nodded. 'James had to learn to swim before he could start basic training. I wasn't involved myself, but I understand he only passed the swimming test in the nick of time.'

Lauren was aghast. 'James can *swim*? That's practically a miracle.'

Dante cut the speed as the buggy splashed through a couple of inches of water alongside a football pitch. Exhausted looking teenagers were running through the mud, doing shuttle runs while carrying fifteen-kilogram weight discs high above their heads. All the while a female instructor screamed abuse at them.

'We have strict discipline here,' Zara explained, as they watched the training. 'That lot smuggled eighty cans of beer on to campus, held a wild party and then tested positive for marijuana the following Monday. We have a zero tolerance policy for all illegal drugs.'

'So what's the deal?' Lauren asked. 'Are we being asked to join CHERUB or what?'

'That's it exactly,' Zara said. 'The circumstances that brought you here are slightly different, but Jennifer Mitchum has given both of you a preliminary assessment and we think you both stand a good chance of qualifying as CHERUB agents.'

'Why's that?' Dante asked.

'Agents have to be exceptional in all areas,' Zara explained. 'Physically strong, emotionally mature and of well-above average intelligence. You both have potential, but I'm sure you'll also have shortcomings. If you choose to join CHERUB . . .'

Lauren interrupted. 'So it's our choice?'

'Absolutely,' Zara said. 'I know you were brought here without your knowledge, but that's only because our location is a secret. If you're not interested in becoming a spy and living on campus, all you have to do is tell us and we'll drop you home.'

'But isn't this place a massive secret?' Dante asked. 'I mean, once you've told us we could blab to anyone.'

'Who would believe you though?' Zara pointed out. 'You don't know where we are. You won't be able to prove anything. In fact, you probably ought to be careful because if you start telling people about being recruited by a secret spying organisation, people are likely to think you've gone mental.

'Anyway, going back to what I was saying before. We believe that you both have the potential to become CHERUB agents. However, before you reach that stage we have to iron out all your flaws. We'll work on your fitness levels, we'll start you off with intensive language and combat courses. You'll be astonished at what our training can help you to achieve, but I'm not going to pretend that it's for everyone. Becoming a CHERUB agent is probably the toughest thing you'll ever do – Dante, next left into the trees and keep the speed down. The road up to the basic training compound is bumpy, and I don't fancy going into an early labour.'

'Have you got any other kids?' Dante asked, as he steered the buggy on to a narrow path between the trees.

Zara shook her head. 'Joshua will be my first and after *this* pregnancy my last.'

Lauren smiled. 'So you've named him already?'

'Yes,' Zara said. 'My husband Ewart and I both liked the name. He's been Joshua since the day we found out he was a boy.'

'So you said my brother's in basic training,' Lauren said. 'How does that work?'

'Careful, Dante!' Zara said urgently, as the buggy clattered into branches at the side of the path. 'Ten mph, no faster.'

Dante enjoyed driving the buggy. It reminded him of what Ross' daughter Tina had said after he'd woken in the night: about how his life would go on and how he'd be able to do special things that would have made his parents happy.

Zara continued her explanation. 'Anyone over ten years old who's reached the required fitness level will go into basic training. It's a one-hundred-day course and the idea is that your mind and body are pushed to the limits every minute of every day. Once you pass you've earned your grey CHERUB T-shirt and you'll be qualified to go on undercover missions.

'If we stop here we should be able to see the trainees doing their morning combat session through the fence.'

Dante stopped the electric cart. After he'd helped Zara out of the buggy, she led the trio over muddy ground. They ended up behind some bushes, with the mesh fence around the training compound in front of them.

'Keep your voices down,' Zara whispered, as she glanced at her watch.

Thirty metres away stood a massive fellow with a bristly moustache and a white CHERUB T-shirt stretched over vast muscles. In front of him stood six trainees. They wore light blue shirts with numbers on the back, but you could barely read them because they were so muddy. The kids had bare feet and the giant instructor had them all in a line, endlessly repeating a complicated combo of four Karate moves.

'That's Norman Large,' Zara explained. 'He's not exactly the most loved member of campus staff amongst you kids, but he does a *bloody* good job of turning out highly trained agents.'

It took Lauren several seconds to recognise her twelve-year-old brother. Not only was James filthy, but his blond hair had been shaved down to a number one and he had a dirty bandage over a wound on his cheek. He'd lost a lot of puppy fat since the last time Lauren saw him and she was impressed by the way he strung together the rapid sequence of Karate moves.

'Partners, sparring,' Large shouted.

'Which one's your brother?' Dante whispered as the trainees split into three pairs.

'In the middle,' Lauren said. 'Squaring up to the little Asian girl.'

'That's hardly fair,' Dante noticed. 'He's miles bigger.'

'That's Kerry,' Zara explained. 'And I wouldn't worry on her behalf.'

Zara didn't need to explain her remark because Instructor Large blew his whistle for the sparring to begin. Lauren watched aghast as Kerry ducked below her brother's clumsy kick, then drove her body upwards, lifting James off the ground, throwing him over her back and dumping him in the mud. Kerry then jammed her heel between James' shoulders and ruthlessly wrenched his arm into a painful lock.

Lauren clutched her hand over her mouth in awe as James moaned in pain and thumped on the mud in submission.

'That Kerry girl is awesome!' Dante said. 'She could be a pro wrestler with skills like that.'

Zara smiled at Dante. 'I heard that you liked wrestling and who knows? With the skills you learn here, maybe you could be a pro wrestler some day.'

As the six trainees started a second round of sparring, Dante stepped back from the fence and broke into a relieved smile. For the first time since the night his parents died, he felt like he had some kind of future without them.

12. RED

After their tour of campus, Zara took Dante and Lauren into the dining-room for a very late breakfast. The space was big enough to seat three hundred around its maple-topped tables. There were serving areas and trays for mealtimes, but agents and staff came and went at odd hours so fresh cooked food could be ordered at any time, day or night.

Hands were cold after the ride in the open cart, so Lauren and Zara warmed themselves with soup and freshly baked bread, while Dante went for a hot turkey and bacon baguette which he opened up and drenched with three sachets of ketchup.

Dante was keen to join CHERUB, Lauren less so.

'Training and fighting in mud,' she said warily as she broke off a piece of warm bread. 'I'm not a skirts-and-glitter type, but that training looked mental.'

'It's tough,' Dante nodded. 'But when your brother finishes basic training he's gonna be rock hard. Like, he can just walk into a room and beat the crap out of anyone he wants to.'

'James is training to defend himself, Dante,' Zara smiled. 'And Lauren, we're not suggesting that you make an absolute commitment to becoming an agent today. I'd suggest that you agree to move here on a trial basis and see how you settle in. You'll start off with regular lessons, along with beginners' fitness training and combat programmes. You're not the first girl who's seen what goes on here and baulked, but once you've settled in and made friends I expect you'll be much more relaxed about it. And if you decide not to stay, we'll find you a foster home and you can still be near your brother.'

'If I join, what happens about Holly?' Dante asked.

'Holly can grow up on campus,' Zara explained. 'We have an excellent nursery unit and you'll be able to see her every day. At four we'll start her off with some combat and language training. At ten, she'll be able to make her own decision about entering basic training and becoming an agent.'

'What if one of us doesn't pass basic training?' Lauren asked. 'Or if my brother doesn't pass?'

Zara shifted awkwardly in her chair. 'Sometimes it takes two or three attempts, but it's rare for someone to fail basic training completely. We can't plan for every possible outcome, but we have had situations where one sibling has become a CHERUB agent while another lives with a foster family near to campus.

'What I *must* stress is that no CHERUB agent is ever forced to do anything against their will. You can quit a training exercise, quit a mission or even leave campus and decide to lead a normal life if that's what you choose.'

Lauren was reassured by this. Dante was delighted that he'd be able to live alongside Holly again, and although it would be nine years into the future he liked the idea that one day she'd have the opportunity to become a highly trained spy too.

'So you both want to take the next step and go for the ability tests and medical?' Zara asked.

'I guess,' Lauren said.

Dante's mouth was crammed with food, but he nodded eagerly.

*

After giving the new recruits half an hour for their food to settle Zara took them to the campus medical centre where they stripped down to their underwear. A grey-haired German doctor named Kessler gave them a full body x-ray, a dental x-ray and then took blood samples.

Doctor Kessler assured them that the muscle biopsy wouldn't hurt that much and called them both whiners as a spring-loaded tube punched through their skin and sucked out a tiny lump of their thigh muscles.

'The tissue will be examined under a microscope,' Kessler explained. 'Your training will be tailored to your body composition. We'll know what your bodies are capable of. So we won't push you too hard, but also we'll know if you're slacking off.'

Kessler led them into a space equipped with a pair of treadmills and a variety of high-tech gadgets designed to test vision, reflexes and co-ordination.

Dante and Lauren began an unofficial competition. They were evenly matched: Dante the stronger, while Lauren better at technical tasks such as being asked to balance on one leg while holding a glass brimming with water and to shoot as many mini footballs as possible through a basketball hoop in one minute.

The final test was the most gruelling: thirty minutes on a treadmill while strapped to a heart monitor and with oxygen masks over their faces. The machine was programmed to alter speed and climb depending upon their level of exhaustion. Kessler told them to push through the pain barrier and only to press the emergency stop button if they thought they were going to pass out.

Lauren felt huge relief when the treadmill motor ground to a halt. She clutched her sides, fighting a stitch, with sweat pouring down her face and dark patches on her orange shirt. Dante looked far worse and staggered towards the wall before retching turkey and bacon into a bucket hastily provided by a nurse.

They got twenty minutes to recover while a dentist prodded and scraped. Lauren's teeth were perfect but Dante would have to come back for a filling and the possible extraction of a crooked rear tooth.

After the dentist they were led out to a waiting room, where Zara had been resting her swollen ankles on a coffee table the whole time.

'Two more or less perfect specimens,' Dr Kessler said

when he emerged twenty minutes later. 'Dante might benefit from contact lenses for reading. Lauren is slightly overweight and her fitness level is poor, but we have ten months to work on that before her basic training starts.'

Zara found an empty classroom in the main building for the academic test. The ninety-minute paper covered maths, general knowledge, spelling, IQ puzzles and a final section that asked you to write a short essay on what you thought would be your main strengths and weaknesses as a CHERUB agent. The questions were tough, and the fact that they were both stressed and exhausted after the physical tests didn't make things easier.

Zara left Dante and Lauren in the dining-room while she marked the papers. It was just after three and the red-shirt cherubs, who were all aged ten or under, had finished lessons for the day. Some had after-school activities, but about thirty were hanging around in the dining-room eating buttered toast and chocolate bars.

Dante felt out of place because all the red-shirt kids seemed to know each other. They were chatting and teasing one another, and leaning over each other's shoulders, borrowing rubbers and copying from homework sheets. None of them could speak to Dante or Lauren because they wore orange T-shirts, and the idea of settling into another new home and trying to make friends with another new bunch of kids filled Dante with dread.

'How do you think you did on the test?' Lauren asked quietly, as she stared down at the table.

'Not bad,' Dante shrugged. 'That stupid essay . . . I

hate it when you have to say what's good and bad about yourself.'

'I know,' Lauren nodded, but before she finished speaking a mound of balled-up toast crusts whizzed in front of her eyes. They hit the table spinning and ricocheted upwards, breaking up and pelting Dante.

A group of six- to eight-year-olds a few tables across started laughing, and Dante and Lauren could tell who was responsible from his body language. It was Jake Parker, the kid they'd seen waiting outside the chairman's office earlier in the day.

Dante shot out of his seat and roared, 'Hey, midget, you want me to come over there and stick your head through the wall?'

Jake swaggered between the tables towards Dante. 'You might be bigger than me,' Jake grinned. 'But I'm a black belt in Judo and Karate, so I'd *suggest* you watch your mouth.'

One of Jake's friends came up behind and tugged him back towards the table. 'Jake, you're talking to orange. You'll get punishment laps!'

Jake realised that his friend was right and started backing up.

'Pussy,' Dante taunted, and he gave Jake the finger.

This was more than Jake could handle. He reared forward, swung at the hips and launched an explosive kick. Tables and chairs ground against the floor as Dante dodged out of the way, but Jake kept coming, dropping into a fighting stance with his hand ready to launch an explosive Karate chop. Dante was a full head taller, but

Jake's moves were lightning fast and Dante suspected he'd bitten off more than he could chew.

But before Jake made contact an older girl with dark hair grabbed him around the waist. She hitched him up by the elasticised waistband of his tracksuit bottoms and threw him across a table top.

Dante sensed the opportunity and threw a punch as Jake straddled the table. But he only hit air because Lauren was dragging him the other way.

'No trouble,' Lauren said anxiously as she hauled Dante back to their table. 'Come on. Sit down.'

As a wall of red T-shirts formed between Dante and Jake, one of the chefs yelled from behind the counter: 'You lot, pack it in!'

Jake yelped as the girl who'd thrown him over the table called him a moron and deadened his arm with a brutal punch.

As suddenly as the fracas started, everyone hurried back to their seats because Zara had entered the dining-room. Something had happened, but all she saw were twenty young faces with *what, me?* expressions.

Jake groaned as the older girl threw him back towards where he'd been sitting.

'Bethany,' Zara said firmly. 'What have I told you about fighting with your brother?'

'It's nothing,' the girl said. 'We were just messing around, weren't we?'

Jake clutched his arm and scowled, but he confirmed his sister's story with a nod.

As Dante sat down he noticed that Zara was holding

a pair of red CHERUB T-shirts sealed in polythene bags.

'Since you've got so much energy, Bethany,' Zara said, 'I'd like you to take our two new recruits Lauren and Dante across to the junior block. Find them some beds and help them to settle in. They'll need clothes, towels and I expect they'll want a shower after all they've been through today.'

As Zara handed over the red T-shirts, Bethany reached across and tapped Lauren on the shoulder.

'Welcome to CHERUB,' Bethany said. 'There's an empty bed in my room if you'd like to bunk in with me.'

In the background, a couple of boys came across to say hello. Dante and Lauren said a quick goodbye to Zara before Bethany led them out into the hallway.

'All us red shirts live in the junior block,' Bethany explained as they walked. 'It's pretty cool. We've got our own classrooms, and a big home-cinema room where we watch movies and if you like animals there's a pet lounge with guinea pigs and mice, frogs and stuff.'

'I'm sorry about what happened with your brother,' Dante said. 'It was only bread. I should have ignored it.'

'It's best not to get into too many fights until you've got a few months' combat training under your belt,' Bethany warned. 'But you don't have to apologise to me. Jake's a *total* dickhead.'

Part Two
Four and a half years later . . .

13. COFFEE

May 2008

Sealclubber was the wrong side of forty, with a white beard, a gallery of tattoos and a taste for huge silver rings. The head of the London Brigands looked out of place in the basement of a Starbucks near King's Cross station.

'Coffee here costs more than a pint,' Sealclubber complained, glancing at the elderly Seiko on his wrist as a twenty-year-old Asian man sat down opposite. 'Twenty minutes I've sat here. This better be worth it.'

Dressed in trainers and a muscle tee, the Asian plopped a raspberry mocha Frappuccino on the table top and dropped a backpack to the floor between his legs.

'Northern line sucks,' he shrugged. 'Hopefully I was worth the wait.'

The surrounding tables were covered with crumbs and empty mugs, but the lunchtime rush was over and the nearest person was a suit and tie using his laptop in a booth five metres away.

Sealclubber took a square note that the Asian man fed across the table and read it to himself: *70 AK47 assault rifles, 12 cases of 24x Swiss Army issue grenades, 40 generic .357 revolvers, 20 H&K machine pistols, 18,000 rounds M43 type ammunition, 5000 rounds .357 ammunition. Price £632,000 for delivery to specified UK location.*

'You starting World War Three?' Sealclubber asked quietly, as he leaned further across the table. 'Because this is a lot of shit, you know? My compadres down in Devon, their business is mostly villains: drug dealers and nightclub bouncers who like a piece of metal by their sides. *Ten* guns is a big order for them.'

The Asian man looked disappointed. 'Can you supply this or not? I can have the ten per cent deposit delivered to your clubhouse as soon as you need it.'

Sealclubber was torn: he wanted to say yes on the spot and grab the commission, but he had no idea who the Asian man was and in the criminal world the more money someone has the worse an idea it is to mess them about.

'I've got to talk with my people,' Sealclubber said. 'You don't need to worry. Don't start looking for alternative suppliers or anything like that, but I'm a businessman and I'm not gonna make you promises I can't keep.'

'We're offering you a lot of money,' the Asian

man said. 'You can buy these guns in the USA a tenth of this price.'

Sealclubber flexed his fingers and his silver rings dazzled the Asian as he smiled. 'You can buy most of this shit in any gun shop in the USA,' he laughed. 'Go to some African shithole and you can pick AK47s off street vendors for less than I paid for my coffee. But in case you haven't noticed, this little island has the tightest gun controls in the world and you can't smuggle a hundred guns and twenty-three thousand rounds of ammunition on a P&O ferry under your jumper.'

The Asian paused, as if he was wavering over the deal. The day was a scorcher and he downed a third of his Frappuccino in three long sucks on the straw. 'I respect the fact that you don't want to make rash promises. When can you let us know?'

'This business is all face to face,' Sealclubber explained. 'It's too risky picking up a cellphone and talking about this. But I'll set up a meeting and get back to you. You'll know within three days, five at the outside.'

'OK,' the Asian said, as he stood up to leave.

'Just one thing,' Sealclubber said. 'This better not be for some terrorist shit.'

'It's Birmingham street shit,' the Asian laughed. 'A lot of money in my community. A lot of drugs and protection rackets. There's a war in the offing and when it starts I'm gonna be right there selling guns and ammo to whichever son of a bitch wants to buy them.'

'You sound like my kind of guy,' Sealclubber grinned.

'Sell the guns to all them Pakis, then sit back and let the bullets fly.'

The Asian looked narked.

'No offence,' Sealclubber said awkwardly. 'It's what we call brown people in my neck of the woods.'

'None taken,' the Asian lied. 'Call me what you like, just get me the guns.'

Sealclubber wished he either had a calculator or had paid enough attention in school maths class to work out what his fifteen per cent cut of £632,000 would be, but he was sure it was a lot of money.

The Asian sucked his Frappuccino dry and dumped it in a bin as he walked back out into the bright sunlight. He lucked out and dived into a black cab waiting at the lights.

'Hornsey Road swimming pool,' he told the driver.

There was a bit of traffic and the ride in the unair-conditioned taxi lasted twenty sticky minutes.

'Could do with a dip myself on a hot day like this,' the cabbie said, as he pulled up outside the pool and wrote a receipt. But once the cab was out of sight the Asian crossed the street and walked into Hornsey police station, directly opposite.

The desk sergeant pressed a buzzer to let the Asian behind the counter. He headed up to an open-plan office on the third floor that belonged to the National Police Biker Task Force (NPBTF). It was a grand name for a squad with eleven officers, two cars and no budget for overtime.

Everyone looked towards the Asian man as he stepped

into the room. 'I think we're in,' he smiled. 'Security's a joke. I wasn't patted down for a bug or anything.'

'Nice one, Georgie boy,' a female officer answered and a couple of other officers celebrated by banging on their desks and hurling compliments.

'He called me a Paki though,' George grinned. 'So I'm Tasering the prick when we bust him.'

Chief Inspector Ross Johnson had been in charge of NPBTF for the last nine months. 'How'd it go, George?' he asked, as he sauntered out of his office.

'Not too shabby, guv,' George admitted, as he stopped in front of his boss and rested an elbow on a beige partition. 'He baulked when he saw the size of the order. Just hope we didn't over-egg it.'

Ross shrugged and smiled. 'I'd hug you if you didn't look so damned sweaty. If the Führer can't deliver that quantity of weapons, he'll still try and sell us as much as he can. That's gonna push his supply chain to the limits and our boy at the other end of the line should get drafted in to help out.'

George cracked a big smile. 'Either that or we'll screw up, lose half a million in cash, get our undercover cop killed and direct traffic until we're old enough to retire.'

14. PROGRESS

Lauren Onions – now known as Lauren Adams – stepped out of the lift on the eighth floor of the main building on CHERUB campus. She wore a black CHERUB T-shirt. Her best friend Bethany Parker was alongside, wearing a navy shirt she'd earned during an eight-month mission in Brazil the previous year.

'Crappy maths homework,' Bethany complained. 'We should start a petition for a *no homework on your birthday* rule.'

'No homework ever would be better,' Lauren smiled, as the pair headed towards the doors of their adjoining bedrooms. 'And free butterscotch ice cream in every classroom.'

'Yay,' Bethany agreed. 'And all lessons to be taught by Rafael Nadal look-alikes with their shirts off.'

'I like the way you think,' Lauren laughed.

Bethany opened her door, and then shot backwards in fright as a bang and a blue flash blasted out of her doorway. It was followed by orange and green sparks, a whizzing sound and a wall-trembling thud. As she stood shielding her ears a grey cloud billowed into the corridor and set off a smoke alarm.

'What the *bloody* hell?' Lauren gawped.

Bethany's twelve-year-old brother Jake and his friend Kevin Sumner had jumped out of the room directly opposite and videoed the firework display on a camera phone.

'Takedown!' Jake shouted.

'You little dickhead,' Bethany shouted back as she wafted the smoke away from her face. 'Look at my room! Everything's gonna stink of smoke. You could have started a fire!'

'It was only a few fireworks in a biscuit tin,' Jake grinned. 'We had fire extinguishers on standby.'

As Bethany rushed into her room to open the balcony doors and clear the smoke, a pair of hands grabbed her from behind, giving her a second fright. The hands were followed by a gentle kiss on the neck.

'Didn't you appreciate that?' Bethany's fourteen-year-old boyfriend Andy Lagan grinned. 'If you think it was loud out there you should have been in here. My ears are *ringing*.'

'Serves you right,' Bethany yelled indignantly, as Andy peeled off a set of eye goggles. 'At least you were expecting it.'

But she managed a smile as her bathroom door came

open and bodies began to pour out singing *Happy birthday to you.* All of her friends were there, including Lauren's boyfriend Rat, a whole bunch of girls and a few older kids.

Lauren's sixteen-year-old brother James Adams stood in the middle of the gathering holding a chocolate cake with candles ablaze and *Happy Fourteenth Birthday* piped across the top in icing.

'You look like a tomato and you smell like dog poo,' Jake sang noisily, as he followed Lauren into the room. Andy sheepishly phoned down to ground-floor reception to explain that the building wasn't on fire and that the siren was a false alarm.

'I hate you evil bastards,' Bethany giggled, and she plunged two fingers into the cake and wiped a brown smear across James Adams' cheek. She licked chocolate frosting off her fingers and told everyone that it tasted great before hugging a couple of the girls.

'Why wasn't I in on this?' Lauren complained.

'You and your humongous trap,' Jake answered.

James placed the cake on Bethany's desk beside a pile of forks and paper plates. She'd already opened some gifts at breakfast time, but there were more presents on her bed.

Feeling happy, Bethany put an arm around boyfriend Andy and brother Jake and smiled for another picture.

'My idiot brother and my idiot boyfriend,' Bethany grinned. 'But I love 'em both really.'

*

Eight floors down, thirteen-year-old Dante Welsh –

formerly Dante Scott – sat in Zara Asker's office. Zara had been promoted to chairman of CHERUB two years earlier and was currently five months pregnant. Pictures of four-year-old Joshua and two-year-old Tiffany adorned the desk and the window ledge behind her head.

'What's it feel like being back?' Zara asked.

'Weird,' Dante admitted, speaking with a slight Belfast accent as he ran his hands through shoulder-length red hair.

'I looked up the stats,' Zara said, moving away from her desk towards a roll-top cabinet beside the fireplace at the opposite end of the office. 'Thirty-four months is the second longest mission on record and *easily* the longest of any agent currently serving on campus.'

'I was only supposed to be gone for six weeks,' Dante smiled. 'I met some good people, but I wouldn't be too sorry if I never went near another Belfast housing estate again.'

'And the thumb?' Zara asked.

Dante held his left thumb in the air, showing a nasty scar and stitch marks that ran all around. 'Feeling's almost back to normal. That surgeon did a blinding job sewing it back on.'

'Your mission controller, Eimer, said you worked hard to keep your fitness levels up.'

'Yeah,' Dante said. 'I didn't want to come back to campus and have old Mr Large get his teeth into me. So I bought some discs and a weight bench. I went running whenever I could and I even got some sparring in with Eimer to keep our combat skills fresh.'

'Great,' Zara smiled. 'It's really impressive that you stuck with your training discipline over such a long mission. Though you don't have Mr Large to worry about, he's no longer with us.'

'Praise God!' Dante whistled. 'Glad to see the back of that creep. What I can't believe is that I come back after all this time and Holly's off skiing in New Zealand. I've spoken to her on the webcam every week and we squeezed in a couple of weeks together at the hostel last summer, but I was really looking forward to us being properly back together.'

'Your sister's a brilliant little kid,' Zara said. 'My oldest Joshua has started lessons on campus. Holly's that bit older and he says she's a real bossy boots.'

'So your kids are going to be CHERUB agents?' Dante asked. 'I didn't think that was allowed.'

'We got the rule change approved by the Intelligence Minister three months back. We're always short of recruits. We conducted an informal survey and a surprising number of ex-cherubs said they'd be happy to let their children become CHERUB agents some day.'

'So one day my kids could be CHERUB agents too?' Dante laughed.

Zara nodded. 'Though to start with, we're only considering kids who have two parents working on campus, or if *both* parents are former CHERUB agents.'

'Plenty of pretty girls on CHERUB campus for me to start breeding with,' Dante grinned.

'Not for a few years I'd *very* much hope,' Zara said, adopting a stiff tone but keeping up her smile. 'Speaking of rules, you know that even though you performed outstandingly on a three-year mission I can't award you a black shirt? It's only for outstanding performance on *more* than one mission.'

Dante nodded. 'I don't care. I'm still only thirteen, there's plenty of time.'

'I think it's a stupid rule,' Zara admitted. 'I'd change it, but it has to be approved by the ethics committee and the Intelligence Minister and frankly I have higher priorities. However, in your case I did get the ethics committee to approve an extra mission. Specifically, this arduous mission involves a missing green marker pen, somewhere in my office. Your mission is to find it and return it to my pen pot. I believe that it was last seen somewhere underneath the chair you're sitting on.'

Dante looked down at the carpet and picked up the marker pen between the chromed legs of his chair.

'This one?'

'An *outstanding* mission performance if ever I saw it,' Zara said cheerfully, before reaching into her cupboard and pulling out a brand new CHERUB tee. 'Congratulations, you've earned your black shirt.'

Dante was startled and felt a tear welling up in his eye. 'You have no idea how desperate I was when I came here nearly five years ago,' he said. 'Making friends and the whole thing of getting ready for training really gave me focus. Without CHERUB I don't know who I'd have been or where I'd have ended up.'

'I just hope you're not too old for a hug,' Zara said. Dante stood up and Zara wrapped her arms around his back. 'If your parents were alive they'd be bloody proud of you, Dante. Now go upstairs and go find all your friends.'

Dante was on a high as he left Zara's office, but his mood dimmed as he hooked a large backpack over his shoulder and pulled a wheelie case towards the lift. Although he had a room on the eighth floor, he'd spent less than two months there after passing basic training.

The East Belfast estate and the people he'd known during his mission felt more like his real friends. The people he'd met on campus three years earlier had probably forgotten all about him.

There was a curious whiff of gunpowder in the eighth-floor hallway as Dante stepped from the lift.

Zara had sent one of the cleaning staff up to his room the previous day to clean it and put fresh sheets on his bed. There were also new sets of CHERUB uniform on the bed and new boots on the floor, but people change a lot between ten and thirteen. The casual clothes in his wardrobe were way too small and Dante felt a mixture of embarrassment and nostalgia at the wrestling posters on his walls and the action figures displayed on the shelf above his sofa.

The unopened black T-shirt was crammed into the pocket of Dante's hoodie. After stripping to his waist, he couldn't resist eyeing himself in his mirrored wardrobe door. He liked his dramatic red hair and muscular torso, but he wished his skin wasn't so pale and he tutted at the sight of a burgeoning zit on his shoulder blade.

'I'll get the Hoover,' a girl out in the hallway shouted.

'It'll be fine as long as nobody treads it into the carpet.'

The voice took Dante back to his first day on campus. He grabbed the handle of his bedroom door and made the girl scream.

'Oh my god! I thought I'd seen a ghost!' Lauren blurted, placing both hands over her heart before breaking into a huge smile. 'Dante, where the bloody hell have you been?'

'Ducking and weaving,' he grinned. 'Here and there, around and about.'

'You've got an Irish accent!'

'I guess if you spend three years anywhere you'll pick up an accent,' Dante explained. 'You smell better than the last time I saw you.'

'When was that?'

'You'd spent the day on ditch-digging punishment after you hit Mr Large with a spade,' Dante grinned. 'You were muddy and smelled vaguely like a cow's bottom.'

'That was so awful,' Lauren groaned. 'It was impossible to get the stench out of my hair.'

'You were about to restart basic training and I got sent off to Belfast before you qualified. Judging by the black T-shirt and your beautiful smile you've done OK since then.'

Lauren was flattered. 'Oh aren't you a charmer?' she grinned. 'You look like you've been hitting the weights. Do you still want to be a wrestler?'

Dante laughed. 'It's been a *long* time. I've even heard a rumour that some of that wrestling is faked.'

'Get *out* of town,' Lauren giggled. 'We're in the

middle of Bethany's birthday party,' she continued, as she grabbed Dante's wrist and gave him a tug. 'Come to her room, everyone's in there.'

So Lauren forgot all about fetching the Hoover and Dante found himself stepping into Bethany's crowded room, bare-chested with the new black T-shirt in his hand.

'Look who it is,' Lauren said enthusiastically.

Some kids like Rat and Andy had joined CHERUB after Dante went off on his mission and had no clue who he was. Others knew Dante, but they'd all aged three years and it was tricky putting names to faces.

'Oooh, a hunky boy on my birthday,' Bethany grinned as she approached Dante. 'Are you gonna strip for me?'

'I was just changing,' Dante said. 'Lauren practically dragged me in here.'

'This is definitely the best present so far,' Bethany smiled.

Over by the balcony, James positioned himself behind Andy and Rat. 'Are you boys sweating?' he teased. 'Because I think you have competition for your girlfriends.'

'You're full of shit, James,' Andy said dismissively.

'I'll kick his arse if he tries anything with Lauren,' Rat added.

Once Dante had shaken some hands and hugged a few girls, Bethany noticed that Dante had his black T-shirt in his hands.

'Put it on,' Bethany squealed. 'Oh my god, you're the black-shirt superstar!'

Dante had five girls watching as he theatrically ripped the cellophane packet open with his teeth and pulled the shirt over his head. When the shirt was on there was a bit of clapping, and Lauren and Bethany kissed Dante on opposite cheeks.

James saw the annoyed looks on Rat and Andy's faces and whispered in their ears in a feminine tone: 'Oh that Dante's so gorgeous! I want to strip down to my little pink panties and let him ravish me.'

Andy gave James an angry stare and told him to shut up.

Rat's Australian accent always grew thicker when he got annoyed. 'Well, I've never had a conversation with this Dante fellow,' Rat growled, 'but he's clearly a total git.'

15. DEVON

The London Brigands are the largest UK chapter with thirty-nine full-patch members, but the South Devon chapter run by Ralph 'the Führer' Donnington is the wealthiest and most influential. Successful property developments in the Salcombe area have made Donnington a millionaire and many long-standing South Devon Brigands are also wealthy men.

Although South Devon only has nineteen full-patch members, the chapter effectively controls two large puppet clubs: the Dogs of War based in Exeter and a three-chapter Devon and Cornwall gang known as the Monster Bunch. These have a combined total of more than one hundred full patches and up to three times that number of associates.

Wealth generated by the successful redevelopment of the Salcombe clubhouse has not stopped the bikers from engaging in criminal activity. Local police say that South Devon Brigands exercise ruthless control over the local drug trade. They own companies that provide door security on every major pub and nightclub venue in South Devon and members of their puppet gangs have been linked to a variety of crimes from organised prostitution to armed robbery.

In recent years South Devon has developed a reputation as a place to purchase illegal firearms and ammunition. Criminals from as far north as Newcastle and Glasgow are known to source weapons from South Devon. The lucrative trade and linked smuggling operations are thought to be controlled by members of the Brigands.

Police investigations into the firearms dealing activities of South Devon Brigands have been hampered by the tight-knit nature of the biker community and the fact that the Devon police are a rural force without the resources necessary to deal with major criminal activity.

In early 2006 a decision was taken to place an undercover police officer inside the South Devon motorcycle gang community. A twenty-eight-year-old officer began hanging around with the Monster Bunch. After three months he was voted into the club and in early 2007 he was made treasurer for the Salcombe chapter. The next stage of this undercover operation will be the most difficult: to infiltrate the Brigands themselves.

Excerpt from a confidential Home Office Briefing Document, written by Chief Inspector Ross Johnson, March 2008

*

Sergeant Neil Gauche had been undercover for two years under the alias Neil Smith. He rode his Harley Davidson like a pro, he'd grown his hair long and had a twenty-centimetre Monster Bunch tattoo inked on his shoulder.

The police had even helped to establish Neil's criminal credentials by allowing him to take part in drug deals and setting up an elaborately faked truck robbery.

After two years living a lie Neil felt comfortable around most Monsters and Brigands, but the Führer could still put the shits up him. Presently the pair sat in the back of a silver AMG Mercedes, with a tan leather arm rest between them.

They'd pulled off a country road on to a farm track, with wheat growing high on either side. Teeth sat in the driver's seat. The engine was off and the only sound was a gentle tap-tap-tap of something cooling down in the engine bay.

The Führer held a razor blade and Neil had no doubt that he'd be sliced open if the fancy took. The Brigands President might have grey hair and a beer gut, but after a few pints he could match any drunken teenager for craziness.

'So you want to be a Brigand?' the Führer asked, his words slurred with booze and his breath smelling like chips and vinegar.

'All my life,' Neil said.

'Take the blade then,' the Führer said. 'Get that Monster Bunch shit off your jacket.'

It was a hot night, so Neil's leather jacket was balled up on the carpet between his boots. He took the loose razor blade and used it to slice the nylon thread that he'd used to sew on his Monster Bunch patch less than a year earlier. Once a few stitches were cut, Neil dug his thumb under the patch and ripped it away.

The Führer pulled an embroidered patch with *South Devon* written on it. This would go on the bottom of Neil's jacket and would mark him as a prospect. It was another step into the world of the Brigands, but he'd only earn the right to wear the Brigands logo after several months of doing the gang's dirty work and a unanimous vote by the nineteen existing members of the chapter.

'Thanks,' Neil said, but as he reached for the badge the Führer pulled it back.

'Dirty Dave said you're a good man,' the Führer smiled. 'He made a lot of money on that cigarette truck you turned over together. But we had to check you out. Your background. Old schools, ex-employers, inmates at that young offenders' institute.'

NPBTF had done an enormous amount of work building up Neil's false background. Getting into Brigands puppet gangs like the Monster Bunch was easy, but becoming a full-patch Brigand was a major deal that involved application forms devised by the Brigands mother chapters in the United States and the attention of private investigators if there was the slightest suspicion about your past.

'I've got nothing to hide, Führer.'

'The guys we had looking into your past say that your job at the clutch centre checks out, as does your prison record and arrest sheet. They broke into your place last week and had a rummage. Nothing untoward there either.'

Neil smiled inwardly. There had always been the possibility of a break-in, or that one of the bikers who occasionally slept over in his flat after a night's partying would look for something to steal, so he kept the investigation notes he wrote each day along with anything else that gave a clue to his real identity behind a false panel in the base of a kitchen cabinet.

But Neil didn't like the fact that this scene was playing out in the middle of nowhere. Why would the Führer do this out here at 2 a.m., instead of making the offer of prospect status back at the clubhouse over a round of drinks?

It was hard to judge anything when you were dealing with the Führer. He was a borderline psychopath, and Neil knew he made people squirm for the fun of it.

'You know it's hard looking for a man named Smith,' the Führer explained. 'It's the most common name in the country. I mean, if your name is Eustace Von Hasselhoff, or even Ralph Donnington it's pretty easy to track through the records. But there are thousands of people called Neil Smith in the country. So if you were an undercover cop, you'd probably want to pick a name like Smith, or Jones, or Edwards.'

Neil felt his heart quicken. The mention of undercover cops made him uneasy, but snitches and deep-cover police officers had caused the demise of gangs all over the world. You'd rarely spend more than a few hours in biker company without someone suggesting that a certain person was a nark or a snitch.

'We've never had anyone infiltrate a Brigands chapter,' the Führer continued. 'Not in the UK, or abroad. And it goes without saying that any cop or snitch found in our ranks is going to suffer a slow and painful death.'

'I'm an open book,' Neil said. 'I've been hanging with the bikers around here for two years. Anything you want to know about my life before that, just ask. You want more personal details so you can check up on me? Just ask. If you think it's too soon for me to become a prospect I'll wait. You know I want this, but I respect the Brigands and the need for all of your security precautions.'

The Führer twisted on the seat so that he was facing Neil. He placed a hand on each of Neil's shoulders and pulled him forward so they were almost nose to nose.

'Admit it,' the Führer said. 'You're a cop. I know you're a cop.'

Neil was nervous, but he managed to make a laugh. 'You're busting my balls. Scout's honour, on my mother's life, pinkie swear. What can I say, boss? I can only say it so many times. Believe me, don't believe me. To be frank, I think the work I've done as treasurer of the Monster Bunch and the money I've earned means I deserve a shot at becoming a Brigand.'

'You're a cop,' the Führer said, as he slumped back against the tan leather.

Neil was alarmed by the change in the Führer's voice. Property deals had made the Führer into a wealthy man who could have lived comfortably off his legitimate income for the rest of his life. But he got a bigger kick out of scaring someone, whether it was a person who owed him money, or a terrified waitress threatened with a punch in the face for delivering the wrong dish. And the Führer didn't sound like he was playing games any more.

'It's funny, Neil,' the Führer smiled. 'The cops must have taken hundreds of man hours. Writing you into the archives: national insurance, tax records, speeding convictions, criminal record bureaux. And then they screwed it all up with your bike.'

Neil jolted as Teeth took an automatic out of the glove box and pulled back the muzzle to load a bullet.

'Cat got your tongue?' Teeth asked, as he gave Neil his trademark gummy grin.

'Come on Neil,' the Führer said gently. 'Play along with me. Why don't you ask how we figured that you're a cop?'

If this was for real, Neil knew he was a dead man. 'Whatever information you've got, it's bullshit,' he said, desperately trying to keep the nerves out of his voice. 'Tell me what it is.'

'Three years ago there was a court case,' the Führer explained. 'Four stolen bikes were shipped to the UK from Canada to be stripped down and sold over here where Harleys are more expensive. Two bikers from some hillbilly gang up north were arrested, and served two years. The owners in Canada had been paid off by their insurance company and rather than ship the bikes back to Canada the insurers sold them at auction here in the UK. Three were bought by a second-hand bike dealer. The fourth was bought by the Metropolitan Police purchasing department and delivered to Hornsey police station, which just *happens* to be the headquarters of NPBTF.'

'It's a plant or something,' Neil explained.

The Führer smiled. 'The chassis number of the bike you've been riding matches the number in the auction catalogue.'

Neil tried not to gasp. Could the police really have spent all that time creating his false identity, only to send him undercover with wheels purchased openly at a bike auction?

'I think the private investigator we hired earned his money, don't you Neil Smith? Or should that be Leicestershire police sergeant Neil Gauche, currently on attachment to the National Police Biker Task Force?'

Neil realised there was no point pretending any more. For two years he'd lived with the possibility that his cover would be blown. He'd played out the scene a million times in his head, but now it was for real his mouth was dry and his brain as dead as a walnut.

'Get out of the car,' the Führer said, as he pulled his jacket open to reveal a gun. 'I don't want your blood all over my leather.'

Neil looked around as he stepped into the verge with the corn towering up alongside him, but there was no escape. Teeth was already out of the car and he'd be shot in the back the instant he made any move.

'Hands on your head,' the Führer shouted. 'Start walking into the corn.'

Neil felt like crying as he imagined how it would pan out. He was due to report in to his handler at 6 a.m.

Once his bosses knew he was missing they'd start a search. If he was left in the corn field they'd probably find the body within a few days, but more likely the Führer would already have made arrangements for a burial site hundreds of kilometres away, or to have his body chopped into a dozen pieces and fed to a batch of hungry pigs. Maybe some day they'd figure it out. Or maybe there would be a TV show about the disappearance of a heroic undercover police officer . . .

Neil considered his mum. She was in her sixties. She'd make a big fuss, but they weren't close. He'd only seen her a couple of times a year since leaving for university at eighteen and he didn't have a wife or kids. The lack of close family was one of the reasons Neil got accepted for undercover work, but he'd always seen himself settling down into less demanding police work and doing the wife, mortgage and brats thing.

The corn rustled until the trio reached a break in the planting.

'Time to kneel, Neil,' the Führer said, smiling at his own pun as he screwed a silencer to his pistol. 'This is going to be a proper pain in the arse, you know? Have you any idea how much heat we'll take when an undercover cop turns up dead?'

'So don't shoot me then,' Neil trembled. 'You're a smart man. You kill a cop and you'll have detectives so far up your arse you won't be able to operate.'

'Cop's gotta die,' the Führer said. 'Anything else sends the wrong message.'

A wasp buzzed close by Neil's head and stubbly grass

pricked through the frayed knee of his jeans. *Bollocks*, he thought to himself as the Führer pressed the silencer against the back of his skull.

16. BREAKFAST

By the next morning Dante had stopped worrying about making friends on campus. Bethany's birthday party made a great ice-breaker. After everyone ate cake and got yelled at by one of the campus caretakers for setting off fireworks indoors and potentially burning the building down, they headed into town in one of the campus minibuses, went bowling and finished up eating in a big group in the Nandos that opened up after Chicken Deluxe went bust.

Dante woke up late. After his mission he was entitled to a week off before resuming lessons and training, but he regretted missing the chance to have breakfast with everyone else. The only people he knew in the canteen were James Adams and Kerry Chang, but they sat together reading the music reviews in the *Guardian* and it didn't look like the kind of scene you were supposed to interrupt.

Dante grabbed potato waffles, bacon and a packet of Crunchy Nut, but as he sat at an empty table James called him over. 'Do we smell or something?'

'I thought you were together,' Dante explained awkwardly.

'We're just mates,' James explained, but Dante wasn't convinced: James and Kerry sat with their chairs close together reading the same newspaper, and although Kerry's arm wasn't actually around James' back she had it hooked around his chair.

'No lessons?' Dante asked, as he bit the corner off a potato waffle.

'Free period,' James explained. 'We've taken a bunch of GCSEs and our handlers haven't *quite* noticed that our schedules aren't very full.'

'Long may it last,' Kerry added, as she gave James a smile and flicked crumbs off his T-shirt with her little finger.

'Sneaky,' Dante laughed. 'I'm almost fourteen, so I'm guessing they'll start me off with a bunch of GCSE courses.'

'Most likely,' James nodded. 'Just avoid history. It's all long essays and you have to read *so* much boring crap.'

'I like history,' Dante said. 'Battles and stuff.'

'Me too,' Kerry agreed. 'The thing is, James is a maths geek. He has such an easy time that he resents putting work into anything else.'

'I think I'm screwed on languages,' Dante explained. 'I did intensive French and Spanish for a year before basic training, but I've been off campus for three years and all I've had are normal school French lessons.'

'That's rough,' Kerry said. 'Like, I speak Spanish, French, Japanese and a bit of Mandarin. Because I've learned them from when I was six I could easily pass A-levels in them and get into university without doing any hard work.'

Dante looked at James. 'And I guess you're the same with maths?'

'Oh he's a smartass,' Kerry smiled. 'He's *already* got three maths A levels, plus physics.'

'Maths is easy,' James said.

Kerry wapped him around the back of the head. 'Oh shut up, you smug git.'

James moved his pointing finger as if he was going to poke Kerry in the ribs and she burst out laughing.

'You try it and I'll break that finger off.'

'You two remind me,' Dante smiled. 'A nice fit campus girlfriend is another item on my to-do list.'

'We're just friends,' Kerry emphasised.

'Obviously,' Dante said wryly, as he crammed a rasher of bacon into his mouth.

'There's something else I never got a chance to talk about last night,' James said. 'I'm friendly with Terry Campbell, do you know him?'

'CHERUB technical director,' Dante nodded. 'White beard, bit of a boffin.'

'That's him,' James nodded. 'You see, I'm really into motorbikes and there's a battered old Harley stored in the vehicle workshop that I'd love to fix up. Terry says it's yours.'

Dante nodded. 'It belonged to my dad.'

'I've been learning about bikes,' James explained. 'I read all the motorbike magazines. I could buy it off you. You'd get a fair price.'

Dante looked surprised. 'Nah, sorry James. It was my dad's bike. Our house burned down after he died and the bike is about the only thing of his that's left.'

'So your dad was into bikes?' James asked.

Dante stopped eating and his face flushed red. 'Sorry,' he said clearing his throat. 'It's complicated and I'd rather not talk about my family to be honest.'

James was surprised by how upset Dante looked and felt really bad. 'No worries,' he said. 'Everyone on campus has a past and you're not the only one who doesn't like dwelling in it.'

Kerry thought it would be tactful to change the subject and tapped on the CD reviews on the paper in front of her. 'So, Dante,' she said. 'What kind of music do you like?'

*

When Neil Gauche woke up the first thing he saw was ants crawling up the arm spread in front of his face. His head throbbed, his ear rang and a bloody cut ran from his temple across to his right eyebrow.

It was some kind of miracle. He remembered everything, right up until the gun fired next to his ear and the bullet punched the ground a few metres from where he now lay. Then he'd been knocked cold, with a boot or more likely the butt of the gun. But why?

Maybe the Führer had listened to what he said about

the heat he'd bring down if he killed a cop. Or maybe he'd only ever planned to scare him and rough him up. Neil felt his pockets and realised his cellphone and wallet had stayed in the Führer's Mercedes when he'd stepped out.

A shocking pain ripped through his head as he rolled on to his back and sat up. The sun was rising, his arm and cheek were pockmarked with the shapes of dry grass and pebbles where he'd lain still for five or six hours.

The corn was chest high, so all he could see without standing were treetops and sky. A belch came up his throat and a night on tex-mex food, Sol lager and tequila shots sent burning acid up his throat.

Neil had lost blood and felt weak. But he found his feet, and as he turned around he realised what the Führer had done. Two hundred metres down a mild slope stood a house. Its new owners used it as a holiday home and had spent a lot of money on refurbishment, but Neil recognised it from police photographs and news reports.

It was the scene of the Scott family murder. Bringing Neil out here and staging a mock execution was the Führer's way of telling the police that he thought he could get away with anything.

'Arrogant little prick,' Neil muttered to himself, as he headed towards the house.

*

While Neil Gauche and his two man backup crew waited in a Devon casualty unit, the rest of the NPBTF team had been put on alert and arrived in their office

154

at Hornsey police station before 9 a.m.

Ross Johnson was a trained psychologist. He wasn't prone to strong emotions and this was the first time many colleagues had seen him lose his cool. A slim female sergeant came into the office as Ross stood brooding by his window.

'Coffee,' she said, placing a cup on the table.

'Cheers, Tracy,' Ross said curtly. 'I need you to get on to Scotland Yard. The Brigands use private investigators. They know Neil's bike was delivered here and for all we know they have us under surveillance. We need new offices. I don't care if it's a rat-infested basement somewhere, but we can't run a covert operation when our enemy can watch us coming and going.'

'If they've had us under surveillance, they could know George Kahn's identity too,' Tracy pointed out.

'Possibly,' Ross nodded. 'But he's only been with us three weeks and there are a lot of Asian men coming and going around here.'

'I'll call the property office as soon as they open and try to get an emergency relocation,' Tracy said. 'What's happening down in Devon? Are we going to arrest the Führer for assaulting Neil? Maybe a firearms charge?'

Ross shook his head. 'It's tough to prove who did what, especially when you're up against the kind of heavy lawyers that the Brigands always use. And the Führer's not stupid, he won't have left any clues, we'll never find the gun and he'll have a dozen witnesses willing to swear that he was with them at the time of the incident.'

'It's like he's above the law,' Tracy sighed. 'What about the bike?'

Ross sighed harder, then grabbed his coffee. 'Neil could have been killed, but if we start a formal investigation into who purchased his Harley in such an obvious way we're going to get bogged down with months of bad feeling. Put the word out: I want the officer who purchased the bike to own up. If they're still part of my squad, I want them to come into this office with a completed transfer request form before the end of today.'

'Yes, guv,' Tracy said. 'What if nobody owns up?'

'Let's not go down that road unless we have to. It wasn't you was it?'

'No,' Tracy said.

Ross smiled with relief. 'Thank Christ for that. You and Neil are my two best people.'

'Does my head in thinking how close we came to a dead officer,' Tracy said. 'So what do we do now? Our whole operation relied on George making a big gun purchase and Neil being on the ground in Salcombe trying to sniff out how the Brigands brought the weapons into the country.'

Ross ran a hand through thinning hair. 'Maybe I should have stuck to my job interviewing child witnesses. Do the interviews, write a report, then pass the whole thing across for the detectives to tie up all the loose ends. Did I ever tell you that it was the Scott family murder that first got me interested in outlaw bikers?'

'When I first came over from drug squad,' Tracy

nodded. 'You even had the boy who survived living with you for a while, didn't you?'

'Dante was a great little kid,' Ross remembered. 'Absolutely tragic. He still e-mails my daughter Tina once in a while.'

'It's game over unless we can find another way to infiltrate the South Devon Brigands quickly,' Tracy said. 'No disrespect sir, but I think you should go out and give the team a pep talk or something. Everyone's been working so hard on this and the mood out there is suicidal.'

'Later,' Ross said, as his eyes widened with a sense of purpose. 'Maybe we're not as far up shit creek as everyone seems to think. Close my door on the way out, I need to make a phone call.'

Once the sergeant was gone, Ross pulled an address book out of the jacket hooked up by the door and looked up M for Mitchum. Jennifer Mitchum's office said that she'd retired, but one of the administration staff at Nebraska House children's home called back a couple of minutes later and gave him a home number.

'You came to my rescue when I needed somewhere safe for Dante,' Ross explained into the handset, after a brief exchange of pleasantries. 'You only spoke in the vaguest terms about where Dante would go and what CHERUB does, but my investigation just came to a grinding halt and I'm wondering if they might be able to help.'

17. CHOPPER

Six days later

The Bell 430 had taken off from an airfield in North London seventy-five minutes earlier. With a jet engine mounted a few metres behind the cockpit, helicopter travel is never genteel and for police officers Neil Gauche and Ross Johnson the experience became more alien ten minutes after take-off when the co-pilot ordered them to don full-face helmets with blacked-out visors.

They were only allowed to remove helmets after they'd landed on the helipad in front of the main building on CHERUB campus. With a top speed of more than 250kph Ross realised that the helicopter could have taken him anywhere in England and Wales, or even into the southern borders of Scotland.

The co-pilot pointed the two officers towards a man

in high-visibility white who stood in front of a sinister concrete bunker. Ross felt oddly powerless as he walked, blinded by the sunlight as his eyes adjusted from the blackness under the helmet.

'Steep stairs,' the man in white warned. 'Hold the railing.'

Ross gripped a metal rail and clanked below ground, into a structure that reminded him of Victorian fortifications he'd seen while holidaying on the south coast.

Inside, another burly guard stood up from behind a desk. Ross and Neil exchanged a glance and Neil quipped, 'Where do they keep the flying saucers?'

'Welcome to CHERUB campus,' the guard said. 'I'm sorry if our security procedures have disturbed you in any way. Now I need you to confirm that you're carrying no recording equipment, mobile telephones or other electronic devices including hearing aids or pacemakers.'

'The pilot stripped 'em before we left,' Neil explained, as the guard waved a metal detector wand over their clothing before pointing them towards a row of booths.

'Please step into a booth and remove your clothing, including your underwear, and jewellery including watches and earrings. Then put on the orange suits and sandals provided.'

The booths were similar to shop changing rooms, apart from the lack of privacy curtains. While Neil and Ross stripped, the guard carefully went through the photographs and documents inside Ross' briefcase, before transferring the contents to a clear plastic bag.

The guard then weighed the bag, and attached a sticky label.

'Don't dispose of anything from the bag while on campus,' the guard said, adopting a flat tone that made it clear he'd done the speech a hundred times before. 'It will be weighed and inspected again when you leave. If you're given anything to take away from campus, keep it separately and present it for inspection when you leave. Do *not* remove anything from campus without authorisation. By entering campus, you agree never to mention its existence to anyone.

'You also agree that you may be x-rayed, searched, or given a rectal or oral examination by campus staff. In the event of any security breach before or after today's visit you may be arrested and detained for an indefinite period. If you agree to all of the following sign the form and proceed through the x-ray barrier. Your liaison is waiting on the other side of the barrier. Have a nice day.'

The plastic sandals and baggy orange suits didn't make it easy to move quickly. As police officers, Neil and Ross were used to being in control, but the hooded flight and intimidating security arrangements left them both out of their depth.

After the x-ray they entered a more familiar space. The waiting room had a filter coffee jug, magazines and a water cooler, but the two cops didn't need it because a woman and a boy were waiting alongside.

'You must be Chloe,' Ross said, as he reached across to shake the woman's hand, before looking at the boy and smiling. 'And *you* are a heck of a lot bigger than the last time I saw you.'

Chloe Blake was CHERUB's youngest full mission controller. Like most CHERUB staff, she'd once been an agent herself. She kept herself in shape with a tough fitness and combat training routine that manifested itself in a slim but muscular frame, currently clad in Nikes and a cotton sweatsuit.

Dante smiled and gave Ross a hug. 'Sorry about the clothes and the security.'

'I don't mind,' Neil grinned. 'I think the *prisoner in transit* look suits me. Do you kids have to go through these shenanigans?'

Dante shook his head. 'Security sometimes do random searches and stuff when we come in and out, but agents and staff don't have to go through all that and of course we know where campus is.'

Chloe cleared her throat and glanced at her watch. 'We need to go over to the mission control building, it's a ten-minute walk. And Dante, you really *shouldn't* discuss any aspect of campus security with guests.'

*

Across campus, Lauren Adams glanced at her watch as she headed out of a girls' changing room with damp hair and a plastic bag filled with wet swimming kit and rolled-up towel. She was a good swimmer, but she'd just completed a ninety-minute aqua-fitness session, comprising lengths, sprint swims, water aerobics and repeated dives into the deep end to retrieve bean bags and weights from the bottom of the pool. Her shoulders and thighs ached and her face was red from the exertion.

Her boyfriend Rat waited for her in the hallway. 'Took you long enough,' he grouched as they headed towards the exit.

'Of course I take longer,' Lauren tutted. 'Your hair is two centimetres long and takes about thirty seconds to dry. I have to shampoo to get the chlorine smell out, then I have to comb it or it dries all straggly.'

'So you want to do homework together or what?' Rat asked. 'We could stop off in the dining-room. I fancy one of those hot chocolate croissants they've started doing. Or we could go to the library and research that history thing.'

'Can't,' Lauren said. 'I told you, dummy, I've got a mission briefing.'

They passed out of the pool complex and turned south as a group of overheated red shirts passed on either side, heading for an after-school splash in the leisure pool.

'Why are you even going on this mission?' Rat asked.

Lauren looked slightly incredulous. 'Why did I spend all afternoon busting my guts in a swimming pool? What's the point of being a cherub if you turn down missions?'

'But we were going to the summer hostel together,' Rat whined. 'We can't if you're going off on some mission . . .'

'Missing summer hostel is a bummer,' Lauren admitted. 'But if I miss out, I'll get a winter break. I'll be able to go skiing or something.'

Rat tutted. 'But not with me.'

'Well we're not *married*, Rat. I've always thought that's the best thing about us. Bethany's been through about six boyfriends since you and me have been together. She's all over someone, then it's finished three weeks later. We just sort of plod along.'

'We did until your red-headed pretty boy came along.'

Lauren laughed. 'Dante?'

'Who else?' Rat said angrily. 'The way you act around him: *Oh Dante, that's such a funny story. Oh Dante, you've got really firm biceps. Oh Dante, I bet your poop tastes like Nutella.*'

'Give us a break,' Lauren sighed. 'How can you be jealous of him? The guy's come back after being away from campus for three years. What's wrong with making him welcome?'

'I'm not jealous,' Rat said. 'But the way you fawn over him is *totally* blatant. And now you're going off on a mission with him. And instead of going to the summer hostel, you'll get a winter break. And who's that gonna be with? Oh yes, the carrot-headed wonder boy.'

The pair turned on to the main path through the centre of campus that led towards mission control and the main building. At this time of day it was busy with kids heading towards the lake to do homework in the sun, or going the other way towards the tennis courts with rackets in their hands.

'I just don't know what to say,' Lauren said. 'I thought you were more mature.'

'I'm mature,' Rat said angrily. 'That doesn't mean I

want my girlfriend slobbering all over someone else and making me look like a fool.'

'Slobbering!' Lauren gasped. 'When was I slobbering?'

'I just want to go to the summer hostel with my girlfriend,' Rat yelled. 'What's so wrong with that?'

'You're changing the subject,' Lauren said. 'When was I slobbering over Dante? When did I do anything, apart from try to be nice and welcome back someone who's been away for a long time?'

'It's everything,' Rat shouted. 'The way you look at him. The flirty little smiles.'

'You're jealous,' Lauren shouted back, as she stopped walking and put her hands on her hips. 'And *totally* immature. And I can't believe you're accusing me of cheating on you.'

'I can't believe that you're denying it when you're so blatantly trying to get off with him.'

Lauren looked at her watch. 'I'm late for my briefing. I'm going on a mission with Dante and my brother. I'll probably go for a late holiday with them afterwards too and maybe I *will* ask Dante out, because I'm not putting up with you acting like a moody jealous creep.'

Lauren stormed off, cutting across the grass because it was a more direct route to mission control.

'See if I care,' Rat shouted after her. 'Why don't you go off and shag the stupid red-headed wanker?'

'He's got more chance than you'll ever get, you brainless Aussie twerp,' Lauren shouted back, before turning around and giving Rat a two-fingered salute with both hands.

James Adams was sitting inside Chloe Blake's office in the mission control building when she arrived with Dante, plus Ross and Neil in their orange suits. The office was large, with a suede sofa that was starting to show signs of wear and a floor-to-ceiling window that had a view of the satellite dishes on the grass outside.

'I picked up the platter from the dining-room,' James said, standing up to shake Ross and Neil's hand before pointing to the food. 'Fresh coffee, sandwiches, cakes. Help yourselves.'

'Your sister not here yet?' Chloe asked.

'Nope,' James said. 'But she's got to come right across from aqua training on the opposite side of campus.'

Dante took obvious pleasure in catching up with Ross. He couldn't tell the policeman anything about his mission in Northern Ireland, but he gave some vague details about life on campus and asked questions about Tina, who was now training to be a solicitor.

'I'm worried about Dante's appearance,' Ross said, giving Chloe a serious look.

Chloe nodded as she sat behind her desk and took a cup of tea from James. 'We looked at some video footage of the interviews you conducted with Dante back in 2003. He's obviously grown physically, the long hair and his new accent also help. But we're going to give him a complete dye job. Not just the red hair on his head but his body hair too and we'll show him how to keep the colour consistent so that he doesn't show any red roots.'

'We did a computer mock-up,' Dante said, handing

across a colour image. 'That's what I could look like.'

'Blond to match me and my sister,' James put in.

'And obviously I can't be called Dante,' Dante added. 'I'll go for John, it's a nice bland name.'

'Looks good,' Ross nodded. 'I definitely think it's an advantage having Dante on the mission. He's not been around Salcombe for five years, but he probably knows more about the Führer and how the Brigands operate than any one of us.'

Dante smiled. 'There's nobody in the world more motivated to see the Führer's arse behind bars than me.'

'After my experience in that field last week, I think I'll run you a close second,' Neil said.

'All of us will need some degree of physical transformation to infiltrate the South Devon Brigands,' Chloe explained. 'James is sixteen, but he'll have the identity of a seventeen-year-old for the mission.'

'Which means I can have my motorbike licence and try hanging around with the younger members of the Monster Bunch,' James said gleefully. 'I've ridden motorbikes before, but I've been out on the roads around campus with an instructor for the last few nights.'

'Lauren will pretty much be herself,' Chloe added. 'But I'm only ten years older than James, so I'll have to age myself a few years so that I can pretend that I'm his mum. A change of wardrobe and a couple of grey highlights should do the trick.'

'Speaking of Lauren, she should be here by now,' Dante said.

Lauren was fifty metres away and had just used the iris

scanner to enter the mission control building. She was knackered after the swimming and the walk across campus in bright sunshine.

The argument with Rat was doing her head in. They'd been together almost since they'd first met three years earlier. This was their biggest row ever, but Lauren wasn't sure if they'd really broken up for good. She didn't think she'd shown any particular fondness towards Dante, but wondered if she had flirted without meaning to because she'd liked him from the morning they'd woken up on campus together and she dug his muscular frame and exotic red hair.

'Sorry I'm late,' Lauren said, dumping her wet swimming stuff in the doorway and quickly shaking hands with Neil and Ross.

'OK,' Chloe said. 'James, Lauren and Dante have all read a lot of background information on the South Devon Brigands over the last week. Ross has brought a lot more information with him which you'll need to study and he's going to brief you on the nature of the mission.'

Ross got up from the sofa and propped himself on the corner of Chloe's desk. 'I think you're all aware of the basic situation,' he said brightly. 'We're ordering a large shipment of arms through a man named Sealclubber who is the president of the London Brigands chapter. We're hoping that such a large shipment will stretch the resources of the South Devon Brigands and in particular their weapons-dealing business. Originally it was Neil's job to get himself involved in the deal, but his cover was blown so now that job falls to you three.'

Chloe interjected. 'Obviously, Neil was going to try and get involved with the Brigands themselves. You three will have to penetrate the smuggling operation in a less direct way.'

Ross nodded. 'First James. You're going to be seventeen. You'll have an unreliable motorbike, that gives you plenty of excuse to hang around with the motorbike dealership located in the retail development near to the Brigands clubhouse. Hopefully, a groovy young cat such as you shouldn't have too much difficulty getting involved with other young bikers who hang around the fringes of the Monster Bunch and Dogs of War gangs.'

'Those two gangs have a much younger membership and are much easier to infiltrate than the Brigands themselves,' Neil explained. 'Rather than trying to join, concentrate on the dodgiest young characters who hang around the gangs. I know for fact that some of those lads earn money doing the Brigands' dirty work, whether it's selling marijuana to the local school kids or going across country on a train to deliver a handgun to someone in London or Manchester.'

James nodded. 'Do you reckon I'll have time to join a gang?'

Neil shook his head. 'We've already set the wheels in motion for our gun purchase. We're going to get our undercover buyer to say he's having cash problems and delay his purchase for a few weeks, but we can't mess Sealclubber around forever. Your job is to try getting information as quickly as possible. If it doesn't work out, we'll pull the whole operation.'

Ross took up the story. 'Lauren and Dante are going to attack the problem from a different angle through the Führer's son Joe. Dante's job is to become Joe's best friend . . .'

'Again,' Dante interrupted. 'He was my best mate for years.'

Ross nodded. 'Lauren's job is the same, but hopefully she's going to appeal to Joe as potential girlfriend material.'

'Unless he's gay,' James grinned. 'In which case Dante will have to try snogging him.'

'Gross,' Dante complained.

'James, be serious,' Chloe said firmly.

'OK,' James smiled. 'A *serious* question. We know that the Führer is a criminal who's stayed out of trouble for years. He wasn't even charged when he wiped out Dante's whole family. What makes us so sure that his fourteen-year-old son is going to know anything about his dodgy dealings?'

Neil answered. 'We know the Führer is close to his younger son. Who knows if Joe flaps his mouth too much when you give him a couple of beers? Or if he mentions something he shouldn't when he's trying to impress a girl?'

'We can give it a go,' Lauren nodded. 'What about electronic surveillance? You know, if we get in his house, or the Brigands clubhouse and plant bugs and stuff?'

Ross shook his head. 'It's a dead end. We've had

electronic surveillance in place for over two years. The Brigands speak in codes when they use a telephone or have a meeting in the clubhouse. But anything sensitive gets discussed face to face, usually in some field out in the open.'

'So that's the basis of your mission,' Ross said. 'We were hoping that Neil was going to have penetrated the Brigands organisation at a much higher level than you'll be able to. I'm not going to pretend that our chances of success are particularly great, but I hope you three are willing to accept the challenge because South Devon Brigands are bringing a lot of guns into the country. As far as I'm concerned, even a twenty per cent chance is worth taking because these guns are killing people on the streets.'

Chloe nodded approvingly. 'I don't know how much attention you three pay to the newspapers, but gun crime amongst teenagers is exploding in British cities.'

'Well, you know I'm in,' Dante said, and James said the same.

'Lauren?' Chloe asked.

Lauren kept thinking about the argument with Rat. She'd really been looking forward to going to the summer hostel with him, but on the other hand even if she *had* flirted a little with Dante he'd totally overreacted.

'Sorry,' she said finally. 'I'm just knackered after swim training. I'm in, of course.'

18. SALCOMBE

It took three days for Chloe to sort out accommodation in the Salcombe area and finalise all the minor details for their mission.

It was a Sunday morning. James stood in his room, rummaging through a packed bag to make sure he hadn't forgotten anything when Kerry came in to say goodbye. She sounded sad and James decided it was time to find out where their relationship was heading.

'This mission's all tied into a weapons buy that the police have already set in motion,' James explained, relieved to find his iPod in a side pocket. 'I can't see it lasting much more than a month or two, and you and me seem to be getting along pretty well these days.'

Kerry laughed. 'We *always* do until we actually start going out with each other.'

James zipped the side pocket. 'We're older now,

though. We've been out with other people. I know we've broken up twice before, but I think it had more to do with the fact that we were so young than anything else.'

Kerry took a step so that her nose almost touched James' chin. It was early and Kerry only wore the T-shirt and baggy pyjama shorts she'd slept in. Her smell turned James on and he imagined shoving her on to the bed and ripping her shorts down, but Kerry would break his neck if he judged that move wrong so he went for a simple kiss on the lips.

After a half-minute snog and a good grope of Kerry's bum, she backed away and they stared open-mouthed at each other.

'Why'd you stop?' James asked.

Kerry shrugged. 'I'm not getting into this just as you're leaving,' she explained. 'Especially with your reputation.'

'What reputation?' James said, acting as if butter wouldn't melt.

'Your reputation for snogging or bonking every girl that comes near you,' Kerry said. 'When you come back we'll talk about getting back together.'

'So you think we should?' James asked. 'And what if you get sent on a mission before I come back?'

'That's *exactly* my point,' Kerry said warily. 'I don't want some big long-distance relationship thing starting up. I don't want to cheat on you, I don't want you to cheat on me. For all we know I'm about to get sent off on some year-long mission where some bronzed millionaire stud will sweep me off my feet.'

'That's *me*' James grinned. 'I'm bronzed, I'm a stud and you can have me right now. I'll even put a Durex on if you ask nicely.'

Kerry knew James wasn't being serious and burst out laughing. 'You might be cute from some angles, but the man of my dreams doesn't have a zit the size of a Rolo on the back of his neck.'

'Hormones,' James said, rubbing the zit self-consciously. 'It's just a sign that I'm brimming over with masculinity.'

'You can call it masculinity, but it looks more like pus to me,' Kerry replied, as she gave James a quick kiss and turned towards the door. 'I'm training some red shirts in the dojo at eight-thirty so I'd better get ready. Have a good mission, text me, yeah?'

'Of course,' James said, feeling a bit sad as Kerry disappeared around the door.

He kicked his door shut, then grabbed a ruler off his desk. He thrust it high into the air and stood in front of his wardrobe mirror with his legs wide apart. He thrust his hips forward and spoke in a deep voice. 'Using the power vested in me by the great god Helix I swear that I shall one day make love to the fine maiden Kerry Chang.'

James felt dumb laughing at his own silliness, but he was still sniggering when he carried his bags towards the lift five minutes later.

*

Dante had gone blond and Chloe had a few touches of grey and a new wardrobe of posh-mum clothes for the mission.

Chloe and the three teenagers did the half-day drive in the comfort of a Range Rover. James had a driving licence for the mission and despite Lauren protesting that he was a terrible driver who'd get them all killed, Chloe let James drive the last leg of the journey after a nice outdoor lunch at a gastro-pub just past Bristol.

Their home was a modern four-bed house a twenty-minute walk from the beach and the centre of Salcombe. The wealthy seaside town was chock full during the summer and the Security Services Emergency Relocation Bureau had paid a small fortune to rent the house and furnish it in a style that fitted in with their background story.

The family name was Raven. Chloe Raven, the divorced thirty-seven-year-old wife who'd moved away from London and an ex-husband who worked in the City. James was seventeen-year-old James Raven, a sixth-form student. Lauren Raven was James' sister and in Year Eight. To avoid similarity with his birth identity Dante had become John Raven, and Lauren's twin brother.

James was the biggest, so he helped carry Lauren and Chloe's bags up to the first-floor bedrooms.

'Your ladyship's case,' he said, when he saw Lauren lying on her bare mattress. She had a large room, with a balcony overlooking a landscaped garden.

'Ta,' Lauren grunted, scratching under her armpit.

'You OK?' James asked. 'You've hardly said anything all day.'

'I'm depressed,' Lauren announced dramatically.

James hadn't seen his sister sulk like this since before their mum died.

'You'll sort it out with Rat,' James said, trying to sound cheerful but not *too* cheerful. 'You've had rows before.'

Lauren sat up sharply. 'What makes you think I want to sort it out with him? He acted like a jealous dick.'

James grinned. 'I'm not surprised, the way you were fawning over Dante.'

'I *so* wasn't,' Lauren said indignantly. 'You boys are all the same. You ogle girls, you have pictures of women with tits the size of footballs draped on your bedroom walls and then you accuse us of being sluts just because we speak to someone else.'

James was only trying to be nice and didn't want to get involved with Lauren's love life. 'Whatever,' he said. 'I'm sure it'll sort itself out one way or another.'

Lauren tutted and folded her arms across her chest as James backed out of the room. He saw Lauren's other bag at the bottom of the stairs, but was buggered if he was carrying it up to her room if she was only going to shout at him.

'Nice house, eh?' Dante said, as he came into the hallway holding a cooler box filled with food for the kitchen. 'You seen your bike, James? It doesn't look too bad.'

'Oh!' James said excitedly. 'I forgot, where is it?'

'Garage,' Dante said. 'Chloe rolled the car in next to it.'

James rushed out the front door, passing Chloe who

held a big carrier bag filled with wellies and umbrellas.

'Can I give the bike a spin?' James asked eagerly.

'I was going to have a cup of tea and a biscuit,' Chloe said. 'Don't you want anything?'

'Just ten or fifteen minutes to get a feel for it,' James begged.

'Go on then,' Chloe smiled. 'Put your protective gear on and take things easy until you're used to riding it.'

She broke out laughing as she walked into the house.

'What's funny?' Dante asked.

'You teenagers,' Chloe explained. 'One minute James is all cool and sophisticated, the next he's beaming like a six-year-old on Christmas morning.'

'James loves his bikes,' Dante said, as he heard a little bike engine buzzing to life.

James had ridden a variety of motorbikes on a mission in America three years earlier. Terry Campbell had let him ride motorbikes around campus and over the past six days he'd had some intensive motorbike instruction on real roads. But this was the first time James had experienced the freedom of his own bike.

The 250cc Honda was a few years old and only had twenty-two horsepower, but powerful bikes are illegal for riders under twenty-one and the machine could still out-accelerate most cars and cruise comfortably at seventy-five miles an hour. What's more, James had experienced larger bikes and in many ways a nippy 250cc was more fun on twisty British roads than the big beasts driven by gangs like the Brigands.

James whizzed up a gently sloping hill. The luxury

houses on either side of the road were all part of the same upscale development. The street was a dead end, so James turned back and hit fifty miles an hour as he passed their house and swung out into a lane.

He drove half a mile, but was trapped behind a motor home plodding at a steady thirty miles an hour. The main road into central Salcombe was clogged with traffic, so he pulled on to a grass verge and turned around.

As he turned he recognised a large piece of land with a tasteless mock-Tudor house and a detached triple garage. James recognised it from a police surveillance photo, but he only twigged that it was the Führer's house when he saw the house name *Eagles' Nest* written in a heavy Germanic font on a wooden sign.

James rolled through a break in the traffic to take a peek down their target's driveway. There was a rusty World War Two-era German light tank aiming its gun towards the street and a sign that read: *Trespassers will be shot.*

'Subtle,' James muttered to himself, as he opened the throttle and headed for home.

*

It was a warm evening. Chloe had no intention of cooking a meal after the long drive, so they headed into town. Dante's head flooded with memories as they cruised Salcombe streets in the Range Rover. He saw low walls and post-boxes and remembered jumping out from behind them to surprise his mum when he was little. He remembered the baker's where she'd buy sausage rolls and donuts and even recognised some of the older yachts bobbing on the quayside.

The road that once led up to the Brigands clubhouse hadn't changed. Dante choked as he realised that the last time he'd been through here was on the night his parents had been killed.

'You OK, Dante?' Lauren asked.

'Memories,' Dante shrugged. 'Nothing I can't handle.'

'I think it's best if you start calling him John all the time,' Chloe said. 'We can go back if it's too much for you, mate.'

Dante shook his head. 'No way. I want to be *here* doing my job, not sitting around the house brooding.'

What was once the entry gate to the Brigands compound was now a curved concrete ramp that led towards parking spaces behind and beneath the long two-storey development called Marina Heights on their right. At street level there was a paved promenade – *no cyclists, no skateboarding* – populated with people taking an evening stroll. A dozen upmarket shops sold things like yachting accessories, surf boards and designer walking gear.

The last and largest shop was called Leather and Chrome. Its plate-glass frontage had a display of custom-built motorcycles. People with smaller budgets could go inside and buy items ranging from toy motorbikes to books and motorbike-themed jigsaw puzzles. A Brigands Motorcycle Club Supporter T-shirt could be purchased for twenty-five pounds, along with Brigands mugs, drink coasters, key fobs and leather-jacketed teddy bears.

James had travelled ahead of the others on his bike. Once they'd parked up Lauren found him staring through glass at a £28,000 Arlen Ness custom bike, finished in green metallic paint with a padded seat barely half a metre off the ground and a set of custom-built front forks that made the bike four metres long.

'Thought I'd find you here,' Lauren said cheerfully. 'Is it me, or is that bike not *terribly* practical?'

James grinned. 'It'd certainly be a bitch in a traffic jam.'

'Didn't mean to bite your head off earlier,' Lauren said. 'Sorry.'

'Meh,' James shrugged. 'You can't expect tiny female brains like yours to stay rational all the time.'

'Let me check my sides,' Lauren replied, 'they might have split. Chloe looked on the Internet and apparently the tapas bar upstairs is really good.'

There were staircases at either end of the promenade of shops, which led up to a first-floor courtyard with a fountain in the centre and restaurants behind. The more upmarket places were at one end, with diners in suits and ties eating olives and watching the yachts. At the other end was a fifties-style American Diner and a row of kiosks including a juice bar and a donut shop.

'Martin Donnington,' Dante said quietly, as he recognised the Führer's oldest son working behind the counter in a crêpe stand. 'The last time I saw that face I beat the crap out of it in a boxing ring.'

Lauren and James both nodded.

While Chloe headed across to the tapas bar to try and get a table, the three teenagers studied the rest of the development. To their left was a six-storey luxury apartment block called Marina View. Its air-conditioned and balconied apartments were some of the most desirable residences in one of the country's most expensive seaside towns.

'You can see why the Führer wanted to build this,' James said. 'They must have made millions.'

Dante found James' comment slightly tactless, but couldn't help thinking the same thing himself. Maybe if his dad hadn't opposed the development, he'd still live here. His parents and siblings would all be alive and they'd probably be rich to boot.

The three teens eventually reached the back of the courtyard, which had less appealing views over the car park and the rubbish bins behind the shops and restaurants. Beyond the cars was a bland two-storey brick box with a huge neon Brigands M.C. logo on it. Above the main entrance a plastic sign read: *Whatever happens in this clubhouse, stays in this clubhouse.*

'Forty minutes for a table,' Chloe said, as she found the kids again. 'Do you want to wait? Or you can go down to the diner, or get donuts or something if you ate enough at lunchtime.'

'There's a whole bunch of kids down that end,' Lauren noted, as her eyes fixed on a group of people her own age. Most of them wore beach shorts, either with surf shoes or barefoot and one of them had even lugged a surf board uphill from the beach.

James saw a slightly older girl leaning on a railing; he couldn't see her face but the wind was blowing against her long skirt and she had a nice figure. 'It might be best,' James said. 'Show our faces. See who's who.'

'OK,' Chloe said. 'I'll hang around, have a look in the shops for an hour or something. I might try the Italian place. It didn't look as busy as the tapas bar.'

Chloe started to walk, but James and Lauren followed her, coughing noisily. She turned around and saw all three kids holding out their palms.

'You're forgetting your motherly duty,' James grinned.

Chloe laughed as she gave each of them a twenty-pound note from her purse and told them to make it last. Lauren and Dante followed the surfer kids, who'd all headed into the diner, while James made a beeline for the girl with the long skirt and long hair.

'Hey beautiful,' he said. 'Where have you been all my life?'

The girl turned around and cracked a smile. Fortunately her face lived up to the rear view. 'Nice pick-up line,' she said. 'I've *never* heard that one before.'

'Sorry,' James said, smiling and shrugging. 'It's kind of awkward. My name's James. I just moved here from London, so I don't know anyone and you looked kind of lonely.'

'Ashley,' the girl said, as she held out a slender hand for James to shake. 'I like your accent. You're a proper cockney boy.'

'Yeah,' James nodded. 'Salt of the earth, London geezer, my old man's a dustman, gawd blimey guvnor and all that. So how come a pretty girl like you's standing here all alone staring out to sea?'

Ashley laughed. 'I'm waiting for my boyfriend to park his car.'

'Oh,' James said awkwardly. 'We could elope together before he gets here.'

Ashley laughed again.

'Sorry, I'm being dumb,' James said. 'Are you in the sixth form?'

Ashley nodded.

'Do you know Crossroads Sixth Form college? That's where I've got to go and register for my courses tomorrow.'

Ashley nodded again. 'That's where I go. It's pretty much the only sixth form around here to be honest, apart from a couple of posh private schools.'

'I thought everyone around here was posh.'

'Not really,' Ashley said. 'Most of the houses on the harbour front and in the centre of town are second homes. But those people live in London, or wherever. We've got some rich people like anywhere else. Julian's parents are pretty loaded. His dad is a judge, and he lives up there in Marina View.'

'That's your boyfriend?'

Ashley nodded. 'They're coming up the stairs now.'

James looked over the railing and was pleased to see that he wouldn't be breaking up a couple: Julian was part of a group made up of five girls and three boys.

'We're gonna hang around in the diner,' Ashley explained, as the friends gathered around her. 'It's pretty boring and the food isn't great, but you can come with if you want.'

James nodded as the tall and curly-haired Julian gave Ashley a kiss. He had a set of Fiat keys hooked over his finger. 'Hi Ash,' he said, in a plummy voice. 'Took ages. Some dick took about ten minutes to get into his parking spot. Had a queue of cars a mile long.'

'This is James,' Ashley said. 'He just moved here, he's enrolling at Crossroads tomorrow. You're coming into the diner with us, aren't you?'

'If that's OK,' James shrugged.

James had clearly been hitting on Ashley, so Julian didn't look impressed. 'Hey James,' he said curtly. 'You're always picking up refugees, aren't you, Ash?'

As James headed towards the diner, Julian put his arm around Ashley's waist, making it clear who she belonged to.

19. HEY

Monday

Salcombe had stirred a lot of old memories, but seeing Joe had made Dante catch his breath. They'd been best friends from toddling around in nappies until the night his family was murdered. He'd often wondered what Joe's reaction had been when he found out that his father had killed his best friend's family.

In the early days after the murder Dante even fantasised that Joe would come out on his side and back up his story about being made to fight Martin in the boxing ring. But he'd never really expected it: Joe idolised his dad, and even if he hadn't he'd have been insane to go to the police against the Führer's will.

The thirteen-year-old Joe was recognisably an older version of the boy Dante had known which made him paranoid that someone would see through his new identity, despite reassurance from the experts on CHERUB campus that four years, a new name, an accent and a change of hairstyle were sufficient.

The school didn't have uniform, so each clique had adopted its own. Joe hung with a crowd of cool boys in designer-brand polo shirts, baggy cargo shorts or jeans, complemented with Vans or Converse. Dante reckoned his old-skool Adidas T-shirt with Diesel Jeans would pass muster, but he hadn't even been assigned to Joe's class because despite Chloe's best efforts, the school had a policy that siblings weren't allowed in the same class.

So while Dante stood alone in the Year Eight common room, trying not to make it obvious that he was watching the boys around Joe and hoping some of them would be in his class, Lauren could make a direct approach. She acted baffled, then walked up to one of the girls sitting cross-legged on a table top at the fringe of Joe's group.

'Excuse me,' Lauren said, as she held out the timetable she'd been given in the Head of Year's office fifteen minutes earlier. 'I'm in class 8C and Mr Brankin said it was easiest if I tagged along with someone to find my form room.'

'I'm 8C,' the girl nodded, as she played with her hair. 'I'm Anna. I like your shoes.'

'Lauren,' Lauren smiled. 'There's a cool shop in Covent Garden, they do all limited edition Nikes and stuff that you never see in the chains.'

The boys around Joe were more interested in Lauren's

bare legs and tits, and while it felt creepy knowing that they were all checking her out, it was exactly what she'd intended when she'd put on short shorts and a tight vest.

Everyone in the group seemed curious. A girl and two boys edged back, making room for Lauren to join the circle. A few kids including Joe told her their names, or made little welcome gestures like nods or wrist flicks.

The boy standing next to Lauren was the tallest. He had a stooped posture and loomed over the edge of the group. He kept quiet, but laughed noisily at the cooler kids' comments, making it obvious that he was a hanger-on rather than part of the core group. Sensing an opportunity to get a cheap laugh, he offered Lauren a handshake, which she took suspiciously.

'My name's Chris,' the kid said, speaking loud so that you could tell he was building up to something. 'Can I put my penis inside you?'

The boys all started laughing hysterically, while a girl called Jane booted Chris' ankle and called him a pig. Lauren's first urge was to snatch her hand away and swear at Chris, but she was an experienced CHERUB agent and she'd been through the *making friends with strange kids* scenario enough times to recognise a golden opportunity.

After freeing herself from the handshake, Lauren gave Chris a shove and snatched the Reebok backpack that had been standing on the ground between his feet. She glanced outside, making sure nobody was around, and then hurled the pack through an open window.

'You're a dog,' Lauren grinned, as Chris caught his balance. 'Go fetch.'

Chris faced Lauren off with bulging eyes. 'Bitch,' he said furiously. 'What did you do that for?'

But the gang was now laughing at Chris rather than with him, and there was no way he could kick off against a girl in the middle of a crowded common room. His face turned red as he steamed towards the fire doors to retrieve his pack before anyone else got hold of it.

'Nice move,' Jane said triumphantly. Anna gave Lauren a big smile. 'Chris has been asking for something like that all year.'

When Chris came back in with his pack, Joe conveniently forgot that he'd laughed as loud as any of the other lads when Chris had first cracked the penis line.

'Why don't you go and annoy someone else?' Joe asked acidly.

Although Chris was the biggest in the group, Joe was clearly the alpha-male and everyone bunched up so that Chris had nowhere to stand.

'Gotta go to the toilet before registration anyway,' Chris said pathetically, and he walked away.

Dante was still on his own and Lauren realised she could introduce him now that she'd won the group over.

'John, come over here,' Lauren shouted, before looking back at Anna and Jane. 'This is my baby brother,' she explained.

Dante smiled as he sidled up to the table beside Anna. 'So how come you're Lauren's baby brother if you're both in Year Eight?' Anna asked.

'Twins,' Dante explained. 'I'm a whole sixteen minutes younger.'

'Love the Irish accent,' Jane said. 'How come you're different?'

'Got expelled from my school in London,' Dante explained. 'So my dad booted my butt into some boarding school in Ireland for two and a half years.'

Dante saw that the other boys were looking his way. Joe narrowed his eyes.

'You look vaguely familiar,' Joe said. 'Have we met before?'

Dante's heart sped up, but he'd been told to expect this. 'Have you ever lived in London?' he asked.

Joe shook his head. 'Nah, you just look a bit like some kid I used to know. But he was a carrot head and he wouldn't show his face in these parts.'

The bell went for first lesson a few seconds later. Dante was pleased to find that Jane and a couple of the lads were in his class, but he hung back and whispered to Lauren before they split up.

'Fast work, sister.'

'Relax and be confident,' Lauren nodded. 'Don't be pushy, make them want to be your friend, not the other way around.'

Dante had done the same training as Lauren and was tempted to tell her that he could have done the same thing. But Lauren had done a textbook job, ingratiating herself with the coolest kids in Year Eight before they'd even heard the school bell.

*

James had to register for his courses at Crossroads Sixth Form Centre. To make life easy he picked maths and physics courses that he'd already passed. He sat a maths catch-up test to assess where he was in relation to his classmates and deliberately flunked several questions so that he didn't appear overly smart.

At lunchtime he found some of the kids he'd met at Marina Heights the night before. They all sat on the grass around a big tree with salads and sandwiches brought from home and took the mickey out of James because he was the only one who ate a dodgy burger and cold fries from the canteen.

He made a point of sitting near Ashley and smiling a lot whenever her boyfriend Julian was around. James didn't particularly fancy her, but he was a good looking guy and it amused him to piss Julian off. But for the purposes of the mission, Julian's friend Nigel was more interesting.

Although it was warm, Nigel wore boots and a black leather jacket. The sixth-form centre was in a remote location and kids who didn't want to wait for buses or parental pick-ups needed their own wheels. Battered Citroens and Fords ruled the car park. A few kids lived near enough to ride push bikes and there was an area given over to motorbikes and scooters.

James' 250cc Honda might not impress outlaws like the Brigands, but in a sixth-form car park it looked full-on amidst 100cc mopeds and cheap Chinese and Indian scooters. After they'd eaten, James wandered amongst the bikes to show Nigel his Honda.

Nigel introduced James to a boy called Ben who owned a 600cc Kawasaki. He was in the upper sixth. He kept a cigarette packet tucked in the sleeve of his T-shirt, sported a triangular beard and a wafer-thin girlfriend called Daisy.

'So how'd you get a six-hundred?' Nigel asked. 'That's gotta be illegal.'

Ben was cool, but nowhere near as cool as he liked to think he was and he acted like it was a big mystery. But James bought and read motorbike magazines all the time.

'You've got a restrictor kit,' James said. 'But the price of insurance on a six-hundred must be horrendous.'

'Restrictor kit?' Nigel asked.

'It limits the power of the bike,' James explained. 'Our licences say we can only ride a thirty-horsepower bike until we're twenty-one, but you can buy a more powerful bike and have a restrictor kit fitted.'

Nigel scowled at Ben's bike. 'So this thing is no faster than mine?'

Ben burst out laughing. 'The new kid is *almost* right, but I'll race you for any money you like. I've had this bike up to a hundred and thirty on the motorway.'

'What, did you break the laws of physics or something?' Nigel asked disbelievingly.

'You buy the bike,' Ben explained. 'Then get the dealer to fit the restrictor kit and get your power output certificate. Then you ask the dealer's mechanic politely and he turns a couple of screws and deactivates the kit.'

'Sweet,' Nigel said.

'Not if you get pulled over and the cops nail you it won't be,' James warned.

Ben shrugged. 'It's a risk, but once you've ridden a proper machine like mine, those little two-fifties are like Lego bikes, or something.'

Nigel started to laugh. 'What dealer will do the dodgy modifications?'

'Any second-hand bike dealer,' Ben said. 'Even some of the franchise dealers who sell new bikes. If you go in willing to spend a few grand and make it crystal that you're *only* buying if they issue the power output certificate and then disable the restrictor.'

'You bought your six-hundred from Leather and Chrome, didn't you?' Nigel asked.

'Sure,' Ben answered.

'I looked in their showroom last night,' James said. 'It's all like custom paint jobs and twenty-grand bikes for fat blokes who need a bike 'cos they're too old to get an erection.'

Nigel laughed. 'That's the irony with expensive bikes and sports cars: by the time you're rich enough to afford it, you're old and bald and you look damned stupid driving it.'

James, Ben and Daisy all laughed. Daisy's laugh was weird and James looked at her glazed eyes and guessed that she'd had a few puffs on a joint.

'That showroom's for tourists and second-home wankers,' Ben said. 'But they've got a workshop over by the Brigands clubhouse and a whole room full of second-hand bikes.'

'I noticed a couple of Brigands last night,' James said. 'Scary looking bastards.'

'You don't wanna start any trouble with them,' Nigel said. 'But they're OK. My big brother says if you like bikes and you get on their right side they'll buy you drinks all night long.'

'Good mechanics too,' Ben said. 'I mean, they're enthusiasts more than capitalists. If you go into Leather and Chrome, and you're a kid and you don't have a lot of money they'll treat you fair. Sort you out with a good bike and not rip you off for servicing.'

'They're really decent,' Nigel nodded. 'Especially with my brother 'cos he's one of the Monster Bunch.'

'The what?' James asked, though he knew of course.

'Monster Bunch,' Nigel explained. 'It's a bike gang. They ride with the Brigands, but they're mostly younger and it's ten times easier to join. My older brother is a member, though he's away at uni at the moment.'

'My cousin is in the Monster Bunch, so I knew a few people,' Ben said. 'Leather and Chrome set me up with the bike, the financing. They even helped me get a job so that I could make the payments.'

'So if I went down to Marina Heights I could get my Honda looked at?' James asked.

Ben nodded. 'What's up with it?'

'I think it's got a bit of a brake imbalance,' James lied. 'It was OK when I first had it, but now if I brake hard the front wheel does next to nothing, then it suddenly bites, locks up and I get tyre smoke.'

Ben laughed. 'I'm amazed that bike ever goes fast enough to get tyre smoke.'

'I've had it up to eighty-five,' James lied again. 'I've got no class this afternoon. I might ride down to Salcombe and see if a mechanic will look at it.'

Nigel looked at his watch. 'You mind if I ride with you, James? I got nothing going on. I might even have a word about that restrictor kit thing.'

20. ER5

It was a thirty-minute ride from the sixth-form centre to Marina Heights. Nigel led the way, showing James a couple of neat shortcuts down farm tracks and walking paths. At two on a Monday afternoon Marina Heights was dead and they parked two bikes into a single space near the back of the shops.

The two teenagers strode towards the bike shop with their helmets in hand. Giant steel bins overflowed after the weekend and the heat amplified the smell of waste food as they walked past the dead neon sign on the Brigands clubhouse. James noticed video cameras pointing in all directions, bars over all the windows and heavy steel bollards that would prevent anyone from trying to smash their way inside with a vehicle.

'What do you reckon about the Brigands?' James asked.

'They're intense,' Nigel explained. 'I mean, I've lived around here my whole life and I still shit myself a little bit when I see one of them.'

'Ever seen any trouble?' James asked.

'Nah,' Nigel said. 'But you read stuff in the local paper. Some guy got his head bashed in on the pavement out here a few weeks back. There's one blind spot where the video cameras can't see, and that just *happens* to be where you'll get stomped if the Brigands take a dislike to you.'

'So, best avoided?' James smiled.

'They're friendly with the locals,' Nigel said. 'They even do charity open days and stuff in the clubhouse. Just don't piss them off. To be honest, I prefer them to image bikers like Ben.'

James was confused. 'Ben seemed nice enough.'

Nigel shrugged. 'He's a nice guy, sure. But for Ben it's *all* about the image. You can tell he spends half an hour every morning spiking his hair and trimming that beard. And he's always got that cigarette packet tucked in his sleeve like he thinks he's James Dean or something.'

'Tries too hard,' James guessed.

'Exactly,' Nigel nodded. 'Real bikers don't give a shit. They smoke, do drugs, shag skanky women, drive awesome bikes and pulp anyone who disses them. Once I'm eighteen my brother says he'll sort me out getting into the Monster Bunch. I might even be going on my first run this summer if I can arrange transport.'

'Nice,' James smiled. 'But what's wrong with your bike?'

Nigel shook his head. 'The gangs cruise in formation at eighty or even a hundred miles an hour. You can't do a run on a two-fifty. Even if you *could* keep the pace the older guys would all take the piss so bad you'd end up miserable. I'd have to get a seat on a coach, or in the run truck.'

'I've read about runs in magazines,' James nodded. 'They sound awesome. What about your mate Julian, would he go?'

'Nah,' Nigel laughed. 'We've grown up together, but he's only a school mate nowadays. His dad is a judge, he's pretty spoiled but he's also on a tight leash. Like, he pranged his car not long after he got it and they went spare. And when they found spliff in his room he was grounded for a whole month.'

By this time James and Nigel had passed the clubhouse and reached the bike workshop. The space was immaculate, with tools in wheeled cabinets and hydraulic lifts that raised the bikes up high so that the mechanics could work without having to crawl around on the floor. Lynyrd Skynyrd came out of a boom box resting against the wall.

Up back there was a custom shop with expensive parts lining the walls. Along one side three Harley Davidsons were suspended in mid air in various stages of being stripped and rebuilt. One was an extraordinarily shabby rat bike with a Brigands M.C. badge painted on the fuel tank.

James moved in for a closer look and found himself confronted by a shirtless man with bushels of hair growing from every orifice.

'Never touch a Brigands bike unless you don't like the way your face looks,' the man barked.

'I wasn't touching,' James said warily. He saw that the man's Levis were stiffened black with oil and filth. James knew he was a Brigand called Heartbreaker. He looked like he'd last bathed several decades earlier and his cologne was eau-de-petrol.

'If you boys are here about a bike you need to go up them metal steps and speak to Rhino.'

James knew Rhino's name from a police file. He was thirty-eight, a long-term biker and Brigands associate with a string of petty convictions. According to Neil Gauche he'd turned down the opportunity to become a prospect Brigand many times because he took pride in his status as a lone rider and didn't care for the infighting and squabbles that came with club membership.

After passing two well groomed mechanics in turquoise overalls, they headed upstairs and found Rhino at a desk in jeans and an AC/DC T-shirt. Behind him was a large room, with its white tile floor streaked with tyre marks. The space was crammed with bikes ranging from battered Harleys and Ducatti racers to pink Lambrettas and quad bikes.

After James had explained about his brakes, Rhino gave him a card and told him that he'd need to phone the service department and make an appointment for later in the week. Nigel had wandered off and found half a dozen mid-sized bikes, similar to Ben's. They were all a few years old, but most only had a few thousand miles on the clock and prices on the right side of £2,000.

'You've got a two-fifty haven't you?' Rhino asked, as he sniffed a sale. 'You're Will's brother?'

Nigel nodded. 'Some nice bikes here, but I'm just looking.'

'Look all you like,' Rhino smiled.

James sat astride a £1,800 498cc Kawasaki ER5 and bounced the suspension.

'That's a perfect bike for a young man like you,' Rhino said. 'Easy to ride, fifty horsepower, it'll cruise at a hundred miles per hour.'

'You'd need one of those restrictor kits,' Nigel said. 'That'd slow it down.'

Rhino smiled. 'Between you and me, on a fifty-horsepower bike we'll fit you the kit, give you the certificate and make *sure* you feel no difference if you see what I mean.'

'It's academic,' James smiled. 'I haven't got eighteen hundred quid.'

'Maybe you don't need it,' Rhino explained. 'Your old bike will count as a deposit of at least four hundred. Then you'll have fourteen hundred outstanding. Zero per cent finance over three years, that's less than ten pounds a week.'

'Can you lend *us* money?' Nigel asked incredulously.

Rhino shook his head. 'You'd have to get a parent to sign the paperwork. But that's a formality. All our bikes are guaranteed rock solid. You've seen the mechanical set-up we've got down there and all these bikes have been stripped and tested. Your friend is sitting astride a bike that's done less than six thousand miles. It's barely run in, but you're paying a third of what some sucker paid in a showroom less than three years ago.'

James smiled, imagining himself blasting the motorway on a 500cc bike. 'Maybe I'll ask my mum.'

'I'll need a bigger bike if I'm going on a run in the summer,' Nigel said. 'But the insurance is gonna be the killer.'

Rhino switched out of being a salesman and sounded more genuine when he heard this. 'Who you going on a run with?'

'Monster Bunch, hopefully,' Nigel said. 'My brother said he'll try and sort something out when he gets back from uni in a couple of weeks.'

'Has Will still got that raggedy 883 Sportster?'

Nigel nodded. 'Spent a lot of money fixing it up. It looks the business, but he's had chronic breakdowns.'

'We have a philosophy here when it comes to selling motorcycles,' Rhino said, dropping back into salesman mode. 'You're teenagers. You don't have much money now, but enthusiasm for motorcycles is a lifelong thing. I'm more interested in sending you out of here on a good reliable bike. Then I can bleed you dry when you're older and you come in here to drop ten grand on a Harley.'

James and Nigel both laughed.

'Do you know Teeth?' Rhino asked.

James knew the name, but he shook his head.

'I know *of* him,' Nigel said.

'Well Teeth is the Führer's right-hand man these days,' Rhino explained. 'He runs Marina Heights promenade. Cleaning crews, maintenance, the diner and the fast-food kiosks. He can't offer glamorous work, but it's a minimum six quid an hour. You can work Saturdays, and once the school holidays start you can do forty hours or more a week. If you're prepared to graft you can easily pay for a bike like this over a single summer.'

Nigel snorted. 'Do you know how hard it is to get Marina Heights jobs? Every kid in town wants them, along with about a million older dudes who come to the beaches to surf.'

Rhino nodded. 'But in case you haven't noticed, Marina Heights is run by the Brigands. We're motorbike people, you're motorbike people. If you're buying a bike out of here, I'll go to Teeth and your names will go to the top of the list for Saturday work and summer jobs. All you've got to do is pick out a bike, get one of your parents down here and we'll sort the whole deal. You could be riding home on one of these bikes *tonight*.'

James was a bright kid, but he'd never faced a hardcore salesman like Rhino before and the prospect of driving an unrestricted 500cc Kawasaki around all summer pressed all his buttons.

'I could *so* go for that ER5,' James smiled, walking back out into the sun with Nigel. 'Do you think you'll get one?'

Nigel shook his head. 'No bike is worth a summer of cleaning toilets, serving burgers and scraping gum off of furniture. Besides, I've got a little gig selling spliff to Julian and that whole crowd of kids. I only make thirty or forty quid a week but it pays for my own weed and my bike insurance and I don't have to lift a finger.'

'Nice,' James nodded. 'So why don't you buy the bike with your drug money?'

Nigel laughed. 'Oh yeah, I come home on a 500cc bike and my ma's not gonna ask where I got the money from, is she?'

'Good point,' James admitted.

'And if you want to buy some shit to smoke anytime, just ask.'

James shook his head. 'I tried marijuana a couple of times but I couldn't get into it for some reason.'

'Probably some cheap crap is why,' Nigel said. 'The stuff I sell is *great*. It's all grown down here in Devon. Hundred per cent organic, THC levels are through the roof.'

'I'll bear it in mind,' James said warily, as he reached his bike. 'What you gonna do now?'

'I stink,' Nigel said. 'I'll go home and take a shower and I've got an essay to write. I think everyone's meeting up on the beach this evening. If you give me your cell number I'll text you the where and when.'

21. HANG

Chloe spent the afternoon supermarket shopping, and when the kids got home she told them that dinner was whichever ready meal they picked from the selection crammed inside their American-style fridge-freezer.

James got first dibs on the microwave and did a lasagne. He headed into the living-room after claiming that the curry Lauren and Dante were heating up was stinking the place out. But the smell followed him into the living-room when they brought their food through a few minutes later.

'You not eating?' Lauren asked Chloe, who sat on an armchair with her feet under her bum.

'I had lunch at the tapas bar,' Chloe explained.

'Good?' Lauren asked.

'Very,' Chloe nodded. 'This old boy sitting next to me started chatting me up. He had pots of money judging by the gold Rolex and the offer of a day out on his yacht.'

'Oooh, Chloe's got a boyfriend,' Dante laughed as he dipped naan bread into his chicken korma.

'So have you,' Lauren grinned. 'Or it won't be long judging by the way you were canoodling with Anna on the bus ride home.'

James perked up at the mention of a girl. 'Good tits?' he asked.

Dante laughed. 'Not huge, but nice.'

'What are we talking?' James asked. 'Kiwi fruit, apples, oranges, mangos, melons?'

Lauren tutted. 'James, not all boys are animals like you.'

But Dante surprised her. 'Big firm oranges, heading towards grapefruits,' he grinned. 'Although *nothing* compared to this girl I went out with when I was in Ireland.'

Lauren's heart sank as she watched Dante cupping his hands in front of his chest. 'Jesus, you're worse than my brother,' she complained, as she wapped him with a rolled-up TV guide.

'It's just tits,' James smirked.

'Tits, tits, wonderful tits,' Dante sang.

Chloe sounded cross. 'I'm *not* sitting here listening to you two talking about breasts,' she said firmly. 'Show some respect. How would you like it if we sat here talking about penises?'

James looked down at his plastic dish, chasing the last piece of lasagne with his spoon. 'How's the mission budget coming?' he asked. 'Only I might need a couple of grand for another bike, plus the insurance.'

Lauren scoffed. 'Why would you *need* another bike?'

'I might get invited on a run with the Monster Bunch,' he explained. 'If I do, Nigel says I'll need a bike that can cruise at seventy or eighty miles an hour.'

James wanted the bike badly and had left out two important facts: Nigel *hadn't* mentioned anything about him being invited on a run and he'd said that the Brigands cruised at up to a hundred, not at seventy or eighty.

Chloe didn't look too impressed as she straightened up. 'So what kind of bike would we be talking about?'

'Five hundred cc. It's a real beauty with less than six thousand miles on the clock.'

'You've already looked?' Chloe laughed. 'You were supposed to ask the mechanics to check your brakes. And I can't see it. I already had to write up a special report for the ethics committee on whether it was safe to let a sixteen-year-old ride around on the bike you've got.'

James shrugged. 'But big bikes are safer in a lot of ways. I mean, imagine you're on the motorway and there's a big truck in the way spraying rain in your face. On a small bike you're stuck behind it. On a bigger machine you can open up the throttle and overtake.'

Chloe blew air between her teeth. 'Don't get your hopes up, James.'

'I think you should let him have a massive racing bike,' Lauren grinned. 'If he splats into a wall at a hundred and sixty miles an hour I'll inherit twice as much money from my mum's estate when I turn eighteen.'

'If you can't say something useful, Lauren, why don't you shut the hell up?' James asked irritably, before speaking to Chloe and trying not to make himself seem too desperate. 'I'm not an idiot, you know? I'll treat the bike with respect. And if I get the bike on finance, Rhino says he'll let me speak to Teeth who'll set me up with a summer job at Marina Heights so that I can make the payments. That way I'll have a chance to get much closer to the Brigands clubhouse.'

Chloe seemed much more positive about this angle. James realised he should have used this argument first, because it didn't look like he was just trying to get his hands on a cooler bike.

'I suppose I can see the benefit of that,' Chloe admitted.

'Cool,' James said. 'The dealership is open until seven tonight. You have to sign some papers for the finance.'

'Not bloody likely!' Chloe said. 'I'm not taking sole responsibility for letting a sixteen-year-old ride around on a hundred-and-twenty-mile-an-hour motorbike. I'll have to speak to the chairwoman and the ethics committee.'

James felt slightly disappointed, but it had always been a long shot that he'd get the bike of his dreams immediately and at least Chloe was open to the suggestion.

*

Two dozen sixth formers hung out on the concrete platform above a sandy cove a couple of kilometres from the centre of Salcombe. The beach and the gentle waves coming off the sea were a novelty for James, but for the rest of the kids it was a regular hang-out where they could chill out, mess around, flirt and catch the last of the day's sunshine.

Nigel dealt marijuana to a couple of kids and James got the impression that he could have sold way more if everyone wasn't broke after the weekend. James' real and fictional background was as a Londoner and everyone asked him questions about places to shop and places to stay.

Julian and his group of friends spoke vaguely of travelling to London for a few days in the summer, but they had nowhere to stay and they were all going on foreign holidays at different times with their parents so James got the impression that it was one of those things that would never come together.

After a while he sat with his back against a set of railings with Ashley and her friend Caitlyn on either side. Caitlyn wasn't with anyone. She had straight dark hair and a short but chunky body. James thought about making a move, but reckoned it was best to concentrate on the mission for a day or two before trying it on with any girls, plus he was highly amused by the dirty looks he got off Julian every time he made Ashley laugh.

Once the sun dropped the wind came up and everyone headed through the centre of Salcombe to get something to eat at Marina Heights. Julian practically had steam venting out of his ears when James gave

Ashley a lift on the back of his Honda and he confronted James angrily in the Marina Heights car park.

'I don't think it's safe, her riding without a crash helmet,' Julian said, as he got out of his car. 'I noticed you wore yours.'

'Whatever,' James shrugged. 'She's a big girl, Jules.'

'To be honest I think you should bugger off, James.'

Ashley made a deep sigh as James mocked Julian's posh accent. 'Well I think you're the one who should jolly well bugger orf.'

Ashley stepped between the two lads. 'For Christ's sake, he only gave me a lift.'

'I play rugby you know,' Julian said, as he poked the pocket of James' shirt. 'So I'm warning you to back off.'

The other kids who'd ridden in Julian's car were all clambering out. They could all see that he was jealous and a couple of them told him to leave it out.

'This is such a dumb argument,' James said, before turning his back and heading for the steps leading up to the restaurants. But Julian threw a punch.

'Stop it!' Ashley shouted, as the fist glanced the back of James' head. 'Stop being an arse.'

The blow was nothing but James couldn't ignore it without looking like a pussy. He turned fast, grabbed Julian around the neck and thumped him against his little Fiat.

The group might not approve if James did something too physical, but he needed to make a mark and he'd just seen Julian dropping his car keys into his jacket pocket. James pulled out the keys and backed off before athletically tossing them on to the metal roof of the Brigands clubhouse.

'Come at me again and I'll flatten you,' James warned, as the keys juddered down a couple of metres of sloped metal and came to rest nestling against a clump of moss.

Julian didn't want to look weak, but he'd felt James' strength when he'd been bundled against the car.

'Christ,' Julian shouted. 'How the hell do I get up there?'

James grinned. 'Knock on the front door and ask the Brigands if they've got a ladder.'

Ashley shook her head contemptuously as she started walking towards the stairs. James was worried that the group would see him as the bad guy, but as he walked up the stairs with Nigel and Ashley, three boys were laughing about Julian's predicament. Caitlyn summed up the mood by telling James that he'd shown admirable restraint in not punching back.

When they got upstairs they headed into the diner. It was two-thirds full and they got nods and smiles from a bunch of other sixth-form kids who sat eating at the tables next to the open front of the restaurant. Fifties pop belted out of a tacky jukebox as Nigel handed James a tenner.

'Got business to do,' Nigel smiled. 'Get me a cheeseburger, fries and Coke plus whatever you want.'

But when James turned around with the money Ashley was already being served. 'You gave me a lift, so I'll get the food,' she said sweetly.

She paid for Nigel too, and when they headed towards

a table to wait for their order Ashley sat next to James and put her hand in his lap. James liked her black nail varnish and the wispy hairs up her arm.

'You should speak with Julian,' James said quietly. 'I'm the new kid in town. I don't want some major beef blowing up.'

'Screw him, treating me like his personal possession,' Ashley said, as she gave the Formica table top the finger. '*I play rugby*,' she mocked. 'You bent him over that car like he was a twig.'

'I've been known to hit the weights,' James grinned. 'Plus some Karate, a little kickboxing. I'm not a violent person. I've not been in a fight since I was twelve, but it's best not to mess with me.'

Ashley purred approvingly as Nigel joined Caitlyn on the other side of the table.

'Will Julian be OK?' James asked.

Nigel burst out laughing. 'Well his car keys are on a rooftop and you've got his girlfriend's hand in your lap. I'm sure he'll be *just* fine.'

'He's your mate though,' James noted.

'A mate who owes me two hundred quid,' Nigel said. 'Never pays for his shit. If I hadn't known him since primary school I'd have got one of the Monster Bunch to beat it out of him.'

'His dad's a judge,' Caitlyn noted.

'That as well,' Nigel smiled.

Caitlyn wasn't eating, but when the food arrived she moved closer to Nigel and picked at his chips. James realised they were drifting towards a double-date situation. His mind was split. Part of him thought about the mission and the talk he'd had with Kerry. On the flipside Ashley was quite sexy and James' moral compass always flew out of the window when he was within ten metres of an attractive girl.

When their plates were empty the foursome drifted out into almost dark. Distant yachts caught the moonlight and candles glowed on tables inside restaurants at the grown-up end of the promenade. James hadn't paid any attention to the younger kids sitting out by the fast-food kiosks, but Nigel zoomed in on a snogging couple, one of whom was Dante.

'Look at these lovebirds,' Nigel teased. 'Don't forget your nine o'clock curfew, little Anna.'

Anna broke away from Dante and told Nigel to go screw himself.

James stood behind Nigel and laughed. 'Is that your little sister snogging my little brother? How cute!'

'Leave 'em alone,' Ashley grinned, as she dragged James away. 'You can tell he's your brother, he's got the same jaw line.'

'I like oranges,' James said cryptically as they backed away. Dante tried not to laugh as he closed in to resume his snogfest with Anna.

'You girls fancy a ride back to my place?' Nigel asked. 'My mum's serving at some dinner party. I can build a monster spliff and we can get totally monged out of our skulls.'

James baulked at the suggestion of smoking marijuana. CHERUB agents are banned from using illegal drugs.

Fortunately Ashley solved his dilemma. 'I'm not getting stoned tonight,' she said. 'I've got my stats mock tomorrow. I got a C at the end of last term and that won't be getting me into a decent uni.'

James grinned. 'And I've got my first proper day at college tomorrow.'

But Caitlyn was giving Nigel a big smile. 'I'm up for a smoke.'

Nigel seemed happy with that result: him and Caitlyn alone and stoned. James didn't know Caitlyn all that well and wondered whether they'd end up shagging.

James looked back as he followed Ashley and Nigel down metal steps to the car park. Dante had started snogging again and he spotted Lauren sitting on a railing with girls and boys on all sides. She looked happy and Joe was part of the group. It seemed that everyone was hanging with the right people and the mission couldn't have started any better.

James looked at Ashley as they moved off to the steps into an empty disabled parking bay. 'I'm good at stats,' he smiled. 'I could help you study. Your place, my place, whatever.'

'Are you *really* good, or are you just saying that to get into my house?' Ashley asked teasingly.

'I'm good,' James said, as he moved in for a kiss. But Nigel yelled before they made contact.

'James, you'd better look at this.'

He jogged across the car park and saw pink stuff streaked all over his bike. When he got close he saw that a chocolate and strawberry ice cream had been mashed everywhere. A crushed cornet lay in a pool of melted ice cream on the seat and more dribbled down the side on to the engine.

'Julian,' James cursed. 'I'll break his bastard spine when I get hold of him. Where's his car? I'm gonna kick out every piece of glass.'

'It's gone,' Caitlyn noted.

Nigel nodded. 'Julian lives over in Marina View. He probably went back to his apartment and grabbed his spare keys. They've got secure parking underground.'

'I'll run up to the donut stand and grab some napkins,' Ashley said.

Nigel crouched down and inspected James' Honda. 'I'd get her home and sponge all that off. If you leave it it's gonna set hard. It could even mess up your electrics.'

'Shit,' James said.

Nigel stood back up and Caitlyn put her arm around his back. 'Not much I can do to help,' Nigel said. 'You mind if we split?'

The couple rode off as Ashley clanked down the steps with a five-centimetre wedge of napkins in her hand. They worked together to clear off the worst, though the ice cream was sticky and the tissue broke up into tufts that ended up stuck all over the seat.

'God, Julian's a jealous arsehole,' Ashley said. 'I'm really sorry about this.'

'I'll have to drive this home and give it a proper clean. I'd offer you a ride, but it's gonna ruin your nice dress.'

'No worries,' Ashley said. 'I can get a cab, or it's only fifteen minutes' walk to my house.'

'Sorry,' James said again, as he dropped a soggy ball of tissue into the gutter.

Ashley took a phone out of her canvas bag. 'There'll be other nights,' she smiled. 'What's your number? I hardly know you. I'll call you, we can do something tomorrow.'

22. FRIDAY

Friday morning

The weather had changed for the worse and drizzle pelted the glass as James laid out on his bed dressed in the socks and briefs he'd slept in. He held his mobile up to his face with Ashley on the other end.

'So what are you wearing?' James asked. A big grin erupted on his face. 'Black is sexy! You know what I'd like to do? I'd love to get up close to you on your bed and . . .'

James stopped talking abruptly as Lauren burst in through the open door. 'Stop talking dirty to your girlfriend and get downstairs.'

'Gotta go,' James said, sliding his phone shut and glowering at Lauren. 'Haven't you heard of knocking?'

Lauren grinned. 'Haven't you heard of closing your

door when you're playing with yourself?'

'I was on the phone,' James protested.

'Chloe wants a conference downstairs before me and Dante go off to school.'

James put on jeans and a T-shirt and was surprised to find Chloe at the stove making scrambled eggs.

'We've been here six days now,' Chloe said, as she took the egg off the gas ring and grabbed four plates from the cupboard. 'I need progress reports. Lauren, Dante, what's the situation with Joe?'

'Friendly,' Lauren said. 'I've been making my move. He doesn't have a girlfriend, so I've been putting myself in the frame. He's mouthy, but I get the feeling that he's actually quite shy around girls.'

'The weekend's coming up,' Chloe noted. 'Maybe it's time to go for broke and ask him out.'

Lauren nodded. 'I'm thinking the same way. The tricky part is picking a moment when he hasn't got sixteen gormless mates surrounding him.'

'Well make that your priority,' Chloe said. 'Remember, this mission needs to move quickly. I'd rather we took a few risks and blew it than not take any and guarantee that we achieve nothing. What about you, Dante?'

'Getting closer to Joe is difficult,' Dante said. 'I'm not in his class. I've had a couple of conversations but he's a popular kid and it's hard to force it.'

Lauren helped Chloe bring four plates of scrambled egg on toast across to the breakfast bar.

'You're spending a lot of time with Anna,' Chloe said bluntly. 'Is that for the mission's benefit, or yours?'

Dante looked ticked off. 'I'm having a good time Chloe, but in case you've forgotten *I've* got more incentive to make this mission work than any of you.'

'Point taken,' Chloe said, holding her hand up defensively. 'What I'm wondering is, can we use your relationship with Anna to help Lauren get closer to Joe? For instance, what if you whisper in Joe's ear and say that you think Lauren likes him. Then you can arrange some kind of double date, or a shopping trip. If you want to do something on the weekend I'd be available to drive you to the shops in Exeter, or the cinema, or something.'

'That could work,' Lauren nodded.

'OK, that's your job for today at school and the weekend,' Chloe said. 'Now James, what about you?'

James shrugged. 'I go to sixth-form centre, some nights I'll hang about with them at Marina Heights or go to the beach. If I had six months I'd be confident that I could make some connections and work my way up to the fringes of the Brigands organisation. But you want it done quickly and you've got me fighting with one arm tied behind my back.'

Lauren groaned. 'Don't start on about that bloody Kawasaki again.'

'What about Nigel?' Chloe asked. 'He deals drugs. We know that the Brigands control the drug trade around here. Can you find out where he buys from?'

'Eventually,' James nodded. 'But you can't ask questions like that after four days. And why would I be curious when I've had to keep telling him that I don't smoke dope?'

'What if there was a buy going on?' Dante asked. 'You know, you mention some friends you had in London who'd be interested in buying some of Nigel's good shit. Either he wants to handle it himself, or he puts you in touch with someone higher up the chain.'

'Could work,' James agreed. 'I'd only be making a contact with someone slightly further up the chain, though. Probably a junior member of the Monster Bunch who supplies weed to a few other kids like Nigel. I still say if we're looking for fast results our best bet is the option I gave you on Monday that you've sat on all week.'

Lauren tutted. 'James, you've wanted a flash motorbike since you came back from Arizona three years ago. That's all this is about.'

'Crap,' James said, close to losing his temper. 'I've explained how it works. We turn up, Chloe makes it clear that she can't afford the bike unless I get a part-time job. Rhino talks to Teeth who sets me up with some crummy job working at Marina Heights. That's where all the Brigands and the other gangs hang out.'

'Why can't you just apply for a job?' Dante asked.

'Because this is Devon,' James said. 'Maybe in London a kid can walk into any fast-food joint, fill in a form and get a job, but Devon and Cornwall have the highest unemployment in the country. There's like a hundred kids at my college who would *die* to have a part-time job.'

Chloe sighed noisily. 'I spoke to Zara about this. She said it was my decision and I had to be *certain* that I trusted you to be responsible with such a powerful bike.'

'So let's bloody well do it then,' James yelled, slapping his thighs as he jumped up from his seat.

Chloe backed off and James felt bad. He'd reached the age where he could physically intimidate adults – especially women – but he didn't always account for the fact.

Chloe was an ex-cherub, and after the initial shock caused by James' outburst she stepped up to James and jabbed him in the chest.

'I've read your file, James Adams,' Chloe said angrily. 'You're a good agent, but your decision-making processes can leave a lot to be desired. If I let you have this bike and then you go off and do something crazy, I could lose *my* job. And since I live on campus, I'll lose *my* home and most of *my* friends too.'

'Sorry I shouted,' James said, holding up his hands and sitting back down on his bar stool. 'I'm trying to make the point that you're pushing me to get things done. Maybe you're right. Maybe I'll get this job and find that it gets me nowhere. All I know is that the Brigands own Marina Heights and if I'm working evenings and weekends I'm in a much better position to see what's going on up there than if I'm hanging around with Nigel and Ashley.'

Chloe shook her head, then sighed. 'OK,' she said finally. 'You've got lessons this morning, but I'll take you down to Marina Heights and try sorting out the job and the bike. But if I catch you messing around I'll have your balls on a platter.'

James wasn't sure whether to gulp or smile as Chloe glowered at him.

Lauren tutted. 'You're *such* a con merchant, James.'

*

Chloe's scheme worked. Joe sat next to Lauren on the bus home from school. He held her hand across the arm rest, and Lauren leaned her head in to rest on Joe's shoulder. He seemed chubby compared to the highly trained boys on CHERUB campus and also charmingly naive. Joe might have been cool and acted Jack-the-lad in class when his mates were around, but his clammy hands and bumbling sentences made her suspect that his love life had never advanced beyond a few snogs at the school disco.

'What do you want to do?' Joe asked, as he led Lauren, Dante and Anna off the bus at a stop a kilometre from the centre of Salcombe.

'John and Lauren live about ten minutes that way,' Anna said. 'And their mum is always cool when I come over.'

Lauren panicked because her objective was to get into the Führer's house. 'I've driven past your house,' she said to Joe. 'You've got that cool tank on the front lawn. Can you climb up inside it?'

Joe looked awkward. 'You can open the hatch, but it's just a hulk. It's all rusty and flooded with water.'

Lauren squeezed Joe's hand and whined like she was five years old. 'I wanna see the tank!'

Joe laughed and relented. 'My mum'll probably be home, but she's cool. The only thing is, my house is kind of embarrassing.'

'Intriguing,' Lauren said. 'How so?'

'You know my dad's the Führer, right?' Joe asked.

Everyone nodded, it was frequently mentioned at school. 'He's cool in some ways, but he buys up all this Nazi shit. I mean, it's not just the tank. We've got rugs with swastikas and there's a bust of Hitler on the mantelpiece.'

Anna smiled awkwardly. 'Freak show!' she grinned.

'Freak show's what it is,' Joe agreed.

Lauren sensed that Joe wasn't keen, so she kissed him on the neck. 'Nobody picks their parents,' she said soothingly. 'Our dad is a total idiot.'

'Grade-one penis,' Dante agreed. 'Cheated on our mum four times before she finally ditched his sorry butt and moved us down here.'

Lauren's kiss gave Joe a boost and his usual cockiness crept back into his voice. 'OK then,' he grinned. 'Let's go visit the freak show. I've also got X-box, and DVDs in my room and stuff.'

The busy country road had no pavement, so they walked single file until they reached the gates of the Eagles' Nest. After a brief stop to climb on the tank the kids walked into the hallway. Joe's mum rushed out from the kitchen. The Führer had moved to a bigger house after making a mint from the development of Marina Heights, but Dante knew Joe's mum.

Marlene Donnington had always been heavy, but she'd gained more weight over the past five years and thick make-up and a deep sun-bed tan did nothing to improve her looks. But Joe's mum had always been nice to Dante and her face reminded him of Brigands barbecues, shopping trips and sleeping out in a tent with Joe when he was little.

'So nice to see some of your friends,' Marlene said cheerfully. 'Would you like some Pepsi and crisps, or I could make ham sandwiches if any of you are hungry? And I'm sorry to be a fusspot, but if you wouldn't mind taking your shoes off inside the house.'

As Dante pulled off his Converse he remembered that he'd always liked Joe's mum's sandwiches because she used butter while his mum could only ever afford margarine.

'Yeah I'm starving,' Joe said.

'I'm vegetarian actually,' Lauren said.

'Me too,' Anna added.

'Can you do some different ones?' Joe asked. 'Ham, cheese and pickle or whatever you've got, and maybe some crisps.'

'So many of you teenagers are vegetarian these days,' Marlene said, as she smiled at the girls. 'I'll bring the sandwiches up to Joe's room.'

'Your mum's so nice,' Anna said as they started up the stairs towards Joe's room.

The house was neatly decorated and could have been the home of any wealthy executive, apart from the framed photos of bikers and the occasional bust of Hitler.

'So is your dad actually a Nazi?' Lauren asked.

'Nah,' Joe said. 'He's mainly interested in the history and stuff.'

'I heard that the Brigands don't let anyone who isn't white in their gang,' Anna said.

Joe pointed at Lauren. 'It's like she said, you can't pick your parents. My dad has done a bunch of shit. Some of it like going on runs and the bikes and stuff is cool, but some of the more extreme stuff pisses me off.'

Dante wondered if the murder of his parents had anything to do with Joe's opinions. Or maybe it was the standard thing of teenagers reaching a certain age and realising that their parents aren't gods. Either way, it made Dante feel a lot better about hanging about with his old friend, but a lot worse about his prospects of wringing useful information out of Joe.

'So this is my room,' Joe said, as he opened up. His mess was disguised behind the doors of fitted wardrobes. He had a big bed, a cool Alienware gaming PC and a big LCD screen with surround speakers.

'You spoiled bastard,' Dante grinned. 'These speakers must be *so* loud.'

'Yeah,' Joe said, as he picked Green Day's *Bullet in a Bible* DVD out of his cupboard. 'Surround sound is awesome, you wanna hear it?'

'American Idiot,' Dante nodded. 'That song is fricking awesome.'

As the DVD went through its copyright warnings Lauren crashed out on a beanbag. Anna and Dante sat together on the sofa and kissed until the music started.

'Jesus this is *so* loud,' Lauren screamed, but nobody heard a word. She burst out laughing when she turned around and saw Dante jumping up and down, playing air guitar and rocking his head back and forth. His long hair flew wildly.

After turning the sound up even louder, Joe threw down the remote and jumped on his bed where he went into competition dancing even more crazily than Dante. Lauren stepped up and they held hands and jumped into the air together, high enough for Lauren's hair to flick against the ceiling.

They repeated this until on the third jump Joe's foot missed the edge of the bed and he stumbled sideways into Anna and Dante. Lauren got dragged off the bed and wound up crashing down on top of Joe, with Anna's legs trapped beneath them and Dante's funky sock in her face.

They were all giggling and trying to clamber out of the heap when Joe's mum came into the room holding a tray stacked with four glasses, a bottle of Coke and a plate of little sandwiches and crisps.

'Turn the music down!' she yelled, as she grabbed the remote off the carpet and tried to find the button. When she got the volume down all she could hear was the four teenagers laughing, but also slightly embarrassed.

'Sorry,' Joe said, as he took the remote off his mum and pressed the mute button.

'Mad bloody lot, you are,' Joe's mum laughed. 'I don't mind you having fun but I could hear *that* down in the kitchen.'

23. LONDON

There were Brigands chapters in twenty-three countries. They all wore the same patch and obeyed a club rulebook set down by the mother chapter in Long Beach, California. All members had to own a Harley Davidson motorcycle and go through an elaborate recruitment process. They had to pay membership fees, attend weekly meetings, go on two mandatory runs per year and contribute generously to the club's legal fund.

The chapters also had rules to follow. Each had to have a minimum of six full-patch members, including a president, a treasurer and a sergeant-at-arms. The clubhouse had to be permanent, with an area for socialising, an area for working on motorcycles and a bunkhouse to accommodate guests. A full-patch Brigand was entitled to enter and stay at any Brigands clubhouse in the world.

Beyond these rules, much depended upon a chapter's wealth. There were chapters in Argentina whose clubhouses were little more than tin sheds, while chapters like Long Beach and South Devon had custom buildings, with elaborate security, air-conditioning and accommodation that was comfortable, if unlikely to impress anyone's mother in terms of cleanliness.

The London chapter fitted between the two extremes. Its clubhouse was a canalside pub, near King's Cross station. It was bought for a few hundred pounds in the 1960s when it was surrounded by bombsites. Now its security cameras and bricked-up windows stood out amidst low-rise offices and budget hotels. Tourists occasionally wandered off the canal path to have their pictures taken in front of the painted Brigands logo and chromed bikes parked outside.

The London chapter had 24/7 security, with the cameras manned by an elderly biker called Pikey who lived in an attic room. Pikey had lost a lung to pneumonia and he wheezed as he leaned over a banister and shouted to the cramped bar downstairs.

'Paki on the intercom. Says he's here to see you, boss.'

Sealclubber stank of booze and cigarettes. He'd played poker until 3 a.m. and crashed out on a mattress on the floor of his president's office without even bothering to remove his boots.

The steel-reinforced entrance had an electronic lock and undercover officer George Khan shoved it when the intercom buzzed. The door opened into a shabby pub, the carpet black with filth and cigarette burns. The pool table and fruit machines looked new while the bar had been ripped out to make space: food and drink were free in Brigands clubhouses, although non-members who didn't slide paper money into one of the donation jars before leaving were liable to find themselves on the end of a fist or boot.

'We used to have a problem with rats in here but they walked out in disgust,' Sealclubber explained, as George stepped inside. 'I'm gonna have to ask you to strip down.'

This kind of search was standard for anyone entering a clubhouse to do business. The two other Brigands sitting at tables across the room gave evil stares as George pulled his T-shirt over his head and dropped his shorts so that Sealclubber could see there was no recording device strapped to his body.

'Leave your keys and mobile over on the table,' Sealclubber said. 'Just in case.'

He then led George through a low door off the side of the room. The walls of his office were layered thick with pinned-up photographs, newspaper clippings and scrawled messages. George was horrified by the stained mattress and knocked back by the overpowering combo of cigar smoke and Sealclubber's BO.

'Is it safe to talk here?' George asked, sitting in a wrecked armchair as Sealclubber settled behind the mounds of paperwork on his desk.

'The office is locked when I'm not here,' Sealclubber

said. 'Whole clubhouse gets swept for bugs every week and I've been doing business out of this office since eighty-three without any shit happening.'

George produced a bundle of cash from a Nike gym bag. 'It's only forty-two grand here,' he said nervously.

Sealclubber reared forward in his seat. 'Sixty-three,' he growled. 'I'm fronting you for six hundred grand and you can't even put up a ten per cent deposit?'

'I could have had it Monday,' George said. 'It's not a question of *having* the money, but of moving it around so that it doesn't get detected by money laundering controls.'

Sealclubber tutted. 'I'm going to Devon *today*. I've told my contact that I'll be bringing the full deposit in cash.'

'All I can do is apologise,' George said. 'But I'll make it right. You'll have the other twenty-one thousand by Tuesday. Then I'll pay you another five hundred for the trouble of sending an extra person down there.'

'Five hundred *plus* expenses,' Sealclubber said. 'First-class train fare and taxis, might as well call it a grand all in.'

George knew this was a shake-down, but he wasn't going to start an argument. 'I appreciate your flexibility.'

Sealclubber noticed a half drunk bottle of Rebel Yell bourbon on his desk and tipped some into a filthy tumbler. 'Your people don't drink, do they?'

'No, thank you,' George said.

'Takes all kinds,' Sealclubber smiled. 'You realise if I'm not going down with the full deposit your delivery date is going back a few days too.'

The CHERUB agents needed as much time as possible and these were the words George had come to hear.

'Shit happens,' Sealclubber said. 'But my contacts might not be as sympathetic as I am. If you delay another payment they could bump the price, or even snatch your deposit and as far as I'm concerned that's entirely between you and them. I'm just brokering this deal.'

'I know,' George nodded. 'Once the deal is done and we have a delivery date in place I'll start making arrangements for the transfers.'

Sealclubber grunted. 'The next payment will be forty per cent, as soon as we agree a delivery schedule. Then the last half on delivery.'

'I can live with that,' George said.

'Right,' Sealclubber nodded. 'I've got a bunch of people coming in before we set off and officially I'm not even supposed to let non-whites in here, so you'd better scoot.'

Before George stood up, he gave a fake cough, spat a piece of gum with a tiny listening device inside into his hand and pressed it against the underside of the chair. Out in the bar he saw that his keys and phone had been moved, and as he stepped into the sun he saw that someone had redialled his last call.

But the phone had been supplied by CHERUB and all the personal contacts and text messages inside it were fake. As soon as George was clear of the building he tapped in #611042# which turned his phone into a listening device.

As George walked along the canal bank Pikey and Sealclubber were talking.

'Forty-two grand,' Sealclubber said. 'I'm tempted not to mention this to the Führer and keep the cash.'

Pikey sounded wary. 'You don't know who these Asians are. For all we know, if you rip these guys off we're gonna have a swarm of Pakis come down from Birmingham to start a fight. Or a price on our heads.'

'He's barely a kid,' Sealclubber said.

'But who's behind him?' Pikey asked. 'The only thing we know about them is that they can lay their hands on six hundred grand. Which means they're deep in the drug trade and they're not gonna be too scared to take on a few fat blokes in leather jackets.'

'You're right,' Sealclubber laughed. 'Let's take our fifteen per cent and let South Devon deal with all the shit. You fancy coming down to Devon with us?'

'Rather keep watch here,' Pikey said. 'Bike plays merry hell with my piles these days.'

*

Rhino turned on the charm as Chloe sat across his desk and flicked through a credit agreement set in six-point text.

'It's all very reputable,' Rhino said reassuringly. 'It's a standard agreement between yourself and Midland Retail credit services.'

Chloe smiled. 'So I won't have a biker on my doorstep threatening to bust my kneecaps if I miss my payment?'

'No indeed,' Rhino laughed, as Chloe signed her name in a box. 'And twice on the back,' he added. 'And finally we need an adult's signature on young James' insurance form.'

James stood in the background and broke into a big smile as a mechanic came and wheeled his new 500cc pride and joy down a ramp to have the restrictor kit fitted. 'Make sure it *doesn't* work,' James whispered, and the mechanic gave him a wink.

'So you just moved down here?' Rhino asked.

'Split from my husband,' Chole explained. 'I got a nice fat divorce settlement and I needed to get out of London.'

'I hear that,' Rhino smiled. 'You don't look old enough for James to be your son.'

'You flatter me,' Chloe answered. 'Look at this grey hair!'

'There's a big bash at the Brigands clubhouse tonight. Would you be interested?'

Chloe knew it might help with the mission, but she was playing the ex-wife of a stockbroker and she couldn't jump at the prospect of a biker party, so she hesitated.

'Come on, let your hair down,' Rhino said cheerfully. 'When was the last time you went to a *really* crazy party?'

Chloe laughed. 'It's been a while and I'm guessing the Brigands clubhouse is livelier than a cocktail party in Primrose Hill.'

24. RIDE

'So how's your little Jap rocket?' Teeth asked, as he stood in the staff canteen, off the mezzanine between Marina Heights' two floors. The windowless space had a few tables and chairs, a fridge, sink and a coffee machine, but on a warm day everyone took their breaks outside.

'Haven't ridden it yet,' James explained. 'They're fitting the restrictor kit right now.'

'Fitting it badly, I hope,' Teeth smiled.

'Course,' James nodded.

'Your basic salary is five an hour,' Teeth explained. 'Seven quid after eight at night and eight if you work after midnight. If you have a problem with your hours *don't* leave it until the last minute to let me know. How does a full Saturday and a couple of evenings after school sound?'

'I guess,' James said. 'What'll I do?'

'Everyone starts on clean-up and odd jobs: toilets, bins, litter. Next stage is serving in one of the kiosks. The top rung is working in the diner or as a kiosk manager. You get an extra two-fifty an hour for that.'

'Cool,' James nodded. 'I've actually worked in a Deluxe Chicken before now, so I've got some experience serving customers and stuff.'

'I'll bear that in mind,' Teeth said. 'You never know.'

James remembered a few details about Teeth's past and decided to flatter his new boss. 'You look slightly familiar. Didn't you use to be a wrestler?'

Teeth broke out in a huge smile. 'How'd you know that?'

'From when I was little. You were Gumdrop McGlone, on one of those early-morning wrestling shows they used to have on the sports channel. I used to lap that up.'

'I only did three televised bouts,' Teeth smiled. 'You've got *quite* a memory.'

'Do you still wrestle now?'

'Nah,' Teeth said. 'I used to do holiday camps and stuff, but now I run Marina Heights and you can't disappear for weeks at a time during the summer season. Plus I'm a few years past my prime. I ran a club for a while teaching young 'uns boxing and wrestling moves, but I turned it in. Some guy tried to sue me after his son broke his arm. Plus they brought in all these regulations and criminal checks for people working with kids, and I've got a bit of a past.'

'Pity,' James said.

'I've got a full complement of staff today,' Teeth said, 'but I could start you off on a special job if you want to earn straight away.'

James wanted to ride his new motorbike as soon as it was ready, but putting in some hours would be more likely to impress his new boss. 'I'll do anything,' James said. 'I'm a hard worker.'

Teeth gave James a security pass, a walkie talkie and a blue boiler suit to put on, then disappeared to collect a water jet sprayer. After leading James to the underground car park below the Marina View apartments they walked between lines of expensive cars to a patch of wall covered with the partially filled outline of a graffiti tag *Eklipz 08*.

'We spotted the man with the spray can and gave him a good kicking,' Teeth explained. 'But the only way you'll get that lot off the concrete is to blast it.'

After showing James where to rig up the hose and plug in, Teeth demonstrated how to blast off the spray paint.

'Spray paint *does* shift, but concrete is porous so it takes a lot of doing,' Teeth explained. 'You're looking at a good four or five hours' work. Take a break when you're halfway through, then come and find me when you're done.'

As James took the face visor from Teeth and began blasting with the hose, the walkie talkie hooked to his waist began to crackle. '*Cleaning team one to Donut Shack,*' it announced. '*Kid puked up on the promenade. Let's get it scooped before people start treading through.*'

It was half three when James finished. The building manager's office was behind the restaurants. Teeth sat at a cluttered desk. James recognised the Führer's sixteen-year-old son Martin as he entered.

'This is the kid I was telling you about,' Teeth explained to Martin.

Martin was taller than James, but thin. He wore skinny-fit black jeans, a short-sleeve blue shirt with a thin leather tie loose at the neck and scruffy emo hair. He reached out and James shook a spindly hand.

'Hey,' Martin said. 'Having fun?'

'Spraying graffiti for four and a half hours,' James smiled. 'How could I not?'

Teeth looked at the area James had cleaned on one of the security screens behind his head. 'Looks like you did OK.'

'I hear you've got a new bike,' Martin said. 'What's it like?'

'Dunno,' James said. 'I'm itching to give it a blast.'

'We just had Martin's assistant call in sick for tonight,' Teeth explained. 'Saturday night is always busy, tonight particularly so because it's a Brigands open night. Martin needs someone to help on the crêpe kiosk between six and midnight. Have you got any plans?'

James shrugged. 'I was gonna phone my girlfriend Ashley, but nothing's fixed so I guess I could.'

'It's best to get there early,' Martin explained. 'That way I can show you the ropes and let you practise cooking before we get busy.'

'No problem,' James grinned. 'So if I'm serving food

I'd better get home and clean up and stuff.'

'Enjoy the bike,' Teeth said, as James and Martin headed outside together.

James threw his wet overalls into a locker in the staff room and belted downstairs to the Leather and Chrome garage. The mechanic recognised him from earlier and dangled the key under his nose.

'Good to go,' he smiled. 'Your mum took all the paperwork home. Just be careful, I'd feel guilty about taking that restrictor off if you wrap yourself around a tree on the way home.'

After putting his riding leathers over his shorts and T-shirt James fired up the bike. Everything about it from the weight and engine noise felt bigger than the Honda he'd arrived on that morning. He felt apprehensive as he opened the throttle and pulled away.

The Kawasaki growled as he cut down the side of the cars queuing to get out of Marina Heights. The streets were crowded with Saturday shopping traffic and James spent several minutes hemmed behind a white van in the high street. But once the traffic broke on to the A-road heading towards home he caught a break in the oncoming traffic and pulled out to accelerate.

The exhaust made a beautiful rumble and before James knew it he'd touched sixty miles an hour and had to dab the brakes to slow down as he dodged back into his own lane. He was tempted to gun the bike and see how fast he could go, but he wanted to get a feel for it, so for now he was content to roll at forty with the wind blasting him and the sun toasting his back.

'I think Teeth likes you,' Martin said, as James stood inside the crêpe kiosk wearing jeans, a white polo shirt and a Marina Heights apron.

'I recognised him from his wrestling days,' James explained, watching as Martin ladled batter on to one of the three circular hot plates used for cooking the French-style pancakes.

'He'd have *loved* you mentioning that,' Martin said, using a wide plastic paddle to spread the batter into a thin circular layer. 'The trick is to make sure there's enough fat to stop the batter sticking. Then watch until the top of the batter starts to harden. That's when you flip her over with the paddle to brown the other side.'

'It's boiling hot here,' James said, wiping the beads of sweat off his brow as he studied the tubs of ingredients and machines on all sides. Crêpe fillings ranging from banana ice cream to chilli-beef were lined up under a glass counter. Behind was a coffee and tea machine and a fridge full of cold drinks.

'You get used to the heat,' Martin said. He moved his steaming crêpe across to a plastic shelf where they added the fillings and sauces. 'OK, grab the ladle and have a try. No pressure, but the girl who called in sick tonight is worse than useless, so if you get this right you might find yourself in here permanently, rather than with your rubber-gloved mitt unclogging a toilet.'

James misted the hotplate with oil before carefully ladling out some pancake batter. As he spread it with the paddle a couple of drips ran off the side of the plate.

'You used a *bit* too much,' Martin explained, 'but it's spread nicely. Now you just need to flip it before it burns. You see how the batter glistens when it's wet? As soon as that stops, that's your cue to flip it over.'

'Ah-ha, look at the working man!' Julian laughed from the other side of the counter.

'Hey cock stain,' James said, as he glowered at Julian's curly hair and grinning face.

'Keep your eye on the hotplate,' Martin cautioned. 'Now, get the skillet under and flip her before she burns.'

'I saw you cleaning graffiti earlier,' Julian said with a superior tone as James flipped the crêpe. 'I don't have to work because *my* family aren't poor.'

'Piss off, Julian,' Martin said.

Julian grinned. 'What was that, my little gay friend? Have you come out to your daddy yet?'

'I'm not ashamed of my sexuality, Julian,' Martin said.

'Oh and I saw your new motorbike, James. I might buy an ice cream and stroll across for a proper look at it later on.'

James was determined to get his first crêpe right, but as soon as he dropped it on to the prep board he lunged across the counter so fast that Julian couldn't move back. James grabbed a handful of Julian's shirt and yanked him forward so that his face squished against the clear plastic display cabinet.

'Touch my new bike and I'll drag you over this counter and fry your head on the hotplate,' James warned, before letting go.

Julian straightened his shirt up and tried not to look flustered as he backed away. 'Have a nice night,' he grinned.

'I will,' James said. 'Especially after my shift when I'm banging your ex.'

As Julian walked away Martin cracked a big smile. 'Julian's the biggest moron. If he touches your bike again, tell Teeth. That whole car park is covered with CCTV and the Brigands have no time for people who vandalise motorbikes.'

'I'll remember that,' James nodded, as his attention turned back to his crêpe. 'So how did I do?'

'Good,' Martin said. 'It's a bit doughy in the middle because you used too much batter, and when we get a real customer I'd recommend more pleases and thank-yous and slightly less of the threatening to fry their face and shag their ex-girlfriend.'

*

The South Devon Brigands had an open night every third Saturday. For poorer chapters open nights were a way of getting people through the door and making money selling food and drugs. For the South Devon chapter it had more to do with community relations.

Closed doors, security cameras and noisy bikes scared the public, especially when Devon police regularly described the Brigands as a menace. But for many locals and tourists, their only contact with South Devon Brigands was on the open nights when the Führer put his crew on their best behaviour.

There was free food and drink, while the outdoor

compound behind the clubhouse was opened up for local kids and teenagers to have a separate party. The events were capped off with midnight fireworks, after which the public was kicked out and the clubhouse went back to being a private club.

By 9:30 the sky was dark and Marina Heights throbbed gently with rock music coming out the back of the Brigands compound. Lauren walked across the promenade with Joe, Dante, Anna and a few other mates. She had sand in her trainers after paddling on the beach and a chocolate, banana and nut crêpe burning her fingertips.

'This is good,' Lauren grinned. 'I can make better pancakes than this, but when you consider that my brother cooked it . . .'

'Your brother *definitely* didn't like it when you kept calling him *boy* and clicking your fingers,' Joe smiled.

They'd only get soft drinks in the Brigands clubhouse, so the thirteen- to fifteen-year-olds had all boozed on the beach before heading uphill to Marina Heights.

For Lauren it was a can of beer and a couple of slugs from Joe's vodka bottle. Joe and Dante were more adventurous. They were sucking breath mints and behaving themselves because they wouldn't get into the clubhouse if they were obviously drunk.

But they needn't have worried. As soon as Joe approached the clubhouse he got a hug and a pat on the back from a thuggish looking Brigands prospect named Fluffy.

'Your dad told me to send you over if you came in,'

Fluffy said. 'He's in his usual spot.'

Joe looked worried and wondered if it was to do with a letter home from school about a teacher he'd sworn at earlier in the week.

All the kids except Lauren and Dante had been in the clubhouse before. The main hall was as bland as the brick exterior. A polished wooden floor, fold-out tables piled with food, seats around the edge and a small stage with a DJ and little kids bopping in front of the disco lights. All it needed was a couple of basketball hoops and it could have passed for a secondary school gym.

The free bar was decorated with giant signs telling people to support their local Brigands by buying raffle tickets, and even with the Brigands on their best behaviour it still took a brave soul to take drinks without contributing.

Lauren's biggest surprise was a group of frail oldies by the door, tapping feet and drumming walking sticks as they sat in plastic seats or wheelchairs. They were being looked after by some of the youngest members of the Monster Bunch and Dogs of War. No biker wanted to spend his Saturday night this way, but the Führer ordered them to keep smiling because the man from the local paper was due and bikers hugging grannies made perfect publicity.

Joe had disappeared to find his dad, but came running back before his gang crossed the room to join the other youngsters outside.

Joe looked at Lauren. 'My dad wants to meet you,' he said awkwardly.

Lauren raised an eyebrow. 'Why?'

'Don't know, but he's the big cheese around here, so it's best to do what he says.'

Joe took Lauren's hand. As they cut between people standing at tables eating and a few groups of dancing women Lauren spotted Chloe on one of the leather benches around the edge of the room having an intense conversation with Rhino.

'This is her,' Joe said.

Lauren looked uncomfortable as she stood in front of circular tables and leather armchairs. The Führer was a small man, with his Hitler moustache and his long leather coat draped over the back of the chair. But you could tell he was the boss by the way the other bikers had their chairs facing towards him.

She recognised full-patch Brigands from the London and South Devon chapters, along with senior Dogs of War and more exotic guests wearing Brigands patches from Australia and South Africa.

'My son's got his first girlfriend,' the Führer roared proudly. 'And about time too.'

Teeth laughed noisily. 'Your boy Martin hasn't had one for *some* reason, has he?'

'That poof's not my son,' the Führer grumbled. 'My theory is that Marlene was being humped by the milkman just before that one was born.'

Lauren and Joe both burned red with embarrassment. The Führer pointed at the fat man sat next to him. 'You remember this man, don't you Joe? Sealclubber, President of the London chapter?'

'Course,' Joe nodded. 'Good to see you again.'

'We're just debating who has the best clubhouse,' Sealclubber said. 'Our thirty-five years of history versus your sterile brick box.'

'You gotta hand it to South Devon,' one of the other London Brigands said. 'We've got Fords while these boys are riding Mercs that they park up in garages bigger than my flat.'

'Look at my boy,' the Führer roared, making all the other bikers-laugh. 'I've never seen Joe so quiet. Why so shy, son? Tell your girl to come here and give her future father-in-law a kiss.'

Lauren stepped up nervously and pecked the Führer on the cheek. He smelled of some weird aftershave, but Sealclubber's rank odour was competing. The Führer made a big gesture of pulling out his wallet and giving Joe two twenties.

'Show her a good time,' the Führer grinned. 'You're beautiful, Lauren, it was good to meet you.'

Joe took the money, then turned anxiously to Lauren as they walked away. 'I'm *so* sorry,' he grovelled. 'I had no idea that my dad was gonna make me do that.'

'I've survived worse,' Lauren shrugged.

As if to prove this, the Führer stood up, punched the air and shouted so that half the room could hear. 'Go on my son, give her one from me!'

The Brigands all roared with laughter as a blushing Lauren and Joe dashed across the floor to meet their friends outside.

25. SCOUTS

Twelve nights after first working the crêpe stand, James had mastered the circular hotplates, knew how to make cappuccinos and lattes without burning his fingertips on the steam nozzle and how to look busy when Teeth or one of the other managers came by wanting an extra hand to wipe tables or empty bins.

James had become friendly with his new boss Martin. Getting a job alongside the Führer's sixteen-year-old son had been an unexpected bonus, but Martin kept distant from his old man and despite hours of conversation inside the kiosk James hadn't picked up any useful information.

Martin had been badly bullied at school because he was gay. He'd dropped out before taking GCSEs and worked on the crêpe stand seven days a week saving up to travel the world with a friend.

The Führer wasn't proud of having a homosexual son, but Martin's mum Marlene protected him and the family name counted for something: as a kiosk manager Martin earned decent money, and compared to the much busier diner or the fish and chip stand the crêperie was a doddle.

'So how's it going with Ashley?' Martin asked. It was just after eight and the sky was orange. He stood on the pavement outside the kiosk, smoking a hand-rolled cigarette. James was inside, leaning on the counter and trying to cool down in the blast of a small plastic fan mounted atop the drinks cooler.

'She's nice,' James said. 'A good laugh.'

'Gettin' any action?'

'No such luck,' James sighed. 'She might smoke a lot of dope on Saturday night, but she goes to confession on Sunday morning and her parents have indoctrinated her with all that love and marriage bullcrap.'

Martin laughed as he flicked his cigarette end over the edge of the promenade and stepped into the stiflingly hot kiosk. 'At least I'm not the only one suffering from sexual frustration then,' he smiled.

James broke into a big grin. 'Tell you what, bend over the counter, pull your trackies down and I'll sort you out.'

'Oh I wish!' Martin said, putting on his campest voice.

James turned around to hear a fifty pence being tapped on the counter top. A thirty-something mum holding a little girl stood at the counter frowning.

'I don't think that talk's appropriate, do you?' she said irritably.

'Yeah, sorry,' James said, clearing his throat and putting his hand over his mouth to disguise a smirk. 'What would you like?'

'Do you sell ice cream?'

James shook his head and pointed out the front of the kiosk to a queue of people. 'Two along,' he explained.

The woman pointed to the tubs of ice cream. 'What's that then?'

'If you want it in a hot crêpe, I'm your man,' James said.

'They're fresh cooked, very nice,' Martin added. 'But if you want ice cream we don't have cornets or anything to put them in.'

'You could put a scoop in a cardboard coffee cup.'

James and Martin exchanged glances. 'Can't,' Martin said. 'There's no button on the till.'

The woman shook her head. 'I'm sure you'd be a lot busier if you sold ice cream,' she said, before reluctantly heading over to join the queue two kiosks over.

'And that's *exactly* why we don't sell it, you dippy tart,' Martin said, as he yawned and stretched theatrically.

'Now you've had your smoke, you mind if I take a break?' James asked.

'Dead here,' Martin said, as he checked his watch. 'Take half an hour, but check back just in case I get busy.'

'Cheers, boss,' James smiled, and opened the kiosk door.

But he only made five steps before his smile got wiped

by a woman called Noelene. She had *duty manager* embroidered on a tight-fitting red polo shirt and she had the kind of sparkly, upbeat, hard working attitude that made her teenage workers hate her guts.

'Where you going, James?' she asked, with a heavy New Zealand accent.

If James had engaged his brain he would have told Noelene that he was going to the larder fridge behind the diner to get fresh pancake batter or ice cream, but instead he mumbled weakly about going for a ten-minute break.

'Oh no you're not, sweetie pie,' she grinned as she pointed into the diner with painted nails that matched her shirt. 'I've got a big food order needs taking over to the Brigands clubhouse, right now. And look around and see how busy we are: there's a dozen or more tables need cleaning. Do you think it's right to swan off on a break when your co-workers are busy?'

James huffed. 'I'll go get the food.'

'I don't like your attitude, Mr Raven,' Noelene said as James sauntered towards the restaurant. 'And pull your trousers up so that I can't see your underwear. This isn't a skateboard rink.'

Skateboard park, you fat arse, James thought to himself. He stepped into the restaurant. The diner bustled with noise, and James nodded to a couple of Lauren and Dante's mates as his nose caught the smell of frying oil and pickles. There was a two-tier serving trolley stacked with donut boxes, fried chicken, burgers and also foil dishes from the Chinese restaurant at the upmarket end of the promenade.

A black chef came out of the kitchen and squeezed on three large pizza boxes. 'Better run with that,' he grinned. 'You serve cold food to the Brigands and they might just stick a boot in your arse.'

'Gotcha,' James said.

The clubhouse wasn't far, but it was only when James got outside that he realised he couldn't take the trolley downstairs. He had to take a tortuous route down a long disabled ramp at the front of the building and then walk all the way around the shops before going back to the clubhouse at the rear.

Five minutes had passed by the time he'd got inside the clubhouse and crossed the deserted main hall. A few Brigands prospects, girlfriends and members of puppet gangs sat at the clustered tables where Lauren had been embarrassed by the Führer two Saturdays earlier. The full-patch members were meeting in a back room and James felt anxious as he knocked.

The door opened and the Führer roared 'Boy!' from his seat at the head of the table.

Cigarette smoke curled up towards the ceiling. More than twenty Brigands sat in walnut-trimmed leather chairs. It could have been a corporate boardroom, but for their clothes and the array of medieval weapons and torture implements displayed along the side wall.

The trolley wheels dug into thick green carpet as James pushed it towards the Führer. He recognised Teeth and noted the presence of Sealclubber and two other London Brigands, which almost certainly meant that they'd brought the next forty per cent instalment of the money for the weapons deal.

James was freaked as the Führer stood up, ripped a twenty-centimetre blade out of his boot and stepped up to face James off.

'Is this everything we ordered?' he demanded. 'Is it *piping* hot?'

To James' alarm, another Brigand stood up behind him and pulled an even bigger knife. 'I didn't cook it,' James bumbled. 'But I ran over here as fast as I could.'

He tried to rationalise that even the Brigands wouldn't randomly stab some teenager who'd been sent to deliver their food, but it still wasn't easy to feel comfortable being hemmed in by two crazy men holding out huge knives.

The Führer flipped open a pizza box, skewered a slice of Hawaiian with the end of his blade and took a bite off the end.

'Tepid,' the Führer complained, and grabbed James' Marina Heights polo shirt.

The other Brigands all hissed. 'Kill the delivery boy,' one shouted, but a few were giggling which pretty much gave the game away.

The Führer held the knife at head height, right in front of James' eyes. 'This time I'll show you mercy, but next time you bring my food you'd *better* be out of breath.'

As the Führer said this, he plunged the knife into the plaster behind James' head and let the handle go. As James backed away from the swaying knife, the Brigand standing behind told James to cup his hands, then passed over a pile of coins and a couple of five-pound notes. James guessed it was at least twenty quid.

'Your tip,' the Brigand explained.

'You didn't handle yourself too badly either,' the Führer laughed. 'Remember that kid we had down on his knees, begging us not to kill him?'

Laughter rolled around the room as James quickly transferred all of the food boxes on to the table and backed towards the door with his empty trolley. When he got out of the room all the drinkers sitting at the tables were looking his way.

'They give you a hard time?' smiled a sweet-looking woman in a tight pink top. 'They like having their fun when a new delivery boy comes through the door.'

James didn't appreciate having a roomful of leather-clad nutters waving knives in his face, but his job was to make friends with as many bikers as he could and that meant he had to find their jokes funny. He nodded, smiled and acted like it was no big deal as he pushed the empty trolley towards the exit.

When he was almost at the main door a vaguely familiar face emerged from the gents in front of him. He wore an odd mix of studenty-retro clothes, including tight black cords, a long scarf and a three-quarter-length leather jacket with a Monster Bunch patch on the back. James nodded to him.

'Are you James?' the man asked. 'I'm Nigel's brother.'

James saw the resemblance as they shook hands. 'It's Will, right? Back from uni?'

'Got home yesterday morning,' Will said. 'My brother said you were interested in running your bike up to Cambridge for the Rebel Tea Party.'

James nodded. 'I'd love to give her a proper run, but Nigel's only got two-fifty cc so I guess it's a non-starter.'

Will shrugged. 'I offered Nigel a ride in my mate's car, but he says he's got something going on this weekend anyway. He says you're cool though, so you can ride behind the Monster Bunch if you like. I can't be your nursemaid, but I'll introduce you to lots of faces and once you get known by the other members, who knows where it'll lead?'

James wanted to go on the run, not just for the good of the mission but also as an excuse to take a long ride on his bike. 'Sounds really great,' he smiled, while trying not to sound too excited. 'I'll have to clear it with my mum but I'm sure she'll be cool.'

26. TEXT

Lauren, Joe, Dante and Anna spent most of their spare time hanging together. They'd taken the train to Exeter to go shopping, they'd been to the cinema and Joe even spent a Sunday morning at the beach trying to teach Lauren how to surf. On weekdays things were more mundane: going to school and doing homework together afterwards.

If the weather was good they'd go to the beach most evenings, usually hanging with other kids from school in a rowdy group that caused strolling couples to cross the street to avoid them. After the beach they'd walk up to Marina Heights and get something to eat from the kiosks.

The road between the beach and Marina Heights was paved, but it zigzagged to minimise the slope. The kids always took a more direct route, cutting across sandbanks, ignoring a *falling rocks* sign, hopping over a wall and then scrambling up a steep pathway.

There had been accidents over the years and several kids, including Joe, were banned by their mums but used the path anyway. Girls could excuse themselves if they had heels or sandals on, but any boy taking the safe route left himself open to merciless ribbing.

As usual, the boys had raced ahead taking precarious shortcuts, shoving each other and making loads of noise. Lauren and Anna walked the path with three other girls, placing their trainers carefully on the crumbling earth and talking about a handsome student art teacher.

'Everyone fancies Mr Zipf,' Anna noted. 'But he's kind of gross. I mean the way he flirts with that group of Year Eleven girls is blatant.'

'He's a man though,' Lauren said. 'All men are basically hairy balls of sperm.'

Lauren's friends all laughed.

'I'd rather have your brother James than Mr Zipf,' a girl called Penny said. 'He can make me a crêpe any day.'

'It's the apron,' Anna nodded. 'Guys in aprons are sexy.'

'Don't talk about my brother like that,' Lauren shuddered. 'Eww.'

Dante, Joe and two other boys were sitting on a roadside crash barrier at the top of the path about fifteen metres further up.

'I'm starving,' Dante complained. 'Move those fat cans, you skanks.'

Before Lauren could return the abuse she was distracted by a text message from Rat: *Can we AT LEAST talk?*

Lauren wasn't sure if she was going to make up with Rat when she got back to campus, but she *had* decided to make him sweat and deleted the message without replying.

Once the nine kids had stepped over the crash barrier, they crossed Marina Heights' single-lane exit road, then ran up a grass embankment and on to the promenade. One of Joe's mates risked the wrath of the security staff by taking a run and shooting off on his skateboard.

'Show off,' Joe said, as he tried to slip his arm around Lauren's back. But Anna grabbed Lauren's arm and tugged her out of reach.

'We need the bathroom,' Anna said forcefully. 'See you upstairs by the kiosks, boys.'

'Where are we going?' Lauren asked.

'Undo your buttons,' Anna said. 'Show some cleavage.'

Lauren realised they were heading towards Anna's brother Nigel and his friend Julian. 'Why?' she asked.

'I need to borrow money off Nigel,' Anna explained. 'And it's been scientifically proven that a boy's IQ drops by thirty points when he can see breasts.'

'What's wrong with *your* breasts?' Lauren said indignantly.

'Nigel's my brother!' Anna said. 'That'd be creepy.'

Lauren reluctantly undid the top two buttons of her shirt as they approached Julian and Nigel, who seemed to be involved in an intense debate.

'You don't need the money,' Julian said to Nigel. 'I'll pay you back.'

'I need someone with a car,' Nigel said. 'Come on, I'll wipe half your debt and front you half an ounce of spliff on credit. That's a *bloody* good deal.'

'I don't know,' Julian said, shaking his curly locks. 'Gimme a second.'

Lauren realised that a biker associate like Nigel talking about money and cars might be an interesting lead. Unfortunately Anna interrupted them.

'Hey, Nigel,' she said sweetly.

'Piss *off*, Anna,' Nigel snapped. 'I already told you, I'm not lending you money.'

'Come *on*,' Anna begged. 'I'm so broke.'

Nigel looked at Lauren. 'You've got half your shirt buttons undone,' he smiled. 'You'll have a bunch of pervs ogling you.'

Anna thumped her brother on the arm as Lauren sheepishly did her buttons up. 'Nigel, if you don't lend me twenty quid, I'm gonna tell Mum where you keep your stash and that you're skipping school tomorrow to deliver something very naughty with Curly there.'

Nigel scowled at his sister. 'How'd you know about that?'

Anna grinned. 'Well, if you take a message on the pad beside the telephone and write with a biro, you can read every word on the next sheet.'

'Oh *shit*,' Nigel gasped. '*Please* tell me you tore that off before Mum saw it.'

Anna smiled. 'Of course I did,' she said. 'Because brothers and sisters help one another out when they need each other, *don't* they?'

Nigel reluctantly pulled his wallet from the back of his jeans and handed Anna two ten-pound notes.

'Can I keep it?' Anna asked.

'I've gotta go, Nige,' Julian said, as he backed away.

'No you don't, you slippery eel,' Nigel said, grabbing Julian by the arm. 'I'm not bullshitting, Julian. If you go back on what you promised I'm in the shit, and if you do, I'm selling your debt to Dirty Dave. See what happens if you don't pay him what you owe.'

Lauren was intrigued by Julian and Nigel's mysterious and illegal activity, but Anna only cared about the money. 'Can I keep it?' she repeated, giving her sweetest *little sister* smile.

'Keep it,' Nigel groaned. 'And Lauren, I won't be in school tomorrow. Can you tell James to get me the homework sheets from my maths class tomorrow morning?'

'Sure,' Lauren nodded.

'Oh I *do* love shaking down my big brothers,' Anna grinned.

'Fine, I'll do it,' Julian hissed at Nigel. 'Just let go of me, you dick.'

Lauren was struggling to work out what Nigel and Julian were up to and she pumped Anna for info as they headed upstairs to meet up with the boys.

'What's your brother doing tomorrow?' Lauren asked.

'Dunno exactly,' Anna shrugged. 'All I know is that some Brigand wants him to deliver something in Bristol. Julian was supposed to take him in his car, but he welched at the last minute.'

Asking too many direct questions might seem suspicious, so Lauren tried a different tack. 'What if your brother ends up in prison or something?'

'He probably will,' Anna said matter of factly, before cracking a smile. 'Which means I can have the big bedroom.'

Lauren laughed. 'You're cruel! But seriously? Is he into a lot of shit?'

'He might be,' Anna said, as they reached the top of the stairs. 'Probably deeper than my older brother Will, truth told. And yes I do get scared, but I can't run my brother's life and what's the point worrying about things you can't control?'

The information was too fresh for Lauren to have worked out all the consequences, but she needed to tell Chloe as soon as possible.

'Back in a second,' Lauren said, as she saw James standing in the crêperie. 'I'll go tell my brother about that worksheet thing before I forget.'

Martin was outside clearing tables, so Lauren explained as much as she could while James cooked a pair of chocolate orange and pineapple crêpes and only charged her for one.

'The car is what makes it interesting,' James said. 'Nigel's a small-time drug dealer and you don't need a car to deliver a few bags of cannabis.'

'I'm going back over to try getting more info out of Anna,' Lauren said, as she grabbed the two hot crêpes in their cardboard trays. 'Can you disappear for a few minutes and go phone Chloe?'

'I've got Noelene trying to bite a chunk out of my arse, but I'll try,' James said.

James phoned Chloe from the seclusion of Marina Heights' disabled bathroom. She sounded positive about the information and said she'd call Ross Johnson and let him know what they'd decided to do. Ten minutes before his shift in the crêperie ended, Chloe called and said she was waiting in the car park.

'Eww,' Chloe said, as James climbed into the Range Rover beside her and closed the door. 'You can smell that pancake batter on your clothes.'

'Ashley moans about that as well,' James nodded.

'Does your Marina Heights security pass get you down into the car park under Marina View?' Chloe asked as she placed a small paper bag in James' lap.

'Sure,' James nodded. He unravelled the bag. It contained a black box with two buttons, a screw-top jar filled with brown gloop, a device that looked like a staple gun and a smaller grey box.

'You recognise everything in the bag?' Chloe asked.

'Except the brown stuff,' James said.

'It's mud from our garden mixed with a couple of egg yolks to make it dry on hard. Rub it on the number plate.'

'Gotcha,' James said. 'By the way, I saw Sealclubber in the clubhouse with the Führer earlier, so I'm guessing that they came down with George's two hundred and fifty grand.'

Chloe nodded. 'George had a meeting in London before Sealclubber left. He said that his first batch of weapons will be delivered within a week.'

'So what's the plan for Nigel and Julian's trip?'

'Neil Gauche and one of our junior mission control staff will tail Julian's car. We'll also have backup from Devon police. Neil will listen to the conversations inside the car and decide whether to pull them over.'

'Right,' James said, as he popped the door open. 'I'll sort this lot out and see you back at home.'

Chloe nodded. 'You'd better clear out, I'm supposed to pick up Lauren and Dante and a couple of their friends in five minutes.'

James hopped out of the Range Rover and walked briskly along the promenade. It was ten past ten, so while the restaurants and bars upstairs were still moderately busy, the shops were all closed and the lower floor was deserted apart from a cleaning crew and a young couple making out on the grass verge between two rose bushes.

James swiped his security pass at a recessed door between two shop fronts and walked down a corridor that ran behind the shops. The floor and walls were bare concrete, and pipes and electrical cables hung from the ceiling centimetres above his head.

He'd only been down here once before, on his first day when Teeth took him to blast graffiti. A door at the end of the corridor opened on to a set of metal steps. These led down into the secure parking area beneath the Marina View apartments where Julian lived.

Each parking bay was assigned to a specific apartment, so James easily found Julian's red Fiat parked next to a Jaguar XF that belonged to his father. James knew that one security man watched the whole Marina Heights complex, so his concern was being detected by a civilian rather than by the CCTV cameras at the end of each line of cars.

James pulled the small black box from his jeans and pressed the button. Chloe had pre-programmed the device to send out a master radio frequency that would unlock Julian's car. James was reassured by a flash of Julian's indicator lights.

With the car unlocked, James opened the door and sat in the driver's seat. He used the staple gun-type device to fire three needle-sized bugs into the fabric-lined roof before stepping outside. He took a wary glance over his shoulder before using the plipper to relock the car.

Next he crouched down by the front tyre, reached under the wheel arch and fitted the magnetic grey box. This acted as a remote tracking device and as a signal amplifier for the tiny bugs inside the car.

James' final task was the messiest. He unscrewed the lid on the pot of egg yolk and mud, then dipped in two fingers and spattered it on the front number plate, obscuring three letters. Because the bumper was up against the car-park wall, there was no way Julian would see this when he drove off.

James wiped his fingers on a crêperie napkin and dropped it inside the paper bag before standing up and walking back to the stairs. He said hello to a cleaner in the corridor, before heading into the staff locker room to grab his helmet and riding gear.

Before zipping his leather riding jacket he pulled out his phone and sent Chloe a text message: *Job done!*

27. STAGED

Friday

Julian and Nigel set off from Marina View at half-eight, blissfully unaware that two cars were tailing them from a kilometre behind. One was a Devon police vehicle containing two uniformed officers. The second car was unmarked. From inside, NPBTF officer Neil Gauche and burly assistant CHERUB mission controller Jake McEwen listened to every word Julian and Nigel said.

Nigel's drug dealing and Julian's role as an indebted customer regularly brought the two seventeen-year-olds into conflict, but their friendship ran back to primary school and as Julian drove they reminisced about sleepovers, birthday parties, boy scouts and PS2 games.

The A38 was busy but the traffic moved freely. It took eighty minutes to reach Exeter and the beginning of the

M5 motorway. Julian kept the Fiat in the middle of three lanes and the needle glued on seventy miles per hour.

'How's things with Caitlyn?' Julian asked, as he overtook a truck. It was a bright day. The Smiths *How Soon is Now?* was coming out of the radio, but mostly drowned out by the engine noise.

'Caitlyn's wild,' Nigel smiled. 'Smokes most of my profits, but I'm being compensated in other ways, if you get my meaning.'

'You hang with James Raven much?' Julian asked.

'I spend most of my time with Caitlyn, but I see him around. He's bloody clever, you know? He spent a couple of hours sorting out some maths stuff that I couldn't get my head around.'

'I messed it up with Ashley,' Julian admitted.

Nigel nodded. 'Get all macho when someone hits on your bitch and you'd better be pretty sure that he's not a third dan Karate black belt and kickboxing expert.'

'No bullshit?' Julian asked.

'Well that's what he claims and he looks the business,' Nigel smiled. 'So I've got no intention of finding out.'

'Jesus Christ,' Julian moaned, as he thumped the steering wheel. 'What are the odds on this?'

Nigel looked over his shoulder and realised they were being flashed by a police BMW. 'Were you speeding?'

Julian pointed at the speedometer. 'Seventy, dead on.'

'It's probably just routine,' Nigel said. 'Pull over and play it cool.'

Julian had only been driving six months and racked his brain trying to think what he'd done wrong. It took a half mile for a break to open up on the inside lane. He pulled across behind a Shell tanker and into the hard shoulder.

When he'd completely stopped, a tannoy blasted out from between the flashing blue lights in the cop car's radiator. 'Turn off your engine and place your hands on the steering wheel.'

One officer stayed at the wheel of the patrol car, while the Asian officer on the passenger side got out and walked towards the Fiat. Nigel rolled down his window, and the officer crouched down and spoke across him to Julian.

'Do you know why you were stopped?'

Julian shook his head. 'I was doing seventy, dead on. There were cars whizzing past me in the fast lane.'

The officer shook his head. 'I want you to step carefully from your vehicle, then come around to the front with me. Bring your licence and vehicle papers with you.'

Trucks and coaches thundered by in the lane alongside as Julian opened his door and edged out. His jaw dropped as he saw the mud obscuring three letters of his number plate.

'I had no idea,' he gasped. 'It must have sprayed off the back of another car, or something.'

The policeman gently scraped the mud with the tip of his boot and shook his head. 'That's dried on hard. I'd say it's been there for a day or two.'

'I've got a window scraper,' Julian said. 'I can take it right off.'

'You do that, but I've still got to write you a ticket.'

Julian looked surprised. 'For a muddy number plate?'

'Zero tolerance,' the cop explained. 'We get a lot of people trying to pull that stunt to avoid getting detected by speed cameras.'

As the cop said this, his colleague came running across from the car. 'The number plate runs clean,' he said, before whispering something in the Asian officer's ear.

The Asian studied Julian's licence and eyed him suspiciously. 'Where did you come from this morning?'

'Salcombe,' Julian said.

'You're not in school today?'

'It's a study day.'

The officer smiled. 'Doesn't look much like studying to me. Where are you headed?'

'Bristol,' Julian answered. 'Visiting friends.'

'There was a serious incident at Exeter airport this morning,' the officer said. 'Two young males were involved in a violent theft and left the airport in a red hatchback. Have you got anything to say about that?'

'Would you object if we searched your car?' the other officer said, as he looked in the back at a pile of cardboard boxes marked *Josie's Florist*.

Julian raised his hands anxiously. 'That's got *nothing* to do with us.'

The traffic was too noisy for Nigel to pick up words, but his heart fluttered as he saw Julian's increasingly nervous body language.

The white police officer spoke into his radio,

explaining what he'd found and asking for more details on the suspects. But the airport incident was a fiction, created to give the officers the *reasonable grounds* they needed to legally search someone's car.

'Suspects described as two men, eighteen to twenty,' the officer explained to his colleague, as he pocketed the radio. 'One dark hair, one blond.'

The Asian officer raised one eyebrow and looked at Julian. 'Are you sure you're telling the truth?'

Julian shook his head violently. 'This is *utter* crap. I'm seventeen and I've not been anywhere near the airport.'

'Don't worry then,' the Asian man said soothingly. 'We need your permission to quickly search the car.'

'What if I refuse?' Julian asked.

'It was a serious incident,' the officer explained. 'We have to arrest you if you refuse, but once that happens there's a whole procedure to follow. Instead of a few minutes, you could be held up for hours.'

Julian reluctantly passed his car keys to the Asian officer, who told Nigel to step out and stand with his hands on the roof before walking around and opening the boot. The five long florist's boxes were stacked up and the officer immediately noticed that their weight had crushed the box at the bottom.

Suspicious, he pulled a plastic glove over his right hand before lifting the flap that held the cardboard lid in place. His eyes widened as the lid popped up, revealing four partially assembled AK47 assault rifles.

*

Twenty minutes later, Julian and Nigel found themselves stripped of shoes and belts, sitting in front of a desk in an interrogation room with their hands cuffed behind their backs.

'I demand a lawyer,' Julian shouted, as Jake McEwen walked into the room and slammed the door. 'I'm a juvenile. I have special rights.'

'The only right you have is to shut your pie hole before I stick your stupid curly head through the wall,' McEwen yelled.

McEwen was a twenty-two-year-old ex-CHERUB agent. His official job title was junior mission controller. Most of the time he worked on campus, researching mission backgrounds, writing briefings and doing all the stuff his more senior colleagues didn't want to. But McEwen's aggressive manner and a heavyweight boxer's physique meant he got an occasional trip off campus when CHERUB wanted to scare someone.

'You two boys are in deep shit,' McEwen boomed. 'How old are you, sixteen, seventeen?'

'Seventeen,' Nigel answered.

Julian turned towards Nigel. 'This is an illegal interrogation. We should have lawyers present. You should be running a tape recorder.'

McEwen walked behind Julian and smacked his head against the table top.

'I'm lodging a complaint,' Julian moaned. 'My father is a judge. This violates my human rights!'

'Every time you use the word *rights* from now on, I'm gonna bang your head against the table top,' McEwen shouted. 'This is an office building, not a police station. I'm with the intelligence service, not the police. And by the time you lodge your official complaint, this room will be stripped bare. You'll have no way to trace me and the two officers who stopped your car will deny all knowledge. To summarise: you two need to get used to the idea that I am god.'

Nigel and Julian looked warily at one another.

'Do you know how this would have played out if we'd done things by the book?' McEwen smiled. 'We arrest you. The Brigands send in some smart lawyer who tells you to keep your mouths shut. You claim that you had no knowledge of what was in the boxes. You plead guilty to a minor firearms charge in court and because you're nice middle-class boys with no previous convictions you get three to six months in a young offenders'. When you get out the Führer gives you a few grand as a thank you for keeping your mouths shut.'

'You can't ignore the law, buddy,' Julian said.

'I'm not your buddy,' McEwen shouted, as he picked Julian out of his chair, lifted him high into the air and slammed his body down hard on the table top. 'And you'd better learn to shut your mouth.'

Julian sniffled as he slid back into his chair with blood dripping out of his nose.

'You've got two options,' McEwen said, crouching down low behind Julian and Nigel. 'You're just a couple of kids working as couriers, we're not really interested in you. What we want is information: who supplied you with the guns, who and where you're meeting, how much you're being paid and where you take the money. Plus anything else you think we might like to know. If you give us the information, we'll let you get back in your little Fiat. You can make your delivery and as long as you're honest we'll pretend like this little stop-and-search never happened.'

'If the Brigands found out we'd grassed, they'd kill us,' Nigel said warily.

'They won't,' McEwen said. 'As long as you're not economical with the truth.'

'So what's the other option?' Nigel asked.

McEwen cracked a big smile. 'Like I said, we're not really interested in busting a couple of teenage couriers. So what we'll do is, we'll confiscate your guns as evidence. Then we'll keep you here for five or six hours and escort you back to Salcombe in the Fiat.'

It took a few seconds for the implications of this to hit the two young suspects. 'They'll think we stole the guns,' Nigel blurted. 'Or at the least they'll torture the shit out of us trying to find out what happened.'

McEwen laughed. 'You can tell them about me,' he grinned. 'How you were arrested by a secret agent, who took you to a secret location and then let you off with no charge whatsoever. I'm sure they'll believe you.'

Nigel pressed his hands against his head. 'They'll never believe that story.'

McEwen raised his eyebrows. 'You think, buddy?'

'This is outrageous,' Julian sighed. 'In a democratic society . . .'

Nigel turned sharply towards his friend. 'Stop going

on about your rights. This isn't A-level sociology, you dick.'

'*I'm* a dick?' Julian spluttered indignantly. 'Did I set this up? I must be mad getting involved in this just to pay off a two-hundred-quid debt.'

'Ladies,' McEwen said firmly. 'Stop bitching and whining. It's decision time.'

'Can I get a tissue or something?' Julian asked, as he pinched his bloody nose.

'It's all down to me really,' Nigel said, as he looked at Julian. 'I set it up, he's just driving me as a favour.'

'Like I give a shit about you two,' McEwen said. He tossed Julian a couple of tissues and pulled out a tape recorder. 'Are you ready to start answering some questions?'

Julian dabbed his nose as Nigel nodded reluctantly. 'Like we've got a choice in the matter,' he grunted.

'OK, we'll take it from the top,' McEwen said. 'Speak slowly into the tape recorder. Spell out any difficult names and remember if you tell me any pork pies I'll be paying you another visit. Who first contacted you asking you to deliver the guns?'

28. RUN

Saturday

The run to the Rebel Tea Party in Cambridge was due to leave the Brigands clubhouse at nine. By 8:40 residents who'd paid between one and three million for their Marina View apartments were waking up to bright sunshine and a hundred motorcycle engines.

The beginning of a run was a spectacle. Riders made last-minute checks on oil and tyre pressure, while a few with problems made adjustments in the Leather and Chrome workshop. Girlfriends and kids said goodbye, some waiting to wave the run off, others boarding one of the three coaches packed with luggage, booze and barbecue equipment.

Dante, Lauren and Chloe had driven out to see James off. James was excited, but also a little scared. He'd never ridden a bike over a long distance and he urgently needed to start making connections with older bikers if he was going to be of any use to the mission.

While James wandered off to report to the Brigands road captain and get his place in the running order, Lauren spotted Joe standing in the middle of the Brigands bikes with his parents. The Führer looked like he always did, except his long leather coat had been swapped for a shorter version more suited to riding on a hot day. But Joe's mum had transformed from her usual Marks and Spencer cardigans into a biker chick. She wore a leather jacket with *Property of South Devon Brigands* on the back, a Lycra top that finished several inches above her flabby stomach, tight fitting jeans and red stiletto heels.

'You look amazing,' Lauren gushed.

'Embarrassing, more like,' Joe scoffed.

The Führer kissed his wife before giving Joe a friendly swipe around the back of the head. 'She's the most beautiful girl in the world.'

Lauren smiled at Marlene. 'Do you always go on the runs?'

'Never missed one,' she grinned, as she gave Joe a huge kiss. 'Even when I was pregnant with this little yobbo.'

'Mum,' Joe complained, frantically wiping lipstick off his cheek. 'I'm outta here.'

Marlene wagged her finger in Joe's face. 'Your brother is in charge and don't you dare start fighting with him or you'll be spending the next run at your grandma's house.'

'I'll be good,' Joe grinned. 'I'm *always* good.'

'Yeah, sure,' Marlene said. She looked at Lauren. 'You two have a nice time and I'll see you Sunday night.'

Joe and Lauren walked away from the bikes and headed up to the diner, which had opened early for the bikers and was doing a roaring trade in bacon sandwiches and breakfast muffins.

'Freeeeeeeedom!' Joe grinned, as he kissed Lauren's cheek. 'This is gonna be the best weekend in history.'

A few metres from the Führer, James was trying to get the attention of a Brigand called Vomit. Vomit was unusually clean-cut for a Brigand, with a shaved head, designer sunglasses and boot-cut Diesel jeans instead of the standard Levis. As South Devon road captain, Vomit's job was to organise every detail of the chapter's road trips, from the running order of the bikes, to food, accommodation, coaches and the breakdown truck.

He held a clipboard and looked stressed as James pushed between a couple of leather jackets.

'Raven, James,' Vomit said, as he reached down into a canvas bag and pulled out a set of notes, which had all been laminated in case it rained. 'You're running dead last with a young Monster Bunch hang-around called Orange Bob.'

James nodded as Vomit handed over the paperwork.

'On there you've got your route map in case you get lost, your entry ticket for the Rebel Tea Party, plus emergency phone numbers for the breakdown truck, for me and for our lawyers. Don't call any of those numbers unless you *really* need them.'

'Gotcha,' James nodded. 'Thanks.'

Vomit slapped James on the back. 'Ride safely, have a great weekend.'

Orange Bob was a skinny nineteen-year-old who'd earned his name because of a taste for fake-tanning products. James found him by asking Nigel's brother Will and they shook hands.

'Hey partner,' James grinned.

Vomit began shouting for the riders to start lining up. There was a rash of last-minute kisses and goodbyes before non-riders backed off to the kerb. James found his ER5 and weaved through bikes going in all directions, ending up the very last of one hundred and six bikes lined up side by side.

There was a strict hierarchy, with all the riders going in pairs. The run was led by the Führer and his road captain. Behind them were the other Brigands officers, including Teeth, then the regular full-patch members and then Brigands prospect members.

After the Brigands, there came riders from the Dogs of War and then the Monster Bunch (these two puppet gangs had equal status and a coin was flipped to see who rode first). The final group were riders who didn't belong to a club. They ranged from long-term Brigand allies like Rhino, to kids like James and even a few wives and girlfriends who were barred from club membership but wanted to ride rather than sit on a coach.

On the stroke of nine Vomit blasted an air horn. The Führer gunned his throttle and pulled out of line. Vomit came next, pulling alongside. Teeth was the first rider in the second row and so on, as the bikes pulled off at two-second intervals.

It would have been easier for the bikes to line up in pairs, but starting a run by blasting out of line was an outlaw biker tradition that required good throttle control and timing. Done properly it was a ballet of engine noise and tyre smoke, but one rider skidding, stalling or otherwise messing up could result in mangled bikes, a broken riding formation and a probable kicking for the rider who screwed up. James' bottom-of-the-pack status meant that he only had to worry about dropping in alongside Orange Bob. He flipped down his helmet visor and gave Chloe and Dante a quick thumbs-up as the bikes in front pulled off.

James got away fine, but was surprised to find two late-arriving Dogs of War pulling into formation behind him. He'd got used to riding his new bike in traffic, but it was a different skill to stay in formation, with Orange Bob on his left, two bikes less than four metres in front and two more the same distance behind.

After they'd left Salcombe and reached the A38 the bikes sped up until the hedges along the roadside blurred. Even through a helmet the noise was deafening. People stared out of cars coming in the other direction and James felt exhilarated, but at the same time scared by the speed and the knowledge that it would only take a rider braking too hard, or a tyre catching in a pothole to turn the roaring formation into tangled metal.

*

McEwen's interrogation of Nigel and Julian the previous day had revealed many facts. The most important were the identity of a Newcastle-based drug cartel that was taking delivery of the assault rifles and the name of Paul Woodhead, who'd paid Nigel and told him where to collect the weapons.

Woodhead was an inactive South Devon Brigand. He'd retired after a riding accident and moved to a remote cottage near Dartmouth, twenty kilometres north east of Salcombe. He'd been off police radar for more than a decade and his emergence as an element of the Führer's weapons smuggling operations was a major breakthrough.

This information was useful, but McEwen suspected Nigel wasn't telling him *everything* he knew. McEwen would have liked to spend more time on the interrogation, but Nigel and Julian had to be released or they'd fail to make their delivery in Bristol and the Brigands would become suspicious.

While the boys were under interrogation, Neil Gauche had fitted listening devices inside their mobile telephones and wallets. Nigel told McEwen that they would meet with Paul Woodhead on Saturday morning to receive their payment for the delivery. McEwen planned to follow them to their rendezvous and listen in, hoping that he might glean information on future deliveries and in particular the huge order made by undercover officer George Khan through the London Brigands.

With his beard gone, his hair cropped and the

Brigands out of town Neil Gauche felt reasonably safe parked in a street directly below Marina Heights. The bug in Julian's wallet picked up a muffled version of the teenager's morning routine, including pissing, push ups, Crunchy Nut and a polite conversation with his parents about the chamber orchestra they'd seen in Torbay the night before.

When Nigel called on his mobile, Julian said goodbye to his parents and picked up his friend in his Fiat at the bottom of the road out of Marina View. McEwen and Neil were in a small BMW less than a hundred metres away.

'Dartmouth,' Nigel said. 'I'll navigate. I've done it before on my bike.'

'You see Caitlyn last night?' Julian asked, sounding quite upbeat as he pulled away.

'Yeah,' Nigel said happily. 'You seemed to be getting on pretty good with that girl in the bar.'

'Twenty-five years old,' Julian smiled. 'Got her phone number. I might call her later and ask her out for a meal or something.'

'Cool,' Nigel said.

McEwen pulled away as Julian turned out the end of the street. The tracking device in the Fiat's wheel arch gave an accurate location signal from anywhere in the country, but they had to keep within one and a half kilometres to pick up the audio from the listening devices.

'I didn't sleep,' Nigel said. 'That guy McEwen really put the shits up me.'

'My ribs are black and blue,' Julian said. 'My nose is all clogged with dried blood. I weigh seventy kilos and he wasn't even straining when he slammed me down on that table.'

'Hard bastard,' Nigel nodded.

McEwen and Neil smiled at each other. Serious criminals like the Brigands didn't speak openly in cars, avoided mobile phones and used codes, but Nigel and Julian were just a couple of sixth formers and it hadn't occurred to either of them that their car or possessions had been bugged when they were pulled in.

'We've always been mates,' Nigel said. 'I'm sorry I got you into this.'

'From now on I'm buying my spliff with cash only,' Julian said. 'No debts to repay.'

'This gun-running shit's *too* heavy,' Nigel said. 'My brother fixed up something else for tonight, but I'm gonna speak to Paul about it. You don't get MI6 or whoever it was threatening to drop you in the shit when you're selling weed to a few mates.'

'So we pick up our money and we're free and clear,' Julian said cheerfully. 'Money in our pockets, no debts and a date with that randy little twenty-five-year-old.'

'Like old times,' Nigel said noisily. 'Sex, weed and parties!'

Neil and McEwen kept a kilometre behind until the Fiat pulled into the grounds of Paul Woodhead's farm house. Neil had scouted the location the night before and they passed the front gate and pulled on to a track a few hundred metres from the house.

Woodhead came to his door in wellies and jeans. He was a big man, with a knee that buckled with each step. His thinning hair was combed back and matted down with sweat.

'Another scorcher,' he said as the door came open. 'Let's walk.'

Woodhead was more cautious than his young assistants and rather than inviting them into the house, he took them on a two-hundred-metre walk into an open area with rusting barns on either side. The metal played havoc with the signal from the listening devices, and a generator running inside one of the barns created a background hum.

'Two hundred each,' Woodhead said, as he peeled money off a bundle of fifty-pound notes. 'I hear you were forty minutes late with the delivery. These kind of people don't like being messed about.'

'Traffic on the M5,' Julian said. 'What can you do?'

'For two hundred pounds, you can get your shitty arse out of bed,' Woodhead snapped back. 'Now, about tonight.'

'Yeah, about that,' Nigel interrupted. 'My brother Will's out of town and my girl Caitlyn's parents are out of town, so I'm not gonna be able to make it.'

Woodhead's voice grew into a reedy shout. 'We have a consignment tonight, young man. There's nobody else: the only reason your spotty face got near a job like this is that all my usual people are on the run up to Cambridge.'

'I'm sorry, Paul. Things just spiralled. I'm not gonna make it.'

McEwen and Neil heard a booming sound, which was Nigel getting rammed against the metal barn.

'Now you listen to me, you bag of donuts,' Woodhead shouted. 'We have a deal. Four hundred pounds apiece for two hours out at sea and some loading and unloading back on shore. And you're *going* to be there because if you let me down I'm gonna fix it for some Brigands to pay you a visit. And they'll fix it for you to spend about two months in hospital suffering from agonising pain because every bone in your body got smashed with hammers.'

'OK, OK, I'll come,' Nigel said. 'But I can't bring my brother. He's left already.'

'Him then,' Woodhead said, pointing at Julian.

'I didn't agree to this,' Julian said, sounding stressed. 'This is serious crime. I'm *way* out of my depth here.'

'I appreciate your honesty,' Woodhead said. 'But I need bodies tonight and you're all there is. I'll pay you the four hundred, plus Nigel's four hundred. And since you like a smoke I'll throw in a couple of ounces of the finest shit you'll ever lay eyes on.'

'I'm sorry,' Julian said, audibly trembling. 'This isn't my style.'

Woodhead turned towards Nigel. 'You'd better try persuading your friend, because if you're *not* both on that boat with me, you're the one who's gonna get seriously mangled.'

'I could ring around,' Nigel said. 'Get someone else.'

'Great bloody idea,' Woodhead shouted. 'Why don't you put a card in the newsagent's window while you're at it? *Gun smuggler required, suit teenager, some heavy lifting, applicants with criminal records considered.*'

'Julian, you've gotta help me out,' Nigel begged. 'With my share and the dope that's more than a grand for an evening's work. *Please.*'

'If I help tonight, I want it to be the last time I'm involved with anything like this,' Julian whined.

'You got my word,' Woodhead said. 'I've got no beef with you, Julian. It's this little mother who's made me promises he can't keep.'

With that, Woodhead lunged forwards and punched Nigel hard in the stomach. 'Dumb kid,' he shouted, as Nigel groaned in agony. 'You're out of your depth and after tonight you'd better keep out of my face. Now I'll see you on the fishing wharf at Kingswear, eight o'clock sharp. Boat by the name of *Brixton Riots.*'

Nigel gasped and retched as Julian helped him back towards the red Fiat. The audio quality improved as their voices got picked up by the bugs in the roof of the car.

Julian sounded deeply upset. 'What the hell have you got me into here?'

'I'm sorry, mate,' Nigel said, as Julian started the engine. 'You saved my arse back there. You can have my two hundred from yesterday and you can have all the weed you can smoke from me for two months.'

Julian pounded on the dashboard. 'What if we get caught on this? What if that crazy bastard McEwen springs up again?'

'I don't know,' Nigel said desperately as he buried his head in his hands. 'McEwen left me a card. I could call him and tell him what's going on.'

'I don't trust him,' Julian said. 'I don't know who he is or who he really works for. I say we do what Paul wants us to do, then we keep our heads down and stay the hell away from the Brigands, the Monster Bunch and all the other crazy bastards.'

29. SERVICES

The Führer led his band up the fast lane of the M5, locked on the 70mph speed limit with no one daring to overtake on the inside. The procession had been joined by the North Devon and Plymouth Monster Bunch chapters and a friendly Cornish gang called Branding Iron.

James found himself amidst a kilometre-long train of bikes, topped and tailed by a ragtag fleet of breakdown vans and coaches. Horns blasted, kids waved from their parents' cars and the highlight of James' morning was a team of hockey players squishing bare breasts against the windows of a coach as the bikers roared past.

Riding a motorbike is more physically demanding than driving a car. James had no farings on his ER5 to keep the wind off and the sun gently roasted him inside his helmet, gloves and thick leather jacket. He was grateful to pull into Stoke Gifford service station with half of the three-hundred-mile ride to Cambridge under his belt.

Parents held their children close and nervous arrivals headed straight for the exit gates as two hundred motorcyclists steamed through the automatic doors to queue in the gents and pile into the restaurants. As the Führer entered he was met by the waiting presidents of the Cardiff and Bristol Brigands and six dark-tanned Brigands from Valencia in Spain.

James joined a huge melee of shouting bodies in Burger King, but the counter was swamped and he realised he had no chance of getting served as higher-status Brigands and Dogs of War pushed in front. James was harder than most of them, but he couldn't start a fight with a whole gang so he gave up and headed to the confectionery shop.

Again, the counters had a massive queue but here the bikers had the option to pilfer. It started with a couple of riders pocketing Polos and opening cans of beer, but soon turned into a scrum with more than thirty riders guffawing as they stole food and drinks while pushing, shoving and knocking down display racks.

James felt bad for the two women behind the counter. One of them screamed for help as a crash-helmeted Dog of War bundled her to the floor and tossed armfuls of cigarette packets into the crowd. James desperately needed a drink, and his lowly status meant that stealing was the only way he'd get anything before they all had to remount their bikes.

He left the shop guzzling from a half-litre bottle of

Sprite and holding a king-sized Mars Bar and a tub of mini Pringles. He stepped over a streak of urine where several Brigands had given up on the toilet queue and pissed over the cash machines.

A coachload of scared pensioners were being herded out through a chirping fire door, while another group of Brigands jeered the man serving in Costa Coffee, and the manager of Marks and Spencer earned a bloody nose after trying to stop a Cardiff Brigand from making off with a bottle of freshly squeezed orange and rasberry.

James was alone and wore no gang insignia. This made him easy pickings if the cops arrived and started arresting people, so he decided to head out to his bike and maybe top up with petrol if the queue wasn't too bad. But as he stood in the automatic doorway he saw twenty-five men charging towards the doors waving clubs and lengths of bike chain. A shout of 'Brigand wankers' went up as they began pouring inside.

James dived back into the shop as men came through the door and immediately chain-whipped a Dog of War queuing for the toilets. Blood sprayed several metres from a deep cut running from the biker's ear to the side of his nose.

'Vengeful Bastards,' several people shouted at once.

James had heard the name: the Vengefuls were a small but fearsome gang, founded by two Brigands who'd been expelled for breaking the club's strict rules banning members from using heroin. Now with six chapters, the Vengeful Bastards were the Brigands' sworn enemies.

James' Sprite bottle got knocked from his hand as

members of the Brigands and their support gangs piled out of the shop, the toilets and the restaurant armed with whatever came to hand. A full-patch biker was expected to fight bravely for his gang. Cowardice was grounds for a severe beating, followed by expulsion.

As James backed up into the shop he watched Teeth disarm a Vengeful, sending his bike chain flying towards him. James grabbed the chain, while Teeth lifted his opponent and smashed him head first into a stone pillar.

The twenty-five Vengefuls seemed outnumbered and were getting a pasting. James crouched down, surrounded by cardboard boxes near the till with two female clerks clutching each other and sobbing under the counter.

James pulled on one of his leather riding gloves, then wrapped half the chain around his padded hand. This made a knuckleduster that doubled as a whip if he needed some extra reach.

'Is there a place to hide?' James asked.

One of the terrified clerks answered. 'Our manager's locked himself in the stock room.'

The fighting outside subsided as Vengefuls were knocked down or ran off, then resurged as a second wave arrived. Some Vengefuls came through the front doors, but a second group poured out of an upstairs restaurant where they'd apparently been waiting in ambush and had missed their cue to pile in with the first wave.

As fists, clubs and boots flew, James watched as a man with a bread knife sticking out of his back staggered into the shop. For a second James thought it was his riding partner Orange Bob, but it was a Vengeful

Bastard prospect barely older than himself.

James considered first aid, but before he could do anything the fighting came into the shop. Two fat Vengefuls held the South Devon Brigand Dirty Dave by his arms. They bundled him into a glass rack stacked with souvenir playing cards, china figures and other tat. As the ornaments smashed on the floor a ginger-bearded Vengeful pulled out a hammer with its end sharpened into a vicious looking spike.

As the hammer lunged, James lashed out with the chain, hitting the ginger Vengeful's hand. He then punched the man in the face. As the Vengeful staggered back, Dirty Dave freed himself from the other one and sent him clattering into an open-fronted cooler filled with soft drinks and sandwiches.

James grabbed a large brass model of the Clifton Suspension Bridge, belted his ginger opponent around the head with it and then knocked him cold with his chain-wrapped fist. Dirty Dave was tussling with the other man, but James prioritised grabbing the sharpened hammer before someone else got hold and used it on him.

As James reached down and grabbed the hammer another Vengeful Bastard charged into the shop and swung a punch at his head. James' vision blurred as the big fist knocked his head against a glass shelf, but he swung the hammer and the pointed end sank deep into the man's knee.

James ripped the hammer out, causing a spurt of blood. He dived out of the way as the biker crumpled, smashing through two glass shelves and moaning in pain. Another Vengeful charged in as James stood up. This man was smaller, and James threw an uppercut, plunging his chain-wrapped fist into the man's chin, smashing his jaw and sending him crashing on to the newspapers and cigarette packets spilled across the floor.

While James floored three men, Dirty Dave was still struggling with his original opponent. They had arms around each other's necks and were throwing weak punches. Although James wasn't really on the Brigands' side, he certainly wasn't with the Vengeful Bastards after three of them had attacked him.

Buzzing with fear and shock, James kneed the fat Vengeful in the stomach. The blow doubled him up, enabling Dirty Dave to break loose and punch him in the face. James finished him off by bashing his head against the inside of the fridge so that it buckled a metal shelf.

James looked outside and saw injured men strewn across the tiles. The Brigands and their puppets seemed to have won the battle, but the cost had been heavy and with so many knives and weapons flying about a lot of men would be on their way to hospital, or dead.

Teeth, the Führer and several Brigands from other chapters stood in the doorway shouting orders. The floor around James was covered in blood, the shelves were shattered and there was hardly a piece of stock left on the shelves.

'You did great,' Dirty Dave said, giving James a massive grin and slapping him on the back. 'Saved my arse.'

James knew his fingerprints were all over the hammer,

so he took it with him and carefully avoided stepping in any blood as he left the shop. He followed Dirty Dave outside, where the Führer and the Cardiff president had taken charge.

'I want our bikes riding out of here in formation,' the Führer shouted. 'If anyone gets arrested, don't say a word unless our lawyers tell you to.'

'What about injuries?' Teeth asked.

'If they can walk, stick 'em on a coach. If they look bad leave 'em for the ambulance.'

As the Führer said this a Vengeful stepped through the shattered glass in the automatic doors clutching his stomach. Teeth backed up and knocked him cold with an explosive kick to the head, as two Monster Bunch members arrived carrying an armful of VHS tapes.

'Good work,' the Führer grinned.

'Found the manager and gave him a kicking,' one of the Monsters explained. 'He says this is all the surveillance footage. Do you want me to burn them up?'

'No,' the Führer said. 'They might be useful. Take off your colours and ride to the nearest post office. Send those tapes by Special Delivery to Burnham, Smith and Greaves Solicitors, one-three-three Salcombe High Street. *Don't* let the cops grab the tapes or I'll slit your throat.'

'Gotcha,' the two Monsters said, before jogging off towards their bikes.

As James heard all this he looked around the car park. There were a few scuffles and a lot of Brigands smashing up Vengeful Bastard bikes.

'Roll, roll, roll,' road captain Vomit shouted as he

came out of the doors with nearly thirty bikers in front of him.

James looked at Dirty Dave. 'What about the formation?'

'Just ride,' Dirty Dave said urgently as he followed the Führer and the rest of the bikes over to where all the Brigands had parked. 'We have to get out of the county before the police get their act together.'

James unwrapped the bloody chain from his riding glove and stuffed it inside his jacket as he ran. Quite a few bikes had been tipped over or vandalised and several Brigands' Harleys had been mashed into a wall by a tow truck, so James was mightily relieved to find his bike intact. He grabbed his helmet from the storage box behind his seat and saddled up.

James rolled forward, then gave way to let Vomit, the Führer and several other Brigands through, but Dirty Dave stopped and waved James' bike in out of respect for what he'd done inside.

Some bikes had already fled, but the majority had waited for the Führer and James found himself riding in the sixth row, boxed in by Brigands on their Harleys, with sixty bikes lined up behind him.

James had only managed a few mouthfuls to drink and his knuckles throbbed from the fight. He looked at the torn leather glove over his right hand and worried about the bloody length of chain and the hammer stashed under his seat. If the police pulled him over and found that, he'd have a lot of explaining to do.

30. FISH

As Julian and Nigel drove back to Salcombe, McEwen let the surveillance drop and turned towards the seafront village of Kingswear. By the time they arrived Neil had spoken to the control room on CHERUB campus, where they'd established that the boat *Brixton Riots* was owned and insured by a Bulgarian front company.

The BMW cruised the shore until they spotted the rusting trawler, painted in motorway-sign blue. McEwen parked up behind a line of bollards eighty metres from the boat and took a set of compact Nikon binoculars from under his seat.

'Nobody out there by the looks of things,' McEwen said, as his magnified view scanned the length of the boat and some rotting strands of fishing net on the shore. Then he saw a notice stencilled on the boat's superstructure: *This vessel can be hired by the day or half day for expert guided fishing expeditions call . . .*

McEwen read the mobile number to Neil, who tapped it into his laptop.

'Phone number belongs to a man named Johnny Riggs,' Neil said, as he used the intelligence service central database to bring up more details on Riggs. 'Lives around here. Credit history says he went bankrupt seven years ago to the tune of three hundred grand. No criminal record, three points on his driving licence for doing fifty-eight in a forty zone. Divorced, court order to pay maintenance through the Child Support Agency for a son and two daughters.'

'Sounds like a straight man to me,' McEwen said, as he continued to study the *Brixton Riots*. 'Most likely a bankrupt fisherman, running a boat owned by one of the Führer's front companies.'

'What are you seeing?' Neil asked.

'I know squat about fishing boats,' McEwen said. 'But there's eight boats out there. *Brixton Riots* is the tattiest, but the radar dish is the biggest and newest. I can see a couple of LCD screens inside the bridge and there's a yellow thing on the back of the deck that looks like a missile or something. It's got the name Towmaster on it and a company name, something like ANT.'

Neil tapped *ANT Towmaster* into his laptop. Google asked if he meant *AMS Towmaster*. He clicked yes and the first link on the answers page took him to a page with a picture of a yellow torpedo-like tube.

'Advanced Marine Systems, Towmaster six-sixty,' Neil said, reading from the screen. 'Sensitive sonar system for marine survey. Number one for marine salvage, nautical archaeology and the oil industry.'

'So that's how they're working it,' McEwen breathed as he lowered the binoculars. 'Big boat sails into shallow water and drops off a package of drugs, guns or whatever. Then *Brixton Riots* goes out, picks it off the sea bed and brings it back to shore.'

'How do you think we should play it?' Neil asked.

'Miniature cameras and microphones on the boat,' McEwen said. 'I can sneak on board and stick them somewhere. If anyone asks, we're a couple of tourists interested in a fishing trip. We'll put more cameras on shore to film them leaving and arriving. We'll watch from the car and follow them wherever they take the cargo when they land.'

'That should cover all the bases,' Neil said. 'I reckon we could do with some backup from my department and some crews on standby in case of a lengthy pursuit.'

'Can never have too much manpower on an op like this,' McEwen agreed. 'Speak to Ross Johnson. If he can't do it I'll try getting someone flown down from CHERUB campus.'

'What about surveillance equipment?'

'I've got nothing in the car,' McEwen said, 'but Chloe will have a suitcase filled with surveillance equipment back at the house in Salcombe.'

Neil looked at his watch. 'One o'clock,' he said. 'It's tight, but we should be able to get this sorted.'

*

Just after 1 p.m. Dante, Joe, Lauren and Anna

approached the fortified entrance of the Brigands clubhouse, each dragging a shopping trolley or a wheeled suitcase behind them. Joe looked left and right before swiping a magnetic card through the entry point and giving the door a shove.

The hall inside was ghostly. Their breathing echoed across a high-ceilinged expanse tinged with cigarette smoke. The only light came from sunbeams piercing three skylights in the roof.

'Anybody home?' Anna shouted.

The four teens had made it across to the self-service bar area when a hungover man hobbled down from the bunkhouse upstairs wearing boxers and a pizza-stained vest. The quartet had no business in the clubhouse and Joe decided that attack was the best form of defence.

'Aussie Mike,' Joe said. 'Aren't you supposed to be working security? What if I'd been a crack team of enemy bikers come to burn down the clubhouse?'

Aussie Mike ran his hands through a long tangle of hair. 'What the hell are you doing here?'

'I'm Joe, the Führer's son. He told me to check up on you.'

The Führer's name made Aussie Mike stand bolt upright and point up the stairs. 'Ahh yeah,' he said in his Aussie drawl. 'Saw you coming in, didn't I? I mean, didn't know exactly who you were, but I've seen you about. Got the old shotguns up there if anyone had come looking for trouble.'

'Cool,' Joe said, raising his hands. 'We're having a little get together at my parents' place tonight. My dad said it was OK to come by and pick up some snacks and fizzy drinks.'

'No worries,' Aussie Mike said, as he turned around and started sauntering back upstairs to the bunkhouse. 'I'll leave you to it.'

The four kids all smiled at each other once Aussie Mike was out of sight.

'Sucker,' Joe grinned as he swiped his dad's security pass in a door marked *no admittance* and led the quartet into a sizeable stock room. One end was dominated by the silver doors of a giant fridge and freezer where the Brigands stored meat for their barbecues, but the kids were more interested in the pallets of beer cans on the floor and the spirit and wine bottles lined up on chipboard shelves.

Dante looked at the beer. 'You said about twenty kids, so if we have four beers each we'll need a hundred cans.'

'More than that,' Joe said. 'I'll probably drink twelve or fifteen cans just myself.'

Lauren burst out laughing. 'What are you, a professional darts player?'

Dante laughed as well. 'I'd love to see you drink ten beers, Joe. You'd pass out after three.'

'Three lemonade shandies,' Anna said, as Lauren's eyes fixed on a line of green bottles.

'Pink champagne,' Lauren grinned. 'We've gotta get some of that.'

'No you won't,' Joe said. 'There's only six bottles and it's expensive. We need to mix and match, a few trays of beer, a few bottles of this, few bottles of that. There's so much booze here nobody will notice as long as we don't take too much of one thing.'

Anna opened the top of her gran's shopping trolley and slid in two pallets of beer, then began topping it off with bottles of vodka, gin and bourbon. Across the room, the boys filled their cases with as much beer as they could cram in while Lauren went into the fridge and got lots of fruit juices and bottles of Coke to use as mixers.

'Drunken sex orgy here we come!' Joe grinned as he zipped his case and gave it a tug that almost wrenched his arm off. 'Jesus that's heavy.'

Anna and Lauren had reached the same conclusion about their haul.

'We'll never get this lot on to the bus,' Dante said.

'I could steal my dad's car,' Joe said. 'It's an automatic, he let me drive it around our house a couple of times when he first got it.'

Lauren and Dante had both been trained to drive by CHERUB, but kids driving cars in daylight was dodgy and letting on would blow their cover.

'How about I call a taxi?' Dante suggested, as he pulled his mobile out of his jacket.

Anna giggled and gave Dante a kiss. 'My clever boy,' she grinned. 'And so much less risky than stealing the Führer's sixty-grand Mercedes.'

*

The battle at Stoke Gifford services had been horrifying, but the police didn't have the guts or manpower to stop a hundred-strong convoy of outlaw bikers, so the slightly depleted band cruised on towards the Rebel Tea Party.

At Swindon, Vomit led everyone a couple of miles off the motorway for an unscheduled stop in a Tesco car park. The bikes queued for petrol, while women from one of the coaches headed into the supermarket and cleared the shelves of sandwiches, Scotch eggs and individual fruit pies.

James found himself the centre of attention during the impromptu car-park picnic that followed. Dirty Dave relayed the story to a circle of bikers, their women and a few kids.

'Thought this spiked hammer was going through my skull,' Dirty Dave explained. 'But this hard little bastard comes in and floors him. Then we took out four more of those pansy-arsed girl-guide Vengefuls, didn't we champ?'

Dave put his arm around James' back and gave him a hug that sent his Mr Kipling's cherry slice spilling out of its foil dish and spinning towards the tarmac. James couldn't actually remember Dirty Dave doing any of the fighting, but he let this detail slide.

'This kid's gonna be a kick-ass Brigand some day,' Dirty Dave said. 'I'd bet my own cock on it.'

'Small bet,' one of the women shouted.

Everyone laughed, but James was surprised to find a serious looking Führer pulling him out of the circle.

'What's up?' James asked nervously.

The Führer smiled. 'Sounds like you showed class back there, but we don't want you getting nicked. Have you got the chain and hammer?'

James pulled the chain out of his pocket. 'The hammer's stashed in my bike.'

'So you're smart *and* tough,' the Führer nodded. 'Never leave a weapon at a crime scene. It'll have fingerprints and DNA all over it. I want you to hand them over to me.'

'What for?' James asked.

'The breakdown truck's gonna take a little detour. Friend of a friend runs a scrap yard not far from here. He's gonna burn up or melt anything incriminating.'

'Right,' James said. 'I'll go get them.'

'You need your riding gloves but they might have blood on them, so throw 'em on the fire when we get to the Tea Party. There's stalls there selling all kinds of biker kit. I'll sort you out if you're short of money.'

'Right,' James said. The Führer was evil, but he couldn't help admiring the man's leadership. While other bikers bragged and ate pork pies, the Führer was like a machine, working out the police's strategy, tracking down and destroying evidence and making calls to his legal team, back in Salcombe.

'Most importantly, kid,' the Führer said, wagging a finger in James' face, 'if the cops pull you over, keep your mouth *shut* and wait for our lawyer. They'll never prove you didn't act in self defence unless you let something stupid out of your mouth.'

'I *did* act in self defence,' James pointed out.

The Führer made a crooked smile. 'Well I won't hold it against you, just this once.'

31. CONTESTANT

James had sweat-soaked clothes stuck to his skin and an aching arse from six hours in the saddle as they closed in on the Rebel Tea Party. An AC/DC tribute band belted out from a stage several hundred metres away as bikes snaked down a country lane, with the surrounding fields enclosed by an aluminium fence.

Fluorescent-jacketed cops filmed with video cameras at the roadside. Vomit had warned everyone to expect a stop-and-search on arrival, but it takes a lot of officers to confront a hundred-strong motorbike gang and the Cambridgeshire police were more interested in having the Rebel Tea Party go off smoothly than in questioning a volatile group about an incident in another force's jurisdiction.

The Tea Party was an annual event organised by four London-based motorcycle gangs. What had started twenty years earlier with a few hundred bikers in a London dance hall was now Europe's largest motorcycle festival, held on a disused RAF airfield. It was spread over two days and attended by more than twenty-five thousand riders and enthusiasts.

Like everything else in the world of outlaw motorbike gangs, entering the Tea Party was a hierarchical affair. While the public parked cars and bikes outside, threw away all food and drink and then queued obediently for a security search, the Führer led his party through a specially opened side gate on their bikes.

The area nearest the entrance was a broad strip of tarmac lined with food stands and fairground rides. The Brigands pulled off their helmets and put on a show, gunning throttles and blasting horns as the crowds parted to let them through.

A greasy Rotterdam Brigand came out of the crowd and handed the Führer a Nazi flag, which he took with great enthusiasm. Cameras popped and camcorders swung towards them as an announcement boomed over the PA system:

'Ladies and gentlemen, let's give a warm Tea Party welcome to Brigands M.C., South Devon, Bristol, Cardiff, Monster Bunch M.C., Dogs of War M.C. and the Branding Irons!'

Eighty per cent of the crowd comprised ordinary motorcycle fans and their families, but among them were outlaws from all the major national and international gangs. Friendly outlaws waved fists and clapped, members of weaker gangs crossed arms and nodded respectfully, while enemies gave the finger, thrust crotches and screamed abuse.

After parading the three-hundred-metre strip, the Brigands and their associates peeled off and gathered speed as they followed the signs to Outlaw Hill. This huge expanse of baked grass was divided into campgrounds for all the different gangs. The higher your status the higher the ground you camped on. The Brigands deferred only to one mighty international gang, who marked the top of the hill with a line of two hundred Harleys and an air-conditioned mobile clubhouse.

The Brigands' spot was already well populated, with members from London, the north and various foreign chapters, plus several hundred guests from their respective puppet gangs. A prospect handed James a necklace with a laminated badge reading *Brigands* M.C. – *Guest* and he rolled his Kawasaki into a row of bikes belonging to friends and hangers-on.

The Brigands' Harleys lined up to form a perimeter wall as well as an exhibition for any civilians brave enough to venture up Outlaw Hill.

The three coaches following the Brigands' convoy had skipped the parade and arrived first. James hurried across to grab his tent and overnight bag from a luggage hold. He scouted about trying to find a space for his tent that was far enough away from the action to be reasonably quiet, but not right up the back near the stinking portable toilets.

'James, *baby!*' Nigel's brother Will shouted. 'I hear you a bad-ass now!'

James fought off a smile as he wandered over to Will and three other Monster Bunch members.

'Pitch your tent with us,' Will said. 'These are my boys, Minted, Rhoda and Shampoo Jr.'

They were all stocky lads, aged between eighteen and twenty, and in various stages of removing their riding gear. James shook all their hands and spent the next quarter hour pitching his tent, changing into cargo shorts and a Ramones T-shirt and drinking a beer that had spent six hours getting warm in a coach.

Once everyone was settled Will led James and his three friends downhill past the various outlaw camps, moving extra fast when they passed a small patch filled with Vengeful Bastards.

'You gonna put James' name up for the Monster Bunch?' Minted asked.

'When I do Nigel,' Will nodded. 'That's if you fancy it, James?'

James laughed. 'Maybe the Dogs of War will make me a better offer.'

'Cheeky little bastard,' Shampoo Jr shouted, giving James a gentle punch in the back and making beer spew down his top.

'So what do you boys fancy?' Will asked. 'Hardcore stage for some dancing? Look around the strip, or the swap meet?'

'Flesh Tent,' Minted and Rhoda said in unison.

'What's that?' James asked.

Will laughed and grabbed James by his shirt. 'If you've never been you've *got* to go there first.'

'And it's better while you're still sober,' Rhoda added.

At the bottom of the hill the lads turned away from the strip and headed towards a white hexagonal tent. After stopping to buy bottles of iced Budweiser they paid four quid each, got their hands stamped and headed inside, with James getting teased as the older boys pointed at the *Strictly Over 18s* sign.

Inside there were about a hundred and fifty seats, but the all-male audience stood crushed up at the front. Music blasted out of tinny speakers as six topless women danced limply up on stage.

James and the other lads jostled up close to the stage as the music stopped playing and a seedy looking fatty in a velvet jacket walked up to a microphone.

'OK folks, let's give our beautiful amateur ladies a big round of applause. And a reminder, our winner walks out with a hundred pounds and *you* the audience get to decide.'

'Looks like we've missed most of it,' James said.

Will shook his head. 'It goes on like this all day. Strippers, pole dancers, amateur girls. Last year they had these two Estonian chicks in leather whipping each other.'

'So let's hear some noise for contestant number one,' the compere shouted.

The room stayed quiet as a woman in her fifties dressed in red suspenders stepped forward and wiggled her flabby arms.

James spat out a mouthful of beer. 'Oh that's *gross*,' he moaned.

'They always do that,' Shampoo Jr explained. 'One really disgusting one to rile up the crowd.'

Contestant numbers two and three got some noise from the crowd. Contestant four got a good reception, except from a group behind James who were jeering and calling her a whore. This caused a whole bunch of men to back up from the stage and before James knew it two groups of outlaws were facing off directly behind him.

'Come on folks, it's just a bit of fun,' the compere shouted. 'My old mum used to tell me to hold my breath and count to ten.'

'I'll slit your throat,' roared a huge barrel of a man standing directly behind James, but it all seemed like bravado until James saw the flash of a butterfly knife, which promptly plunged into a stomach.

Will and the others had backed out through a gap, but James found himself trapped between the stage and the fight as a dozen men traded kicks and punches. Folding chairs scraped on the wooden floor as men piled out the back of the tent in a state of panic, then became the weapons of choice as the brawl spread across the room.

James didn't want to get involved, but his only way out was up the three steps at the side of the stage. To his astonishment the fat compere charged towards him and ordered him to get down before swinging a punch.

'I'm just trying to get out,' James shouted, as he ducked the punch and whacked the compere around the head.

The six topless contestants had run off and were

grabbing their tops and shoes from behind a flimsy partition. As James raced across stage to a back exit someone switched on the lights. The smaller of the two fighting groups was running out, there was no sign of Will or the others, but James could see the patches from up on stage and realised that the man who'd been stabbed was a London Brigand.

James jumped off the back of the stage and followed two of the contestants through a rear flap. The tent backed on to the metal perimeter of the Tea Party compound. James stepped gingerly over an air-conditioning pipe and cables, but he heard a girl screaming back inside the tent.

'You dirty bitch,' the compere yelled as he hit the girl again. 'I don't give a shit where your clothes are.'

This seemed wrong, so James rushed back inside where the petite contestant number five stood barefoot and still topless. Her dark hair was wound around the compere's hand.

'Give it up,' the compere shouted.

'Pick on someone your own size,' James said indignantly, as he popped the fat compere in the mouth, before snatching his wrist and bending it up behind his back.

'Let go of her hair or I'll break your arm,' James ordered.

The compere set the girl loose, but when James released his arm he swung at him again.

'You're too fat and too slow,' James explained, as he threw three quick punches, knocking the compere off the stage, where he clattered backwards into a bunch of chairs before landing hard on his arse.

James didn't know who the compere was, but if he ran a tent at an event like this he'd certainly have well-connected biker friends and James didn't intend sticking around long enough to meet them.

He looked behind the stage as contestant number five searched through pom-poms, twirling sticks, a caged parrot and leather whips while swearing loudly in Spanish.

'What was that all about?' James asked. 'Why did he hit you?'

'Someone took my T-shirt,' the girl seethed. 'How do I get back to my caravan like this?'

James could see no sign of the T-shirt, so he pulled his own over his head. 'It's a bit sweaty,' he said, as he offered it. 'But it's better than five thousand people seeing your tits.'

'My hero,' the girl said, giving James a sweet smile as she pulled the T-shirt on and slid her feet into a pair of canvas plimsolls.

James followed her as she hurried out of the tent. 'Some people are such arseholes,' James said indignantly as the sun hit his bare back. 'Fancy hitting you just because you asked him to help look for your top.'

The girl's face lit up with a mischievous smile as she peeled a roll of twenty-pound notes out of her cut-off jeans. 'I think it had more to do with me stealing the prize money,' she explained. 'And I would have gotten away if that slag contestant number three hadn't stolen my top.'

James laughed as they walked clear of the tent. Three bikers wearing vests marked *Security* and a first-aid team with a stretcher were running into the tent, while a couple of London Brigands stood outside using mobiles, clearly relaying what had happened to their bosses.

'Here,' the girl said, as she offered James forty pounds. 'You saved my ass, you deserve a cut.'

James grinned as he took the money. 'I love your accent. Are you Spanish?'

'No shitting you is there, Sherlock,' she grinned.

'I'm James by the way.'

'So why does a good looking boy like you hang around with creepy fat men watching a titty contest?'

James felt embarrassed. 'I got dragged in there by a bunch of mates. I've never been anywhere like that before. And I was *definitely* gonna shout for you, you were the best looking by miles.'

'You need to come back to my caravan with me,' the girl smiled as she led James into the crowds on the strip.

'I do?' James said.

'I'll grab a top,' she explained. 'Then you can have your T-shirt back.'

32. CARAVAN

The radio-controlled Panzer tank clattered through the shabby lawn behind the Führer's house. Its turret swung rapidly towards a Red Army T34 and an orange flash and tinny electronic boom came out of the muzzle.

'Missed me, cock breath!' Dante said, giving Joe the finger before staring down at his radio control unit. 'Which one turns the turret again?'

Dante couldn't find it and Joe was closing in with the Panzer, so he threw it into full reverse and crashed into a bird table. Joe fired and missed again.

Lauren grabbed Joe's controller. 'Gimme that thing.'

Dante had finally worked out where his turret control was. He advanced forward from the bird table and fired.

'*Direct hit*,' a synthesised voice announced from the controller in Lauren's hand. '*Damage level fifteen per cent.*'

'Fifteen per cent damage,' Joe carped. 'You're

on eighty per cent. One more hit on the side and you're toast.'

To simulate the reloading of a shell in a real tank, the electronics only allowed one shot every fifteen seconds. This meant Lauren's Panzer would be ready to fire before Dante's T34, so Dante swerved in front of Lauren's tank and charged through the shaggy grass at full speed before swerving into relative safety behind the skinny trunk of a plum tree.

'Don't go too near the pond,' Joe said anxiously, as Lauren's Panzer skimmed over a bump and briefly left the ground. 'My dad'll break my legs if we wreck 'em.'

Anna batted Dante on the arm as the four teenagers chased after the tanks. 'My turn,' she demanded.

'Nah-uh,' Dante said. 'You're rubbish. I'm trying to pull us back from the brink.'

A green LED lit up on Lauren's controller, indicating that her tank was ready to fire again. She came to a halt and took aim at the sliver of Dante's T34 protruding from the plum trunk.

'You'll never hit that,' Joe warned, as Lauren fired anyway and missed. 'Idiot!'

Anna scowled at Dante. 'Don't screw it up,' Dante warned, as he passed the controller over. 'The firing light just came on.'

After missing, Lauren's tank was vulnerable to attack, but instead of retreating she charged on towards the plum tree. It was a calculated risk, based upon the fact that Anna was going to miss.

'Ooops,' Anna said, as her tank shot backwards.

'That one's the turret,' Dante groaned, as he pointed at the controller.

'Keep your wig on,' Anna shouted back, as Lauren's tank closed to within four metres.

'Shoot now,' Dante yelled.

Anna got the turret pointing towards Lauren's Panzer and pressed the fire button.

'Too soon,' Dante said furiously. 'The turret was still moving.'

The synthesised voices from two control units disagreed. '*Side hit. Tank A, damage level thirty-five per cent.*'

'What!' Joe yelled indignantly. 'That was head on. How could it possibly hit the side?'

'Must have just glanced it,' Dante giggled, as he slapped Anna on the back. 'Nice one.'

Lauren's gun was almost ready to fire, but Anna charged forward recklessly. Lauren threw her Panzer into reverse, but instead of the electric motor churning inside, she got a whimper.

The two tanks crashed face on. The left track of Anna's T34 reared up on to the Panzer. The front track hit the turret hard, before the vehicle tipped sideways and rolled off. As the T34 landed upside down on its turret, Lauren frantically jiggled her controller.

'It's dead,' she said, as she demonstrated the fact to Joe.

'Flat battery,' Joe explained.

'Is there a spare?' Lauren asked, and Joe shook his head.

'Victory!' Dante said, grinning at Anna.

Lauren tutted. 'How can it be a victory if your tank is upside down?'

'And you're eighty-five per cent damaged,' Joe added. 'We kicked your arse.'

'It's a war of attrition,' Dante grinned. 'We conserved energy and ammunition.'

'The only reason your battery lasted longer is that you couldn't use the controller,' Joe said.

'Well they're *your* dad's tanks,' Anna replied. 'You've driven them before.'

Lauren peeled her sweaty top away from her back and grabbed her trainers out of the grass. 'I'm going inside,' she said. 'I'm gasping for a drink.'

Joe carried the dead Panzer, while Dante flipped the T34 back on to its tracks and drove it through the open doors of the conservatory. Lauren followed it and found Joe's brother Martin in a leather armchair reading *The Times*.

'Why is all that booze piled up in the hallway?' Martin asked, when Joe came in. 'Planning a little soirée, are we?'

'You'll be at the crêperie,' Joe smiled. 'So you and your bum-boy friends aren't invited.'

Lauren had grown to like Joe, but she hated it when he trumpeted his dad's homophobic views and she flicked his ear. 'Don't be such a shit,' she said.

'It's OK, Lauren,' Martin said airily. 'Bigotry is a sign of a small mind, and they don't come much smaller than Joe's.'

Dante grinned. 'If you think his mind's small, you

should see his dick in the changing rooms.'

'Trust you to be looking, you bender,' Joe snapped back.

Martin stood up and eyed Joe seriously. 'If this house gets trashed, Dad'll kill you.'

'No he won't,' Joe grinned. 'I'm his golden boy. If he hears that I threw a wild party he'll slap me on the back and tell me I'm a *chip off the old block.*'

Martin sighed. 'The depressing thing is you're probably right about Dad, but if the house gets messed up Mum *will* smack you into next week.'

'I can handle Mum,' Joe smirked. 'Her bark is worse than her bite. And besides, it's all people I know from school. If someone pukes or something I'll get Lauren to put on her Marigolds and scrub up.'

Dante laughed. 'Yeah, girls love cleaning. It's genetic.'

Lauren gave Joe the finger. 'With the sexism and the homophobia I can see one little boy getting smacked into next week *before* his mommy comes home,' she grinned.

*

James lay on a narrow bed in the back of a small Volkswagen camper van. His skin glistened with sweat, he was out of breath and his clothes were strewn over the tiny kitchen cabinets running along the opposite wall. The Spanish girl snuggled naked beside him.

James was grinning from ear to ear. 'That was *bloody* incredible!'

The girl poked out her tongue and licked a bead of sweat off his chest. 'It's not every day you get rescued by a big horny boy. What happened down here?' she asked, poking just below his nipple. 'Did some crazy girl try to bite it off?'

'Nah,' James grinned. 'I got bitten by a snake, about a year back.'

'You lead an interesting life,' she smiled.

'I suppose I do,' James agreed as he nuzzled the back of the girl's neck. 'You know, this is kind of embarrassing but I didn't actually catch your name.'

'That's because I didn't tell you,' the girl said, pushing James' head away and sitting up with her bum balanced precariously on the edge of the bed. 'Did you see where my socks went?'

James laughed. 'So aren't you going to tell me?'

'No,' the girl said, as she picked up the watch lying on the draining board. 'And now I have to go to work.'

James was disappointed. 'How long for? Can we meet up afterwards?'

'This was fun,' she smiled, as she hooked on a black bra and gave James a kiss. 'But it was what it was.'

James wasn't sure exactly what it had been, but he didn't want to sound stupid so he changed the subject. 'So what do you work at?'

'My father and uncle have a van. We make paella.'

'Ahh,' James said. 'So you travel all around?'

'In summer,' the girl nodded. 'All the big festivals. V2, Reading, Glastonbury, Donnington, Notting Hill Carnival, and in Europe too. In the winter we go back to my mother and brothers in Spain.'

'Life on the road,' James said wistfully. 'Sounds cool.'

'Pass my jeans,' the girl said as she looked at her

watch. 'You need to start getting dressed too.'

James reluctantly sat up and reached into the cab where he'd thrown the girl's jeans. As he picked them up, he noticed a dark red triangle sticking out from the pocket.

'A-ha,' James said happily, as he swiped the passport from the pocket and opened the back page. 'Reina Cardinas,' he said in a thick Spanish accent. 'Even your name is sexy.'

But Reina lunged frantically. 'Nosy pig,' she spat. 'Give to me.'

'You were cute.' James smiled at Reina's passport picture, in which she was about twelve. 'Nice pigtails.'

Reina scowled as she snatched the jeans and the passport back. 'Creep!' she said, hooking James' Ramones T-shirt with her big toe and flicking it up into his lap. 'My things are private and you need to leave. My dad will be here soon.'

'How come you're out here on the road?' James asked, as he pulled the Ramones tee over his head. 'Shouldn't you be at college or something?'

He'd hoped Reina would open up, but her tone remained bitter. 'After the third school expelled me, my dad said he'd take me on the road where he can keep an eye on me.'

'He's doing a great job,' James grinned as he slid his trainers on, but Reina didn't smile back and before he knew it he was striding between the tightly parked vans, heading back towards Outlaw Hill.

33. TRAIL

The sun was starting to drop as Chloe parked the Range
Rover in a side street a couple of hundred metres from
the seafront at Kingswear. She walked down a steeply
sloped lane and knocked on the back of a van marked
with the name of a sanitation company.

The door swung open and she hopped inside, joining
McEwen, Neil Gauche and an array of screens and
monitoring equipment.

'Your majesty,' McEwen said sarcastically. 'To what do
we owe the honour?'

Chloe smiled. 'James is in Cambridgeshire, Lauren
and Dante are partying at the Führer's house and there's
nothing on telly, so I thought I'd come along and see if
you boys needed a hand.'

'Cool,' Neil said.

'So what's the state of play?' Chloe asked.

McEwen answered. 'Johnny Riggs arrived and went aboard the *Brixton Riots* about an hour after I fitted the cameras and microphones on the boat. A fuel tanker came by, then he spent some time cleaning up on deck. Paul Woodhead, plus Julian and Nigel arrived just after six. We picked up Nigel asking how long it would take. Riggs said he hoped to be back ashore before nine and all finished by eleven at the latest.'

'What about the equipment?'

'See for yourself,' McEwen said, as he pointed to an LCD screen showing a clear video feed from the rear deck of the boat. 'We've also got cameras set up on the dock, and Neil went out and put recording devices and trackers on Riggs' car and the van Woodhead arrived in.'

'Van,' Chloe smiled. 'So they'll load up into that.'

'I'd guess,' McEwen said. 'The coastguard are going to track the boat on radar, just in case it tries to drop the cargo somewhere else. My biggest worry is that none of our equipment is designed for use at sea.'

Chloe nodded. 'The memory chips will store the video from the deck even if the signal drops out though.'

'Yeah,' McEwen said. 'But what about the weather? Sea, salt spray and all that.'

'At least the sea's calm,' Neil noted, as he dragged a chair across the van's floor towards the monitors. 'We're gonna be here for a few hours, Chloe. You might as well sit down.'

*

By quarter to eight there were about twenty kids in the Führer's house, mostly Year Nines but a couple who were a year or so either side. The teenagers were past the age for sleepovers and birthday parties, but not yet comfortable with the concept of an evening party with no parents, unlimited booze and a chance of getting your hands on members of the opposite sex.

The result was awkward, with boys drinking cans of lager around a pool table and dart board in the back lounge, while a slightly smaller number of girls colonised the kitchen, mixing cocktail recipes from a book belonging to Joe's mum, or sprawled over the chairs in the adjoining conservatory gossiping about their lives and in particular the lies they'd told their parents in order to come to an unsupervised party.

Dante was slightly drunk after two beers, and he bumped into Anna at the top of the first-floor stairs as he came out of the toilet.

'This is dull,' Anna complained, as she went up on tiptoes and gave Dante a kiss. 'Everyone down there is brainless.'

Anna's breath smelled boozy, but Dante didn't complain as she pushed him against the wall and slid her hand down the back of his shorts while they snogged. A couple of girls giggled and said, 'Oooh Anna!' as they walked by and went into the bathroom together.

'Lesbians,' Dante sniggered.

Anna took his hand and gave him a tug. 'Let's find somewhere private,' she said.

'You're braver when you're tipsy,' Dante smiled, as they walked down a corridor covered with a dated turquoise carpet.

The first room they opened was Martin's. The large space was similar to Joe's room, but with fewer gadgets and a big map of the world on the wall with pins marking all the places where he planned to travel.

They skipped Joe's room, then laughed when they opened his parents' bedroom door and saw Marlene's giant underwear and the Führer's baggy Y-fronts lying on the floor.

'Old people's bodies are so horrible!' Anna winced. 'I want to die young and beautiful.'

A loud cheer came up from the lads playing pool downstairs. As it subsided the two girls came out of the bathroom and Dante and Anna dived through the double doors at the end of the corridor to make sure that they weren't spotted.

'Wow,' Anna said, as she stared along the narrow room towards a bay window draped with heavy velvet curtains. The land dropped away sharply where the house ended and there was a view over orange sky and an expanse of fields and countryside.

The room was the Führer's study and it reminded Dante of the German officer's headquarters in a hundred World War Two TV dramas. A painting of Hitler hung over the fireplace, and a shop dummy wore a full Gestapo uniform.

'Joe's dad isn't quite right in the head,' Anna noted, as she looked around. 'He's got guns as well.'

Dante saw the pair of shotguns. He knew that the Führer held a shotgun licence, and the firearms cabinet was fitted with toughened glass and a heavy lock as the law required. Below the case were open shelves containing a selection of crossbows ranging from an expensive handmade bow with an optical sight to a selection of cheap-but-powerful crossbow pistols.

'No psycho's home should be without one,' Dante grinned, picking up a menacing looking crossbow and pointing it at Anna.

'Don't,' she protested, and shielded her face.

'There's no bolt loaded,' Dante smirked, as he put it back on the rack. 'Silly girl.'

Anna put one hand on her hip and adopted a soppy look. 'I'm not silly,' she said.

Her body language said *snog me* and Dante obliged. Anna ended up on a leather armchair in Dante's lap, joined at the lips with their hands roaming. But Dante froze when he noticed a picture on the wall above a filing cabinet.

The Führer had dozens of Brigands pictures around the house, including a few of Dante's dad, Scotty. But this one was different, because Dante's whole family was there. Everything but a few baby photos had been lost when the Führer burned out Dante's house and now he recognised faces he hadn't seen for nearly five years.

Dante recalled the day it was taken outside the old clubhouse. It was the Brigands summer barbecue. Scotty stood proudly alongside the man who would kill him a year later, with the Brigands all around him. Wives stood at the edge of the framed picture, while the kids knelt or stood in front of their fathers.

Holly was a few months old, a bald head buried in her

mother's arms. Dante stood beside Joe, best friends. Dante's older brother Jordan puffed out his cheeks to ruin the picture and his sister Lizzie squatted on one knee with the expression she always had when she didn't want to be somewhere.

Dante had seen the expression a thousand times, but he'd forgotten it. He felt like he'd betrayed his family by forgetting so much about them.

'Are you OK, John?' Anna asked. 'Did I do something?'

Dante remembered that *he* was John and quickly smeared out the tear forming in his eye. 'It's the beer,' he said weakly. 'You're pressing down on my bladder or something, I need to pee again.'

Anna hopped off and Dante rushed down the hallway to the Führer's bedroom, where he bolted himself in the en-suite bathroom and fought off his tears.

*

James had been back at the Brigands compound for an hour, downing more warm beer as he helped to unload firewood and bundles of newspaper from one of the coaches to make a huge bonfire in the centre of camp. It wasn't necessary for warmth, but the various clubs had a friendly rivalry that would turn Outlaw Hill into a series of giant pyres once it got dark.

Less friendly rivalries put menace in the air and as James hauled wood and newspaper he tried to decipher the rumours. The easiest to understand was the Vengeful Bastards wanting revenge after their surprise assault at the service station had ended in defeat. Some said they were planning a second attack. There weren't enough Vengefuls to confront the Brigands, but they had allies and rumours swirled that several gangs were planning to raid the Brigands compound during the night.

It had also emerged that the London Brigand stabbed in the Flesh Tent had been seriously wounded by a member of a gang called Satan's Prodigy. The London chapter and some northern Brigands regarded Satan's Prodigy as enemies, but confusingly South Devon and Cardiff did business with them and wanted the whole thing smoothed over.

Outlaw Hill was a web of shifting alliances and the only conclusion James reached by the time the fire was lit was that it looked set to be a long and violent night. As the flames took hold, James wandered drunkenly through the twilight towards his tent. It was the first time he'd seen Will, Minted and Shampoo Jr since leaving the Flesh Tent more than four hours earlier.

'Where'd you disappear to?' Shampoo Jr asked as James lay back on the grass outside his tent and pulled off his trainers.

'Nowhere,' James said, as he caught a whiff of his own feet. His hands were black with newsprint and his deodorant had been overpowered inside his motorcycle leathers somewhere before Bristol. 'I stink like a dog.'

'This is nothing,' Minted smiled. 'You should have been here last year when it was raining. Outlaw Hill was solid mud. Head to toe, covered in filth and we had to walk the bikes through it.'

'I'm still trying to get to the bottom of our friend's

little adventure,' Will said. 'So we saw you come out the Flesh Tent with the chick wearing your T-shirt.'

James shrugged. 'Yeah, I had to walk to her van so she could get a top and give me my Ramones shirt back.'

'And that's it?' Will said suspiciously. 'Why were you gone for so long?'

'Had to get these,' James explained, as he opened his tent flaps and showed them a newly purchased set of riding gloves. 'The others were all gashed up where I hit that dude with the chain and the Führer told me to burn 'em.'

'Really?' Shampoo Jr said. 'So how come you've got lipstick all over your cheek?'

'Have I?' James said, rubbing the cleanest part of his hand against his face.

'No you haven't,' Shampoo Jr roared. 'But you just gave the game away, didn't you?'

'We followed you,' Will explained. 'And we waited a good few minutes for you to get out so we *know* you did more than swap shirts.'

'I don't get why you're so shy about it,' Minted laughed. 'If I went into the Flesh Tent and scored I'd be screaming it from the rooftops.'

'OK, I shagged her,' James admitted reluctantly as he drained his beer bottle. 'I can't help being gorgeous. It's no big deal, girls throw themselves at me all the time.'

'Big-headed bastard,' Will smiled as he offered James a high five. 'Good on you, mate.'

But before James could raise his hand there was a huge bang near the edge of the Brigands' camp.

Everyone looked around thinking it was early fireworks.

'Oh shit,' Will said as he looked over tents at a pair of flaming Harleys that had been doused with petrol. 'I think World War Three is about to break out.'

Other Brigands rushed forward and wheeled their Harleys away from the flames, while the two London Brigands whose bikes were burning sprinted towards the breakdown truck to grab fire extinguishers.

'That's the two whose mate got stabbed in the Flesh Tent,' Minted said. 'It's gotta be Satan's Prodigy.'

'They've gotta be insane,' Will said, as the faster of the two fat Brigands reached his bike and began blasting it with white carbon dioxide powder. 'Satan's Prodigy are outnumbered ten to one by Brigands.'

'They've teamed up with the Vengefuls,' Minted said. 'They must have done.'

James smiled. 'Unless someone who *wants* us to start a war with Satan's Prodigy did it.'

'Could be,' Will admitted. 'There are some sly people around.'

The heat from the flames expanded the air in the motorbike tyres. As the two owners desperately fought the flames, one tyre blew and the two blubbery men jumped back in fright and tripped over each other. It was high comedy, but nobody laughed.

'Those bikes are wasted,' Will said. 'Even if they get the fire out before the petrol blows everything will be warped from the heat.'

As more extinguishers arrived and the flames were finally engulfed by the clouds of white powder, seven

Brigands chapter presidents gathered for an urgent fireside conference. The voices were angry and James heard every word from thirty metres away.

Sealclubber was the most vocal, demanding that everyone tool up and immediately attack Satan's Prodigy. The Führer urged him to calm down and not act until they were sure who was behind the attack.

'You're full of shit,' Sealclubber screamed into the Führer's face. 'I've got a man stabbed, two of my full-patches' bikes burned up on the grass and you're telling me to hold back. I say we move now, and wipe Vengefuls and Satan's Prodigy off the face of the earth.'

The Führer tried to calm Sealclubber down, but he wasn't having it. The Führer realised that he was in a minority of one as dozens of inflamed full-patch Brigands gathered around him. The presidents took a vote and the Führer lost five to two.

'Guns, knives, bats,' Sealclubber shouted to the cheering crowd. 'Tool up and ship out, the Brigands are going on the warpath.'

34. BUOY

The sea and moonlight gave Nigel and Julian an eerie sense of calm as they came up from the crew quarters and stepped out on to the rear deck. Rods hung over the side, giving the impression of a boat hired for a night fishing trip.

'What's going on?' Julian asked, unaware that his tall frame and curly hair were blocking the lens of a button-sized camera stuck to the doorframe above his head.

Riggs sat up on the bridge, while Paul Woodhead stood on deck shining a powerful lamp over the sea.

'The Towmaster SONAR located our packages on the sea bed,' Woodhead explained. 'We've sent a signal to release the buoys attached to the packages. I need you two to open up the hold and set the ramp.'

The hold was accessed through a hinged metal cover. It took two arms to lift and the stench of rotting fish hit the two seventeen-year-olds as the hatch slammed down on the deck.

'Sighted,' Woodhead shouted up to the bridge, as the first of three fluorescent pink buoys broke the waterline thirty metres from the boat.

Riggs gave the engine a blast of power and threw on full rudder.

Woodhead eyed Julian and Nigel. 'What are you standing there for? One of you get down there and set the bloody ramp.'

Nigel wasn't keen, but Julian had done him a favour by agreeing to turn up, so it seemed fair that he should take the dirty end of the job. The hold's metal floor boomed as his trainers landed in a fine layer of silt, with a centimetre of water sloshing about. He was overpowered by the warm fishy air as Julian passed down an inspection lamp that clipped over a hook on the ceiling.

'You OK?' Julian asked.

Nigel didn't answer because he thought he might puke if he opened his mouth. He reached into the dirt and pulled up a sodden wooden board that latched over the sill of the hatch to make a ramp.

The trawler had slowed to a crawl and the pink buoy now bobbed five metres off the port side. Paul threw out a grappling hook and snared the rope attached to the base of the buoy. He then hauled the buoy in, hooked the rope over a pulley above the deck and looped the end around an electric winch.

The rear of the boat dipped as the winch raised the

package from the sea bed fifty metres below. It emerged from the water, a sandy rectangle the size of a freezer and wrapped in a rubber membrane sealed with epoxy resin.

'Give us a hand here,' Woodhead ordered, as he leaned precariously over the side of the boat and grabbed a rope attached to the bottom of the package to help swing it around on deck. Julian tried to help and almost got his arm crushed as the boat rocked and the package slammed against the hull.

For their second attempt Woodhead snared the rope on the bottom of the package with the grappling hook, Julian took the top end and the pair managed to manhandle it on to the deck.

'Jesus,' Woodhead gasped, groaning from the exertion and wiping the sweat off his brow. 'You did good. Now start slitting and sliding.'

As Riggs lined the boat up with the second buoy, Julian and Woodhead worked frantically. They slit open the rubber membrane and inspected the cardboard boxes inside.

'It's all dry,' Woodhead grinned. 'And that's a lot of shooters.'

The writing on the boxes was mostly in Chinese script, but it didn't take a genius to work out what was inside. Some were plain cardboard, but others were retail packs, printed in colour and advertising the benefits of the guns or bullets inside them.

Pulling up the packages and stashing the cargo was the riskiest part of the smuggling operation, especially on a calm summer Saturday when the yachts and pleasure craft were cruising and coastguard helicopters had plenty of moonlight to work with. Woodhead and Julian worked fast, carrying the heavy boxes across deck and sliding them down to Nigel who stacked them up in the stinking hold.

*

If you travelled with the Brigands you were expected to fight with the Brigands, so James had no choice as everyone piled out from between the tents, grabbing tent pegs, hammers, bike chains or whatever else came to hand.

Although the Führer had voted against the fight, his reputation as an outstanding leader meant that he was in charge of the attack. Two chapters including London would go after Satan's Prodigy, four would attack the more numerous Vengefuls, while the Cardiff chapter would stay back to defend the camp. Most hangers-on and puppet gang members would fight with whatever Brigands chapter had brought them, but Cardiff didn't have much backup so the Führer ordered two chapters of the Monster Bunch to stay behind.

As a hang-around, James could have gone with any group he fancied, but he chose safety over the chance of further fighting glory and stayed back with Will and the other Monsters. As six Brigands chapters led a noisy charge downhill, James joined a defensive line on the edge of camp. He stood two metres from Will, arms folded and wearing his new riding gloves with a length of bike chain wound around his left fist.

Satan's Prodigy were a powerful gang, but their

fourteen chapters were all based in northern England or Scotland and only two of them had come south for the Tea Party. The Brigands arrived to find that the Prodigy had packed up and taken refuge on other parts of Outlaw Hill. It was a victory of sorts, but most likely the start of a bitter feud that would flare up at runs and gatherings over months or years.

The Vengefuls were tougher opponents. The Brigands outnumbered them, but any Vengeful showing his face after the earlier rout was going to be tough and well armed.

The view down Outlaw Hill was lit by motorcycle headlamps and the huge bonfires. James caught glimpses of a medieval style battle, with screams, groans and metal hitting metal.

'We should be down there,' Will said eagerly, as he stood beside James.

But James didn't like it one bit. CHERUB taught you to measure up an opponent and only attack when you knew you could win. In particular he remembered how his friend Gabrielle had almost died after being stabbed in a street brawl and his shorts and T-shirt offered no protection.

'I'm going back to my tent for a second,' James said. 'I'm gonna grab a couple of tent pegs.'

But James really wanted protection. He unzipped his tent and grabbed the jeans he'd ridden up in and a blue hooded sweatshirt from his backpack. This was reinforced with a thin stab-proof lining and he pulled it on quickly.

As James crawled out of the tent he got blinded by three white headlamp beams. The bikes had crept on to Brigands territory from behind the portable toilets. James wasn't the first to notice and as he put on his trainers several Cardiff Brigands were charging towards the invaders. With the headlamps shining in James' face he couldn't tell what the riders were up to until flames erupted over the line of non-Harleys owned by members of the puppet gangs.

The sight of burning bikes set most of the Monster Bunch running out of their defensive positions towards the three riders, who opened their throttles and blasted off downhill. James was one of the first to reach the line of flaming bikes.

His first thought was his own Kawasaki. He couldn't remember exactly where he'd parked and was relieved to spot it five metres clear of the flames. He'd already seen how hard it was to put out the two flaming Harleys and they'd used up the fire extinguishers from the breakdown truck.

'Give us a hand,' James shouted, as he grabbed the bike nearest the flames that wasn't actually burning and lifted the back wheel to push it away.

The bike was heavy and the heat licked his jeans, but he soon had a Cardiff Brigand dragging the bike from the front.

'Good thinking, boyo,' the Brigand said, before shouting orders. 'Get the other bikes out. Make a fire break.'

It didn't take long to shift the bikes, but there was no

water around so the burning bikes were doomed. One desperate owner tried to beat the flames with a branch snapped off a tree, but it was hopeless. The guy was a Monster Bunch member in his early twenties and it was a horrible thing to watch his bike burn. James knew it was probably the most expensive thing he owned.

But there wasn't time for sympathy. The attack from the rear had been a diversion; bikers now swarmed into the Brigands' camp from the front. Someone screamed that they'd been stabbed. James and the Monsters moved warily towards the middle of the camp, where several of the attackers seemed to be holding sticks in the fire.

These caught light instantly, the blue flames they gave off indicating that the ends had been doused in petrol. James realised the Führer's suspicions about leaving camp were correct. Satan's Prodigy and the Vengeful Bastards weren't strong enough to take on the Brigands, but another gang had used the situation to formulate a well planned attack.

A Cardiff Brigand ran towards the fire and gave one of the torch bearers a two-handed shove, knocking him head first into the flames. But this was a minor victory amidst a spectacular defeat as bikers rampaged across the Brigands' camp using their flaming torches to set light to the tents.

Women gathered up kids and ran into the lane behind the camp. The defending Monsters and Brigands fought bravely but either got knocked down or retreated when the numbers overwhelmed them. There were hundreds more Brigands downhill, but by the time they knew what was going on and ran back up to their camp it would be too late.

James unwound some of the chain around his gloved left fist and ran towards his tent. Tents a few metres away were ablaze and he wondered if he should have gone straight for his bike as he stepped over a small gas camping stove. If one of those got hot enough to explode it would cause serious injuries.

But James was committed. He dived inside his tent, grabbed his crash helmet and hooked his backpack over one shoulder. As he backed out a bright blue flame plunged through the nylon over his head and swung towards his chest.

James was thankful for all the hours of combat training he'd done on CHERUB campus as he pulled his legs up to his chin, flipped himself head over heels and sprang gymnastically to his feet.

It was the last thing the attacker was expecting, and the stunned, flame-lit face of a wiry biker made James feel like he was in a dream from some weird zombie movie. He swung with the chain, slicing open the biker's cheek. A Karate kick to the kidneys sent James' attacker crashing to the ground, crushing Shampoo Jr's tent. The burning torch landed alongside and set fire to the nylon fabric.

James' tent and a dozen nearby were burning. The air was getting too hot to breathe and the skinny biker showed no signs of getting up. He'd suffocate, or at least get badly burned, if James left him, so he hooked his helmet over one arm before grabbing the biker's ankle and dragging him between a line of tents on to clear grass.

Half a dozen men fought nearby as James swatted out the flames on his opponent's jeans and rolled him in the dirt to make sure. The patch on the back of his jacket read: *Bitch Slappers, Luton.* He saw that part of the patch had torn off as its owner got dragged through the dirt, and knew that stealing it would earn him kudos from the Brigands.

As James dug his gloved fingers under the stitching and ripped the patch off he heard a gunshot. It was a long way down the hill, but it crushed any lingering doubts about whether he should leave.

James stuffed the patch inside his backpack and dodged behind Shampoo Jr, who was down in the dirt and about to get stomped by three Bitch Slappers. He thought about wading in, but in a mass brawl even the best fighter can get stabbed from behind or knocked out by a stray punch and he'd taken too many risks already.

The worst of the fighting hadn't reached the back of the Brigands' campsite. A couple of the toughest Cardiff Brigands stood by one of the coaches, armed with machetes. The coach itself had its engine running. All the seats were filled with women and sobbing kids, but more were piling on board to sit on laps or stand in the aisle.

James ran up to his bike and saw that someone had worked their way along the line with a hammer, smashing lights and tipping them over. His Kawasaki seemed to be leading a charmed life: the only damage he could see in the dark was an indicator lamp that had shattered when the Honda trail bike next door had been kicked over.

After hauling the Honda back on to its stand, James straddled his Kawasaki and put on his helmet. His backpack hung awkwardly from one shoulder and he wasn't even sure if the zips were done up, but he could stop and fix that later. He needed to get out of the danger zone as fast as he could.

There was a muffled crunch as James kick-started his engine. His heart leapt, thinking that he'd been sabotaged, but he'd actually heard a Bitch Slapper hurling a stone slab at a side window of the packed coach.

The last passengers ran aboard and the driver began reversing with the two Cardiff Brigands leaning from the open doorway. As James pushed off he saw that the slab had ricocheted off the toughened glass, but he could see people screaming in the seats next to it and the coach driver couldn't pull away until he'd made a tricky reversing manoeuvre on to a tree-lined avenue.

The Bitch Slapper was picking up the slab and if it hit the window a second time it might punch a hole and seriously injure the kids inside. James still had the chain wrapped around his glove and he unwound it as he drove off at walking pace. With one hand on the handlebars, he opened the throttle and his Kawasaki accelerated hard. The ground was bumpy and it was a fight to keep the bike under control, but he steered up on to the road beside the coach and lashed the Bitch Slapper across the back with the chain, slicing through his leather jacket and tearing into his back.

As the Bitch Slapper collapsed, James lost control of the chain, which swung around and cracked his visor. He wrenched the brakes, but found his tyres jolting violently over tree roots. He thought he was going head first into a trunk, but he managed to swing past with his jeans scraping bark.

Back on the road the coach driver completed his turn and aligned his front tyres so that his vehicle passed cleanly over the stone slab and the writhing Bitch Slapper. James took a long breath and stuffed the chain into his hoodie pocket before driving in a tight circle and pulling back on to the road.

After a few hundred metres the road broke away from Outlaw Hill and he overtook the coach. Some of the women inside gave him thumbs-up and the Cardiff Brigand in the open doorway waved his machete appreciatively.

James sped on across a taxiway, between the frames of two rusting hangars that hadn't housed an aircraft in thirty years. The moonlit fields on either side were dotted with couples making out and families enjoying a late picnic. But while some corners of the Tea Party remained calm, James saw an air of panic on the main strip, with vanloads of police parked in the middle of the tarmac and ordinary bikers and their families surging towards the exit gates.

James cruised an access road that ran parallel with the strip and gulped when he saw the tatty stall with *Cardinas Spanish Paella – Famous across Europe* written across the back. He felt slightly sad as he imagined Reina standing inside with her hair tied back.

The gate James had entered through with the Brigands was manned by one of the bikers in fluorescent security jackets.

'You want a hand stamp for re-entry?' he asked. 'What's it like up there on the Hill?'

'Mental,' James said. 'Looks like the police are getting ready to go in and I've got no intention of going back.'

The coach closed back up behind James as he pulled through the gate and turned right. The traffic was heavy, but the snarl-ups were all in the public car park behind him. Most of the traffic was coming out of the festival, but the headlamps of the few cars coming the other way reflected horribly off the crack in his visor and blinded him.

James had lost count of the beers he'd drunk and as his adrenaline rush wore off he realised he was in no state to make the three-hundred-mile ride back to Devon. He stuck close to the kerb, let cars overtake and hummed an Arctic Monkeys song to stop himself from falling asleep.

When he reached an out-of-town shopping area he pulled the bike up outside a McDonald's, then checked the area out to make sure that there were no other refugees from the Tea Party around. There weren't, but it was probably only a matter of time and he didn't want to be here on his own when a chapter of riled-up outlaws arrived.

James slid out his mobile and dialled the campus

emergency number. A man with a brummy accent answered: 'Unicorn Tyre Repair.'

'Hey, Ranjit,' James said, relieved to hear a familiar voice. 'It's James, agent twelve-o-three. I'm about fifteen miles from Cambridge with a motorbike. I need you to reserve me a hotel room somewhere nearby. Then arrange for a van to come and pick me and the motorbike up early tomorrow morning and take me back to Devon.'

James waited a few seconds while the emergency mission controller tapped away at his keyboard.

'OK,' Ranjit said. 'I can book you into a three-star or a five-star. Those are both within four miles of your present co-ordinates. Which would you prefer?'

'Oh let me think,' James said. 'The five-star, maybe?'

Ranjit laughed. 'Why ask, eh? I've e-mailed driving directions to your hotel to your handset. Is there anything else you need? Would you like me to contact Chloe Blake?'

'Yeah, give her a call and tell her I'll speak to her once I've checked in and taken a shower.'

'You don't sound so great.'

'Just knackered,' James explained. 'It's been a bloody long day.'

35. COUSINS

Dante tried not to think about his past as alcohol took hold and the party at the Führer's house came to life. By quarter to ten you couldn't get across the conservatory without stepping over teenagers making out. The stereo speakers were out on the lawn and a dozen girls danced barefoot in the grass. The atmosphere in the back lounge was darker, as lads who'd either been blown out or were scared to speak to girls drank hard and bickered over the pool table and dart board.

Joe was in a state. Lauren tried to keep him calm, but all the little problems were stressing him out. The toilet upstairs was blocked, someone had puked on the doorstep, the woman who owned a cottage on the next plot of land phoned to complain about lewd dancing and he'd caught two girls snogging on Martin's bed.

Worst of all one girl had brought an older cousin and

then a bunch of his friends had turned up. Before long there was a group of five sixth-form kids who were acting rowdy and making phone calls urging more friends to come along.

'What are we gonna do?' Joe asked Lauren, as he sat on the bottom of the stairs drumming his leg. 'If I ask them to go they'll just laugh . . . And everyone will think I'm a geek.'

Lauren put a hand on his shoulder. 'I've told you already, me and John will back you up if you want to go in there and ask them to leave.'

A roar of laughter and clapping came out of the front lounge and two people Joe hadn't seen before walked past.

'Who the bloody hell are *they?*' Joe said. 'I didn't see them come in.'

Lauren shrugged. 'I don't think they're bothering with the front door. They're walking around the side and coming in through the French doors.'

'Shit,' Joe said, burying his head in his hands. 'I never should have done this. You and me could have had the house to ourselves. Drunk some champagne, used my parents' Jacuzzi. Instead I had to have this dumb party.'

'Next time, eh?' Lauren smiled, as she kissed Joe on the neck. 'Shall I get you a drink?'

'I suppose,' Joe said. 'Lager or something. I might as well *try* to enjoy myself.'

Lauren stumbled as she got off the steps and only avoided a fall by grabbing hold of the banister. 'Those wine spritzer things are *too* nice,' she giggled, as she ambled down the hallway towards the kitchen.

The kitchen worktop was covered with the residue from the cocktail making, the fridge door hung open and someone had dumped empty beer cans in the washing machine. Lauren grabbed a bottle of Stella for Joe. She wasn't planning to drink another spritzer straight away but she saw that there were only a few left so she grabbed one.

'Hey gorgeous,' a kid with a beard slurred, grabbing a handful of Lauren's bum as his other arm reached in for a beer. 'You're like, cute . . . you know?'

Lauren cracked her head on the inside of the fridge as she shot up. 'Buzz off, you creep,' she snapped as she scowled and rubbed her head.

The guy thrust his hips and flicked his tongue in and out. 'You *know* you want me, baby cakes!' he howled.

He howled again as Lauren jammed her finger in his eye.

'Bitch,' he moaned, as he dropped his unopened beer and stumbled backwards into a cabinet. 'I was only messing.'

'Kiss my arse,' Lauren said, as she slammed the fridge door and stormed off with the two drinks. She was halfway down the hall when she heard a window breaking in the back lounge.

Joe got there first, and found a bunch of his school friends scuffling over the pool table with some of the older kids. The window had broken when two guys fighting over a cue had led to the thick end going through a pane of glass.

'Hey, what the hell?' Joe demanded, as he faced off an overweight kid who looked about James' age.

'These wankers won't let us near the table,' the fat kid explained. 'All I said is that I'll play the winner.'

'These *wankers* are my friends,' Joe answered back. 'Who are you? Why are you even in my house?'

The kid shoved Joe with both hands. 'You starting something, titch?'

'I can batter you, you fat turd,' Joe shouted.

Lauren and Dante had both come into the room, along with a whole bunch of the older kids.

'Are we getting the pool table or not?' one of them demanded. 'These Year Eights need their butts whipped if you ask me.'

'Do you know who owns this house?' one of Joe's mates shouted. 'Start something here, mate, and the Führer will finish it.'

'And where is he?' the fat kid taunted. 'Fat arsed old racist. Probably out lynching some coons with his KKK buddies.'

Joe charged forward. It had been a few years since he'd been coached by Teeth but he could still throw a decent punch and the fat kid hit the floor, unconscious. There was a collective gasp followed by plenty of pushing and shoving.

'I think everyone who doesn't know Joe should show some class and leave,' Lauren suggested.

All Joe's friends agreed, as did some of the older crew who justified themselves by saying things like *It's a kiddies' party anyway*, but were actually shit scared of the Führer.

The majority started heading out of the lounge, but as Lauren and Joe gave each other relieved smiles a kid in a Man United shirt stuck a pool cue through another window.

'This is bullshit, man,' he yelled.

'Dickhead,' Joe shouted, and charged into the older kids. But one good punch and some alcohol-fuelled bravado hadn't turned him into a fighting champion. The sixth former in the Man United shirt clamped Joe's head under his arm and punched him hard in the eye.

As Lauren waded in to save her boyfriend, a whole bunch of Joe's mates charged towards the older kids. Most didn't want trouble, but a hard core of five lads stood their ground and traded punches with eight younger boys plus Lauren.

Dante overbalanced as he dragged the toughest looking kid away from a skinny Year Eight and ended up stumbling forward and slamming a window sash down on the tough kid's head.

Lauren freed Joe from the kid in the Man United shirt, but she was drunk and hopelessly mistimed a Karate kick. She landed up on her arse, but her opponent was all mouth and she launched a savage upwards kick as he tried to punch Joe.

Of the five older kids who'd stayed to fight, Lauren and Dante had nailed one each, two had been knocked to the ground and were getting worked over by all Joe's mates. The last kid stood up on the pool table. Small and squat, with tangled black hair, he swished a cue back and forth and yelled, 'Come and have a go then ya cocky little bastards!'

Lauren and Dante made eye contact and moved in together. As Lauren snatched the swinging cue, Dante jumped on to the end of the pool table and brought him down with a rugby tackle. His chin thumped the corner pocket before Lauren grabbed his neck and dragged him away.

'All right, son,' she said cheerfully as she gave the lad a gentle slap on the cheek. 'Time to go home to mommykins.'

As Lauren escorted the grunting boy towards the door, Dante realised that the two down on the ground were getting serious beats and told the others to back off. Once the fighting stopped some of the older group came back into the lounge to extract the injured.

The cue swinger swore at Lauren as she threw him down on the front porch. There were a few kids squatting nearby, including a girl being sick and a boy with a bloody face. Most of the older kids were heading towards the road, though a few took revenge by ripping up plants and shrubs and one shouted that the Führer was a *Nazi tosser* as he ripped up the *Eagles' Nest* sign and lobbed it over a hedge.

Lauren checked that there were no more older kids upstairs before turning off the music and telling the girls to come inside and lock the French doors until the older kids were gone. Everyone gravitated towards the kitchen and Joe sat on a stool, clutching his eye and trying not to sob.

A whole bunch of girls gathered around and offered sympathy. Lauren was out of breath after grappling with two older kids and she located her unopened wine spritzer.

'Maybe we should all tidy up a bit,' Dante suggested.

A couple of the girls started picking up empty cans and bottles, while Dante found a dustpan and brush to pick up the broken glass in the back lounge. As he walked along the hallway he saw a police car rolling up the drive.

*

When the *Brixton Riots* docked back at Kingswear, Paul Woodhead drove his van up to the dockside and the four-man crew took ten minutes to transfer the boxed guns and ammunition into the rear compartment.

The surveillance team didn't have the resources to follow everyone, so they prioritised. They couldn't lose track of the weapons, so McEwen and Neil Gauche took the BMW and surveillance van respectively and stayed a kilometre behind the tracking signal from Paul Woodhead's van. Chloe stayed behind in Kingswear, monitoring Riggs as he moved from the shore to the village pub and listening to the conversation inside Julian's car.

'My arms feel like they've been stretched on a rack,' Julian complained, as he slammed his door. 'Quite a workout.'

'I'm sorry you got dragged into this,' Nigel said,

getting in next to Julian. 'I reek from inside that hold. I'm gonna stink out your car.'

'Smoke?' Julian asked.

Nigel laughed. 'I need *something* to take the edge off. I hope I never see that bastard Woodhead again.'

Julian's hands trembled with a mix of fear and exhaustion as he put two cigarettes in his mouth and lit them both before passing one to Nigel.

'At least you made a grand,' Nigel said.

'Take your half if you want,' Julian replied, with his voice croaky from the smoke.

'It's your money, Julian. Paul would have had my legs smashed if you hadn't come through and done this for me.'

Julian grunted. 'You did save me from drowning when I fell off that rope swing.'

'I forgot that,' Nigel said. 'How old were we? Eight or nine?'

'I don't want dirty money,' Julian said. 'I'll pay my debts, but making money off guns is bad karma. I'll stick it in a charity box. African babies, or blind pandas or some shit.'

'Sweeeet,' Nigel laughed, as Julian started his engine.

Julian pulled away from the empty seafront. Chloe thought about following them back to Salcombe, but she couldn't see anything useful coming out of it and decided to stick around for a while, just in case Riggs went back to the boat, or McEwen called asking for backup.

'This is some heavy shit,' Julian sighed, as he drove up a cobbled lane heading for the road back to Salcombe. 'I mean, when you think about it a grand seems like a lot for a night's work. But what if we'd been busted gun running?'

'Oh yeah,' Nigel smiled. 'That's prison time for sure. But we're out of it now and we wore gloves the whole time, so there's no prints on those boxes.'

Julian burst out laughing as he made a left turn. 'Man, you *really* stink of fish. You're gonna have to burn those clothes.'

36. COPS

Joe answered the door to a policewoman, while her male colleague walked back to the gate to speak with a group of the older kids who were waiting for a taxi. The policewoman realised that Joe was shaken up.

'Can I step inside?' she asked cheerfully. 'We had a call from a young girl inside the house. She seemed a bit worried about what was going on.'

The police weren't strangers to the Führer's house, but he didn't leave anything incriminating in his home and Joe had instructions to be polite and allow the police to search if they asked to.

'Not much happened,' Joe explained, as the policewoman walked down the hallway past peanut shells and crumpled cans. 'There was a rumble and a couple of windows got broken.'

The officer nodded as she walked into the kitchen

and acknowledged the girls leaning on the cabinets. 'Are you all OK?'

The girls looked sheepish as Joe wondered which one had called the police.

'Well,' the officer sighed, 'if it's any consolation I've seen house parties resulting in much bigger messes than this. But it's a warning to you all the same. If you have an unsupervised party, make sure you only invite people you know and trust. Or better still, don't have one at all.'

The friendly lecture took Lauren back to primary school when the local beat constable turned up to teach her class road safety. The young male officer who came through the front door wasn't as friendly.

'Got a lad up there with a busted nose,' he told his colleague stiffly. 'I've radioed for an ambulance and told him to wait. I don't suppose any of you lot saw what happened?'

Dante shrank back behind Anna, suspecting that it was the guy whose head he'd slammed in the window.

The female officer took Joe back into the hall and spoke quietly. 'I think I know your mum, don't I?'

'You might do,' Joe nodded. 'She's on the neighbourhood watch.'

'I wouldn't want to be in your shoes when she gets home,' the officer smiled. 'I think it's best if I ask everyone to go home, don't you?'

Joe was embarrassed at the way the policewoman was mothering him, but was also relieved to have some of the responsibility taken away.

'Listen up everyone,' the policewoman said, as she

clapped her hands. 'I think it's time you all went home. So call your parents or make whatever arrangements you have to. And while you're waiting, perhaps you can help your friend Joe to pick up as much mess as you can.'

Some of the kids lived within walking distance and left straight away, but a dozen had to wait for pickups and they all mucked in with the clean-up. Lauren loaded the plates and glasses into the dishwasher, Dante hoovered and swept while Anna mopped the kitchen floor.

By half-eleven the two cops and all the kids except Lauren, Anna and Dante had left. The house looked reasonable, but Joe was still going to get in trouble for the things that would take time to fix: three busted windows, torn felt on the pool table, and the huge penis and hairy balls someone had drawn on the wallpaper in the upstairs toilet.

'It's not bad at all,' Lauren said. She sat on a bar stool in the kitchen draining a wine spritzer, with the dishwasher humming in the background.

Joe came in from taking out black rubbish bags filled with empties. He was almost back to his cocky self and moved in to give her a kiss, but Lauren leaned towards him and completely lost her balance. She hit the floor hard. Dante was concerned enough to come running over, but Lauren clutched her sides and began shrieking with laughter.

Joe gave her an arm up as Dante inspected the wine spritzer bottle. 'How many of these have you had?' he asked.

'I love your cute little chops,' Lauren grinned, as she pinched Joe's cheek between her thumb and finger and then stumbled forward. She was heavy and Dante had to grab her waist to stop her knocking Joe over. The two lads then grabbed Lauren under the arms and dragged her to the conservatory where they dumped her over the sofa.

'Those things are delicious,' Lauren hooted. 'Someone go back to the clubhouse and rob more spritzers!'

Anna hovered behind the two boys. 'I could make her some black coffee or something.'

Dante sighed. 'It'd take half the Brazilian coffee harvest to sober that up.'

'Did you phone your mum?' Joe asked.

Dante knew that Chloe was helping with surveillance duty. 'She's on a date and she'll go nuts if she sees Lauren in that state.'

This was completely true. CHERUB agents have to fit in and are allowed to drink and smoke within reason in social situations, but it's easy to make slip-ups with your cover story when you're as drunk as Lauren was, and if Chloe found out she'd be in serious trouble.

'I'll take her home,' Dante sighed. 'Hopefully the walk will sober her up a bit.'

'I'm hardly even drunk,' Lauren protested, as she stood bolt upright with her arms rigid like a soldier about to march.

Joe looked at Anna. 'What about you?'

'I lied and told my mum that I was sleeping over at

Tracy's house,' Anna explained. 'But Tracy's dad picked her up ages ago.'

'You can stay here,' Joe said.

'But no hanky panky,' Lauren snorted, as she bunched a fist. 'He's my man. You keep your hands off!'

'Come on, sister,' Dante moaned as he grabbed Lauren's arm and pulled her forward. 'Let's get you home.'

'We've got a wheelbarrow,' Joe grinned. 'You could stick her in that if you like.'

Anna cracked up laughing as Lauren staggered down the hallway, holding on to the walls and telling nobody in particular that she was perfectly fine and didn't need any help. Then she tripped over the doormat and sprawled out on the patio.

'Ooopsie daisy,' Lauren giggled, as Dante rushed forward and helped her up. 'Who put that stupid thing there?'

'See you tomorrow, maybe,' Dante called back to Joe, as he began walking up the drive with Lauren's arm draped over his shoulder. 'Or maybe at school on Monday.'

'Not if I see you first,' Joe said, giving the thumbs-up as he closed the front door.

Lauren being off her face had seemed funny back in the kitchen, but by the time they'd made it up the long drive and turned towards home the stumbling and giggling was getting on Dante's nerves. When they reached a section of the busy lane with a grass verge he stopped walking, grabbed Lauren's hand and jerked her arm to make sure she was looking at him.

'I don't know if Chloe's home,' Dante warned. 'But if she sees you walking into the house like this you're gonna face suspension from missions. So *stop* mucking about.'

Lauren poked out her tongue. 'Bee boo,' she giggled, showering Dante in spit.

Dante squeezed her hand hard and spoke firmly. 'I'm not mucking about, Lauren. This is serious.'

'You're hurting me,' she whined, as she tried tugging her hand free.

Dante was worried, because even though Lauren was completely smashed she still knew some nifty combat moves. But he kept squeezing Lauren's hand because otherwise she'd ignore him.

'You're being an idiot,' he barked. 'Do you want me to leave you here? Because I will.'

As Dante said this, a big four-wheel-drive Toyota whizzed past, blowing Lauren's hair about.

'If you don't let go of me,' Lauren began angrily, but then her expression changed. 'You know, your eyes are *dead* sexy when you're angry.'

Before Dante knew it she'd grabbed him around the neck and started kissing him. Lauren was fit and he instinctively opened his mouth wide and pulled her in, but after a couple of seconds he saw sense and pushed her back.

'Don't,' he said. 'We've both had a few drinks and imagine if someone drives by. We're *supposed* to be brother and sister.'

Lauren started to walk under her own steam. She was a bit wobbly, but Dante kept close and made sure that she didn't fall or wander out into the traffic.

She turned back with a serious expression and a wagging finger. 'I think you're one of the nice guys, Dante,' she slurred. 'Most boys would have taken advantage. If you'd been like my brother you'd have my top off by now.'

'Watch the cars,' Dante warned, as a Ford skimmed by and blasted its horn.

Dante nudged Lauren back to the side of the road, but at least she was moving quickly and it was much easier going without her arm draped around his back.

The last third of the walk was on a much quieter road with a proper paved sidewalk. It curved up a gentle slope through the estate of luxury homes where they lived. Dante was relieved to be out of the traffic, but now he worried that Chloe would drive past or that Lauren would make a noise and disturb the neighbours.

What he didn't expect was to see her start clambering through the hedge at the bottom of their road.

'Where are you going?' Dante asked.

'I'm absolutely busting,' Lauren said. 'I'll be two seconds.'

Dante tutted. 'We're three hundred metres from home. You *don't* need to go in a hedge.'

But Lauren was full of drunken determination and ploughed through the branches. As she stood up on the other side Dante heard her trainer skid, followed by a yelp and a kind of zipping sound.

'Lauren, are you OK?' Dante shouted, following her through the hedge.

Dante realised that Lauren had tripped over a knee-high railing. She'd then slid two metres down a forty-five-degree concrete embankment and landed in a drainage channel designed to stop the water that ran off the hill from flooding the road.

'Are you OK?' Dante asked anxiously. He cleared the railing and stepped gingerly down the concrete slope. At least the bottom of the channel was dry after all the recent hot weather.

It was almost dark, but the moonlight caught a pained expression on Lauren's face. 'I landed really hard on my hand,' she explained. 'I don't know what I've done but it hurts like shit.'

*

McEwen parked five hundred metres back and watched through binoculars as Paul Woodhead reversed the white van into a dilapidated farm building a kilometre from his Dartmouth home. After padlocking the doors, Woodhead donned a crash helmet and leather jacket before getting on a small Yamaha trail bike and heading back out to the road.

'What do you think?' Neil asked over the police radio from inside the surveillance van.

'I'll stay here and see what we've got,' McEwen said. 'You follow Woodhead's bike. He's almost certainly heading for home, but let's be sure.'

'Copied and understood,' Neil said.

McEwen grabbed a torch, a video camera and a lock

gun from the glove box before stepping out of the BMW and heading towards the barn. He approached slowly and used the binoculars to check the building from all sides, making sure there was no sign of an alarm or surveillance cameras. When he got up close he flicked on the torch and shone it over the dirt outside the shed to see if there were any trip wires or motion sensors.

It all seemed reassuringly low tech. So was the two-lever padlock, which McEwen popped with a filed-down key and a sharp slam from behind. The wooden door was noisy and he jolted as his radio made a bleep.

'He's home,' Neil said. 'Watched him strip off through the bedroom window and head for the bathroom.'

'Might as well come back here then,' McEwen said. 'I'm already inside.'

'See you there,' Neil said.

McEwen kept an eye out for security devices as he circled the van. Once he felt safe, he put on a set of clear plastic gloves and pulled the small video camera out of his pocket. The back doors of the van were unlocked and he caught a whiff of fish as the light mounted on the video camera illuminated the boxes.

'Could start a nice little war with that lot,' McEwen said a couple of minutes later when Neil arrived. 'Grenades, assault rifles, bullets. There's even an RPG launcher in there.'

Neil was shocked. 'George didn't order any RPG launcher.'

McEwen shrugged. 'Maybe they've got other customers. Or maybe it's for the Führer's private armoury.'

'What now?' Neil asked.

'There's some miniature tracking devices in the BMW,' McEwen explained. 'We can use them to follow individual boxes when the weapons are moved. Unfortunately the mini trackers are a lot less reliable than the big suckers we stick on the cars.'

'And then we watch and wait,' Neil said. 'The question is how long? Hours, days, weeks?'

'I expect that the Brigands will want their money ASAP,' McEwen said, as he looked at his watch and yawned. 'All I know for sure is that I've been on duty since I got out of bed this morning, so I hope your boss Chief Inspector Johnson is sending someone down here to relieve us before too much longer.'

'Someone's coming down from our London HQ,' Neil said, shaking his head ruefully. 'But we're gonna have to keep our eyes propped open for a few more hours yet.'

37. HOME

James spent the night on a huge feather mattress and managed breakfast in bed before 8 a.m., when a driver from campus arrived to take him and the bike back to Salcombe. The roads were Sunday-morning quiet and driving a van registered to an organisation that doesn't exist means you can't pick up speeding fines, so they made three hundred and twenty miles in less than five hours.

According to Radio Cambridge the trouble at the Tea Party had resulted in several stabbings, four people with serious burns and one fatality. The story had also made it on to the tail end of national radio news.

James couldn't be seen arriving home in a van, so they pulled over fifteen miles from Salcombe. It was a glorious morning as James rolled his bike down a ramp and he powered off with only a slight headache and his busted helmet visor to remind him of the day before. The clear roads and lush countryside made him feel like he was riding through a TV commercial.

The long journey the day before had boosted James' confidence in the saddle. He rode fast and when he pulled on to the brick driveway he'd have been happy to turn back and do it again. He rummaged in his backpack, but couldn't find his door key and rang the bell.

Lauren came to the door in pool shoes and James' Green Day T-shirt. 'Where's your key, div?' she said dourly.

'I wondered where that shirt disappeared to,' James said. 'You look *seriously* rough.'

'Joe's party,' Lauren explained in a flat voice, before raising her arm to show off a plaster cast.

'Who'd you punch?' James grinned.

'You're *so* funny,' Lauren said, and wandered into the kitchen with James behind her. She reached up into a cupboard and grabbed two fizzy paracetamol tablets from a medicine box. As she dropped the pills into a glass of water, Dante came in from the garden smelling of grass. His bare chest glistened with sweat.

'*How* convenient,' Dante complained. 'Lauren can't push the mower with her broken wrist and you turn up just as I roll it back into the garage.'

Hot from his ride, James filled a mug with tap water and gulped it down. 'You still haven't told me how you did your wrist in.'

'Let Dante explain,' Lauren said, waving her hand in

front of her face. 'I'm going back to bed for a bit. Tell Chloe that if she makes lunch I don't want anything.'

'Not even a nice pickled beetroot and raw liver sandwich?' James teased.

Lauren glowered at her brother. 'James, if I spew up I'm gonna aim at you.'

'You should have seen her,' Dante said quietly, as Lauren padded upstairs to her bed. 'She drank about a dozen wine spritzers. She was *completely* smashed. She tried squatting in the hedge at the bottom of the road to take a piss and she fell into the drainage channel.'

James burst out laughing. 'You're shitting me! She doesn't usually get drunk. She always says she doesn't like the taste of alcohol.'

'I thought she was gonna get in trouble with Chloe,' Dante explained. 'Fortunately the pain from her wrist had sobered her up by the time Chloe got to the hospital.'

James found all this highly amusing. 'Well, that's something else I can wind her up about. Is Chloe in?'

'Sitting on the patio reading the *Sunday Times* while I slaved my guts out in the sun,' Dante explained bitterly. 'I'm gonna dive in the shower.'

James wandered out into the back garden where Chloe lay on a sun lounger wearing big sunglasses. She had the *Style* magazine from the newspaper and James thought she looked sexy in shorts and a lime green bikini top. He'd already called her the night before and explained everything that happened at the Tea Party, minus his two hours bonking in the back of a caravan.

'Get back OK?' Chloe asked.

'Pretty painless,' James nodded. 'And the hotel was nice so I got some kip.'

'You had a call about an hour ago. Dirty Dave.'

James smiled casually. 'He's got a kind of hero-worship thing going with me since I saved his butt at the service station yesterday. I tell you, if I play him right I could get right in close with the Brigands.'

'That's why you're here,' Chloe smiled. She reached towards a bottle of suntan lotion that was just beyond her fingertips. 'Pass that up, would you?'

'Don't strain yourself, girl,' James said, as he kicked the bottle towards her. 'Did you get a number?'

'Written on a Post-it by the phone,' Chloe nodded.

The lotion bottle made a farting noise as Chloe squeezed it. James grabbed the phone in the living-room and dialled Dirty Dave's mobile.

'Are you home OK?' Dave asked.

'Just arrived,' James said. 'I'm sorry I bailed, but it was getting messed up in there. My mum's gonna kick my arse: my helmet's busted, my Kawasaki needs a new indicator lamp and my tent, sleeping bag and everything got cremated.'

'No one's holding it against you,' Dave said. 'The Führer's wife Marlene was on that coach. She says you're a sodding hero the way you chain-whipped that Bitch Slapper.'

'So where are you now?'

'Hotel near Cambridge,' Dave explained. 'There's about fifty refugees here. We pulled out not long after you and the coach. The Führer's livid at Sealclubber. The Brigands' reputation is in tatters.'

'Never should have poured out of camp like that,' James agreed. 'Made us look proper muppets. How's about your bike?'

'I'm one of the lucky ones,' Dave said. 'The Führer lost his bike. Teeth's had his new Speedster less than a month and it's nothing but a charred frame. There's gonna be a war over this. Inside the Brigands *and* out.'

James knew this was bad. When studying the background for the mission he'd read about wars between outlaw biker gangs in Canada, the USA, Holland, Australia and Scandinavia. They'd resulted in shoot-outs, bombings and dozens of dead bodies. Out of all the countries with large biker communities Britain was the only one that had never seen a major turf war, but the Tea Party incident looked set to change that.

'You know I'm loyal,' James said. 'So did you call to check on me, or was there something else?'

'I did have a proposition,' Dave nodded. 'It's something that could earn you a good deal more than your crêpe flipping job, but it's a matter for face to face conversation. I should be back in Salcombe by this evening. Could you meet me at Marina Heights sometime tomorrow?'

'I've got school,' James said. 'But I can be there by about four.'

*

McEwen and Neil had spent the night in the BMW, taking turns to watch the shed, making sure that the weapons weren't moved. When it got to one in the afternoon and they still hadn't been relieved, Neil called his boss, Ross Johnson.

'I do understand your position, sir,' Neil said into his handset. 'But we've been on duty twenty-seven hours straight. We need to be relieved. If someone comes in and grabs those weapons now, McEwen and I are in no proper state to follow them. We're in the middle of nowhere. I've barely put a crumb past my lips since yesterday afternoon.'

Neil relayed his boss' explanation to McEwen. 'Ross says he's had problems because there's no overtime budget and he's had to send six of his best people to start an investigation into the trouble at the Rebel Tea Party. Our relief has arrived, but they've just gone to check into their hotel.'

McEwen's eyes shot open. To Neil's alarm McEwen snatched the mobile from his hand. 'McEwen here,' he shouted. 'Now listen here, you candy-arsed penguin-poking bottom-bandit. I haven't eaten, slept or shat. I'm sitting here in a car that's as hot as hell, and you're telling me that my relief has gone to check into a bastard hotel! What the hell else are they gonna do before they make it up here? Sit down for a cheese ploughman's? Play nine holes at the seafront pitch-and-putt?'

As a Chief Inspector, Ross Johnson wasn't used to being spoken to like that, especially by a twenty-two-year-old like McEwen.

'Now you listen here, young man,' Johnson roared.

'Don't you *young man* me, you goat's dangler,'

McEwen bellowed, as Neil shrivelled into his seat with embarrassment. 'When you work with CHERUB you do what *we* say. And I'm saying get your people to stop whatever they're doing and drive here and relieve my arse *now* . . . Who goes and checks into their hotel when the surveillance team hasn't eaten for eighteen hours?'

McEwen threw the phone at Neil so hard that it bounced off his lap and hit the door, making the battery compartment fly off.

'Glad to get that off your chest?' Neil inquired.

'No offence,' McEwen said. 'But I spend a lot of my time working with the police and the great majority of them are dipshits.'

Neil sighed. 'Ross isn't a bad guy. We just don't have the budget or manpower that we really need.'

McEwen got out to stretch his legs as Neil reassembled his mobile. Standing up gave McEwen a better view and he couldn't believe what he saw.

'Binoculars,' McEwen yelled, as he leaned into the car.

The magnified view confirmed that there was a police van parked by the trees on the far side of the shed, plus two armed officers taking up positions behind a hedge.

'What are they doing here?' McEwen shouted into the car desperately. 'They'll blow our whole operation.'

McEwen grabbed his security services ID from a jacket thrown over the back seat and started running flat out across the field. By the time he'd reached the front of the shed there were six uniformed officers coming towards him and a megaphone blaring out.

'This is the police, stand still and raise your hands.'

'Go swivel,' McEwen shouted as he carried on steaming towards a sergeant.

A warning shot fired out of the bushes, hitting the grass about five metres behind McEwen. They were in the middle of nowhere and even if the locals hadn't seen the police driving up to the fields, half the neighbourhood would have heard the gunshot.

'Do not move,' the megaphone blared. 'Drop to your knees and place your hands on your head.'

McEwen swore as he dropped to his knees and the cops surrounded him. The senior officer was a burly sergeant all done up in riot gear. He directed four men towards the shed before pulling his baton and glowering at McEwen.

'Think you need all that gear to storm a wooden barn?' McEwen asked sarcastically, as he waved his ID. 'I'm intelligence service. That barn is under surveillance and you just blew a major operation.'

The sergeant snatched McEwen's ID and stared at it sceptically. He wasn't the first policeman who didn't recognise a security service identity card when he saw one.

'Where'd you get this, sonny? Did you buy it in the pub, or laminate it yourself?'

The sergeant laughed as his colleagues used a battering ram to smash the door off the barn.

'You're gonna be in the shit when my people hear about this,' McEwen shouted.

'Cuff *that*, and stick him in a van,' the sergeant told a

female colleague as he swaggered uphill towards the barn. But by this time Neil Gauche had arrived, waving a more recognisable metal police badge.

'He's with me. Sergeant Neil Gauche, National Police Biker Task Force. What's happening here?'

A cop shouted out from the barn. 'We've got the guns, sarge. Whole van is packed with 'em.'

The sergeant looked at Neil and shook his head. 'I don't know who you are or what's going on here. All I know is that this got called in by the Chief Constable for Devon. So if you want to know why we're here, you'd better ask him.'

Neil pointed at McEwen. 'He's with me, can you let him up?'

'I suppose,' the sergeant said, and gave McEwen back his card. 'Intelligence service, eh? You don't exactly look like James Bond, do you? Or even very intelligent for that matter.'

The sergeant laughed at his own joke, but stopped abruptly as McEwen grabbed his riot clothing and nutted him.

38. FISHES

Chairwoman Zara Asker had cooked her Sunday roast, but instead of eating it with her family she'd had to drive to the RAF airfield near CHERUB campus and take a small jet down to Exeter.

Chloe met her in the terminal and they drove to a conference room she'd booked at short notice in a nearby hotel. As one of CHERUB's most junior mission controllers Chloe was nervous around her boss.

'Ross Johnson can't make it,' Chloe explained as they walked across a sunny car park and into the hotel's bland lobby.

Zara wasn't in a good mood. 'If I can make it all the way from campus when I'm seven months pregnant, why the hell can't he get from London?'

'He's in Cambridge,' Chloe said. 'He's got the press on his back after the Tea Party riot.'

'So who is here?'

'Ross' deputy, an Inspector named Tracy Jollie.'

'And she's cleared to know about the CHERUB operation?' Zara asked.

'We cleared the three,' Chloe said. 'Ross Johnson, who knew about CHERUB already, Neil Gauche and Tracy Jollie. The rest of Ross' team know about the fake weapons buy, but not about the CHERUB operation.'

Zara nodded as they turned out of the lobby and began walking down a long corridor lined with the closed doors of banqueting suites.

'This was the only place I could find near to the airport at short notice,' Chloe explained.

'I'm sure it's fine,' Zara said, sensing Chloe's nerves. 'What about the three kids? How are they taking the news of the police raid?'

'Lauren and James have been on enough missions to expect things to go wrong, Dante's more of a worry. He has such a big personal investment in this mission. He really wants to see the Führer go to prison.'

The conference room had windows overlooking the runway of Exeter's small airport and all the standard features: long table, overhead projector and flip chart, plus a plate of biscuits and a Thermos of hot water for making drinks.

Everyone had waited more than forty minutes for Zara. Neil and McEwen still hadn't slept and stayed alert by pouring sachets of Nescafe coffee granules on to their tongues. Lauren sat with her head slumped on the desk, while James and Dante had built a tower out of miniature UHT milk cartons.

Zara came in and quickly shook hands with Tracy, then sat at the head of the table.

'OK,' Zara said, as she pulled in her chair. 'What do we know about these police raids? How and why did they happen?'

Police inspector Tracy Jollie began to answer. 'I've been on the phone with the Chief Constable for Devon and I've met with the inspector who ordered this morning's raid. Last night Neil and McEwen watched four men unloading weapons from the trawler *Brixton Riots*. One of the crew was a young lad named Julian Hargreaves. Our teams dropped surveillance on him after he left the scene.'

'Why?' Zara interrupted.

'Manpower,' McEwen said. 'It was me, Neil and Chloe. We chose to follow the weapons.'

Tracy continued. 'It's my understanding that Julian left his friend Nigel and then went to his home in the Marina View apartments. When Julian arrived he started thinking about what he was involved in and got worried about what the guns and weapons he'd smuggled would be used for.'

James had heard the story already and snorted dismissively. 'Julian isn't the kind of guy who lets his conscience keep him awake. It's more likely that he smoked enough dope to scramble his brain, then got paranoid about getting nicked.'

'Maybe,' Tracy nodded. 'It doesn't really matter. What matters is that Julian decided to approach his father and confess to what he'd done. Jonty Hargreaves is a crown court judge with a background in criminal law. He set about doing what any father with a legal background would do, which was to find the best possible outcome for his son.

'So the Honourable Jonty Hargreaves got Julian to write and sign a statement, explaining how he'd been dragged into the smuggling operation by Paul Woodhead in order to save his friend Nigel from a beating. Jonty then called his old friend the Chief Constable for Devon, and they carved up a deal.'

'How did Julian know where the weapons were stored?' Lauren asked.

'Woodhead must have mentioned something when he was on the boat,' McEwen suggested, before Tracy continued her story.

'First thing this morning, Jonty and Julian presented themselves at the police station. Julian handed his written confession to an inspector hand-picked by the Chief Constable. Julian had admitted to a serious crime, *but* his father knows that his son is seventeen years old, Julian has no previous criminal convictions and he's making a confession that will lead to the seizure of a large shipment of illegal weapons and the arrest of Riggs and Woodhead.'

Zara nodded. She understood how the law worked with juveniles better than most lawyers and finished the story herself. 'So Julian will have to go to court and plead guilty to a couple of minor charges, but the judge will give him credit for confessing. And, as Julian's still seventeen, he's a juvenile so he won't even have a criminal record beyond his eighteenth birthday.'

'That's it in a nutshell,' Neil sighed. 'But Judge Hargreaves' *get out of jail free* scheme for Julian has wrecked any chance we had of following the weapons to their destination and getting evidence that links the Führer and other senior Brigands to the smuggling racket. The icing on the cake for us is that we've paid a three-hundred-grand deposit which we'll probably never see again. It's a *massive* embarrassment.'

Dante sprang up, making his chair shoot backwards, then slammed his palm on the table top. 'That bastard,' he shouted. 'The Führer's gotta be the luckiest dirtbag on the planet. Nothing ever sticks to him. Give me a gun, I'll stick it in his face and spray his brains all over his front doorstep.'

Chloe stood up and moved towards Dante. 'Calm down, mate,' she said soothingly. 'Everyone here wants to see the Führer put behind bars, but we always knew that this mission was a long shot.'

'Don't give me that,' Dante said furiously. 'For all you lot the Führer is a target. Some you win, some you lose and if you lose you'll get on with the next job. But I watched him take a gun and kill four members of my family.'

Zara stood up and spoke in a firm voice. 'Dante, I know you're having a hard time with this. But even CHERUB isn't totally above the law. There are countries in the world where the government goes around killing anyone they don't like, but I'm glad that I *don't* live in one of them.'

'I'm sorry,' Dante said, stepping back from Chloe and picking up his chair. 'I'm not being professional. It just *pisses* me off that the Führer keeps on getting away with everything.'

'Completely understood,' Zara nodded. 'So how was the CHERUB part of the mission going before this happened?'

Lauren answered first. 'Me and Dante were getting nowhere fast. We did get the tip-off about Nigel being involved in the weapons smuggling through his sister Anna, but that was a fluke to be honest. Our main target was Joe Donnington, on the basis that he'd know a lot about what his dad was up to, but he doesn't. He finds having a father who goes around dressed like Hitler embarrassing and keeps his distance.'

'Joe's a good kid,' Dante said. 'He was my best friend back in the old days and if my parents were alive he probably still would be. But he doesn't know any more about Brigands weapons smuggling or drug dealing than I do.'

'Disappointing,' Zara said. 'What about you, James?'

James straightened up in his chair and cleared his throat. 'It was going really slowly,' he said. 'On Friday I'd have said that I was no closer to penetrating the Brigands organisation than when we first arrived. But the run out to the Rebel Tea Party changed everything. Dirty Dave loves me, the other Brigands are starting to think I'm an asset and I'm a shoo-in for Monster Bunch membership if I hang around over the summer.'

'It's so frustrating,' Chloe said. 'James made the

breakthrough we've been desperate for just as the other end of the operation blew up in our faces.'

'I've got this meeting with Dirty Dave on Monday,' James said. 'He said he's going to offer me a way to start making some money.'

'Any idea how?' Tracy asked.

James shook his head. 'But he said he didn't want to talk about it over the phone, so it's going to be something illegal.'

Zara nodded and locked her fingers together. 'Well,' she said, as she drew a sharp breath, 'none of you are going to like this but I think CHERUB has to pull the plug on this one.'

'For god's sake,' Dante moaned.

'*Don't* bite my head off,' Zara said. 'Every CHERUB mission is authorised by our ethics committee. Your mission briefings cleared you to infiltrate the Brigands and work with the Biker Task Force in order to help them link a shipment of weapons to the Führer and other full-patch Brigands. That mission ended when the weapons were seized by Devon police.'

'I could have been stabbed or worse at the Tea Party last night,' James protested. 'I'm happy to take risks, but what's the point if the rug gets pulled from under you? Especially with this meeting on Monday.'

'I know,' Zara nodded. 'I don't think we should forget all about the Brigands, especially as the three arrests probably won't stop their weapons smuggling. What I am saying is that the mission you were sent here for is over. You kids can tell your friends that your parents are reconciling and that you're going back to your father in London on a trial basis.

'Chloe can work with Ross Johnson. Maybe they can devise another mission that takes advantage of James' burgeoning relationship with the Brigands. We'll keep the house in Salcombe and with the school summer holidays coming up, it's perfectly credible for you all to disappear back to London for a few weeks.'

'What about my meeting with Dirty Dave on Monday?' James asked. 'I might as well go and listen to his offer.'

'Agreed,' Zara nodded.

'So who would come back?' Dante asked. 'All of us, or just Chloe and James?'

Zara shrugged. 'Probably just Chloe and James, but it obviously depends upon the new mission and its objectives.'

'If there is one,' James said.

Tracy spoke enthusiastically. 'If James is on the cusp of penetrating the Brigands it could be a huge breakthrough. Especially with a biker war on the horizon.'

Zara stood up. 'So, does anyone else have anything to add?'

Nobody said anything, although Dante groaned to remind everyone how cheesed off he was. Zara shook Tracy and Neil's hands before they left the room.

'I'll drive the kids back to Salcombe,' Chloe said.

Zara pointed at McEwen. 'You *stay* here,' she said firmly. 'The Chief Constable isn't very happy about one of his sergeants ending up with a fractured cheek and neither am I.'

McEwen shrugged and looked like a little boy who'd been caught stealing cookies. 'I blame it on stress,' he said. 'And extreme sleep deprivation.'

'Really,' Zara said, clearly not convinced. 'Well, the good news is that you'll have six months to recover from stress and sleep deprivation while you work in the basement of the main building. I believe there are five thousand boxes of archives to be re-catalogued and digitised.'

39. CHARRED

When his Monday afternoon maths class finished, James headed straight off to the Leather and Chrome workshop where he'd booked in his bike to have the rear indicator replaced. The twin garage doors were open and James was shocked to see a dozen charred Harleys along one wall. They ranged from blackened hulks to less serious cases that had suffered minor damage from being near the flames.

'Not a pretty sight,' James said, sucking air between his teeth as Rhino came down the steps from the showroom. 'That's gotta be over a hundred grand's worth of damage.'

Rhino nodded. 'And these are just the bikes that are salvageable, or that have some parts worth stripping. We left four more up there that were nothing but scrap metal.'

'Tragic,' James said. 'Did you come out OK?'

Rhino pointed towards his yellow Harley Softail. 'It doesn't look too bad, but it got near the flames and heat is a killer. All the wiring's got to be stripped out and replaced. You're looking at two or three days' work and a lot of money for parts.'

'Not good,' James said. 'I was lucky, for sure.'

'I've got another ER5 upstairs in the showroom,' Rhino explained. 'I'll take the lamp from that one if that's OK? It'll be Friday before the new unit arrives.'

'Sounds OK,' James said. 'How much is it gonna set me back?'

'Fifty-six quid for the part is all,' Rhino said. 'The Führer said not to charge you any labour on account of what you did with the coach.'

'Cool,' James smiled. 'That's appreciated. How long will it take?'

'It's a twenty-minute job, I'll do it myself while you wait.'

'Brilliant,' James said. He pointed towards Marina Heights. 'I've got to meet Dirty Dave. Will it be OK if I swing by and pick it up in half an hour?'

'Course,' Rhino nodded. 'By the way, I've not seen your mum for a week or so. Give her my regards.'

James took off his leather riding jacket and slung it over his back as he walked up the back steps towards the restaurants. It was another glorious day and Dirty Dave waved from one of the tables outside a French restaurant that was closed for a break between lunch and dinner. He had a bottle of fizzy water and an ashtray stuffed with dog ends in front of him.

As James sat down he noticed an open-faced motorbike helmet finished in black carbon fibre resting on an empty chair. Most outlaw bikers wore open face helmets. They provided less crash protection than fully enclosed helmets, but gave better visibility and looked ten times cooler.

'That's for you,' Dirty Dave said.

James cracked a big grin. He'd seen a similar helmet advertised in a magazine for over three hundred quid. 'That's awesome,' he gasped. 'But I can't take this, it's too much.'

Dave shrugged as he sucked on his hand-rolled cigarette. 'That sharpened hammer would have gone through my skull,' he said. 'Besides, Brigands get trade price in the Leather and Chrome showroom. The mark-up on those things is like a hundred and fifty per cent.'

James gave the helmet's soft leather trim a sniff and admired his reflection in the chromed chin bar. 'I just did what anyone would have done.'

'The other thing I've got to ask you about could earn you a lot more than cooking crêpes,' Dave said. 'You interested?'

'I'm always interested in making money.' James reckoned it was most likely to be drug related, but if it was to do with weapons smuggling they might be able to extend the mission.

Dave smiled. 'I saw you walking around at the Tea Party with your shirt off and you've got a great physique. Do you work out?'

'Some weights and stuff,' James nodded, wondering if

Dave wanted him to work as a bouncer or something like that. 'And I did a lot of Karate and kickboxing when I lived back in London.'

'You see, in my business youth is *everything*. Someone your age can make a heck of a lot of money.'

James was slightly baffled. 'What business is that?'

'I thought you knew: I run half the strip joints in Devon. Why do you think I'm called *Dirty* Dave?'

James' jaw practically hit the table top and Dave caught his expression.

'I know what you're thinking,' Dave said. 'But being a male stripper doesn't make you gay. What it makes you is *minted*. You're seventeen, but you look younger. I can put you on stage in a skimpy costume at my club in Taunton. You dance around a bit, flash your biceps, wiggle your bum in some dirty old sod's face. I'll pay you fifty quid for a four-hour shift, but on top of that you'll get blokes giving you tips and for someone your age that could be a *lot* of money.'

James looked aghast. 'Are you on a wind-up?'

'Absolutely not,' Dave insisted. 'I can take you up to my club for a look if you want to check it out. The manager and the other boys will find you a costume, teach you a few dance steps and show you how to handle the customers.'

James had been through all kinds of stuff on CHERUB missions, but nothing in his training had prepared him for this moment and his face was going bright red.

'Oh,' he said weakly. 'I mean, this is a surprise. So,

like . . . How about I think about it for a day or two and give you a call?'

'You're flustered,' Dave said, as he pointed towards the crêperie. 'Embarrassed even, and that's completely understandable. But you can spend all night cooking pancakes and make what? Twenty-five or thirty quid? At your age and with your body you can make twenty times that amount. Why not use your assets to your advantage?'

*

Lauren thought it was the funniest thing she'd ever heard. She laughed so much that she fell off the sofa and ended up on the floor with one hand clutching her stomach and another thumping repeatedly on the carpet.

'Oh please god, stop me laughing,' Lauren shrieked. 'I can't breathe. I'm going to die.'

Chloe was trying to act like a responsible adult and had gone out to the kitchen to calm down, but James could still hear her convulsing with laughter.

'It's not *that* funny,' James protested, as he hurled the TV remote at Lauren.

'Yes it is,' she screamed. 'Oh god, I can't wait to tell everyone on campus.'

Dante had been doing homework at Anna's house and wheeled his bike into the hallway a couple of minutes later.

'What's so funny?' he asked.

'James got invited to become a stripper at Dirty Dave's gay club in Taunton,' Chloe said, as she came back into the living-room.

As soon as she made eye contact with Lauren she started howling again. Dante didn't laugh as hard as the girls until Lauren jumped up on to the coffee table and started dancing.

'I'm James and I'm a stripper, put some money down my pants,' she sang.

'So are you gonna do it?' Dante smirked. 'I can just see you up on stage, with greasy old businessmen leering at you.'

'I think it's the perfect way for him to infiltrate the Brigands,' Chloe smiled. 'He can do it for a couple of years and if it doesn't work out at least he'll have a nice little nest egg.'

Lauren hopped off the table but lost her balance and bent her thumb back as she landed awkwardly on the sofa.

'Serves you right,' James gloated, as Lauren clutched her hand and moaned. 'I'm going upstairs to get changed for work.'

'Leather hat and tanga briefs?' Dante grinned, making Lauren start laughing again.

Chloe stopped James as he stormed towards the door. 'On a more serious note, now that we know Dirty Dave's proposition isn't related to weapons smuggling you'd better start preparing to leave. I want all of you to tell your friends that it looks like I'm getting back with your dad and that you'll be going back to London this weekend. Make sure you don't burn any bridges, in case any of us come back for a second mission.'

40. FLIP

It was Thursday, nine-thirty and James' pancake flipping career would end in half an hour. He dropped a steaming crêpe on to the preparation surface, then laid on vanilla ice cream, tinned orange segments and chopped nuts before folding it in half and dropping it on to a cardboard plate.

'Voilà,' James said cheerfully, as his nine-year-old customer grabbed her food and bolted towards parents and a disabled brother sitting at one of the tables. Then he turned towards Martin and acted like he was crying. 'I'll miss this all so much,' he wailed.

'Sure you will,' Martin said. 'I just hope whoever Teeth sends over as a replacement is as cute as you are.'

'What are the odds of that happening?' James grinned. 'Ten million to one?'

'How'd Ashley take the news that you're going back to London?'

James shrugged. 'She seemed underwhelmed. I don't think it's gonna go down as one of my greatest romantic entanglements.'

'You can knock off now if you like,' Martin said. 'Is there anyone you want to say goodbye to or anything?'

'I've gotta go up and give my security pass to Teeth in the office, but that's about it . . . Oh, and if Noelene's around I might tell her that she's a stuck-up wrinkle-faced ho.'

As James undid his apron he was surprised to see Nigel and his brother Will approaching.

'My sister Anna's heartbroken that your little brother's leaving,' Will complained. 'When are you off ?'

'Tomorrow,' James said, before turning to Nigel. 'How's it going?'

'My life is absolutely and completely down the shitter,' Nigel said, faking cheerfulness.

'I saw the story about weapons getting seized on the local news Monday night,' James nodded. 'There's all sorts of rumours buzzing around college.'

'Cops busted me Sunday morning,' Nigel explained. 'Hauled me in. Searched my house. They found my stash and a bunch of fish-stinking clothes that screwed up whatever chance I had of an alibi.'

'So they've charged you?' James asked.

Nigel nodded. 'I'm out on bail. The Brigands have sorted me a decent lawyer, but even if I plead guilty she says I'll be looking at time locked up in young offenders'.'

'Shit,' James said sympathetically. 'Any idea how long?'

Will answered. 'Lawyer reckons between eighteen months and three years. With so much publicity around gun crime she says it's a bad time to stand in front of a judge on a weapons smuggling charge.'

'And finding three ounces of spliff under my bed doesn't help,' Nigel sighed. 'I already got a caution for possessing marijuana last year.'

James liked Nigel, but struggled to find something suitably grave to say. In the end he gave up and went with, 'I'm sorry for you, mate.'

'Not as sorry as me, I'd bet,' Nigel grunted.

'So, has anyone seen that snitching sack of shit Julian?' Will asked.

'Nah,' James said. 'Not at school or around here.'

'He won't show his face,' Nigel said. 'There's too many bikers around and he knows he'll get his head caved in. It's my own stupid fault for getting Julian involved: way out of his depth. It's no surprise that he panicked and went running to his dad.'

'He might be getting a slap on the wrist from the law, but he'd better start running when he sees me,' Will growled. 'I understand his daddy's Jaguar has already had an unfortunate encounter with some pickaxe-wielding Dogs of War.'

'Ashley says she overheard one of the teachers talking about Julian going private for his last year of school,' James explained.

'Figures,' Nigel said. 'Boarding school probably, and his dad owns a flat in London, so I'd say the chances of seeing Julian's face in these parts are about zero.'

'Paul Woodhead is a retired full-patch Brigand,' Will noted. 'So he'd better watch his back.'

James shrugged. 'But on the other hand, with Julian's dad being a judge and the Brigands focused on repercussions of the Rebel Tea Party, they might lay off him.'

'It's barely even registered with my dad,' Martin agreed. 'Priority one is dealing with Sealclubber and the London Brigands. Then he's got to re-establish the Brigands' status in the pecking order by waging war with the Vengefuls and the other gangs.'

James was surprised by Martin's comment. In all the hours they'd worked together in the crêperie this was the first time he'd ever heard him comment on Brigands affairs.

'So anyway,' Nigel said, tapping a pound coin on the counter top. 'Before I'm locked up eating soggy shepherd's pie with dead bugs in it, I might as well treat myself. Gimme a banana, almond and honey filled crêpe, with extra cream and rum-raisin sauce.'

*

Back at the house Dante was in his room, packing tops and underwear into a blue crate. When it was full he clipped on the plastic lid and grabbed the handles to go stack it up in the hallway downstairs, but he stopped when he passed Lauren's room. Her door was slightly open because of the heat and he could see her lying on her bed, facing the wall.

'Are you OK?' Dante asked, as he leaned in the doorway.

'Yeah,' Lauren said, but an involuntary sniff gave the game away.

Dante stepped inside, dodging four half-packed crates. 'What's the matter?' he asked.

Lauren hesitated for a few seconds. She considered telling Dante to mind his own, or pretending like nothing was wrong, but realised she needed to talk to someone.

'I was thinking about Joe,' Lauren explained, as she sat up. 'I know it's stupid. I'm a trained agent and I'm supposed to be wary of forming close bonds on missions and blah, blah, blah.'

'Anna's pretty sad that I'm leaving too,' Dante nodded.

Lauren smiled. 'It's funny, all the boys on campus brag about going on missions and getting off with girls. And for the girls it's supposed to be like, *oh god some horrible boy is gonna try and get his hands on me.*

Dante laughed. 'Either that or you're labelled a maneater or a slut.'

'Exactly,' Lauren said, smiling and sniffing at the same time. 'But Joe is *such* a nice guy. When I first met him, with all his mates and his designer label clothes and his cockiness I thought he was a knob. But now we really get along. At first he was *so* sweet. He'd never had a girlfriend before and he was really nervous.'

'He's a good guy,' Dante agreed. 'I'm surprised you're

not together for your last night.'

'I know,' Lauren sulked. 'His aunt's just had an operation. He got dragged to visit her with his mum.'

'That's really shit,' Dante said. 'Anna's got swimming club, but she said she'll drop by on her way to school tomorrow.'

'So, have you got feelings for her?'

'Some,' Dante said awkwardly. 'But – and don't spread this around on campus, this is between you and me – there was a girl called Harriet when I was on my mission in Belfast. We went out for over a year and because of the way my mission ended, we never even got to say goodbye.'

'Oh that's *really* sad,' Lauren said.

Dante pulled a Velcro wallet out the back of his shorts. He dug his fingers inside and took out a crumpled passport picture of a dark haired girl with a round face and big brown eyes.

'She's beautiful,' Lauren said. 'I guess I've been lucky, really. Unless you include horses, this is the first mission I've been on where I've really fallen for someone.'

'I'm sure we'll both survive,' Dante smiled, as he backed up towards the door. 'I'd better get my box downstairs.'

Lauren pointed out the boxes spread over her floor. 'I think I'm with you on that score,' she grinned.

Out in the hallway, Dante put his photograph back in his wallet and picked up the box of clothes. As he walked down he thought about Joe and his mum being out. After stacking his clothing on top of the other crates in the hallway, he took his mobile out of his shorts before stepping on to the doorstep.

The sun was down and a hairy moth circled around the carriage lamp beside him. He slid his mobile open and dialled Joe's house. Joe and Marlene were at the hospital and Martin was working with James at Marina Heights. But where was the Führer?

Just as Dante expected an answerphone to cut in, he heard the Führer's voice. 'Yeah, who's this?'

Dante didn't speak, but his heart quickened. He hung up. The sky was black and the fields behind the house rustled in a gentle breeze, just like the night his parents died five years earlier. He thought about his recurring nightmare: running through the fields, with the Führer wielding his gun and his baby sister's body slippery with blood.

Now the Führer was home alone and with the mission over this was his only chance for revenge. After racing up to his room, Dante dragged a backpack filled with espionage equipment out the bottom of his wardrobe and unzipped to make sure he had everything he needed.

Dante pulled a hooded sweatshirt over his head, then put a knife, a lock gun and pair of disposable plastic gloves into his front pockets before slinging the pack over his shoulder.

Lauren was packing in the room next door, and Chloe was in the dining-room typing up a mission report on her laptop. He could go out the front door, but thought it was best if he appeared to be home if either came looking for him, so he dashed into his en-suite bathroom and let his shower run cold. Back in the bedroom he switched on his bedside radio and laid a set of clothes out on his bed so that it looked like he'd put them on when he came out.

Dante thought about timings as he opened his bedroom window. He could run the kilometre to the Führer's house in four minutes. If he was in the house for six minutes and ran back again his trip would take about the same amount of time as a leisurely shower.

The knife dropped out of Dante's pocket as he landed on the hard ground outside his first-floor window. He'd made quite a noise, but looked up at Lauren's room and was relieved to see her moving a stack of hanging clothes from her wardrobe on to her bed.

Seeing Lauren made Dante pause for thought. He was trained well enough to kill the Führer without leaving conclusive evidence, but even though the Führer had lots of enemies, if Chloe and Zara were smart enough to join the dots he'd be kicked out of CHERUB.

But looking up at the window reminded Dante of his sister Lizzie and how she'd spent the last seconds of her life lowering Holly to safety. Scotty had always told his sons that men fought their own battles and Dante couldn't help but agree as he started running: for all the good intentions and hard police work, the Führer had got away with four murders and lived in a luxurious house, with millions in the bank and loyal followers prepared to fight and kill for him.

At the bottom of the street, Dante crossed over the

road and vaulted a fence. The cross-country route would add a couple of minutes to his trip, but he wouldn't be seen by passing traffic.

The ground was hard as he ran flat out across open fields, slowing only for a low hedge and a metal gate. The Führer owned a good stretch of the sloping land beyond his house. Dante could have vaulted the wooden fence with a short run-up, but he'd damage plants and might leave footprints if he landed in soft earth, so he cut back on to the road. He used the main gate and walked up the front drive, taking cover only when he got to within twenty metres of the house.

The lights were off, except the front hallway, the kitchen and an upstairs bedroom. It was a warm night and he'd hoped one of the downstairs windows would be open, but they were all locked.

He considered ringing the front doorbell, but after recent events the Führer would be cautious about opening up, so Dante crept around to the conservatory. He peered through the French doors towards the kitchen and saw that nobody was inside. The sliding glass had locks that were only accessible from within, so he moved towards the wooden door at the back of the kitchen.

After putting on plastic gloves, Dante tried the handle and found it locked. This wasn't a huge problem: the door only had a basic lock. He clipped the right sized pick to the end of his lock gun and a squeeze of the trigger and two seconds of jiggling saw the door opening up into the kitchen.

Dante stepped inside, closed the door quietly, then

checked his watch. He'd left home less than six minutes earlier. The next task was to find the Führer before the Führer found him. He moved stealthily into the hallway that led towards the front door. The back living-room was open. He noticed that the windows had been fixed and the pool table had been stripped down to its slate base in order to have the felt replaced.

The front living-room door was shut. No light crept from around the door frame and there was no sound when Dante put his ear to the door so he headed upstairs. After passing Joe and Martin's rooms, Dante saw that the Führer's bedroom door was ajar. The hallway light was off, but there were flashes of blue and pink light and the sound of a voiceover from a TV.

Dante moved swiftly towards the bedroom, then crouched down low and peered through the gap. The Führer sprawled on his bed in a towelling robe with a beer can in hand and a bag of kettle chips wedged between his thighs. The window was open and the net curtain wafted into the room as an F16 launched off a carrier deck on the TV.

'As well as being the most modern ship in the Nimitz Class, the Ronald Reagan is home to more than seventy of the world's finest fighter pilots and the qualified mechanics who keep their lethal war birds in the sky . . .'

The Führer's presence made Dante feel sick. If he'd been forced into a surprise encounter, Dante would have gone for a knock-out blow and then used his knife, but from the point of view of leaving forensic evidence it was better to use something from the house.

Dante jogged down the hallway to the study at the rear end and flipped on the light. He paused for an instant in front of the picture of the Brigands 2002 Summer Barbecue before grabbing a crossbow pistol with an optical sight – deliberately avoiding the one he'd handled in front of Anna on Saturday – and loaded three bolts into the firing mechanism.

After flipping out the light, Dante walked back towards the Führer and crouched in the doorway. The door wasn't open far enough to give him a good shooting angle so he nudged it a few centimetres and the hinges creaked.

The Führer saw the movement out the corner of his eye, but attributed it to the breeze. As his attention turned back towards Nimitz Class carriers, Dante looked through the magnified sight and aligned the crosshairs over the Führer's neck.

Dante pushed his shoulder up to the door and took a deep breath to steady his aim. Once the first bolt hit, he'd barge into the room and shoot the second through the Führer's heart.

41. NUMB

James took a twenty-mile detour on the way home, blasting down unlit lanes with the exhaust roaring and his single headlamp showing the way. He scared himself a couple of times and arrived home sweaty and exhilarated.

He felt mournful as he rolled his Kawasaki up the brick driveway and parked it in the double garage beside the Range Rover. He'd used the bike in conjunction with a secret identity, so even if he offered to buy the bike out of his savings there was no way he'd be allowed to keep it. And as James was only sixteen it might be a while before he got another shot at riding a motorbike, especially one as powerful as his ER5.

James stripped the riding gloves he'd bought at the Rebel Tea Party and the fancy carbon-fibre helmet Dirty Dave had given him three days earlier. The motorised garage door did its thing as James walked towards the front door, dipping into his jeans for a set of house keys. His nose caught something sweet and he smiled: one thing he wouldn't miss was coming home tainted by the sweet steam that rose off hot crêpe batter.

'That you James?' Dante said, making him jump.

James looked up, then behind before realising that Dante was slumped against the wall in the brick corridor between the house and garage. There was enough light escaping from the bedrooms upstairs to see that he looked pretty sad.

'You OK?' James asked, as he noticed a small crossbow pistol resting on Dante's lap. 'Where'd you get that from?'

'The Führer's house,' Dante explained. 'You killed someone once, didn't you?'

'On my second mission,' James nodded. 'I snatched his gun. It was him or me.'

It was only as James said this that his brain linked Dante's hatred of the Führer with the fact that Dante had visited the Führer's house and the fact that he had a crossbow pistol loaded with deadly metal bolts in his hand.

'Dante, what the *hell* have you done?' James gasped.

'He was home alone,' Dante explained. 'I broke in, found the Führer laying on his bed. Lined him up in the crosshairs and went to pull the trigger, but I dunno . . . It wasn't in me.'

James exhaled with relief, but couldn't find any words. He agreed with the principle that CHERUB didn't go around assassinating people, but knew he'd feel differently if the Führer had killed *his* family.

'I had it all worked out,' Dante said. 'I made sure I wore the same trainers that I had on at Joe's party, so my shoe prints wouldn't prove anything. By using the Führer's own weapon and leaving it at the scene there'd be nothing you could trace back to me. Zara and Chloe would have suspected, but unless I'd been severely unlucky with an eye witness, they never would have proved a thing.'

'Maybe it's for the best,' James said softly. 'I still wonder about the bloke I shot. It really plays on your mind.'

Dante got out of the gravel and looked thoroughly disgusted with himself. 'I'm weak,' he said. 'If there's an afterlife, my dad's sitting up there now with his head in his hands because he just found out that I'm the biggest chicken-shit coward that ever lived.'

As Dante turned away, a rolled-up photograph dropped out of his sweatshirt. James picked it up.

'Don't you want this?' James asked.

'Bin it,' Dante said bitterly, as he walked towards the back garden.

James opened out the photo and saw that it was a Brigands barbecue. He recognised the Führer in the middle, with Joe standing proudly in front of him. Dante looked very different with short red hair, but the teenage girl on the edge of the picture looked remarkably like him.

'You know, Dante,' James said, as he followed the

younger boy on to the back lawn, 'maybe the reason you couldn't pull the trigger wasn't because you're a coward. It's not like shooting someone in the head is something to be proud of, is it?'

They'd kept their voices down to avoid being heard by the girls inside the house, but now Dante shouted. 'James, *please* just leave me alone.'

'You couldn't kill the Führer because you're a better person than he is,' James explained. He held out the photo for Dante to see. 'Look at your mum and your sister in this picture. Do you think they'd want you to be torturing yourself over revenge, or to get on with your life?'

James wondered if his argument sounded too sappy, but Dante stopped walking and snatched the picture back.

'Give us that,' Dante said, managing a half smile. 'It's weird looking at Lizzie and thinking that she'd be twenty-one now. And I only remember her as my bossy big sister, but when I look at this picture you can see she was dead sexy. She was really funny as well.'

James nodded. 'You know the weirdest thing about being a cherub? We get to do all this great stuff and our lives are amazing compared to ordinary kids, but I reckon most of us would go back to our boring old lives if we had the chance.'

'In an instant,' Dante nodded. 'And at least the Führer's gonna get a shock the next time he goes into his study.'

'The missing picture,' James nodded.

'Not just that,' Dante smiled. 'I fired a crossbow bolt between the eyes of his Hitler painting and scratched *Dante Scott is a Vengeful Bastard* into his desktop with my hunting knife.'

James smiled, then smiled some more as the complexity of this message sunk in. 'If he thinks you're part of the *Vengefuls* and he knows that you were walking around his house with a crossbow . . .'

'I might be too chicken to blow the Führer's brains out,' Dante said ruefully. 'But at least I've given him something to mull over.'

42. FRIDAY

Twenty-four hours later James, Lauren and Dante were all back on campus. Friday night always had a good atmosphere and this one was better than usual because loads of kids on campus were flying off to CHERUB's summer hostel the following Monday.

Just after five, Rat came back from playing tennis with Andy. He'd kicked off his trainers and was peeling a sweaty shirt over his head when Lauren erupted out of his wardrobe and screamed, 'I'm back!'

Rat flew up in the air and jolted back towards his bed, before bursting out laughing. 'You scared the living crap out of me,' he gasped.

'I got your text messages,' Lauren said. She stood teasingly in front of Rat, so that her bust almost touched the beads of sweat running down his chest.

'Pity you didn't answer them then,' Rat said frostily.

'I reckon me and you have something pretty special going,' Lauren grinned. 'And besides, with my wrist in plaster I'll need someone to carry my luggage on to the plane next week.'

'And what makes you think I want you back?' Rat sneered. 'For all *you* know I've been having a torrid affair with some bimbo while you've been away.'

'Two reasons,' Lauren answered. 'First of all, I've got spies all over campus. Second, what other girl would put up with your stupid hair?'

'How can I turn down an offer like that?' Rat smiled. 'I'd kiss you but I'm all sweaty.'

'There's a fine line between manly ruggedness and BO,' Lauren grinned, as she moved closer and pecked Rat on the lips. 'Just this once I'll give you the benefit of the doubt.'

*

Two floors down James was sitting on the sofa in Kerry Chang's room. He'd only been back on campus for two hours, during which time he'd managed a late lunch, a shower and a change into shorts and a CHERUB T-shirt.

Kerry smiled as she came out of her bathroom, towelling her long black hair, dressed in a matching white bra and knickers.

'Third time lucky for us,' James said. 'That's what I reckon.'

Kerry threw the towel back inside her bathroom as she sat on her bed. 'So you never got up to anything on your mission?'

'Nah,' James shook his head. 'Well, there was this girl

Ashley, but she was just someone I made friends with and she was religious so I wouldn't have got anywhere even if I'd wanted to.'

Kerry laughed and rubbed a hand against her duvet. 'Why are you hiding over there on the sofa?'

James grinned as he stood up. 'I feel like a drug addict. I've been cold turkey on Kerry Chang for almost two years, but now I'm about to start injecting again.'

Kerry burst out laughing. 'So you're saying I'm like a cheap fix?'

'No,' James grinned. 'I'm saying you're irresistible and highly addictive.'

'Remember when we used to wrestle?' Kerry said. 'You used to get pissed off because I *always* won.'

'I remember no such thing,' James smirked. 'Besides, back then I was only a few centimetres taller. Now I'm all butch and manly.'

Kerry thought this was hilarious. 'Tell you what, big man,' she grinned. 'If you can pin me, you can do anything you like to me.'

James' eyes boggled. 'Does that include naked stuff?'

'You've got to pin me first,' Kerry said. 'And of course, you've got to do whatever *I* want if you lose.'

'You mean I'll be your love slave?' James checked.

Kerry smiled. 'Is it a bet, or not?'

James had forgotten how playful Kerry could be and she looked really sexy, dressed just in her underwear.

'Sure,' James said. He was proud of his upper body so he ripped off his T-shirt and hurled it up in the air. 'I won't be needing that again for a couple of hours.'

Kerry got off her bed and dropped into a fighting stance, with James looming over her.

'You *really* mean anything?' James asked.

Kerry blew a kiss. 'I'll belong to you.'

'Jesus Christ,' James said excitably. He charged forward, trying to get Kerry around the waist. But she spun out of the way, hooked her foot around James' trailing leg and tripped him over. Almost before James knew it, Kerry sat across his back with his neck in an agonising choke hold.

'Same old, same old,' Kerry said cheerfully. 'All that bulk, but you still move like a geriatric snail.'

'Christ,' James gasped, as Kerry tightened the hold. 'I can't breathe.'

'Do you know how much you hurt me when you dumped me?' Kerry asked. 'If you break my heart again James, I'll break you.'

James had watched Kerry batter a man with a baseball bat while they were on work experience, so he knew what she was capable of.

'I'm sorry,' James whimpered. 'For god's sake. This *really* hurts.'

'We might break up or fall out,' Kerry continued. 'That's acceptable, but if you cheat on me again, you're a dead man. So decide now whether you want to go out with me, but those are my terms.'

'I'm more mature now,' James whined. 'Come on, let me go.'

'Promise,' Kerry said. 'Or get the hell out of my room.'

'OK, I promise,' James said, then whooshed with relief as Kerry let his neck go. 'Jesus, I'd forgotten how fast you are.'

Kerry laughed as she kissed the back of James' neck and stood up. He rolled over and caught his breath as she stood astride him. James wondered if he was nuts to start going out with Kerry again, but as he looked up at smooth legs and swaying black hair he wanted her more than anything else in the world.

*

It was quarter past eight when Dante dragged a small mattress into his eighth-floor bedroom. His five-year-old sister Holly trailed behind. She had long red hair, wore CHERUB uniform and held a duvet which was bundled up so high that she could barely see over it.

'How many nights can I stay in your room?' Holly asked excitably, as Dante dropped the mattress on his floor.

'You are such a worrier,' Dante soothed. 'Why don't we just see how it goes? I expect you'll want to go back with your friends in the junior block in a few days.'

'If I have a bed in your room, and a bed in the junior block I can just sleep in whichever one I like,' Holly suggested. 'And you could come and sleep in my room sometimes.'

Dante smiled. 'We're going to the summer hostel in a few days, anyway.'

Holly threw her duvet out over the mattress, and grabbed the pyjamas that had been rolled inside as Dante lobbed a pillow at her head.

'Oi!' Holly giggled. 'You hooligan.'

'Do you need help getting undressed?' Dante asked.

Holly looked at her brother like he was a Martian. 'I'm five,' she said indignantly.

'Sorry,' Dante said. 'I haven't seen you properly for ages. Last summer you got your giant head stuck every time you tried taking your shirt off.'

To prove her point, Holly deftly pulled off her T-shirt, then dropped her shorts and showed Dante the back of her leg. 'See my bruises?' she said proudly. 'I got them at skiing.'

'I've never been skiing,' Dante said. 'I'd probably be useless and crash.'

Holly laughed, making a noise like an explosion. 'I could teach you,' she said. 'I'm the second best skier out of all the girls who hadn't been before.'

Once Holly had her pyjamas on she went into the bathroom to brush her teeth. Dante had spent all the time since he arrived with Holly, so he used the break to grab his dirty laundry and dump it into his washing basket. Then he unpacked his PSP and some of his other things, until Holly came out and stood in front of him with her mouth open.

'Clean?' Holly asked, as she blew toothpasty breath over him.

Dante realised that this must be something the carers in the junior block did to make sure all the little kids were brushing properly. 'Looks good to me,' he smiled. 'Come and sit on the bed for a minute. Let me show you this.'

As Holly jumped on the bed, Dante unrolled the photograph from the Brigands' barbecue and pointed to the boy standing in the centre of the picture. 'Do you know who that is?' he asked.

Holly shook her head, but then put a hand over her mouth. 'Was that *you*?'

'Yep,' Dante said, before pointing his finger up at Scotty. 'And that's your daddy.'

Holly had seen a couple of blurry police surveillance photographs of her father and nodded.

'That's your sister Lizzie sulking, your brother Jordan pulling a silly face and that's our mum,' Dante said. 'And what do you think that tiny lump she's holding is?'

Holly moved her head closer to the picture. 'Me,' she said, before smiling and resting her head on Dante's shoulder. 'But now it's you and me and we both live at CHERUB.'

Dante gave his little sister a squeeze and kissed the top of her head.

'I'm getting in bed,' Holly yawned, almost headbutting Dante as she shot up and dived excitedly on to her mattress. 'It's really cool having my big brother back. We can do everything together when we get to the summer hostel.'

Dante flipped out his main light and lay across his bed watching Holly going to sleep. Every so often she'd open one eye and then giggle naughtily when Dante poked his tongue out at her. The photo lay on the bed and Dante couldn't not look at the Führer. His mind drifted back to the night before and he tried figuring out why he hadn't pulled the trigger.

Seeing the Führer's flabby body through the crosshairs had transformed him from the figure of doom who chased Dante through his nightmares into a middle-aged man who was only breathing because Dante had spared his life.

The mission had gone wrong and the Führer wasn't behind bars. Maybe people like Chloe Blake and Ross Johnson would find a way to bring the Führer to justice. Maybe he'd rot in jail, maybe he'd meet a violent end at the hands of another biker, or maybe the Führer would die blissfully happy at the age of a hundred and five.

Dante thought about this and was shocked to realise that he no longer cared. As he watched Holly sleep, Dante understood that revenge wouldn't have brought his family back. He hadn't gone to the Führer's house to kill him, he'd gone to say goodbye to his past.

EPILOGUE

The 2008 Rebel Tea Party marked the beginning of a major war, both within the Brigands and with rival gangs such as the Bitch Slappers, Satan's Prodigy and Vengeful Bastards.

One of the first casualties was London chapter president SEALCLUBBER, who was found murdered in his London home. RALPH DONNINGTON (AKA THE FÜHRER) was questioned in connection with the killing and later replaced Sealclubber as the Brigands' National President.

The Dutch Brigand and explosives expert JONAS HAARDEN (AKA DOODS) is still thought to be at large, possibly within the United Kingdom.

Ex-Brigand PAUL WOODHEAD was sentenced to

fifteen years in prison for his role in weapons smuggling operations. Trawler captain JOHNNY RIGGS was sentenced to seven years. NIGEL CONNOR was sentenced to thirty months in a young offenders' institution.

JULIAN HARGREAVES pleaded guilty to all weapons smuggling charges but was released unconditionally and praised by the trial judge for his bravery in coming forward to give evidence. Following a series of instances of vandalism and harassment against his family, Julian now attends a fee-paying school in London, while his father JONTY HARGREAVES has sold his apartment in Marina Heights.

Devon police say that these sentences and the seizure of the trawler *Brixton Riots* have had a significant effect on the Brigands' ability to smuggle weapons into the United Kingdom.

MARTIN DONNINGTON continues to manage the Marina Heights crêpe stand. He has booked a round-the-world air ticket and hopes to have saved enough money to spend the whole of 2009 travelling the world.

His younger brother JOE DONNINGTON paired off with ANNA CONNOR after Dante and Lauren returned to campus.

In an internal police report, Chief Inspector ROSS JOHNSON was criticised for continuing the weapons purchase operation after the undercover role of Sergeant NEIL GAUCHE was unearthed and for the consequent loss of £316,000.

The role of CHERUB agents in the latter stages of the operation could not be revealed to the team that wrote the report. Johnson was saved from demotion following the personal intervention of CHERUB chairwoman Zara Asker.

Johnson continues to work with CHERUB mission controller CHLOE BLAKE with a view to staging another anti biker mission.

Neil Gauche's attachment to the National Police Biker Task Force has now ended and he has returned to work as a detective in his native Leicestershire.

Ex-CHERUB agent and child psychologist JENNIFER MITCHUM is partially retired, but works part time on CHERUB campus studying the background of potential recruits and counselling agents who have returned from difficult missions.

CHERUB chairwoman ZARA ASKER gave birth to her third child, a boy, JONAH EWART ASKER.

In its report on the biker mission, the CHERUB Ethics Committee criticised JAKE McEWEN for his assault on the police officer, and his excessively violent interrogation of Julian Hargreaves. McEwen is slowly archiving five thousand files in the basement of the main building on CHERUB campus. Zara Asker has also sent him for anger management training.

JAMES ADAMS, LAUREN ADAMS and DANTE WELSH all flew off to the CHERUB summer hostel the week after they returned from their mission. James Adams and his Kawasaki ER5 remain on standby for a possible reprisal in the role of biker James Raven.

In 2010, James Adams will be back
for one final adventure . . .

CHERUB: SHADOW WAVE

After a tsunami causes massive devastation to a tropical island, its governor sends in the bulldozers to knock down villages, replacing them with luxury hotels.

Guarding the corrupt governor's family isn't James Adams' idea of the perfect mission, especially as it's going to be his last as a CHERUB agent. And then retired colleague Kyle Blueman comes up with an unofficial and highly dangerous plan of his own.

James must choose between loyalty to CHERUB, and loyalty to his oldest friend.

Plus:

James gets back on his ER5 to tidy up unfinished business from Brigands M.C.

James and Kerry – how will it end?

James meets his dad.

Uncle Ron gets out of prison.

The final epilogue – find out what happens to all the major characters.

Robert Muchamore takes us back to World War Two, where the very first CHERUB adventure will soon begin . . .

THE ESCAPE

Summer, 1940.
Hitler's army is advancing towards Paris, and millions of French civilians are on the run. Amidst the chaos, two British children are being hunted by German agents.

Spy Charles Henderson tries to reach them first, but he can only do so with the help of a twelve-year-old French orphan.

EAGLE DAY

Late summer, 1940.
Hitler has conquered France. Now he intends to cross the Channel and defeat Britain before winter arrives. A group of young refugees led by British spy Charles Henderson faces a stark choice: to head south into the safety of neutral Spain, or go north on a risky mission to sabotage the German invasion plans.

The British secret service is about to discover that kids working undercover will help to win the war.

www.hendersonsboys.com

Coming next from Robert Muchamore:

SECRET ARMY

CHERUB campus, 1941.
The government is building a secret army of intelligence agents to work undercover, gathering information and planning sabotage operations in Nazi-occupied Europe.

Henderson's boys (and one girl) are part of that network: kids cut adrift by the war, living in a disused school and training together for the fight of their lives.

They'll have to parachute into unknown territory, travel cross-country and outsmart a bunch of adults in a daredevil exercise.

In wartime Britain, anything goes.

This is the story of how CHERUB began.

JAMES ADAMS' ROOM 12/08/09